Charles Percy Snow was born in Leicester in 1905. He was educated as a chemist and physicist at the universities of Leicester and Cambridge. After scientific research he turned to administration and then to writing and later held many important public posts and was made Baron Snow of Leicester.

Snow's first novel *Death Under Sail* was published in 1932. His successful novel sequence portraying English life from 1920 onwards is *Strangers and Brothers*. This sequence spans the life of its narrator, Lewis Eliot, barrister – and took over 30 years to write. Snow describes the rarefied worlds of academia, Cambridge, the Jewish community and Westminster. In addition to fiction, Snow also wrote several critical works including a biography of Trollope. He married the novelist Pamela Hansford Johnson in 1950 and died in 1980.

BY THE SAME AUTHOR
ALL PUBLISHED BY HOUSE OF STRATUS

GENERAL FICTION:
THE AFFAIR
A COAT OF VARNISH
CORRIDORS OF POWER
THE CONSCIENCE OF THE RICH
DEATH UNDER SAIL
GEORGE PASSANT
HOMECOMINGS
IN THEIR WISDOM
LAST THINGS
THE LIGHT AND THE DARK
THE MALCONTENTS
THE MASTERS
THE NEW MEN
THE SEARCH
THE SLEEP OF REASON
NON-FICTION:
THE PHYSICISTS
TROLLOPE

C P SNOW

Time of Hope

HOUSE OF
STRATUS

This edition published in 2000 by House of Stratus, an imprint of Stratus Holdings plc, 24c Old Burlington Street, London, W1X 1RL, UK.

www.houseofstratus.com

Typeset, printed and bound by House of Stratus.

A catalogue record for this book is available from the British Library.

ISBN 1-84232-428-4

To
DICK

CONTENTS

Part One – SON AND MOTHER

1	Chime of a Clock	3
2	Mr Eliot's First Match	11
3	An Appearance at Church	20
4	My Mother's Hopes	28
5	A Ten-shilling Note In Front of the Class	36
6	The First Start	46
7	The Effect of a Feud	53
8	A Sunday Morning	65
9	At a Bedside	71
10	The View Over the Roofs	76

Part Two – TOWARDS A GAMBLE

11	Discontent and Talks of Love	83
12	Pride at a Football Match	88
13	The Hopes of Our Youth	96
14	An Act of Kindness	103
15	An Intention and a Name	109
16	Denunciation	116
17	The Letter on the Chest of Drawers	124

Part Three – THE END OF INNOCENCE

18	Walking Alone	131
19	The Calm of a September Afternoon	137
20	In the Rain	146
21	Deceiving and Pleasing	158
22	Christmas Eve	165
23	The Lights of a House	174
24	The Key In the Lock	180

Part Four – THE FIRST SURRENDER

25 A Piece of Advice   187
26 Meeting by Accident   196
27 'I Believe In Joy'   207
28 Results of a Proposal   218
29 Second Meeting With a Doctor   226
30 The Examination   236
31 Triumph and Surrender   242

Part Five – THE HARD WAY

32 Two Controllers   249
33 Manoeuvers   257
34 A Friend's Case   266
35 A Freezing Night   273
36 A Stroke of Luck   277
37 Value In Other's Eyes   282
38 Some Kinds of Suffering   291
39 Sheila's Room   302
40 Listening to Music   311

Part Six – A SINGLE ACT

41 The Sense of Power   319
42 Steaming Clothes Before the Fire   327
43 Mr Knight Tries to be Direct   332
44 Beside the Water   341

Part Seven – THE DECISION

45 An Autumn Dawn   347
46 The New House   355
47 Another Night In Eden's Drawing-Room   360
48 Two Men Rebuild Their Hopes   370
49 Parting   376
50 Walk In the Garden   382

Part One

SON AND MOTHER

1

Chime of a Clock

THE midges were dancing over the water. Close to our hands the reeds were high and lush, and on the other side of the stream the bank ran up steeply, so that we seemed alone, alone in the hot, still, endless afternoon. We had been there all day, the whole party of us; the ground was littered with our picnic; now as the sun began to dip we had become quiet, for a party of children. We lay lazily, looking through the reeds at the glassy water. I stretched to pluck a blade of grass, the turf was rough and warm beneath the knees.

It was one of the long afternoons of childhood. I was nearly nine years old, and it was the June of 1914. It was an afternoon I should not have remembered, except for what happened to me on the way home.

It was getting late when we left the stream, climbed the bank, found ourselves back in the suburb, beside the tramlines. Down in the reeds we could make-believe that we were isolated, Camping in the wilds; but in fact, the tramlines ran by, parallel to the stream, for another mile. I went home alone, tired and happy after the day in the sun. I was not in a hurry, and walked along, basking in the warm evening. The scent of the lime trees hung over the suburban street; lights were coming on in some of the houses; the red brick of the new church was roseate in the sunset glow.

At the church the street forked; to the right past the butcher's, past a row of little houses whose front doors opened on to the pavement;

to the left past the public library along the familiar road towards home. There were the houses with 'entries' leading to their back doors, and the neat, minute gardens in front. There was my aunt's house, with the BUILDER AND CONTRACTOR sign over the side gate. Then came ours: one of a pair, older than the rest of this road, three storeys instead of two, red brick like the church, shambling and in need of a coat of paint to cover the sun blisters. Round the bend from the library I could already see the jessamine in the summer twilight. I was in sight of home. Then it happened. Without warning, without any kind of reason, I was seized with a sense of overwhelming dread. I was terrified that some disaster was waiting for me. In an instant, dread had pounced on me out of the dark. I was too young to have any defences. I was a child, and all misery was eternal. I could not believe that this terror would pass.

Tired as I was, I began to run frantically home. I had to find out what the premonition meant. It seemed to have come from nowhere; I could not realize that there might be anxiety in the air at home, that I might have picked it up. Had I heard more than I knew? As I ran; as I left behind 'good nights' from neighbours watering their flowers, I felt nothing but terror. I thought that my mother must be dead.

When I arrived, all looked as it always did. From the road I could see there was no light in the front-room window; that was usual, until I got back home. I went in by the back door. The blinds were drawn in the other sitting-room, and a band of light shone into the back garden; in the kitchen there was a faint radiance from the gas mantle, ready for me to turn it up. My supper was waiting on the table. I rushed through the passage in search of my mother. I burst into the lighted sitting-room. There she was. I cried out with perfect relief.

She was embarrassed to see me. Her face was handsome, anxious, vain, and imperious; that night her cheeks were flushed, her eyes bright and excited instead of, as I knew them best, keen, bold, and troubled. She was sitting at a table with two women, friends of hers who came often to the house. On the table lay three rows of cards, face upwards, and one of my mother's friends had her finger pointing to the king of spades. But they were not playing a game – they were telling fortunes.

These séances happened whenever my mother could get her friends together. When these two, Maud and Cissie, came to tea, there would be whispers and glances of understanding. My mother would give me some pennies to buy sweets or a magazine, and they left to find a room by themselves. I was not told what they did there. My mother, proud in all ways, did not like me to know that she was extremely superstitious.

'Have you had your supper, dear?' she said that night. 'It's all ready for you on the table.'

'I'm just showing your mother some tricks,' said Maud, who was portly and good-natured.

'Never mind,' said my mother. 'You go and have your supper. Then it'll be your bedtime, won't it?'

But in fact I had no particular 'bedtime'. My mother was capable but preoccupied, my father took it for granted that she was the stronger character and never made more than a comic pretence of interfering at home; I received nothing but kindness from them: they had large, vague hopes of me, but from a very early age I was left to do much as I wanted. So after I had finished supper I came back along the passage to the empty dark front room; from the other sitting-room came a chink of light beneath the door, and the sound of whispers from my mother and her friends – their fortune-telling was always conducted in the lowest of voices.

I found some matches, climbed on the table, lit the gas lamp, then settled down to read. Since I had arrived at the house, found all serene, seen my mother, I was completely reassured. I was wrapped in the security of childhood. Just as the misery had been eternal, so was this. The dread had vanished. For those moments, which I remembered all my life, had already passed out of mind the day they happened. I curled up on the sofa and lost myself in *The Captain*.

I read on for some time. I was beginning to blink with sleepiness, the day's sun had made my forehead burn; perhaps I should soon have gone to bed. But then, through the open window, I heard a well-known voice.

'Lewis! What are you doing up at this time of night?'

It was my Aunt Milly, who lived two houses down the road. Her voice was always full and assertive; it swelled through any room; in any group, hers was the voice one heard.

'I never heard of such a thing,' said Aunt Milly from the street.

'Well, since you are up – instead of being in bed a couple of hours ago,' she added indignantly, 'you'd better let me in the front door.'

She followed me into the front room and looked down at me with hot-headed, vigorous reprobation.

'Boys of your age ought to be in bed by eight,' she said. 'No wonder you're tired in the morning.' I argued that I was not, but Aunt Milly did not listen.

'No wonder you're skinny,' she said. 'Boys of your age need to sleep the clock round. It's another thing that I shall have to speak to your mother about.'

Aunt Milly was my father's sister. She was a big woman, as tall as my mother and much more heavily built. She had a large, blunt, knobbly nose, and her eyes protruded: they were light blue, staring, and slightly puzzled. She wore her hair in a knob above the back of her head, which gave her a certain resemblance to Britannia. She had strong opinions on all subjects. She believed in speaking the truth, particularly when it was unpleasant. She thought I was both spoilt and neglected, and was the only person who tried to govern my movements. She had no children of her own.

'Where is your mother?' said Aunt Milly. 'I came along to see her. I'm hoping that she might have something to tell me.'

She spoke in an accusing tone that I did not understand. I told her that mother was in the other room, busy with Maud and Cissie – 'playing cards,' I fabricated.

'Playing cards,' said Aunt Milly indignantly. 'I'd better see how much longer they think they're going on.'

Through two closed doors I heard Aunt Milly's voice, loud in altercation. I even caught some of her words: she was wondering how grown-up people could believe in such nonsense. Then followed a pause of quiet, in which I imagined my mother must be replying, though I could hear nothing. Then Aunt Milly again. Then a clash of doors, and Aunt Milly rejoined me.

'Playing cards!' she cried. 'I don't think much of cards, but I wouldn't say a word against it. If that was all it was!'

'Aunt Milly, you have — ' I said, defending my mother. Aunt Milly had reproved her resonantly for suggesting whist last Boxing Day. I was going to remind her of it.

'Seeing the future!' said Aunt Milly with scorn, as though I had not made a sound. 'It's a pity she hasn't something better to do. No wonder things get left in this house. I suppose I oughtn't to tell you, but someone ought to be thinking of the future for your father and mother. I've said so often enough, but do you think they would listen?'

Outside, in the hall, my mother was saying goodbye to Maud and Cissie. The door swung slowly open and she entered the room. She entered very deliberately, with her head high and her feet turned out at each step; it was a carriage she used when she was calling up all her dignity. She had in fact great dignity, though she invented her own style for expressing it.

She did not speak until she had reached the middle of the room. She faced Aunt Milly, and said: 'Please to wait till we are alone, Milly. The next time you want to tell me what I ought to do, I'll thank you to keep quiet in front of visitors.'

They were both tall, they both had presence, they both had strong wills. They were in every other way unlike. My mother's thin beak of a nose contrasted itself to Aunt Milly's bulbous one. My mother's eyes were set deep in well-arched orbits, and were bold, grey, handsome, and shrewd. Aunt Milly's were opaque and protruding. My mother was romantic, snobbish, perceptive, and intensely proud. Aunt Milly was quite unselfconscious, a busybody, given to causes and good works, impervious to people, surprised and hurt when they resisted her proposals, but still continuing active, indelicate, and undeterred. She had no vestige of humour at all. My mother had a good deal —

7

but she showed none as she confronted Aunt Milly under the drawing-room mantel.

They had been much together since my parents' marriage. They maddened each other: they lived in a state of sustained mutual misunderstanding; but they never seemed able to keep long apart.

'Please to let my visitors come here in peace,' said my mother.

'Visitors!' said Aunt Milly. 'I've known Maud Taylor longer than you have. It's a pity she didn't get married when we did. No wonder she wants the cards to tell her that she's going to find a husband.'

'When she's in my house, she's my visitor. I'll thank you not to thrust your opinions down her throat.'

'It's not my opinions,' said Aunt Milly, loudly even for her. 'It's nothing but common sense. Lena, you ought to be ashamed of yourself.'

'I'm not in the least ashamed of myself,' said my mother. She kept her haughtiness; but she would have liked to choose a different ground.

'Reading the cards and looking at each other's silly hands and –' Aunt Milly paused triumphantly, '– and gaping at some dirty tea leaves. I've got no patience with you.'

'No one's asked you to have patience,' said my mother stiffly. 'If ever I ask you to join us, then's the time for you to grumble. Everyone's got a right to their own opinions.'

'Not if they're against common sense. Tea leaves!' Aunt Milly snorted. 'In the twentieth century!' She brought out those last words like the ace of trumps.

My mother hesitated. She said: 'There's plenty we don't know yet.'

'We know as much as we want to about tea leaves,' said Aunt Milly. She roared with laughter. It was her idea of a joke. She went on, ominously: 'Yes, there's plenty we don't know yet. That's why I can't understand how you've got time for this rubbish. One of the things we don't know is how you and Bertie and this boy here are going to live. There's plenty we don't know yet. I was telling the boy –'

'What have you told Lewis?' My mother was fierce and on the offensive again. When Aunt Milly had jostled her away from propriety and etiquette and made her justify her superstitions, she had been secretly abashed. Now she flared out with anxious authority.

'I told him that you've let things slide for long enough. No wonder you're seeing it all go from bad to worse. You never ought to have let – '

'Milly, you're not to talk in front of Lewis.'

'It won't hurt him. He's bound to know sooner or later.'

'That's as may be. I won't have you talk in front of Lewis.'

I knew by now that there was great trouble. I asked my mother: 'Please, what is the matter?'

'Don't you worry,' said my mother, her face lined with care, defiant, protective, and loving. 'Perhaps it will blow over.'

'Your father's making a mess of things,' said Aunt Milly.

But my mother said: 'I tell you, you're not to talk in front of the child.'

She spoke with such quiet anger, such reserve of will, that even Aunt Milly flinched. Neither of them said another word for some moments, and one could hear the tick of the clock on the mantelpiece. I could not imagine what the trouble was, but it frightened me. I knew that I could not ask again. This time it was real; I could not run home and be reassured.

Just then the latch of the front door clicked, and my father came in. There was no mystery why he had been out of the house that night. He was an enthusiastic singer, and organized a local male-voice choir. It was a passion that absorbed many of his nights. He came in, batting short-sighted eyes in the bright room.

'We were talking about you, Bertie,' said Aunt Milly.

'I expect you were,' said my father. 'I expect I've done wrong as usual.'

His expression was mock-repentant. It was his manner to pretend to comic guilt, in order to exaggerate his already comic gentleness and lack of assertion. If there was clowning to be done, he could never resist it. He was a very small man, several inches shorter than his wife or sister. His head was disproportionately large, built on the same lines as Aunt Milly's but with finer features. His eyes popped out like hers, but, when he was not clowning, looked reflective, and usually happy

9

and amused. Like his sister's his hair was on the light side of brown (my mother's was very dark), and he had a big, reddish, drooping moustache. His spectacles had a knack of running askew, above the level of one eye and below the other. Habitually he wore a bowler hat, and while grinning at his sister he placed it on the sideboard.

'I wish you'd show signs of ever doing anything,' said Aunt Milly.

'Don't set on the man as soon as he gets inside the door,' said my mother.

'I expect it, Lena. I expect it.' My father grinned. 'She always puts the blame on me. I have to bear it. I have to bear it.'

'I wish you'd stand up for yourself,' said my mother irritably.

My father looked somewhat pale. He had looked pale all that year, though even now his face was relaxed by the side of my mother's. And he made his inevitable comment when the clock struck the hour. It was a marble clock, presented to him by the choir when he had scored his twentieth year as secretary. It had miniature Doric columns on each side of the face, and a deep reverberating chime. Each time my father heard it he made the same remark. Now it struck eleven.

'Solemn-toned clock,' said my father appreciatively. 'Solemn-toned clock.'

'Confound the clock,' said my mother with strain and bitterness.

As I lay awake in the attic, my face was hot against the pillow, hot with sunburn, hot with frightened thoughts. I had added some codicils to my prayers, but they did not ease me. I could not imagine what the trouble was.

2

Mr Eliot's First Match

FOR a fortnight I was told nothing. My mother was absent-minded with worry, but if she and my father were talking when I came in they would fall uncomfortably quiet. Aunt Milly was in the house more often than I had ever seen her; most nights after supper there boomed a vigorous voice from the street outside; whenever she arrived I was sent into the garden. I got used to it. Often I forgot altogether the anxiety in the house. I liked reading in the garden, which was several steps below the level of the yard; there was a patch of longish grass, bordered by a flower bed, a rockery and some raspberry canes; I was specially fond of the trees – three pear trees by the side wall and two apple trees in the middle of the grass. I used to take out a deckchair, sit under one of the apple trees, and read until the summer sky had darkened and I could only just make out the print on the shimmering page.

Then I would look up at the house. The sitting-room window was a square of light. Sometimes I felt anxious about what was being said in there.

Apart from those conferences, I did not see any change in the routine of our days.

I went as usual to school, and found my mother at midday silent and absorbed. My father went, also as usual, to his business. He took to any routine with his habitual mild cheerfulness, and even Aunt Milly could not complain of the hours he worked. We had a servant-girl of about sixteen, and my father got up when she did, in the early morning, and had left for work long before I came down to breakfast, and did not return for his high tea until half past six or seven.

For three years past he had been in business on his own. Previously he had been employed in a small boot factory; he had looked after the books, been a kind of utility man and second-in-command, and earned two hundred and fifty pounds a year. On that we had lived comfortably enough, servant-girl and all. But he knew the trade, he knew the profits, he reported that Mr Stapleton, his employer, was drawing twelve hundred a year out of the business. To both my parents, to Aunt Milly, to Aunt Milly's husband, that income seemed riches, almost unimaginable riches. My father thought vaguely that he would like to run his own factory. My mother urged him on. Aunt Milly prophesied that he would fail and reproached him for not having the enterprise to try.

My mother impelled him to it. She chafed against the limits of her sex. If she had been a man she would have driven ahead, she would have been a success. She lent him her savings, a hundred and fifty pounds or so. She helped borrow some more money. Aunt Milly, whose husband in a quiet inarticulate fashion was a good jobbing builder and appreciably more prosperous than we were, lent the rest. My father found himself in charge of a factory. It was very small. His total staff was never more than a dozen. But there he was, established on his own. There he had spent his long days for the past three years. At night I had often watched my mother look over the accounts, have an idea, ask why something had not been done, say that he ought to get a new traveller. That had not happened recently, in my hearing, but my father was still spending his long days at the factory. He never referred to it as 'my business' or 'my factory' – always by a neutral, geographical term, 'Myrtle Road'.

One Friday night early in July my mother and father talked for a long time alone. When I came in from the garden I noticed that he was upset. 'Lena's got a headache. She's gone to bed,' he said. He gazed miserably at me, and I did not know what to say. Then, to my astonishment, he asked me to go with him to the county cricket match next day. I thought he had been going to tell me something painful: I did not understand it at all.

Myself, I went regularly to the 'county' whenever I could beg sixpence, but my father had not been to a cricket match in his life. And he said also that he would meet me outside the ground at half past eleven. He was going to leave Myrtle Road early. That was also astonishing. Even for a singing practice, even to get back to an evening with a travel book, he had never left the factory before his fixed time. On Saturdays he always reached home at half past one.

'We'll have the whole day at the match, shall we?' he said. 'We'll get our money's worth, shall we?'

His voice was flat, he could not even begin to clown.

Next morning, however, he was more himself. He liked going to new places; he never minded being innocent, not knowing his way about. 'Fancy!' he said, as he paid for us both and we pushed through the turnstiles. 'So that's where they play, is it?' But he was looking at the practice nets. He was quite unembarrassed as I led him to seats on the popular side, just by the edge of the sight-screen.

Soon I had no time to attend to my father. I was immersed, tense with the breathtaking freshness of the first minutes of play. The wickets gleamed in the sun, the bail flashed, the batsmen played cautious strokes; I swallowed with excitement at each ball. I was a passionate partisan. Leicestershire were playing Sussex. For years I thought I remembered each detail of that day; I should have said that my father and I had watched the first balls of the Leicestershire innings. But my memory happened to have tricked me. Long afterwards I looked up the score. The match had begun on the Thursday, and Sussex had made over two hundred, and got two of our wickets for a few that night. Friday was washed out by rain, and we actually saw (despite my false remembrance) Leicestershire continue their innings.

All my heart was set on their getting a big score. And I was passionately partisan among the Leicestershire side itself. I had to find a hero. I had not so much choice as I should have had, if I had been luckier in my county; and I did not glow with many dashing vicarious triumphs. My hero was C J B Wood. Even I, in disloyal moments, admitted that he was not so spectacular as Jessop or Tyldesley. But, I told myself, he was much sounder. In actual fact, my hero did not often let me down. On the occasions when he failed completely, I wanted to cry.

That morning he cost me a gasp of fright. He kept playing – I think it must have been Relf – with an awkward-looking, clumsy, stumbling shot that usually patted the ball safely to mid-off. But once, as he did so, the ball found the edge of the bat and flew knee-high between first and second slip. It was four all the way. People round me clapped and said fatuously: 'Pretty shot.' I was contemptuous of them and concerned for my hero, who was thoughtfully slapping the pitch with the back of his bat.

After a quarter of an hour I could relax a little. My father was watching with mild blue-eyed interest. Seeing that I was not leaning forward with such desperate concentration, he began asking questions.

'Lewis,' he said, 'do they have to be very strong to play this game?'

'Some batsmen', I said confidently, having read a lot of misleading books, 'score all their runs by wristwork.' I demonstrated the principle of the leg-glance.

'Just turn their wrists, do they?' said my father. He studied the players in the field. 'But they seem to be pretty big chaps, most of these? Do they have to be big chaps?'

'Quaife is ever such a little man. Quaife of Warwickshire.'

'How little is he? Is he shorter than me?'

'Oh yes.'

I was not sure of the facts, but I knew that somehow the answer would please my father. He received it with obvious satisfaction.

He pursued his chain of thought.

'How old do they go on playing?'

'Very old,' I said.

'Older than me?'

My father was forty-five. I assured him that W G Grace went on playing till he was fifty-eight. My father smiled reflectively.

'How old can they be when they play for the first time? Who is the oldest man to play here for the first time?'

For all my Wisden, it was beyond me to tell him the record age of a first appearance in first-class cricket. I could only give my father general encouragement.

He was given to romantic daydreams, and that morning he was indulging one of them. He was dreaming that all of a sudden he had become miraculously skilled at cricket; he was brought into the middle, everyone acclaimed him, he won instantaneous fame. It would not have done for the dream to be absolutely fantastic. It had to take him as he was, forty-five years old and five feet four in height. He would not imagine himself taken back to youth and transformed into a man strong, tall and glorious. No, he accepted himself in the flesh, He grinned at himself – and then dreamed about all that could happen.

For the same reason he read all the travel books he could lay his hands on. He went down the road to the library and came home with a new book about the headwaters of the Amazon. In his imagination he was still middle-aged, still uncomfortably short in the leg, but he was also paddling up the rainforests where no white man had ever been.

I used, both at that age and when I was a little older, to pretend to myself that he read these books for the sake of knowledge. I liked to pretend that he was very learned about the tropics. But I knew it was not true. It hurt me, it hurt me with bitter twisted indignation, to hear Aunt Milly accuse him of being ineffectual, or my mother of being superstitious and a snob. It roused me to blind, savage, tearful love. It was a long time before I could harden myself to hear such things from her. Yet I could think them to myself and not be hurt at all.

My father treated me to gingerbeer and a pork pie in the lunch interval, and later we had some tea. Otherwise there was nothing to occupy him, after his romantic speculations had died down. He sat there patiently, peering at the game, not understanding it, not seeing the ball. I was not to know that he had a duty to perform.

After the last over the crowd round us drifted over the ground.

'Let's wait until they've gone,' said my father.

So we sat on the emptying ground. The pavilion windows glinted in the evening sun, and the scoreboard threw a shadow halfway to the wicket.

'Lena thinks there's something I ought to tell you,' said my father.

I stared at him.

'I didn't want to tell you before. I was afraid it might spoil your day.'

He looked at me, and added: 'You see, Lewis, it isn't very good news.'

'Oh!' I cried.

My father pushed up his spectacles.

'Things aren't going very well at Myrtle Road. That's the trouble,' he said. 'I can't say things are going as we should like.'

'Why not?' I asked.

'Milly says that it's my fault,' said my father uncomplainingly. 'But I don't know about that.'

He began to talk about 'bigger people turning out a cheaper line'. Then he saw that he was puzzling me. 'Anyway,' he said, 'I'm afraid we may be done for. I may have to file my petition.'

The phrase sounded ominous, deadly ominous, to me, but I did not understand.

'That means', said my father, 'that I'm afraid we shan't have much money to spare. I don't like to think that I can't find you a sovereign now and then, Lewis. I should like to give you a few sovereigns when you get a bit older.'

For a time, that explanation took the edge off my fears. But my father sat there without speaking again. The seats round us were all empty, we were alone on that side of the ground; scraps of paper blew along the grass. My father pulled his bowler hat down over his ears. At last he said, unwillingly: 'I suppose we've got to go home sometime.'

The gates of the ground stood wide open, and we walked along the road, under the chestnut trees. Trains kept passing us, but my father was not inclined to take one. He was quiet, except that once he remarked: 'The trouble is, Lena takes it all to heart.'

He said it as though he was asking me for support.

As soon as he got inside the house and saw my mother, he said: 'Well, I've seen my first match! There can't be many people who haven't seen a cricket match until they're forty-five – '

'Bertie,' said my mother in a cold angry voice. Usually she let him display his simplicity, pretend to be simpler than he was. That night she could not bear it.

'You'd better have your supper,' she said. 'I expect Lewis can do with it.'

'I expect he can,' said my father. Nine times out of ten, for he never got tired of the same repartee, he would have said, 'I expect I can too.' But he felt the weight of my mother's suffering.

We sat round the table in the kitchen. There was cold meat, cheese, a bowl of tinned pears, jam tarts, and a jug of cream.

'I don't suppose you've had much to eat all day,' said my mother. 'You'll want something now.'

My father munched away. I was ashamed to be so hungry, in sight of my mother's face that night, but I was famished. My mother said she had eaten, but it was more likely that she had no appetite for food. From the back kitchen (the house sprawled about without any plan) came the singing of a kettle on the stove.

'I'll have a cup of tea with you,' said my mother. Neither of them had spoken since we began the meal.

As my father pushed up his moustache and took his first sip of tea, he remarked, as though casually: 'I did what you told me, Lena.'

'What, Bertie?'

'I told Lewis that we're worried about Myrtle Road.'

'Worried,' said my mother. 'I hope you told him more than that.'

'I did what you told me.'

'I'd have kept it from you if I could,' my mother said to me. 'But I wasn't going to have you hear it first from Aunt Milly or someone else. If you've got to hear it, I couldn't abide it coming from anybody else. It had to be from us.'

She had spoken with affection, but most of all with shame and bitter pride.

17

Yet she had not given up all hope. She was too active for that. The late sun streamed across the kitchen, and a patch of light, reflected from my mother's cup of tea, danced on the wall. She was sitting half-in, half-out of the shadow, and she seldom looked at my father as she spoke. She spoke in a tight voice, higher than usual but unbroken,

Most of it swept round me. All I gathered was the sound of calamity, pain, disgrace, threats to the three of us. The word 'petition' kept hissing in the room, and she spoke of someone called the 'receiver'. 'How long can we leave it before he's called in?' asked my mother urgently. My father did not know; he was not struggling as she was, he could not take her lead.

She still had plans for raising money. She was ready to borrow from the doctor, to sell her 'bits of jewellery', to go to a moneylender. But she did not know enough. She had the spirit and the wits, but she had never had the chance to pick up the knowledge. Despite her courage, she was helpless and tied.

It seemed that Aunt Milly had offered help, had been the only relative to offer practical help. 'We're always being beholden to her,' said my mother. I was baffled, since I was used to taking it for granted that Aunt Milly was a natural enemy.

My father shook his head, He looked cowed, miserable, but calm.

'It's no good, Lena. It'll only make things worse.'

'You always give up,' cried my mother. 'You always have.'

'It's no good going on,' he said with a kind of obstinacy.

'You can say that,' she said with contempt. 'How do you think I'm going to live?'

'You needn't worry about that, Lena,' said my father, in a furtive attempt to console her. 'I ought to be able to find a job if you give me a bit of time. I'll bring home enough to keep you and Lewis.'

'Do you think that is worrying me?' my mother cried out.

'It's been worrying me,' said my father.

'We shall make do somehow. I'm not afraid of that,' said my mother. 'But I shall be ashamed to let people see me in the streets. I shan't be able to hold up my head.'

She spoke with an anguish that overawed my father. He sat humbly by, not daring to console her.

Watching their faces in the darkening kitchen, I craved for a distress that would equal my mother's. I was on the point of acting one, of imitating her suffering, so that she would forget it all and speak to me.

3

An Appearance at Church

THAT night, when I went to bed, I took the family dictionary with me. It was not long since I had discovered it, and already I liked not having to be importunate. Now I had a serious use for the dictionary. It was a time not to worry my mother: I had to be independent of her. Through the tiny window of the attic a stretch of sky shone faintly as I entered the room. I could see a few faint stars in the clear night. There was no other light in the attic, except a candle by my bed. I lit it, and before I undressed held the dictionary a foot away, found the word 'petition', tried to make sense of what the book said.

The breeze blew the candle wax into a runnel down one side, and I moulded it between my fingers. I repeated the definitions to myself, and compared them with what I remembered my father saying, but I was left more perplexed.

It was still the month of July when I knew that the trouble had swept upon us. My father's hours became more irregular; sometimes he stayed in the house in the morning and sometimes both he and my mother were out all day. It was on one of these occasions that Aunt Milly found me alone in the garden.

'I came to see what they were doing with you,' she said.

I had been playing French cricket with some of the neighbouring children. Now I was sitting in the deckchair under my favourite apple tree. My aunt looked down at me critically.

'I hope they leave you something to eat,' she said.

'Yes,' I said, resenting her kindness. Then I offered her my chair: my mother had strong views on etiquette, some of them invented by herself. Aunt Milly rebuffed me.

'I'm old enough to stand,' she said. She stared at me with an expression that made me uncomfortable.

'Have they told you the news?' she asked.

I prevaricated. She cross-questioned me. I said, feeling wretched, that I knew there was trouble with my father's business.

'I don't believe you know. No wonder everything goes wrong in this house,' said Aunt Milly. 'I suppose I oughtn't to tell you, but it's better for you to hear it straight out.'

I wanted to beg her not to tell me; I looked up at her with fear and hatred.

Aunt Milly said firmly: 'Your father has gone bankrupt.'

I was silent. Aunt Milly stood, large, formidable, noisy, in the middle of the garden. In the sunlight her hair took on a sandy sheen. A bee buzzed among the flowers.

'Yes, Aunt Milly,' I said, 'I've heard about his – petition.'

Inexorably Aunt Milly went on: 'It means that he isn't able to pay his debts. He owes six hundred pounds – and I suppose I oughtn't to tell you, but he won't be able to pay more than two hundred.'

Those sounded great sums.

'When you grow up,' said Aunt Milly, 'you ought to feel obliged to pay every penny he owes. You ought to make a resolution now. You oughtn't to rest until you've got him discharged and your family can be honest and above board again. Your father will never be able to do it. He'll have his work cut out to earn your bread and butter.'

As a rule at that age I should have promised anything that was expected of me. But then I did not speak.

'There won't be any money to send you to the secondary school,' said Aunt Milly. 'Your father wouldn't be able to manage the fees. But I've told your mother that we can see after that.'

I scarcely realized that Aunt Milly was being kind. I had no idea that she was being imaginative in thinking three years ahead. I hated her and I was hurt. Somewhere deep within the pain there was anger

21

growing inside me. Yet, obeying my mother's regard for style, I produced a word or two of thanks.

'Mind you,' said Aunt Milly, 'you mustn't expect to run away with things at the secondary school. After all, it doesn't take much to be top of that old-fashioned place your mother sends you to. No wonder you seem bright among that lot. But you'll find it a different kettle of fish at a big school. I shouldn't wonder if you're no better than the average. Still, you'll have to do as well as you can.'

'I shall do well, Aunt Milly,' I said, bursting out from wretchedness. I said it politely, boastingly, confidently and also with fury and extreme rudeness.

Just then my mother came down to join us. 'So you've got back, Lena,' said Aunt Milly.

'Yes, I've got back,' said my mother, in a brittle tone. She was pale and exhausted, and for once seemed spiritless. She asked Aunt Milly if she would like a cup of tea in the open air.

Aunt Milly said that she had been telling me that she would help with my education.

'It's very good of you, I'm sure, Milly,' said my mother, without a flicker of her usual pride. 'I shouldn't like Lewis not to have his chance.'

'Aunt Milly doesn't think I shall do well at the secondary school,' I broke in. 'I've told her that I shall.'

My mother gave a faint grin, wan but amused. She must have been able to imagine the conversation; and, that afternoon of all afternoons, it heartened her to hear me brag.

Aunt Milly did not exhort my mother, and did not find it necessary to tell her any home truths. Aunt Milly, in fact, made a galumphing attempt to distract my mother's mind by saying that the news looked bad but that she did not believe for a single instant in the possibility of war.

'After all,' she said, 'it's the twentieth century.'

My mother sipped her tea. She was too tired to be drawn. Often they quarrelled on these subjects, as on all others: Aunt Milly was an enthusiastic liberal, my mother a patriotic, jingoish, true-blue conservative.

Aunt Milly tried to cheer her up. Many people were asking after her, said Aunt Milly.

'I'm sure they are,' said my mother, with bitter self-consciousness.

Some of her women friends at the church were anxious to call on her, Aunt Milly continued.

'I don't want to see any of them,' said my mother. 'I want to be left alone, Milly. Please to keep them away.'

For several days my mother did not go outside the house. She had collapsed in a helpless, petrified, silent gloom. She could not bear the sight of her neighbours' eyes. She could guess only too acutely what they were saying, and she was seared by each turn of her imagination. She knew they thought that she was vain and haughty, and that she put on airs. Now they had her at their mercy. She even put off her fortune-telling friends from their weekly conclave. She was too far gone to seek such hope.

I went about quietly, as though she were ill. In fact she was often ill; for, despite her vigour and strength of will, her zest in anything she did, her dignified confidence that, through the grand scale of her nature, she could expect always to take the lead – despite all the power of her personality, she could never trust her nerves. She had much stamina – in the long run she was tough in body as well as in spirit – but some of my earliest recollections were of her darkened bedroom, a brittle voice, a cup of tea on a little table in the twilight, a faint aroma of brandy in the air.

She never drank, except in those periods of nervous exhaustion, but in my childish memory that smell lingered, partly because of the heights of denunciation to which it raised Aunt Milly.

After the bankruptcy, my mother hid away from anything they were saying about us. She was not ill so much as limp and heartbrokenly despondent. It was a week before she took herself in hand.

She came down to breakfast on the first Sunday in August (it was actually Sunday, 2nd August, 1914). She carried her head high, and her eyes were bold.

'Bertie,' she said to my father, 'I shall go to church this morning.'

'Well, I declare,' said my father.

'I want you to come with me, dear,' my mother said to me. She took it for granted that my father did not attend church.

It was a blazing hot August morning, and I tried to beg myself off.

'No, Lewis,' she said in her most masterful tone. 'I want you to come with me. I intend to show them that they can say what they like. I'm not going to demean myself by taking any notice.'

'You might leave it a week or two, Lena,' suggested my father mildly.

'If I don't go today, people might think we had something to be ashamed of,' said my mother, without logic but with some magnificence.

She had made her decision on her way down to breakfast, and, buoyed up by defiance and the thought of action, she looked a different woman. Almost with exhilaration, she went back to the bedroom to put on her best dress, and when she came down again she wheeled round before me in a movement that was, at the same time, stately and coquettishly vain,

'Does mother look nice?' she said. 'Will you be proud of me? Shall I do?'

Her dress was cream-coloured, with leg-of-mutton sleeves and an hourglass waist. She picked up the skirt now and then, for she took pleasure in her ankles, She was putting on a large straw hat and admiring herself in the mirror over the sideboard, when the church bell began to ring. 'We're coming,' said my mother, as the bell clanged on insistently. 'There's no need to ring. We're coming.'

She was excited, flushed and handsome. She gave me the prayer books to carry, opened a white parasol, stepped out into the brilliant street. She walked with the slow, stylised step that had become second nature to her in moments of extreme dignity. She took my hand: her fingers were trembling.

Outside the church we met several neighbours, who said 'Good morning, Mrs Eliot'. My mother replied in a full, an almost patronizing tone, 'Good morning Mrs –' (Corby or Berry or Goodman, the familiar names of the suburb). There was not time to stop and talk, for the bell was ringing twice as fast, in its final agitated minute.

My mother swept down the aisle, me behind her, to her usual seat. The church, as I have said, was quite new. It was panelled in pitch-pine, and had chairs, painted a startling yellow, instead of pews; but already the more important members of the parish, led by the doctor and his sister, had staked out their places, which were left empty at any service to which they did not come. My mother had not been far behind. She had established her right to three seats, just behind the churchwardens'. One was always empty, since my father was obstinately determined never to enter the church.

To the right of the altar stood a small organ with very bright blue pipes. They were vibrating with the last notes of the 'voluntary' as my mother knelt on the hassock before her chair. The windows were polychromatic with new stained glass, and the bright morning light was diffused and curiously coloured before it got inside.

The service began. Usually it was a source of interest, of slightly shocking interest, to my mother, for the vicar was an earnest ritualist, and she was constantly on edge to see how 'high' he would dare to go. 'He's higher than I ever thought,' she would say, and the word 'higher' was isolated in a hushed, shocked, thrilling voice. My mother was religious as well as superstitious, romantic and nostalgic as well as a snob; and she had a pious tenderness and veneration for the old church where she had worshipped as a child, the grey gothic, the comely, even ritual of the broad church. She was disappointed in this new edifice, and somehow expressed her piety in this Sunday-by-Sunday scrutiny of the vicar's progress away from all she loved.

At that morning service, however, she was too much occupied to notice the vicar's vestments. She believed that everyone was watching her. She could not forget herself, and, if she prayed at all, it was for the effrontery to carry it off. She had still to meet the congregation coming out after service. That was the time, each Sunday, when my mother and her acquaintances exchanged gossip. In the churchyard they met and lingered before going off to their Sunday meals, and they created there a kind of village centre. It was that assembly my mother had come out to face.

She chanted the responses and psalms, sang the hymns, so that all those round could hear her. She sat with her head back through the sermon, in which the vicar warned us in an aside that we ought to be prepared for grave events. But it was no more than an aside; to most people there, not only to my mother, the 'failure' of Mr Eliot was something more interesting to talk about than the prospect of a war. Their country had been at peace so long: even when they thought, they could not imagine what a war might mean, or that their lives would change.

The vicar made his dedication to the Trinity, the after-sermon hymn blared out, my mother sang clearly, the sidesmen went round with the collection bags. When the sidesman came to our row, my mother slipped me sixpence, and herself put in half a crown, holding the bag for several instants and dropping the coin from on high. Those near us could see what she had done. It was a gesture of sheer extravagance. In the ordinary way she gave a shilling night and morning, and Aunt Milly told her that that was more than she could afford.

At last came the benediction. My mother rose from her knees, pulled on her long white gloves, and took my hand in a tight grip. Then she went deliberately past the font towards the door. Outside, in the churchyard, the sunlight was dazzling. People were standing about on the gravel paths. There was not a cloud in the sky.

The first person to speak to my mother was very kind. She was the wife of one of the local tradesmen.

'I'm sorry you've had a bit of trouble,' she said. 'Never mind, my dear. Worse things happen at sea.'

I knew that her voice was kind. Yet my mother's mouth was working – she was, in fact, at once disarmed by kindness. She only managed to mutter a word or two of thanks.

Another woman was coming our way. At the sight of her my mother's neck stiffened. She called on all her will and pride, and her mouth became firm. Indeed, she put on a smile of greeting, a distinctly sarcastic smile.

'Mrs Eliot, I was wondering whether you will be able to take your meeting this year.'

'I hope I shall, Mrs Lewin,' said my mother with condescension. 'I shouldn't like to upset your arrangements.'

'I know you're having your difficulties – '

'I don't see what that has to do with it, Mrs Lewin. I've promised to take a meeting as usual, I think. Please to tell Mrs Hughes' (the vicar's wife) 'that you needn't worry to find anyone else.'

My mother's eyes were bright and bold. Now she had got over the first round, she was keyed up by the ordeal. She walked about the churchyard, pointing her toes, pointing also her parasol; she took the initiative, and herself spoke to everyone she knew. She had specially elaborate manners for use on state occasions, and she used them now.

Her hand was still quivering and had become very hot against mine, but she outfaced them all. No one dared to confront her with a direct reference to the bankruptcy, though one woman, apparently more in curiosity than malice, asked how my father was.

'Mr Eliot has never had much wrong with his health, I'm glad to say,' my mother replied.

'Is he at home?'

'Certainly,' my mother said. 'He's spending a nice quiet morning with his books.'

'What will he do now – in the way of work, Mrs Eliot?'

My mother stared down at her questioner.

'He's considering,' said my mother, with such authority that the other woman could not meet her glance. 'He's weighing up the pros and cons. He's going to do the best for himself.'

4

My Mother's Hopes

AT home my mother could not rest until my father got a job. She pored with anxious concentration through the advertisement columns of the local papers; she humbled herself and went to ask the advice of the vicar and the doctor. But my father was out of work for several weeks. His acquaintances in the boot and shoe trade were drawing in their horns because of the war. The hours of that sunlit August were burning away; somehow my mother spared me sixpence on Saturdays to go to the county; the matches went on, the crowds sat there, though outside the ground flared great placards that often I did not understand. The one word MOBILIZATION stood blackly out, on a morning just after my father's bankruptcy; it puzzled me as 'petition' had done, and carried a heavier threat than to my elders.

It was not till the end of August that my father's case was published. He had gone bankrupt to the tune of six hundred pounds; his chief creditors were various leather merchants and Aunt Milly's husband; he was paying eight shillings in the pound. That news was tucked away in the local papers on a night when the British Army was still going back from Mons. For all her patriotism, my mother wished in an agony of pride and passion that a catastrophe might devour us all – her neighbours, the town, the whole country – so that in wreckage, ruin and disaster her disgrace would just be swept away.

October came, the flag-pins on my mother's newspaper map were ceasing to move much day by day, before my father got a job. He returned home one evening and whispered to my mother. He was looking subdued; and, for the first time, I saw her shed a tear. It was not in gratitude or relief; it was a tear so bitterly forced out that I was terrified of some new and paralysing danger. All this time I had had a fear, acute but never mentioned, that my father might have to go to prison. Perhaps this infected me because my mother had warned me, one evening when we were having tea alone, that he must never contract a debt, and that we had from now on always to take care that we paid in the shop for every single article we bought. As I saw the tears in my mother's eyes, the harsh grimace that she made, I was terrified that he might have forgotten. I was surprised to hear my mother say, in a dull and toneless voice: 'Father will be going to work next week, dear.'

I heard the details from Aunt Milly, when she next came into our house.

'Well, your father's got a job,' she said.

'Yes, Aunt Milly.'

'I can't see him doing much good as a traveller. If they say no, he'll just grin and go away. No wonder they're only paying him enough to keep body and soul together.'

My father's former employer, always known as 'Mr Stapleton', had persuaded a leather merchant to take him on as traveller, so that he could go the rounds of his old competitors.

'I suppose I oughtn't to tell you,' said Aunt Milly, 'but they're giving him three pounds a week. I don't know how you're going to manage. Of course, it's better than nothing. I suppose he wouldn't get more anywhere else.'

It must have been almost exactly that time when my mother realized that she was pregnant again. I knew nothing of it; I saw that she was ill, and moved slowly, but I was used to her being ill; I knew nothing of it, all through that winter and spring, but I knew that she was constantly needing to talk to me.

I used to arrive back from school on an autumn afternoon and find her sitting by the fire in the front room. Outside, the rain fell gently in the wistful dusk, and the flames of the blazing coal began to be reflected in the window panes. My tea was ready, a good tea, for our standard of eating had not been much reduced; we did not have so much meat, we had to go without the occasional 'bird' which had once given my mother a lively social pleasure, but she would have still felt it beneath her to provide me with margarine instead of butter. So I tucked into my boiled egg, had some rounds of bread and butter and jam, finished off with a piece of home-made cake. There was no Vera to take away the tea things, but we left them on the table, for Aunt Milly used to send her own maid round for an hour in the morning and an hour at night.

My mother liked to wait until it was quite dark before we lit the gas and drew the blinds, so that we sat and watched the lavish, glowing fire. In one of the lumps of coal, remote from the red-hot centre, a jet of gas would catch alight and make my mother exclaim with pleasure; she used to want me to imagine the same pictures in the fire.

On those afternoons, as we sat in the dark, the fire casting a flickering glow upon the ceiling, my mother talked to me about the hopes of her youth, her family, her snobbish ambitions, her feeling for my father, her need that I should rectify all that had gone wrong in her life.

The child she was carrying – of which I was innocently ignorant, although she turned to me with an insistence I had never seen before – was to her a mistake, unwanted, conceived after a nine years' interval in defeat and bitterness of heart. Possibly she had never loved my father, though for a long time she must have felt an indulgent half-amused affection for his good nature, his amiable mildness, his singular lack of self-regard. Although she was realistic in her fashion, she may have had her surprises; for he was one of those little men who, unassertive in everything else, are anything but unassertive in their hunger for women. That would have made her love him more, if she had loved him at all. But, without love, with only a shaky affection to rest on, it meant that she was always on the fringe of feeling something like contempt. After failing, after exposing her to a humiliation which she could not forgive, he had lost nothing of his ardour – he had given her another child. She told me, much later, that it was done against her will. It rankled to the depth of her proud soul.

'I married the wrong man,' said my mother as we sat by the fire. She said it with naked intensity. She was nearly forty; and she could scarcely believe that all she longed for as a girl should have come to this.

Her hopes had been brilliant. She had a romantic, surging, passionate imagination, even then, when a middle-aged woman beaten down by misfortune. As a girl she had expected – expected as of right – a husband who would give her love and luxury and state. She thought of herself in her girlhood, and as she spoke to me she magnified the past, enhanced all that she could glory in, cherished her life with her own family now that she looked back with an experienced and a disappointed heart.

Her family had been different in a good many ways from my father's. The Eliots, apart from my father, who was unlike the rest, were an intelligent, capable lot without much sensitivity or intuition, whose intelligence was usually higher than their worldly sense; they were a typical artisan, lower-middle-class family thrown up in their present form by the industrial revolution, who should, but for a certain obtuseness, have done much better for themselves. My grandfather Eliot, my father's and Aunt Milly's father, was a man of force and intellect, who had mastered the nineteenth-century artisan culture, who knew his 'penny magazines' backwards, read Bradlaugh and William Morris, picked up some mathematics at a mechanics' institution. He had died early in the year of my father's bankruptcy. He had never climbed farther than maintenance foreman at the local tram depot.

He had quarrelled with my mother whenever they argued, for he was a serious nineteenth-century agnostic, she devout; he voted radical and she was a vehement Tory; and they were both strong characters. Their temperaments clashed, my mother had no more in common with him than with his daughter Milly; and my mother's family, and all the background of her childhood, had roots quite different from theirs.

31

Her family, unlike the Eliots, had never lived in the little industrial towns that proliferated in the nineteenth century, the Redditches and Walsalls where my grandfather had spent his early years. My mother's family had had nothing to do with factories and machines; they were still living, those that were left, in an older, agricultural, more feudal England, in the market towns of Lincolnshire or, as gamekeepers and superior servants and the like, on the big estates. They were not more prosperous than the Eliots, as my mother admitted. She was entirely truthful and had a penetrating regard for fact, despite her nostalgia and imagination. She did not even allow herself to pretend, although she would have dearly loved to, that they were noticeably more genteel. No, she told me the truth, though she had a knack of making it shimmer a little at the edges. Her father's name was Sercombe, and he had been employed, like his father and grandfather before him, in the grounds of Burghley Park: to my mother, for ever after, that mansion signified the height of all worldly ambition. The Sercombe men often ran true to a physical type. Like my mother, they were dark as gypsies; they were dashing, physically active, fond of the open air, naturally good at games but too careless to learn them properly, gay, completely unbookish – men who loved all the hours of young manhood and were lost when youth ended. Almost all were born with an air of command, and stood out in a crowd. They won much love from women, but had not as a rule the steadiness or warmth of nature to make them good friends to other men. Sometimes they used their boldness, dash, and charm to marry above themselves.

It was these marriages that gave my mother her best chance to stick to the truth, and yet to glorify it. Her own father had married as his second wife someone from a Stamford family which had known better days. My mother was a child of that second marriage; and down to her girlhood, there were Wigmore cousins, who lived in solid middle-class comfort, who had a 'position' in the town and with whom occasionally she was invited to stay. Those visits stayed in her mind with a miraculous radiance. To me, to herself, she could not help embellishing the wonder. She did not know that she was romanticizing – for to her nothing could be more romantic than those visits in girlhood, when she felt transported to her own proper place, when she dreamed of love and marriage, when she dreamed that one day she would find her way to her proper place again.

She could never quite convey the marvel of those Wigmore households. The skating in the bitter winter of 1894, when she was nineteen! The braziers on the ice, a handsome cousin teaching her to cut figures (my mother, like her Sercombe brothers, was adept at dancing and games), music afterwards in the drawing-room! The gigs clattering up the street to her cousin's office – he was a solicitor – and the clients having a glass of sherry at eleven in the morning! How he drove out to 'late dinner' with one or two of the minor gentry! The young officers at a new year's ball! The hushed confidences afterwards with the other girls!

'You never know what's going to happen to you,' said my mother, with the curious realistic humour that came out when one least expected it. 'I didn't bargain on finding myself here.'

Often she felt that she had been deprived of her birthright. She did not ask for pity, she was sarcastic and angry in her frustration, and would have answered with pride if anyone condoled too facilely. She wanted it taken for granted that life had not dealt with her in a fitting fashion; that she was cut out to remain in the houses of those Elysian visits; that she was not designed to stay among the humble of the world. And, with her romantic, surging, passionate spirit she believed – in the midst of heartbreak and disgrace – that there was still time for her luck to change.

I was marked out as the instrument of fortune. Since the bankruptcy, she had invested all her hopes in me. She thought that I was clever; she believed that I was bone of her bone, with the same will and the same pride.

'I want you to remember', said my mother, as the flames danced on the ceiling, 'that you haven't got to stay in this road, I want you not to be content with anything you can find round here. I expect big things from you, dear.'

She looked at me with her keen, luminous eyes.

33

'You're not the sort of boy to be satisfied, are you, Lewis? You're like me in that. Remember, I've seen the things that would just suit your lordship. Please to remember that. I don't want you to be satisfied until you've got there.'

My mother was thinking still of a solicitor's house in Stamford, with the carriages outside, snug and prosperous at the turn of the century – but all seen through the lens of her brilliant imagination.

'You're not going to sit down and let them do what they like with you, are you, dear? I know you. You're going to have your own way. You needn't look as though butter wouldn't melt in your mouth. Your eyes are a lot too sharp. You've just come out of the knife-box, haven't you?'

She grinned. I always enjoyed her mocking, observant grin. Then she spoke with passion again:

'I want to live long enough to see you get there, Lewis. You'll take me with you, won't you? You'll want me to share it, won't you? Remember, I know all about you. I know just what you want. You're not going to be satisfied until you've done everything I've told you, are you, my son?'

I was quick to say yes, to weave fantasies with her, to build houses and furnish them and give her motor cars and furs. Already I loved to compete, I revelled in her pictures of success. Yet I was not easy with her that evening. I was not often easy with my mother.

She meant much to me, much more than any other human being. It was her anxiety and pain that I most dreaded. I always felt threatened by her illnesses. I waited on her, I asked many times a day how she was; and, when in the dark room I heard her answer 'not very well, dear', I wanted to reproach her for being ill, for making the days heavy, for worrying me so much. It was her death that I feared as the ultimate gulf of disaster. She meant far more to me than my father; yet with him I never felt a minute's awkwardness. He was amiable, absorbed in his own daydreams; he was dependent on me, even as a child, for a kind of comic reassurance, and otherwise made no claims. He did not invade my feelings, and only wished for a response that it was innate in me to give, to him and to others, and which I began giving almost as soon as I could talk.

For I was not shy with people. Apart from Aunt Milly, whom at times I hated, I liked those I came into contact with; I liked pleasing them and seeing them pleased. And I liked being praised, and at that age I was eager to have my own say, show off, cut a dash. I had nothing to check my spontaneity, and, despite the calamities of my parents, I was very happy.

I could make the response that others wished for, except to my mother. I was less spontaneous with her than with anyone else, either at this time or later in my boyhood. It was long before I tried to understand it. She needed me more than any of the others needed me. She needed me with all the power of her nature – and she was built to a larger scale than the other figures of my childhood., Built to a larger scale, for all her frailties; most of those frailties I did not see when I was a child; when I did see them, I knew that I too was frail. She needed me. She needed me as an adult man, her son, her like, her equal. She made her demands: without knowing it, I resisted. All I knew was that, sitting with her by the fire or at her bedside when she was ill, my quick light speech fled from me. I was often curt, as I should never have been to a stranger. I was often hard. Yet, away from her presence, I used to pray elaborately and passionately that she might become well, be happy, and gain all her desires. Of all the prayers of my childhood, those were the ones that I urged most desperately to God.

5

A Ten-shilling Note In Front of the Class

WHEN I was eleven, it was time that I was sent to the secondary school, if ever I were to go. There was no free place open for me, since my mother had not budged from her determination not to let me enter a council school. The fees at the secondary school were three guineas a term. My mother sat at the table, moistening a pencil against her lip, writing down the household expenses in a bold heavy hand; she kept the bills on a skewer, and none of the shopkeepers was allowed to wait an hour for his money; she had developed an obsession, almost an obsession in the technical sense, about debt. My father's salary had only gone up by ten shillings a week since the war began. It was now 1917, the cost of living was climbing, and my mother was poor to an extent she had never known. Later I believed that she welcomed rationing and all the privations of war, because they helped to conceal what we had really come to.

She could invent no way of squeezing another nine guineas out of her budget. She had to turn it into shillings a week, for those were the terms in which she was continually thinking. 'Three and eightpence about, it comes out to,' she said. 'I can't manage it, Lewis. It means cutting out the Hearts of Oak, and then I don't know what would happen to us if Bertie goes. And there will be other things to pay for beside your fees, There'll be your cap, and you'll want a school bag and – I don't know. I'm not going to have you suffer by the side of the other boys.'

My mother swallowed her pride, as she could just bring herself to do for my sake, and went to remind Aunt Milly of her promise to pay for my schooling. Aunt Milly promptly redeemed it. Her husband was doing modestly well out of the war, and with the obscure comradeship that linked her to my mother she was concerned about each new sign of penury. But Aunt Milly found it hard to understand the etiquette my mother had elaborated for herself or borrowed from the shabby genteel. My mother would accept the loan of the maid, or 'presents', or 'treats' at my aunt's house; she would have accepted more if Aunt Milly had been careful, but she could not take blunt outright undisguised charity. This 'bit of begging' – as she called it – for my fees was the first she had descended to since she was faced with the expenses of my brother Martin's birth and her illness afterwards. Those would have crippled us entirely, and she let Aunt Milly pay.

Aunt Milly even spared my mother any exhortation when she agreed to find my fees. She saved that for me an hour or two later. She was never worried about repeating herself, and so she gave me the same warning as on the afternoon of my father's bankruptcy, three years before. I was not to expect success. It was likely that I should have a most undistinguished career at this new school.

'You've got too good an opinion of yourself,' said Aunt Milly firmly and enthusiastically, with her usual lack of facial expression. 'I don't blame you for it altogether. It's your mother's fault for letting you think you're something out of the ordinary. No wonder you're getting too big for your boots.'

To the best of Aunt Milly's belief, I should find myself behind all other boys of my age. I should, in all probability, find it impossible to catch up. Aunt Milly would consider that her money had been well invested if I contrived to scrape through my years at school without drawing unfavourable attention to myself. And once more I was to listen to her message. My first duty, if ever my education provided me with a livelihood, was to save enough money to pay twenty shillings in the pound on my father's liabilities, and so get him discharged from bankruptcy.

I was practised in listening silently to Aunt Milly. Sometimes she discouraged me, but for most purposes I had toughened my skin. My skin was not, however, tough enough for an incident which took place in my first term at the new school.

Several of the boys there knew that my father had 'failed in business'. They came from the same part of the town, they had heard it gossiped about; my father might have passed unnoticed, but my mother was a conspicuous figure in the parish. One of them twitted me with it, saying each time he saw me, 'Why did your dad go bust?' in the nagging, indefatigable, imbecile, repetitious fashion of very small boys. I flushed at first, but soon got used to him, and it did not hurt me much.

Curiously enough, until the incident of the subscription list, I was more embarrassed by the notoriety of no less a person than Aunt Milly. Her vigour in the cause of temperance was well known all over the town. During the summer she had organized a vast teetotal procession through the streets: it consisted of carts in which each of the Rechabite tents staged its own tableau, usually of an historical nature and in fancy dress, followed by the Templar lodges on foot and carrying banners. My aunt, and the other high officers, made up the end of the procession; wearing their 'regalia' of red, blue, or green, according to the order, with various signs of rank, something like horses' halters round their necks, they sat on small chairs on a very large cart.

Like all Aunt Milly's activities, the procession had been organized with extraordinary thoroughness and clockwork precision. But some of my form-mates who had seen it – perhaps some had even taken part – discovered that she was my aunt and decided that to have such an aunt was preposterously funny. I then found out that shame is an unpredictable thing. For I should have said that I could take any conceivable joke against Aunt Milly without a pang: in fact, I was painfully ashamed.

The incident of the subscription list took place in November, a couple of months after I first attended the school. Each boy in each form had been asked to make a donation to the school munitions fund. The headmaster had explained how, if we could only give sixpence, we should be doing our bit; all the money would go straight to buy shells for what the headmaster called 'the 1918 offensive – the next big push'.

I reported it all to my mother. I asked her what we could afford to give.

'We can't afford much really, dear,' said my mother, looking upset, preoccupied, wounded. 'We haven't got much to spare at the end of the week. I know that you've got to give something.'

It added to her worries. As she had said before, she was not going 'to have me suffer by the side of the other boys'.

'How much do you think they'll give, Lewis?' she inquired. 'I mean, the boys from nice homes.'

I made some discreet investigations, and told her that most of my form would be giving half a crown or five shillings.

She pursed her lips.

'You needn't bother yourself, dear,' she said. 'I'm not going to have you feel out of it. We can do as well as other people.'

She was not content with doing 'as well as other people'. Her imagination had been fired. She wanted me to give more than anyone in the form. She told herself that it would establish a position for me, it would give me a good start. She liked to feel that we could 'still show we were someone'. And she was patriotic and warlike, and had a strong sense of wartime duty; though most of all she wanted me to win favour and notice, she also got satisfaction from 'buying shells', from taking part in the war at second hand.

She skimped my father's food and her own, particularly hers, for several weeks. After a day or two my father noticed, and mildly grumbled. He asked if the rations were reduced so low as this. No, said my mother, she was saving up for the subscription list at school.

'I hope you don't have many subscriptions,' said my father to me. 'Or I expect she'll starve me to death.'

He clowned away, pretending that his trousers had inches to spare round his middle.

'Don't be such a donkey, Bertie,' said my mother irritably.

She kept to her intention. They went without the small luxuries that she had managed to preserve, through war, through the slow grind of growing poverty – the glass of stout on Saturday night, the supper of fish and chips (fetched, for propriety's sake, by Aunt Milly's maid), the jam at breakfast. On the morning when we had to deliver our subscriptions, my mother handed me a new ten-shilling note. I exclaimed with delight and pressed the crisp paper against the tablecloth. I had never had one in my possession before.

'Not many of them will do better than that,' said my mother contentedly. 'Remember that before the war I should have given you a sovereign. I want you to show them that we've still got our heads above water.'

Under the gaslight, in the early morning, the shadow of my cup was blue on the white cloth. I admired the ten-shilling note, I admired the blue shadows, I watched the shadows of my own hands. I was thanking my mother: I was flooded with happiness and triumph.

'I shall want to hear everything they say,' said my mother. 'They'll be a bit flabbergasted, won't they? They won't expect anyone to give what you're giving. Please to remember everything they say.'

I was lit up with anticipation as the tramcar clanged and swayed into the town. Mist hung over the county ground, softened the red brick of the little houses by the jail: in the mist – not fog, but the clean autumnal mist – the red brick, though softened, seemed at moments to leap freshly on the eye. It was a morning nostalgic, tangy, and full of well-being.

In the playground, when we went out for the eleven-o'clock break, the sun was shining. Our subscriptions were to be collected immediately afterwards: as the bell jangled, my companions and I made our way chattering through the press of boys to the room where we spent most of our lessons.

Mr Peck came in. He taught us algebra and geometry; he was a man about fifty-five who had spent his whole life at the school; he was bald, fresh-skinned, small-featured, constantly smiling. He lived in the next suburb beyond ours, and occasionally he was sitting in the tramcar when I got on.

Some boy had written a facetious word on the blackboard. Peck smiled deprecatingly, a little threateningly, and rubbed out the chalk marks. He turned to us, still smiling.

'Well,' he said, 'the first item on the programme is to see how much this form is going to contribute to make the world safe for democracy.' There was a titter; he had won his place long ago as a humorist.

'If any lad gives enough,' he said, 'I dare say we shall be prepared to let him off all penalties for the rest of the term. That is known as saving your bacon.'

Another titter.

'Well,' he went on, 'I don't suppose for a moment that you want to turn what you are pleased to call your minds to the problems of elementary geometry. However, it is my unfortunate duty to make you do so without unnecessary delay. So we will dispose of this financial tribute as soon as we decently can. I will call out your names from the register. Each lad will stand up to answer his name, announce his widow's mite, and bring the cash up here for me to receive. Then the last on the list can add up the total and sign it, so as to certify that I haven't run away with the money.'

Peck smiled more broadly, and we all grinned in return. He began to read out the names. The new boys were divided into forms by alphabetical order, and ours ran from A to H.

'Adnitt.' 'Two shillings, sir.' The routine began, Adnitt walked to the front of the class and put his money on the desk. I was cherishing my note under the lid of the desk; my heart thudded with joyful excitement. 'Aldwinckle.' 'Two and sixpence.' 'Brookman.' 'Nothing.'

Brookman was a surly, untidy boy, who lived in the town's one genuine slum. Peck stared at him, still smiling. 'You're not interested in our little efforts, my friend?' said Peck.

Brookman did not reply. Peck stared at him, began another question, then shrugged his shoulders and passed on.

'Buckley.' 'A shilling.' 'Cann.' 'Five shillings.' The form cheerfully applauded. 'Coe.' 'A shilling.' 'Cotery.' 'Three shillings and twopence.' There was laughter; Jack Cotery was an original; one could trust him not to behave like anyone else. 'Dawson.' 'Half a crown.' There were several other D's, all giving between a shilling and three shillings. 'Eames.' 'Five shillings.' Applause. 'Edridge.' 'Five shillings.' Applause. My name came next. As soon as Peck called it out, I was on my feet. 'Ten shillings, sir.' I could not damp a little stress upon the ten. The class stamped their feet, as I went between the desks and laid the note among the coins in front of Peck.

I had just laid the note down, when Peck said: 'That's quite a lot of money, friend Eliot.' I smiled at him, full of pleasure, utterly unguarded; but at his next remark the smile froze behind my lips and eyes.

'I wonder you can afford it,' said Peck. 'I wonder you don't feel obliged to put it by towards your father's debts.'

It was cruel, casual, and motiveless. It was a motiveless malice as terrifying for a child to know as his first knowledge of adult lust. It ravaged me with sickening shameful agony – and, more violently, I was shaken with anger, so that I was on the point of seizing the note and tearing it in pieces before his eyes.

'Let me give you a piece of advice, my friend,' said Peck, complacently. 'It will be to your own advantage in the long run. You're a bright lad, aren't you? I'm thinking of your future, you know. That's why I'm giving you a piece of advice. It isn't the showy things that are most difficult to do, Eliot. It's just plodding away and doing your duty and never getting thanked for it – that's the test for bright lads like you. You just bear my words in mind.'

Somewhere in the back of consciousness I knew that the class had been joining in with sycophantic giggles. As I turned and met their eyes on my way back, they were a little quieter. But they giggled again when Peck said: 'Well, I shall soon have to follow my own advice and plod away and do my duty and never get thanked for it – by teaching a class of dolts some geometrical propositions they won't manage to get into their thick heads as long as they live, But I must finish the collection first. All contributions thankfully received. Fingleton.' 'Two shillings, sir.' 'Frere.' 'A shilling.'

I watched and listened through a sheen of rage and misery.

At the end of the morning, Jack Cotery spoke to me in the playground. He was a lively, active boy, short but muscular, with the eyes of a comedian, large, humorous, and sad.

'Don't mind about Pecky,' he said with good nature and a light heart.

'I don't mind a scrap.'

'You were as white as a sheet. I thought you were going to howl.'

I did not swear as some of the boys in the form habitually did; I had been too finically brought up. But at that moment all my pain, anger, and temper exploded in a screaming oath.

Jack Cotery was taken aback. 'Keep your shirt on,' he said.

On the way to the tram stop, where we travelled in different directions, he could not resist asking me: 'Is your old man in debt, really?'

'In a way,' I said, trying to shield the facts, not to tell an actual lie— wanting both to mystify and to hide my own misery. 'In a way. It's all very complicated, it's a matter of — petitions.' I added, as impressively as I could, 'It's been in the solicitor's hands.'

'I'm glad mine's all right,' said Jack Cotery, impressive in his turn. 'Of course, I could have brought a lot more money this morning. My old man is making plenty, though he doesn't always let on. He'd have given me a *pound* if I'd asked him. But' —Jack Cotery whispered and his eyes glowed — 'I'm keeping it in reserve for something else.'

When I arrived home, my mother was waiting for me with an eager question.

'What did they think of your subscription, dear?'

'All right,' I said.

'Did anyone give more than ten shillings?'

'No. Not in our form.'

My mother drew herself up and nodded her head: 'Was ours the highest?'

'Oh yes.'

'What was the next highest?'

'Five shillings,' I said.

43

'Twice as much,' said my mother, smiling and gratified. But she was perceptive; she had an inkling of something wrong.

'What did they *say*, though, dear?'

'They thanked me, of course.'

'Who was the master who took it?' she asked.

'Mr Peck.'

'Was he pleased with you?'

'Of course he was,' I said flatly.

'I want to hear everything he said,' said my mother, half in vanity, half trying to reach my trouble.

'I can't now, Mother. I want to get back early. I'll tell you everything tonight.'

'I don't think that's very grateful of you,' said my mother. 'Considering what I did to find you all that money. Don't you think I deserve to be told all about it now?'

'I'll tell you everything tonight.'

'Please not to worry yourself if it's too much trouble,' she said haughtily, feeling that I was denying her love.

'It's not too much trouble, Mother. I'll tell you tonight,' I said, not knowing which way to turn.

I did not go straight home from school that evening. Instead, I walked by myself a long way round by the canal; the mist was rising, as fresh and clean as that morning's mist; but as it swirled round the bridges and warehouses and the trees by the waterside, it no longer exalted me. I was inventing a story, walking that long way home through the mist, which would content my mother. Of how Mr Peck had said my contribution was an example to the form, of how he had told other masters, of how someone said that my parents were public-spirited. I composed suitable speeches. I had enough sense of reality to make them sound plausible, and to add one or two disparaging remarks from envious form-mates.

I duly repeated that fiction to my mother. Nothing could remove her disappointment. She had thought me inconsiderate and heartless, and now, if she believed at all, she felt puzzled, cast-off, and only a little flattered. I thought that I was romancing simply to save her from a bitter degradation. Yet I should have brought her more love if I had told her the truth. It would have been more loving to let her take an equal share in that day's suffering. That lie showed the flaw between us.

There were nights that autumn, however, when my mother and I were closer than we had ever been. They were the nights when she tried to learn French. She saw me with my first French grammar, and she was seized with a desire to follow my lessons. French to her was romantic, genteel, emblem and symbol of the existence she had so much coveted. Her bold, handsome eyes were bright each time we spread the books on the front-room table. Her health was getting worse, she was having frightening fits of giddiness, but her interest and nervous gusto and hope pressed her on as when she was a girl.

'Time for my French lesson,' she said eagerly when Saturday evening came round. We started after tea and she was downcast if I would not persevere for a couple of hours. Often on those Saturday nights the autumn gales lashed rain against the windows; to that accompaniment, my mother tried to repeat my secondary-school phonetics.

Actually, she found my attempts to retail the phonetic lessons quite impossible to imitate. She learned entirely by eye, and was comfortable when she could pronounce the words exactly as in English. But she learned quickly and accurately by eye, as I did myself. Soon she could translate the simple sentences in my reader. It gave her a transfiguring pleasure; she held my hand, and translated one sentence after another. 'Is that right? Is that right?' she cried wildly and happily, and laughed at me. 'You're not ashamed of your pupil, are you, dear?'

6

The First Start

I BURIED deep the claims my mother made on me and which I could not meet. I could forget them more easily because, in my successes at school, I provided her, for the only time for years, with something actual for her hopes to feed on. She still read the cards and teacups, she had taken to entering for several competitions a week in *Answers* and *John Bull*, but when she studied my terminal reports, she felt this was her solitary promise for the future. As soon as she had received one and read it through, she put it in her bag, changed into her best dress, and, pointing her toes, set off in dignity for Aunt Milly, the doctor, and the vicar.

When I took the Senior Oxford, I gave her something more to flaunt. My last term at school was over and I waited for the result. It was the brilliant summer of 1921, and one night I came home after baking all day at the county ground. As I came up our street in the hot and thundery evenings I saw my mother and brother waving to me from the window.

My mother opened the door herself. She was displaying the evening paper. She looked flushed and well, her eyes were flashing, although she had had a heart attack that summer.

'Do you know, dear?' she cried.

'No. Is it –?'

'Then let me be the first to congratulate you,' she said with a grand gesture. 'You couldn't have done better. It's impossible for you to have done better!'

It was her way, her romantic and superb way, of saying that my name appeared in the first class. She was exultant. My name was alone! – she was light-headed with triumph. I was recklessly joyful, but each time I caught my mother's eye I felt I had never seen such triumph. She had none of the depression of anticlimax that chases after a success; she had looked forward to this moment, one of many moments to come, and her spirit was strong enough to exult without a single qualm.

My mother at once sent my young brother out for foods that we could not usually afford. She intended to have a glorious supper – not that she could eat much nowadays, but for the sake of style and for my sake. My father had, a year past, ceased to be a traveller and had moved back to 'Mr Stapleton's' as a cashier at four pounds a week. He was competent at paperwork, but my mother ground the aching tooth and told herself that it was shameful to return to such a job when he had been second-in-command, that the job was just a bone thrown in contemptuous friendliness and charity. Thus, with the fall in the value of money, our meals were not as lavish as they had been even immediately after my father's bankruptcy. Even so, my mother never lost her taste for the extravagant. She still paid each bill on Saturday morning; but if luxuries were required for a state occasion, such as that night, luxuries were bought, though it meant going hungry for the rest of the week.

That night we ate a melon and some boiled salmon and éclairs and meringues and *millefeuilles*. My mother's triumph would have been increased if she could have had Aunt Milly there to gloat over; but she could not have Aunt Milly as well as a glass of wine, and my mother's sense of fitness would not be satisfied without wine on the table; she wanted to fill the wine glasses which she had received as a wedding present and which were not used more than once a year. So young Martin had been sent on another errand to the grocer, and the glasses were filled with tawny port.

My father, who had changed not at all in the last seven years, kept saying, 'Well, I didn't pass the examination. But I can dispose of the supper as well as anyone,' and ate away with his usual mild but hearty content. My mother was too borne up to say more than, 'Bertie, don't be such a donkey'. She took her share of the meal, which nowadays she rarely did, and several glasses of wine. More than once she put up her spectacles to her long-sighted eyes and read the announcement again. 'No one in the same division!' she cried. 'It will give them all something to think about!' She decided that she must have two dozen copies of the paper to send to friends and relatives, and ordered Martin to make sure and go to the newsagents first thing next morning.

My mother talked to me across the supper table.

'I always told you to make your way,' she said. The room was gilded in the sunset, and she raised a hand to shield her eyes. 'I want you to remember that, No one else told you that, did they?'

She was illuminated with triumph and her glasses of wine, but she asked insistently.

'No,' I said.

'No one else at all did they?'

'Of course not, Mother,' I said.

'I don't expect you to be satisfied now,' she said. 'There's a lot to do. You've got a long way to go. You remember all you've promised me, don't you?'

It turned out, almost at once, very easy not to be satisfied. For I was faced with the choice of my first job. When the examination result came out, I had actually left school, although we had put off the question of my job. And now my mother and I conferred. What was I to do? We had no one to give us accurate information, let alone advice. No boy at the school had ever taken a scholarship to the university; those masters who had degrees had taken them externally through London and Dublin. None of them knew his way about. One or two, wanting to help me, suggested that I might stay at school and then go to a teacher's training college. It meant real hardship to my mother unless I earned some money at once; not that she would have minded such hardship – she would have cherished it, if her imagination had been caught – but she resented stinting us all for years so that I might in the end become an elementary school teacher.

My mother found no more help in the parish. This was the *vie de province*, the life of a submerged and suburban province. The new vicar, though even 'higher', was less cultivated than the old one. The doctor had lived in the district all his life, except when he was struggling his way through a London hospital and the conjoint; from his excessive awe at my passing an examination, I suspected that he had had trouble with his own. He knew the parish like the palm of his hand, but he was quite ignorant of the world outside. He could suggest nothing for me. Perhaps he was anxious to take no responsibility, for my mother, given the slightest lead, would not have refused to let him set me going. My mother had always believed that if I showed promise Dr Francis would interest himself practically in my career. But Dr Francis was a wary old bird.

Aunt Milly took it into her head that I ought to become an engineer. She first of all pointed out that, though I might have done better than anyone from the local schools, no doubt plenty of boys in other places had achieved the same result. Then, in her energetic fashion, she went off, without getting my mother's agreement or mine, and plunged into discussions with some of her father's acquaintances at the tram depot. She obtained some opinions which later I realized were entirely sensible, It would be necessary for me to become a trade apprentice: that meant five years in the works, and working at the technical college at night; it would be easy to get taken as an apprentice by one of the town's big engineering firms. Aunt Milly produced these views with vigorous satisfaction. She felt, as usual, confident that she had done the right thing and that this was the only conceivable course for me. She overlooked two factors. One, that my mother was shocked to the marrow of her bones by the thought that I should become for years what seemed to her nothing but a manual worker. Two, that there was almost no occupation which I should have liked less or been more completely unfitted for. Aunt Milly left the house in a huff, and it was apparent that we could expect no further aid from her.

That aggravated our distress, for up to now my mother had always known that she had Aunt Milly as an ultimate reserve, in the very long run. It was only a few days afterwards, when I had begun answering advertisements in the local paper, that I received a letter from my headmaster. If I was not fitted with what he called a 'post', would I go to see him? At once my mother's romantic hope surged up. Perhaps the school had some funds to give me a grant, perhaps after all they would manage to send me to a university – for, learning from the handbooks on careers that I had discovered, my mother now saw a university as our Promised Land.

In brutal fact, the offer was a different one. The education office in the town hall had asked the school to recommend someone as a junior clerk. It was the kind of job much coveted among my companions – the headmaster was giving the first refusal, as a kind of prize. The pay was a pound a week until seventeen and then went up by five shillings a week each year, until one reached three pounds, the top of the scale. It was a perfectly safe job; there were prospects of going reasonably high in the local government offices, perhaps to a divisional chief at four hundred and fifty pounds a year. There was, of course, a pension. The headmaster strongly advised me to take it. He had himself begun as an elementary schoolteacher in the town, had acquired a Dublin degree, and when our school had been promoted to secondary status he had had his one great piece of luck. He was a full-blooded and virile man, but he was hardened to his pupils having to scrape their way.

I thanked him, and took the job. There seemed nothing else to do.

When I told my mother her face on the instant was open with disappointment.

'Oh,' she said. Then she added, trying to make her voice come full and unconcerned: 'Well, dear, it's better than nothing.'

'Oh yes,' I said.

'It's better than nothing,' said my mother. She was recovering herself. It was only another of her many disappointments. They had taught her to be stoical. And she still kept, which was part of her stoicism, her unquenched appetite for the future; for an appetite for the future was, with her, another name for hope.

She inquired about the job, the work, where it would lead. She liked the phrase 'local government'; she would use that to the doctor and the vicar, for it took the edge off the comedown, it made my doings seem much grander.

'How do you feel about it, dear?' she asked, after she had been imagining how I could turn it all to profit.

'It's better than nothing.' With a sarcastic flick, I returned her phrase.

'You know I only want the best for you,' she said.

'Of course I know.'

'We can't have everything. I haven't had everything I should like, have I? You'll manage as well as you can, won't you?'

'Of course.'

She looked at me with trouble in her eyes, with guilt and with reproach.

'There's still time if you can see anything else to do, dear. Please to tell me. Please – if there's any mortal person I can talk to for you – '

'It's all right, Mother,' I said, and let it stop at that.

My feelings were mixed. I was, in part, relieved and glad, absurd though it seemed only a few months later; but I was glad to be earning a living, and to know that next week I should have a little money in my pocket. I was nearly sixteen, it was irksome to be so often without a shilling, and that trivial relief lightened me more than I could believe.

I disliked the sound of the job – I felt it was nothing like good enough. Yet I was interested, just as I was in any new prospect or change. I had spasms of rancour that I had been so helpless. If I had known more, if I had moved among different people, I could have looked after myself and this would never have happened. But that rancour was not going to cripple me. I was not a good son to my mother, but I was very much her son: I had the same surgent hope. Other disasters might wound me beyond repair, but not anything like this, not anything outside myself that I could learn to master, I knew, with the certainty that comes when one is in touch with a deep part

51

of one's nature, that this setback was not going to matter much. My hope was like my mother's, but more stubborn and untiring. I believed I could find a way out.

7

The Effect of a Feud

AUNT Milly was violently opposed to my 'white-collar job'. 'That's all it is,' said Aunt Milly in her loudest voice to my mother. 'He's just going off to be a wretched little clerk in a white-collar job. I never did believe all that people told me about your son, but he seems to have more brains than some of them. Now he's content to go off to the first white-collar job he sees. Don't complain to me when he finds himself in the same office when he's forty. No wonder they say that the present generation hasn't got a scrap of enterprise.'

My mother recounted the scene, and her own dignified retort, with the humorous haughty expression that she wore when she had been most upset. For, particularly as the months went on, and I had been catching the eight-forty tram for a year, for a year and a half, she wondered painfully if we had made a mistake. She was a little better off, since I paid her ten shillings a week for my keep – but she could not see any sign of the dramatic transformation scene she had always longed for, always in her heart expected, as I came to manhood. She would have been content with the slightest tangible sign for her indomitable spirit to fasten on. If, for example, I had been working for a university scholarship, she would have foreseen fantastic, visible, miraculous success at the university, herself joining me there, all her expectations realized at a stroke. She did not mind how many years ahead the transformation scene took place, so long as there was just one real sign for her imagination to refresh itself upon. As she saw me go to the office, day following day, the months lengthening into a year, she could not find that one real sign.

She had to come to earth now and again, if her excursions into the future were to keep her going. In her fashion, she was both shrewd and realistic, though with a minimum of encouragement she could draw wonderful pictures of how her life might yet be changed. She was too shrewd and realistic to derive any encouragement from my days at the office. She took to filling in more of her competition coupons. Her health became worse, and one heart attack made her spend a whole spring as an invalid, lying all day on a sofa. She stood it all, hope deferred, illness, pride once more wounded, with the fierce steady endurance that did not seem in any way affected by her own quivering nerves.

I used to work through the long, tedious hours in a room which overlooked the tramlines. The trams ran past the office windows in Bowling Green Street; our room, three storeys up, looked down on the tram tops and the solicitors' and insurance offices on the other side of the street. I shared the room with six other clerks and one more senior man, Mr Vesey, who was called a departmental head and paid two hundred and fifty pounds a year. The work was one long monotony for me, interspersed by Mr Vesey's slowly growing enmity. He was in charge of the branch, which was part of the secondary school department; I made lists of the children from elementary schools who won 'free places', and passed the names on to the accountant's room. I also made lists of pupils at each secondary school who left before taking the General Schools or Senior Oxford examinations. I compiled a good deal of miscellaneous statistical information of that kind, which Mr Vesey signed and sent up to the director. Our room did little but accumulate such facts, pass records of names to other departments, and occasionally draw up a chart. Very few decisions were ever taken there. The most onerous decision with which Mr Vesey was faced was whether to allow a child to leave school before the age of fifteen without paying a penalty of five pounds. He was allowed the responsibility of omitting the penalty; if he wished it imposed, the case had to go before the director.

That suited Mr Vesey very well. He had no desire to take decisions, but an insatiable passion for attracting the notice of his superiors. When I first went into the office, I rather liked the look of him. He was a spruce, small man of about forty, who must have spent a large fraction of his income on clothes. His shirts were always spotless, he had a great variety of ties, all quiet and carefully selected. His eyes, which were full and exophthalmic, were magnified still further because of the convex lenses that he wore, so that one's first impression, after seeing his trim suit, was of enormous and somewhat baffled and sorrowful eyes. He told me my duties in a manner that was friendly, if a little fussed, and I was young enough, and enough of a stranger, to be grateful for any kindness and not overcritical of its origin.

It took me some time to realize that Mr Vesey spent fifty-nine minutes in the hour tormenting himself about his prospects of promotion. He was a departmental officer grade one, salary scale two hundred and twenty-five pounds to three hundred and fifteen pounds; his entire activity was spent in mounting to the next grade. As I came to know him, I heard of nothing else. A contemporary of his in another office got promoted. 'Why don't they do something about me?' sounded Mr Vesey's *cri de coeur*. His technique for achieving his aim was, in principle, very simple. It consisted of keeping in the public eye. If ever he could invent an excuse for calling on the director, he did so. So that every child who left school before the age of fifteen secured a visit to the director's room; a trim, spectacled figure, holding a file, knocked briskly on the door, the director was entangled in an earnest consultation, found himself faced with enormous exophthalmic eyes. The director soon became maddened, and sent down minutes about types of case which it was unnecessary for him to see. Mr Vesey went to see him to discuss each minute.

When any senior person came into our room to inspect the work, a trim spectacled figure stood beside him, on the alert, agog and on tenterhooks to seize the chance. The visitor asked one of the clerks a question. Mr Vesey leapt in to answer it. The visitor asked me to describe some of the statistics. Mr Vesey was quicker than ever off the mark.

All lists, charts, notes of any kind going out from our room had to be initialled NCWV. For a time he experimented with hyphenating the W and V, possibly in the hope that it would make the initials impossible to miss. There were rumours that his wife wanted to be called Mrs Wilson-Vesey. However, the assistant director asked him brusquely what the hyphen was put in for. All superiors were important to Mr Vesey, though some were more important than others. The hyphen disappeared overnight.

His worst moments were when, as occasionally happened, the assistant director – instead of asking for information through Mr Vesey as head of the branch – demanded a clerk by name. Mr Vesey's enmity towards me first showed itself after a few such calls. The assistant director found I knew my lists inside out (which was child's play to anyone with a good memory), took a fancy to me, said maddeningly once that if I were still at school the department would make a grant to help me go to a university. Meanwhile, Mr Vesey was raising cries to heaven: how could he organize his branch if people did not go through the proper channels? How could he secure discipline and smooth working if people went over his head? Junior clerks did not understand the whole scope of his responsibilities – they might give a wrong impression and that meant his promotion would never come. There was such a thing, said Mr Vesey in a tone full of meaning, as junior clerks trying to draw attention to themselves.

So it went on, a blend of monotony and Mr Vesey. So it went on, from nine to one, from two to five-thirty, from my sixteenth birthday to my seventeenth and beyond. Often, during those tedious days, I dreamed the ambitious dreams of very young men. Walking past the lighted shops in the lunch hour of a winter's day, I dreamed of fame – any kind of fame that would put my name in men's mouths, in the newspapers, make people recognize me in the streets. Sometimes I was a great politician, eloquent, powerful, venerated. Sometimes I was a writer as well known as Shaw. Sometimes I was extraordinarily rich.

Always I had the power to make my own terms, to move through the world as one who owned it, to be waited on and give largesse.

The harsh streets were lit by my fancies, and I was drunk with them – and yet they were altogether vague. There was a good deal of ambition, I knew later, innate within me; and I had listened since I was a child to my mother's prompting. But those dreams of mine had not much in common with the ambition that drives a man, that in time drove me, to action. These were just the lazy and grandiose dreams of youth. They were far more like the times when, lying awake on windy autumn nights or sitting under the apple tree in the garden after my parents had gone to bed, I first luxuriously longed, through a veil of innocence, for women's love.

Even at sixteen, however, I felt sometimes guilty, because I was only dreaming. The pictures in my mind were so heady, so magnificent – they made all practical steps that I could take seem puny. Puny they seemed, as I took the opportunity one day to talk to my acquaintance, the assistant director. He had sent for me again, inflaming Mr Vesey to transports of injured dignity. Darby was a decent pale man with a furrowed forehead, sitting in his small, plain office. He gave me prosaic but sensible advice. It might be worth while thinking of the possibility of an external London degree. It might be worth while picking up some law, which would be useful if I stayed in the office. I ought to consult the people at the College of Art and Technology.

I did so, and enrolled in the law class at the college – which everyone called 'the School', and which was at that time the only place of higher education in the town – in the summer of 1922, when I was not yet seventeen. The School was the lineal descendant of the mechanics' institution, where my grandfather had learned his mathematics; it was housed in a red-brick building, a building of remarkable Victorian baroque. There was a principal and a small permanent staff, but most of the lecturers had other jobs in the town, were secondary schoolmasters and the like, and gave their school lectures in the evening. The first law class I attended was given by a solicitor from the town clerk's department. It was a course on a dull subject, dully taught. It lasted through the autumn: I used to walk down the Newarke on Tuesday and Friday evenings after the office, wondering whether I was not wasting my time.

I was still wondering, towards the end of the year, whether to give up the law courses, when I happened to see a notice in the School, announcing a new course in the spring term – 'Fundamentals of Law, 1. Criminal, by G Passant'. I thought I would give him a trial. Before I had listened for ten minutes to the first lecture, I knew this was something of a different class, in sheer force, in intellectual competence and power, from anything I had ever heard.

George Passant's voice was loud, strained, irascible, and passionate. He gave the entire lecture at a breakneck speed, as though he were irritated with the stupidity of his class and wanted to get it over. His voice and manner, I thought, were in curious contrast to his face, which wore an amiable, an almost diffident smile. His head was large and powerful, set on thick, heavy shoulders; and under the amiable smile, the full amiable flesh, the bones of his forehead, cheekbones and chin were made on the same big scale. He was not much over middle height, but he was obviously built to put on weight. His hair was fair: he was a full blond, with light blue eyes, which had a knack of looking past the class, past the far wall, focusing on infinity.

After that night, I made inquiries about George Passant. No one could tell me much: he had only come to the town in the previous autumn, was a qualified solicitor, was working as managing clerk in the solid, respectable firm of Eden and Martineau. He was very young, not more than twenty-three or four, as indeed one could see at a glance. Someone had heard a rumour that he led a 'wild' life.

Meeting George Passant was the first piece of pure chance that affected all that I did later. The second piece of chance in my youth happened, oddly enough, within a fortnight.

My mother was one of a very large family – or rather of two families, for, as I mentioned previously, her father had married twice, having four children by his first wife, and seven, of whom my mother was one of the youngest, by his second. For many years she had been on bad terms with her half-brothers and sisters: within her own mother's family there was great affection, and they saw and wrote to each other frequently their whole lives long, but none of them visited their seniors or spoke of them without a note of anger and injury.

I had first heard the story in those talks by the fireside, when my mother let her romantic imagination return to the winter of 1894. It was then that she told me of the intrigues of Will and Za. For a long time I thought she had exaggerated in order to paint the wonder of the Wigmores. In her version, the villain of the piece was my Uncle Will. He was the eldest son of the first family, and my mother described him with hushed indignation and respect. His villainy had consisted of diverting money intended for the younger family to himself and his sisters. My mother had never succeeded in making the details clear, but she believed something like this: her mother had brought some money with her when she married (was she not a Wigmore?). How much it was my mother could not be sure, but she said in a fierce whisper that it might have been over fifteen hundred pounds. This money her mother had 'intended' to be divided among the younger family at her death. But Uncle Will had intervened with their father, to whom the money was left and who was then a very old man. Through Uncle Will's influence, every penny had gone to himself and his two sisters (the fourth of the first family had died young).

I never knew the truth of it. My mother believed her story implicitly, and she was an honest woman, honest in the midst of her temptation to glorify all that happened to her. It was certainly true that Aunt Za, the oldest sister of all, Uncle Will and Aunt Florrie all had a little money, while none of the other family had inherited so much as a pound. It was also true that all my mother's brothers and sisters bore the same grievance.

After twenty years of the quarrel, my mother tried to make peace. She did it partly for my sake, since Aunt Za was the widow of an auctioneer and thought to 'have more than she needed for herself'. She had, since her husband died, gone to live near her brother Will, who ran a small estate agency in Market Harborough. My mother wanted also to repair the breach in order to show me off; but the chief reason was that she had deep instinctive loyalties, and though she told herself that she was making an approach purely for my sake, as a piece of calculation, it was really that she did not want any of them to die unreconciled.

Her move went about halfway to success. She visited Market Harborough and was welcomed by Za and Will. After that visit, birthday and Christmas correspondence was resumed. But neither Za nor Will returned her visit, nor would they, as she tried to persuade them, write a word to any others of the younger family. My mother, however, secured one positive point. She talked about me; it was easy to imagine her magnifying my promise, and being met in kind, for Za and Will had exactly her sort of stately, haughty manner. I was about fourteen at the time, and was invited over to Will's for a week in the summer holidays. Since then I had gone to Harborough often, as an emissary between the two families, as a sign that the quarrel was at least formally healed.

On these visits to Harborough, I did not see much of Aunt Za (her name, an abbreviation of Thirza, was pronounced Zay). Her whole life, since her husband died, was lived in and round the church. She taught a Sunday-school class, helped with mothers' meetings, attended the sick in the parish, but most of all she lived for her devotions, going to church morning and night each day of the year. I used to have tea with her, once and only once, each time I stayed with Uncle Will. She was an ageing woman, stately and sombre, with a prowlike nose and sunken mouth. She had little to say to me, except to ask after my mother's health and to tell me to go regularly to church. She always gave me seed cake with the tea, so that the taste of caraway years later brought back, like a Proustian moment, the narrow street, the dark house, the taciturn and stiff old woman burdened with piety and the dreadful prospect of the grave.

I did not entertain her, as sometimes I managed to entertain Uncle Will. Yet apparently she liked me well enough – or else there was justice in my mother's story, and Aunt Za felt a wound of conscience throbbing as she became old. Whatever her motive, she wrote to my mother in the autumn I entered the office, said that she was making a new will, and proposed in doing so to leave me 'a small remembrance'.

My mother was resplendent with pleasure. It gratified her that she had brought off something for me, that her schemes had for once not been blocked. It gratified her specially that it should come through her family, and so prove something of past glories. As she thought of it, however, she was filled with anxiety. 'I hope Za doesn't tell Will what she intends to do,' said my mother. 'He'll find a way to put it in his own pocket, you can bet your boots. You're not going to tell me that Will has stopped looking after himself.'

My mother's suspicion of Uncle Will flared up acutely eighteen months afterwards – in the spring of 1923, when I was seventeen and a half. My mother had been ill, and was only just coming down again to breakfast. There was a letter for her, addressed in a hand that could belong to no one but Uncle Will, a fine affected flowing Italian hand, developed as an outward mark of superiority, with dashes everywhere instead of full stops. As she read it, my mother's face was pallid with anger.

'He didn't mean us to get near her,' she said. 'Za's gone. She went yesterday morning. He says that it was very sudden. Of course, he was too upset to send us a wire,' she added with savage sarcasm.

However, this hope of hers was not snatched away. My father and I attended the funeral, and afterwards heard the will read in Uncle Will's house. I received three hundred pounds. Three hundred pounds. It was much more than I expected, or my mother in her warmest flush of optimism. Cheerfully, my heart thumped.

My father ruminated with content as we walked to the station: 'Three hundred of the best, Lewis. Think of that! Three hundred of the best. Why, there's no knowing what you'll be able to do with it. Three blooming hundred.'

Almost for the first time in my experience, he was impelled to assert himself. 'I hope you won't think of spending it without consulting me,' he said. 'I know what money is, you realize. Why, every week at Mr Stapleton's I pay out twice as much as your three hundred pounds. I can keep you on the right track, providing you never commit yourself without consulting me.'

I assured him – in the light, familiar, companionable tone that had always existed naturally between us – that we would have long and exacting conferences. My father chuckled. A trifle puffed out by his success, he produced a singular piece of practical advice.

'I always tell people', he said, as though he were in the habit of being deferred to on every kind of financial business, 'never to go about without five pounds sewn in a place where no one can find it. You never know when you'll need it badly, Lewis. It's a reserve. Think of that! If I were you, I should get Lena to sew five of your pound notes into the seat of your trousers. You never know when you'll want them. One of these days you'll thank me for the idea, you mark my words.'

In the train, we found an empty third-class carriage. My father stretched his short legs, I my long ones, and we looked out of the window at the sodden fields, sepia and emerald in the drizzle of the March afternoon.

'I don't like funerals, Lewis,' said my father meditatively in the dark carriage. 'When they put me away, I wish they wouldn't make all this fuss about it. Lena would insist on it, though, wouldn't she?'

His thoughts turned to more cheerful themes.

'I've got to say this for Will, they did give us some nice things to eat,' said my father, as naturally and simply as ever. 'Did you try the cheesecakes?'

'No,' I said with a smile.

'You made a mistake there, Lewis,' said my father. 'They were the best I've tasted for a very long time.'

We did not go straight home, but instead crossed the road from the station and called at the old Victoria, which later became, for George Passant and me and the circle of friends we called the 'group', our habitual public house. My father suggested, feeling a very gay dog, that we should celebrate the legacy. I drank two or three pints of beer; my father did not like beer, but put away several glasses of port and lemon. He became gay without making any effort to control himself. Once he lifted his voice in a song, his surprisingly loud and tuneful voice. 'No singing, please,' called the barmaid sourly. 'Don't be such a donkey, Bertie,' my father muttered to himself, mildly and cheerfully, imitating my mother's constant reproof.

Their relation, I knew, had deteriorated with the years. It was held together now only by habit, law, the acquiescence of his temperament, the pride of hers, and most of all the difficulty of keeping two *ménages* for those as poor as they were. He did not mind very much. So much of his life was lived inside himself; in his own comical fashion he was far better protected than most men; his inner life went on, whatever events took place outside – failure, humiliation, the disharmony of his marriage. That day, for example, he had experienced happy moments as the accomplished financier and, later in the Victoria, as the hard-bitten man of the world. He was simple, he did not mind being laughed at, he was quite happy, the happiest member of the family, all the years of his life.

I got on with him as I had always done, on the same level, with little change since my childhood. He asked for nothing. He was grateful for a little banter and just a little flattery. It would not have occurred to him, now that I was in his eyes grown-up, to ask me to spend a day with him. If one came by accident, such as this outing to Market Harborough, he placidly enjoyed it, and so did I.

At last we went home. We got off at the tram stop and walked by the elementary school, the library, Aunt Milly's house, just the same way as I had run in sudden trepidation that night before the war, when I was a child of eight. Returning from Za's funeral, however, I was, like my father, comfortable with a little drink inside me. A cold drizzle was falling, but we scarcely noticed it. My father was humming to himself, then talking, as I teased him. He hummed away, zum, zoo, zum, zoo, zoo, zoo, pleased because I was inventing reasons for his choice of tune.

We were almost outside our house before I took in that something was not right. The gas in the front room was alight, but the blinds were not drawn. That was strange, different from all the times I had walked that road and seen the light behind the blinds.

I looked straight into the empty, familiar room. Above, in my mother's bedroom, the light was also burning, but there the blinds were drawn.

Aunt Milly let us in. In her flat energetic way she said that my mother had had another attack that afternoon, and was gravely ill.

8

A Sunday Morning

I WENT to see my mother late that night. Her voice was faint and thick, the lids fell heavy over her eyes, but she was quite lucid. I only stayed a moment, and left the bedroom with the weight of anxiety lightened. She seemed no worse than I had often seen her. None of us knew how ill she was, that night or the next day. We were so much in ignorance that, on the next evening, Aunt Milly set about attacking me on how I should dispose of my legacy.

I was sitting in the front room, below my mother's bedroom, when Aunt Milly came downstairs.

'How is she?' I said. I had not been inside my mother's room since early that morning, before I departed for the office.

'About the same,' said Aunt Milly. With no change of expression at all, she went on, her voice loud and vigorous: 'Now you'll be able to start making an honest man of your father. It's high time.'

'What do you mean, Aunt Milly?'

'You know very well what I mean.' Which, though she had momentarily startled me, was true. 'You can pay off another ten shillings in the pound.'

I met her stare.

'It's the honest thing to do,' she said. 'You needn't pay Tom's share yet awhile. You can keep that in the bank for yourself. But you'll be able to pay the other creditors.'

An obstinate resolve had formed, when she bullied me as a child, that I would never pay those debts, however much money I made and however long I lived. Now I liked her better, saw her as a woman by herself not just as a big impassive intruding face, an angry threatening voice, that filled the space round and wounded me. I liked her better; but the resolve had stayed intact since I was eight. However much Za had left me, I should not have used a penny as Aunt Milly wanted.

But I could deal with Aunt Milly by now. Once she used to hurt me, then I had toughened my skin and listened in silence; now that I was growing up, I had become comfortable with her.

'Do you want to ruin me, Aunt Milly? I might take to drink, you know.'

'I shouldn't be surprised. Anyone who doesn't pay his debts', said Aunt Milly unrelentingly, 'is weak enough for anything.'

'I might be able to get qualified in something with this money. You tried hard enough to get me qualified as an engineer, didn't you? You ought to approve if I tag some letters after my name.'

I said it frivolously, but it was a thought that was going through my mind. That too made me hang on to the money, perhaps it determined me more than the resolution of years past.

Aunt Milly had no humour at all, but she could vaguely detect when she was being teased, and she did not dislike it. But she was obdurate.

'You can always invent reasons for not doing the right thing,' she said at the top of her voice.

Soon I went upstairs to my mother. I expected to find her asleep, for the room was dark except for a nightlight; but, in the shadowy bedroom, redolent with eau-de-Cologne, brandy, the warm smell of an invalid's bedroom, my mother's voice came, slurred but distinct:

'Is that you, dear?'

'Yes.'

'What was Milly shouting about?'

'Could you hear?'

'I'm not quite deaf yet,' said my mother, stuffing in the flickering light, smiling with affronted humour, as she did when, at nearly fifty, she heard herself described as middle-aged. Her physical vanity and her instinctive hold on youth had not abandoned her. 'What was she shouting about?'

'Nothing to worry you,' I said.

'Please to tell me,' said my mother. She sounded exhausted, but she was still imperious.

'Really, it's nothing, Mother.'

'Was it about Za's money?' Her intuition stayed quick, realistic, suspicious. She knew she had guessed right. 'Please to tell me, dear.'

I told her, as lightly as I could. My mother smiled, angry but half-amused.

'Milly is a donkey,' she said. 'You're to do nothing of the sort.'

'Of course, I shouldn't think of it.'

'Remember, it's some of the money I ought to have had. Please think of it as money I've given you. You're to use it to make your way. I hope I see you do it.' Her tone was firm, quiet, unshaken, and yet worried, I noticed, with discomfort, how easily she became out of breath. After saying those words to me, she had to breathe hard.

'It's a great comfort to me', she went on, 'to see the money come to you, dear. It's your chance. We shall have to think how you're going to take it. You mustn't waste it. Remember that you're not to waste it.'

'We won't do anything till you get better,' I said.

'I hope it won't be too long,' said my mother, and I caught the tone again, unshaken but apprehensive.

'How are you feeling?' I asked.

'I'm not getting on as fast as I should like,' said my mother.

As I said good night, she told me: 'I'm angry with myself. I don't like lying here. It's time I made myself get well.'

She was undaunted enough to tell Aunt Milly, on each of the next two days, that I was on no account to spend any of the legacy in getting my father's discharge. My mother stated haughtily that it was not to happen. She explained to Aunt Milly that it was only right and just for her son to possess 'her money', and that money must be used to give him a start. In a few years, Lewis would be able to settle Bertie's affairs without thinking twice.

Aunt Milly had to restrain herself, and listen without protest. For by this time she, like all of us, realized that my mother might not live.

She seemed to have, Dr Francis explained to me, the kind of heart failure that comes to much older people. If she recovered, she would have to spend much of her time lying down, so as to rest the heart. At present it was only working strongly enough just to keep her going without any drain of energy whatever.

From our expressions, from the very air in the house, my mother knew that she was in danger. Her hope was still fierce and courageous. She insisted that she was 'better in herself'. Impatiently she dismissed what she called 'minor symptoms', such as the swelling of her ankles; her ankles had swollen even though she lay in bed and had not set foot on the floor for three weeks.

One Sunday morning Dr Francis spent a long time upstairs. Aunt Milly, my father and I sat silently in the front room.

Dr Francis had come early that morning, so as not to miss the service. The church bell was already ringing when he joined us in the front room. He had left his hat on the table, the tall hat in which he always went to church, the only one in the congregation. I thought he had come to take it, and would not stay with us. Instead, he sat down by the table and ran his white, plump fingers over the cloth. The skin of his face was pink, and the pink flush seemed to shade up to the top of his bald dome. His expression was stern, resentful, and commanding.

'Mr Eliot, I must tell you now,' he said. His voice was hoarse as well as high.

'Yes, doctor?' said my father.

'I'm afraid she isn't going to get over it,' said Dr Francis.

The church bell had just stopped and the room was so quiet that it seemed to have gone darker.

'Isn't she, doctor?' said my father helplessly. Dr Francis shook his head with a heavy frown.

'How long has she got?' said Aunt Milly, in a tone subdued for her but still instinct with action.

'I can't tell you, Mrs Riddington,' said Dr Francis. 'She won't let herself go easily. Yes, she'll fight to the last.'

'How long do you think?' Aunt Milly insisted.

'I don't think it can be many weeks,' said Dr Francis slowly. 'I don't think any of us ought to wish it to be long, for her sake.'

'Does she know?' I cried.

'Yes, Lewis, she knows.' He was gentler to me than to Aunt Milly; his resentment, his almost sulky sense of defeat, he put away.

'You've told her this morning?'

'Yes. She asked me to tell her the truth. She's a brave soul. I don't tell some people, but I thought I had to, with your mother.'

'How did she take it?' I said, trying to seem controlled.

'I hope I do as well,' said Dr Francis. 'If it happens to me like this.'

Dr Francis had deposited his gloves within his tall hat, Now he took them out, and gradually pulled on the left-hand one, concentrating on each fold in the leather.

'She asked me to give you a message,' he said as though casually to my father. 'She would like to see Lewis before anyone else.'

My father nodded, submissively.

'I should give her a few minutes, if I were you,' said Dr Francis to me. 'I expect she'll want to get ready for you. She doesn't like being seen when she's upset, does she?'

He was thinking of me too. I could not reply. He gazed at me sharply, and clicked his tongue against his teeth in baffled sympathy. He pulled on the other glove and said that, though it was late, he would run along to church. He would get in before the first lesson. He said good morning to Aunt Milly, good morning to my father, put his hand on my arm. We saw him pass the window in short, quick, precise steps, his top hat gleaming, his plump cushioned body braced and erect.

'Well,' said Aunt Milly, 'when the time comes, you will have to leave this house.'

'I suppose we shall, Milly,' my father said.

'You'll have to come to me. I can manage the three of you.'

'It's very good of you, Milly, I'm sure.'

'You two might have to share a room. I'll set about moving things,' said my aunt, satisfied that there was a practical step to take.

Then the clock struck the half-hour. My father did not repeat his ritual phrase. Instead he said:

'Lena didn't use to like the clock, did she? She used to say "Confound the clock. Confound the clock, Bertie." That's what she used to say. "Confound the clock." I've always liked it myself, but she never did.'

9

At a Bedside

MY mother's head and shoulders had been propped up by pillows, in order to make her breathing easier – so that, asleep or awake, she was half-sitting, and when I drew up a chair that Sunday morning, her eyes looked down into mine.

They were very bright, her eyes, and the whites clear. The skin of her face was a waxy ochreous cream, and the small veins were visible upon her cheeks, as they sometimes are on the tough and weather-beaten. She gave me the haughty humorous smile which she used so often to pass off a remark which had upset her.

Outside, it was a windy April day, changing often from sunlight to shade. When I went in the room was dark; but, before my mother spoke, the houses opposite the window, the patch of ground between them, stood brilliant in the spring sunshine, and the light was reflected on to my mother's face.

'When it's your time, it's your time,' said my mother. She was speaking with difficulty, as though she had to think hard about each word, and then could not trust her lips and tongue to frame it. I knew – with the tight, constrained, dreadful feeling that overcame me when she called out for my love, for in her presence I could not let the tears start, unbidden, spontaneously, as they did when Dr Francis spoke of her courage – that she had rehearsed the remark to greet me with.

'When it's your time, it's your time,' she repeated. But she could not maintain her resignation. Her real feeling was anger, grievance, and astonishment. 'It's all happened through a completely unexpected symptom,' said my mother. 'Completely unexpected. No one could have expected it. Dr Francis says he didn't. It's a completely unexpected symptom,' she kept saying with amazement and anger. Then she said, heavily: 'I don't want to stay like this. Just like an old sack. It wouldn't do for me, would it?'

For once, I found my tongue. I told her that she was looking handsome.

She was delighted. She preened herself like a girl, and said: 'I'm glad of that, dear.'

She glanced round the bedroom, which was covered with photographs on all the walls – photographs of all the family, Martin, me, but most of all herself. She had always had a passion for photographic records: she had always been majestically vain.

'But I shouldn't like you to think of me like this,' she said. 'Think of me as I am in the garden photograph, will you, dear?'

'If you want, Mother,' I said. The 'garden' photograph was her favourite, taken when she was thirty, in the more prosperous days just after I was born. She was in one of the long dresses that I remembered from my earliest childhood. She had made the photographer pose her under the apple tree, and she was dressed for an Edwardian afternoon.

She saw herself as she had been that day. She rejected pity, she would have rejected it even if she had found what she had sought in me, one to whose heart her heart could speak. She would have thrown pity back even now, even if I could have given it with spontaneous love. But she saw herself as she had been in her pride; and she wished me eternally to see her so.

We were silent; the room was dark, then sunny, then dark again.

'I've been wondering what you'll do with Za's money,' said my mother.

'I'm not sure yet,' I said.

'If it had come to me as it ought to have done,' she said, 'you should have had it before this. Then I should have seen you started, anyway.'

'Never mind,' I replied. 'I'll do something with it.'

'I know you will. You'll do the things I hoped for you.' She raised her voice. '*I shan't be there to see.*'

I gasped, said something without meaning.

'I didn't want just the pleasure of it,' said my mother fiercely. 'I didn't want you to buy me presents. You know I didn't want that.'

'I know,' I said, but she did not hear me.

'I wanted to go along with you,' she cried, 'I wanted to be part of you. That's all I wanted.'

I tried to console her. I told her that, whatever I did, I should carry my childhood with me: always I should hear her speaking, I should remember the evenings by the front-room fire, when she urged me on as a little boy. Yet afterwards I never believed that I brought her comfort. She was the proudest of women, and she was vain, but in the end she had an eye for truth. She knew as well as I, that if one's heart is invaded by another, one will either assist the invasion or repel it – and if one repels it, even though one may long, as I did with my mother, that one might do otherwise, even though one admires and cherishes and assumes the attitude of love, yet still, if one repels it, no words or acting can for long disguise the lie. The states of love are very many – some of them steal upon one unawares; but one thing one always knows, whether one welcomes an intrusion into one's heart or whether, against all other wishes and feelings, one has to evade it, turn it aside.

My mother was exhausted by her outburst. She found it harder to keep her speech clear; and once or twice her attention did not stay steady, she began talking of something else. She was acutely ashamed to be 'muddle-headed', as she called it; she screwed up all her will.

'Don't forget', she said, sounding stern with her effort of will, 'that Za's money ought to have been mine. I should like to have given it to you. It was Wigmore money to start with. Don't forget that.'

Her lips took on the grand smile which I used to see when she told me of her girlhood. She lay there, the room in a bright phase of light, with her grand haughty smile.

I noticed that a Sunday paper rested on the bed, unopened. It was strange to see, for she had always had the greatest zest for printed news. After a time, I said: 'Are you going to read it later on today?'

'I don't think so, dear,' she said, and the anger and astonishment had returned to her voice. 'What's the use of me reading the paper? I shall give it up now. What's the use? I shall never know what happens.'

For her, more than for most people, everything in the future had been interesting. Now it could interest her no longer. She would never know the answers.

'Perhaps I shall learn about what's going on here,' she said, but in a formal, hesitating tone, 'in another place.'

That morning, such was the only flicker of comfort from her faith.

We were quiet; I could hear her breathing; it was not laboured, but just heavy enough to hear.

'Look!' said my mother suddenly, with a genuine, happy laugh. 'Look at the ducks, dear!'

For a second I thought it was an hallucination. But I followed her glance; her long-sighted eyes had seen something real, and she was enjoying what she saw. I went to the window, for at a distance her sight was still much better than mine.

Between the houses opposite, there was a space not yet built over. It had been left as rough hillocky grass, with a couple of small ponds; on it one of our neighbours kept a few chickens and ducks. It was a duck and her brood of seven or eight ducklings that had made my mother laugh. They had been paddling in the fringe of one pond. All of a sudden they fled, as though in panic, to the other, in precise Indian file, the duck in the lead. Then, as though they had met an invisible obstacle, they wheeled round, and, again in file, raced back to their starting point.

'Oh dear,' said my mother, wiping her eyes. 'They are silly. I've always got something to watch.'

She was calmed, invigorated, made joyful by the sight. She had been so ambitious, she had hoped so fiercely, she had never found what she needed to make her happy – yet she had had abounding capacity for happiness. Now, when her days were numbered, when her vision was foreshortened, she showed it still. Perhaps it was purer, now her hopes were gone. She was simple with laughter, just as I remembered her when I was five years old, when she took me for a walk and a squirrel came quarrelling down a tree.

I came back to the bedside and took her hand. It occurred to her at that moment to tell me not to underestimate my brother Martin. She insisted on his merits. In fact, it was an exhortation I did not need, for I was extremely fond of him. My mother was arguing with her own injustice, for she had never forgiven his birth, she had never wanted to find her match and fulfilment in him, as she had in me.

There was a flash of irony here – for he was less at ease with others than I was, but more so with her.

Then she got tired. She tried to hide it, she did not choose to admit it. Her thoughts rambled; her speech was thicker and hard to follow; Martin Francis (my brother's names) took her by free association to Dr Francis, and how he had come specially to see her that morning, which he would not do for his ordinary patients. She was tired to death. With perfect lucidity, she broke out once: 'I should like to go in my sleep.'

Her thoughts rambled again. With a last effort of will, she said in a clear, dignified manner:

'I didn't have a very good night. That's what it is. Perhaps I'd better have a nap now. Please to come and see me after tea, dear. I shan't be a bother to you then. I like to talk to you properly, you know.'

10

The View Over the Roofs

MY mother died in May. From the cemetery, my father and I returned to the empty house. I drew up the blind, in the front room; after three days of darkness, the pictures, the china on the sideboard, leaped out, desolatingly bright.

'Milly keeps on at me about living with her,' said my father.

'I know,' I said.

'I suppose we shall have to,' said my father.

'I'm not sure what I shall do,' I said.

My father looked taken aback, mournfully dazed, with his black tie and the armlet round his sleeve.

I had been thinking what I should do, when I sat in the house and my mother lay dying. I had been making up my mind while in the familiar bedroom her body rested dead. I was too near her dying and her death to acknowledge my own bereavement. I did not know the wound of my own loss. I did not know that I should feel remorse, because I had not given her what she asked of me. I was utterly ignorant of the flaw within, which crept to the open in the way I failed my mother.

At the time of my mother's death I was as absorbed in the future, as bent upon my plans, as she might have been. My first decision, in fact, was more in my mother's line than my own of later years. For it was a bit of a gesture. I had decided that I would not go to live with Aunt Milly.

When I told my father that I was 'not sure' of my intentions, that was not true. The decision was already made, embedded in a core of obstinacy. What I said about it, however much I prevaricated or delayed, did not matter. On this occasion, I had already, in the days between my mother's death and the funeral, been looking for lodgings. I had found a room in Lower Hastings Street, and told the landlady that I would let her know definitely by the end of the week.

I should have to pay twelve and six a week for that room and breakfast. I was getting twenty-five shillings from the education office. I calculated that I could just live, though it would mean one sandwich at lunchtime and not much of a meal at night. Clothes would have to come out of Za's money; that was my standby, that made this manoeuvre possible; but I resolved not to take more than ten pounds out of the pool within the next year. In due time I should have made another choice – and then that money meant my way out.

I knew clearly why I was making the gesture. I had suffered some shame through my father's bankruptcy. This was an atonement, a device for setting myself free. It meant I was not counting every penny – and to smile off the last winces of shame, I had to throw away a little money too. I had to act as though I did not care too much about money. And this gesture meant also that I was defying Aunt Milly, the voice of conscience from my childhood, the voice that had driven the shame into me and had, at moments since, trumpeted it awake. If it had been anyone else but Aunt Milly who had offered to take us in, I believed that I should have said yes gratefully and saved my money.

I was fairly adroit, however, in explaining myself to her – more adroit, I thought later with remorse, than I had often been with my mother, and then I thought once more that adroitness would have been no good, neither adroitness nor the tenderest consideration. With Aunt Milly, it was not so difficult. I did not want to hurt her; I had become fond enough of her to be considerate. It would hurt her a little, I knew. For, in her staring blank-faced dynamic fashion, Aunt Milly had always been starved of children. She had felt maternally towards me and my brother, though it sometimes struck me that she used a curious method for expressing it. And she could not understand that she put people off, most of all young children, whom she desired most for her own.

She left my father alone with me after we came back from the cemetery; Martin had stayed at her house since before my mother's death. Aunt Milly did not let us alone all day, however; she came in that night, and discovered us in the kitchen eating bread and cheese. She examined the shelves, notebook in hand. She was marking down the crockery which was to be transferred. It was then that I put in a word.

'I don't know, Aunt Milly,' I said, 'but it might be better if I went off by myself.'

'I never heard of such a thing,' said Aunt Milly.

'I don't want to be in the way,' I said.

'That's for me to settle,' she said.

She had turned round, her face impassive and pop-eyed, but tinged with indignation. My father was watching with mild interest.

'I know you'll put yourself out and never tell us.' I laughed at her. 'And take it out of us because you've done so.'

'I don't know what you're talking about.'

'I should like to come – '

'Of course you would. Anyone in his sense would,' said Aunt Milly. 'You don't get your board and lodging free everywhere.'

'As well as a few home truths now and again. It would be very good for us both, wouldn't it?'

'It would be very good for you.'

'I've looked forward to it.'

'I expect you have. Well, I'm ready to have you. I don't know what all the palaver is about.'

Aunt Milly took words at their face value; to cheek and compliments she returned the same flat, uncompromising rebuff; but sometimes they had just a little effect.

'Listen, Aunt Milly, I'll tell you. I expect I shall want to study – '

'I should think you will,' she said.

'That does mean I ought to be on my own, you know.'

'You can study in my house.'

'Could you study,' I said, 'if you had to share a room with my father – or your brother?'

Aunt Milly was the least humorous of women, and rarely smiled. But she was capable of an enormous hooting laugh. She had also been conditioned to think, all her life, that my father ought to evoke laughter. So she burst into a humourless roar that echoed round the kitchen. My father obligingly burst into a snatch of song, then pretended to snore.

'One of the two,' he said with his clowning grin. 'One of the two. That's me, that is.'

'Stop it, Bertie,' said Aunt Milly implacably.

My father, still clowning, shrank into a corner.

The argument went on. I was ready to stick it out all night. I was as obstinate as she was, but that she did not know. I played all the tricks I could: I flattered her, I was impertinent, I stood up to denunciation, I gave vague hints of how I thought of living.

Those hints made her voice grow louder, her eyes more staring and glazed. I proposed to go into lodgings, did I – and how was I going to pay for them out of a clerk's earnings? I described what I thought my budget would be.

'You're not leaving yourself any margin,' she retorted.

'I've got a little money in the bank now, you know,' I said. I had been careless to speak so. It might have provoked a storm, about bankruptcy, my father's debts, my duty. She would not have been restrained because my father was present. But it happened that my mother, before she died, had made her promise not to deter me from 'taking my chance'. Aunt Milly prided herself on having dispensed with 'superstitious nonsense' – for after all this was the twentieth century, as she asserted in every quarrel with my mother. She would have said that she paid no special reverence to deathbed promises. If she kept this one, she would have said, it was because she always kept her word.

'I won't say what I think of that,' said Aunt Milly, with a thunderous exertion of self-control. Then she indulged in one, but only one, loud cry of rage: 'No wonder this family will come to a bad end.'

The evening became night. To say that she gave in would not be true; but she acknowledged my intention, though with a very bad grace. To say that I had got so far without hurting her would be nonsense. We were set on aims that contradicted each other; they could not be reconciled, and no gloss on earth could make them so. But at least in Aunt Milly's understanding we had not split or parted. She did not consider it a break. I had promised to go and have tea at her house each Sunday afternoon.

It was a warm, wet evening late in May when I first went as a lodger to my room in Lower Hastings Street. The room was at the top of the house, and was no larger than my attic at home. From the window I looked over slate roofs, the roofs of outhouses and sheds, glistening in the rain. Beyond, there was a cloud of sulphurous smoke, where a train was disappearing through a tunnel into the station yard.

I had brought all my possessions in two old suitcases — another suit, two pairs of flannels, some underclothes, a few books and school photographs. I left them on the floor, and stood by the window, looking over the roofs, my heart quickening with a tumult of emotions. I felt despondent in the strange, cheerless room, and yet hopeful with the hope that I saw so often in my mother; anxious, desperately anxious that I might have chosen wrong, and at the same time ultimately confident; lonely and also free.

There was everything in the world to do. There was everything in front of me, everything to do — yet what was I to do that moment, with an evening stretching emptily ahead? Should I lie on my bed and read? Or should I walk the streets of the town, alone, in the warm wet night?

Part Two

TOWARDS A GAMBLE

11

Discontent and Talks of Love

DURING the summer after my mother's death I used to walk to the office in the warm and misty mornings; there was a smell of rain freshening the dusty street, and freshening my hopes as well, as I walked along, chafing at another wasted day ahead.

I ticked off names, names written in violet ink that glared on the squared paper. I read each date of birth, and underlined in red those born before 31 August 1908. I gazed down into the sunlit street, and my mind was filled with plans and fancies, with hope and the first twist of savage discontent. My plans were half-fancies still, not much grown up since my first days in the office, when I walked round the town hall square at lunchtime and dreamed that I had suddenly come into a fortune. I still made resolutions about what to read, or what prospectus to write for next, with an elation and sense of purpose that continued to outshine the unromantic act of carrying the resolution out. But there was some change. I had my legacy. I was angry that I could not see my way clear, I was angry that no one gave advice that sounded ambitious enough. Gazing down, watching the tramcars glitter in the sun, waiting with half an ear for Mr Vesey's cry of complaint, I began to suffer the ache and burn of discontent.

Yet I was sidetracked and impeded by that same discontent. There were days when the office walls hemmed me in, when Mr Vesey became an incarnate insult, when I was choking with hurt pride, when Darby in all kindness gave me grey and cautious advice. Those were the days when I felt I must be myself, break out, not in the planned-for distant future, but now, before I rusted away, now, while my temper was hot.

It was a temptation then to show off, get an audience by any means I could, and at that age I could not resist the temptation. I scarcely even thought of trying, it seemed so natural and I got so fierce a pleasure. I had a quick, cruel tongue, and I enjoyed using it. It seemed natural to find myself at the ILP, getting myself elected on to committees, making inflammatory speeches in lecture halls all over the town. Only the zealots attended in the height of summer, but I was ready to burst out, even before a handful of the converted, and still be elated and warm-tempered as we left the dingy room at ten o'clock of a midsummer evening and found ourselves blinking in the broad daylight. The town was not large enough for one to stay quite anonymous, and some of my exploits got round. A bit of gossip even reached Aunt Milly, and the next Sunday, when I visited her house for tea, she was not backward in expressing her disapproval.

To myself, I could not laugh that attack away as cheerfully as I did most of Aunt Milly's. I was practical enough to know that I was doing nothing 'useful'. As I strolled to my lodgings ('my rooms', I used to call them to my acquaintances, with a distinct echo of my mother, despite my speeches on the equality of man) late on those summer nights, I had moments of bleak lucidity. Where was I getting to? What was I doing with my luck? Was I so devoid of will, was I just going to drift? Those moments struck cold, after the applause I had won a few hours earlier with some sarcastic joke.

But once on my feet again, with faces in front of me, or distracted in a different fashion by Jack Cotery and his talk of girls, I was swept away. My own chilling questions were just insistent enough to keep me going regularly to the law classes at the School, and that was all. I intended to get to know George Passant, and I may have had some half-thought that his advice would be grander than that of Darby and the rest; but my first expectations were forgotten for ever, in the light of what actually happened. I had not, however, forced myself into his notice before the School closed for the summer holidays. Occasionally

I saw him from my office window, for the firm of Eden and Martineau occupied a floor on the other side of Bowling Green Street. On many mornings I watched George Passant cross over the tramlines, wearing a bowler hat tilted back on his head, carrying a briefcase, swinging a heavy walking stick. I was due at nine, and he used to cross the street with extreme punctuality half an hour later.

All that summer, when I was not what Aunt Milly denounced as 'gassing', I spent lazy lotos-eating evenings in the company of Jack Cotery. At school he had been too precocious for me; now he was a clerk in the accounts branch of a local newspaper, he ate his sandwiches at midday in the same places as I did, and we drifted together. He had become a powerfully built young man, still short but over-muscled; he had the comedian's face that I remembered, fresh, lively, impudent, wistful. His large ardent eyes shone out of his comedian's face, and his voice was soft and modulated, surprisingly soft to come from that massive chest and throat. He was eighteen, a few months my senior; and he was intoxicated by anything that could come under the name of love. In that soft and modulated voice he talked of girls, women, romance, passion, the delights of the flesh, the incredible attraction of a woman he had seen in the tram that morning, the wonderful prospect of tracking her down, the delights not only of the flesh but of first hearing her voice, the delight that the world was so made that, as long as we lived, the perfume of love would be scattered through the air.

It was talk that I was ready and eager to hear. Not primarily because of the interest of Jack himself, though, when I could break through the dreams his talk induced, he was fun in his own right. In his fashion, he was kind and imaginative. It had been like him, even as a boy, to try to console me on that shameful morning of the ten-shilling note. When one was in his company, he lavished all his good nature, flattering and sweet as honey.

But he was the most unreliable of friends.

He was also a natural romancer. It came to him, as easy as breathing, to add to, to enhance, to transmogrify the truth. As a boy he had boasted – utterly untruthfully – how his father had plenty of money. And now 'I'm on the evening paper,' he could not resist saying, when someone asked his job, and proceeded – from the nucleus of fact that he worked in the newspaper office – to draw a picture of his daily life, as a hard drinking, dashing, unstoppable journalist. He had enough of a romancer's tact to point out that the glamour of the journalist's occupation had been grossly overdrawn. He shrugged his shoulders like a disillusioned professional.

It was the same with his stories of his conquests. He had much success with women, even while he was still a boy. If he had stuck to the facts, he would have evoked the admiration, the envious admiration, of all his companions, me among them. But the facts were too prosaic for Jack. He was impelled to elaborate stories of how a young woman, obviously desirable, obviously rich and well-born, had come into the office and caught his eye; how she had come in, on one pretext after another, morning after morning; how in the end she had stopped beside his desk, and dropped a note asking him to meet her in the town; how she had driven him in her own car into the country, where they had enjoyed a night of perfect bliss under the stars. 'Uncomfortable at times, clearly,' said Jack, with his romancer's knack of adding a note of comic realism.

He knew that I did not believe a word of it. I was amused by him and fond of him, and I envied his impudence and confidence with women, and of course his success. Chiefly, though, he carried with him a climate in which, just at that time, I wanted to bask; because he was so amorous, because everything he said was full of hints, revelations, advice, fantasies, reminiscences, forecasts, all of love, he brought out and magnified much that I was ready to feel.

For at this stage in our youth we can hold two kinds of anticipation of love, which seem contradictory and yet coexist and reinforce each other. We can dream, delicately because even to imagine it is to touch one of the most sacred of our hopes, of searching for the other part of ourselves, of the other being who will make us whole, of the ultimate and transfiguring union. At the same time we can gloat over any woman, become insatiably curious about the brute facts of the pleasures which we are then learning or which are just to come. In that phase we are coarse and naked, and anyone who has forgotten his youth will judge that we are too tangled with the flesh ever to forget ourselves in the ecstasy of romantic love. But in fact, at this stage in one's youth, the coarseness and nakedness, the sexual preoccupations, the gloating over delights to come, are − in the secret heart where they take place − themselves romantic. They are a promise of joy. Much that Jack Cotery and I said to each other would have been repulsive to a listener who forgot that we were eighteen. The conversations would not stand the light of day. Yet at the time they drove from my mind both the discontents and the ambitions. They enriched me as much as my hope, my anticipation, of transfiguring love.

12

Pride at a Football Match

AUTUMN came, and I was restless, full of expectation. The School reopened. In the bright September nights I walked down the Newarke to George Passant's classes, full of a kind of new-year elation and resolve. Going back to my lodgings under the misty autumn moon, I wondered about the group that Passant was collecting round him. They were all students at the School, some of whom I knew by name; young women who attended an occasional class, one or two youths who were studying full-time for an external London degree. They gathered round him at the end of the evening, and moved noisily back into the town.

Their laughter rang provocatively loud as they jostled along, a compact group, on the other side of the road. I felt left out. I was chagrined that George Passant had never asked me to join them. I felt very lonely.

Not long afterwards I took my chance and forced myself upon him. It happened in October, a week after my eighteenth birthday. I had come out of the office late. There, on the pavement ten yards ahead, George Passant was walking deliberately with his heavy tread, whistling and swinging his stick.

I caught him up and fell into step beside him. He said good evening with amiable, impersonal cordiality. I said that it was curious we had not met before, since we worked on opposite sides of the street. George agreed that it was. He was half-abstracted, half-shy; I was too intent to mind. He knew my name, he knew that I attended his class. That was not enough. I was going to cut a dash. We passed the reference library, and I referred airily to the hours I spent there, the amount of reading I had done in the last few months; I expounded on Freud, Jung, Adler, Tolstoy, Marx, Shaw. We came to a little bookshop at the corner of Belvoir Street. The lights in the shop window shone on glossy jackets, the jackets of the best sellers of the day, A S M Hutchinson and P C Wren and Michael Arlen, with some copies of *The Forsyte Saga* in an honourable position on the right.

'What can you do?' I demanded of George Passant. 'If that's what you give people to read?' I waved my arm at the window. 'If that's what they're willing to take? I don't suppose there's a volume of poetry in the shop. Yeats is one of the greatest poets of the age, and you couldn't go into that shop and buy a single word of his.'

'I'm afraid I don't know anything about poetry,' said George Passant, quickly and defensively, in the tone of a man without an ounce of blague in his whole nature. 'I'm afraid it's no use expecting me to give an opinion about poetry.' Then he said: 'We ought to have a drink on it, anyway. I take it you know the pubs of this town better than I do. Let's go somewhere where we shan't be cluttered up with the local bell-wethers.'

I was bragging, determined to make an impression, roaring ahead without much care of what he thought. George Passant was five years older, and many men of his age would have been put off. But George's nerves were not grated by raw youth. In a sense, he was perpetually raw and young himself. Partly because of his own diffidence, partly because of his warm, strong fellow feeling, he took to me as we stood outside the bookshop. Shamelessly I lavished myself in a firework display of boasting, and he still took to me.

We sat by the fire at the Victoria. When we arrived, it was early enough for us to have the room to ourselves: later it filled, but we still kept the table by the fire. George sat opposite me, his face flushed by the heat, his voice always loud, growing in volume with each pint he drank. He paid for all the beer, stood the barmaids a drink and several of the customers. 'I believe in establishing friendly relations. We shall want to come back here. This is a splendid place,' George confided to me, with preternatural worldly wisdom and a look of extreme cunning: while in fact he was standing treat because he was happy, relaxed, off his guard, exhilarated, and at home.

It was a long time that night before I stopped roaring ahead with my own self-advertisement. The meeting mattered to me – I knew that while living in it, though I did not know how much. I was impelled to go on making an impression. It was a long time before I paid any attention to George.

At close quarters, his face had one or two surprises. The massive head was as impressive as in the lecture room. The great forehead, the bones of the jaw under the blanket of heavy flesh – they were all as I expected. But I was surprised, having only seen him tense and concentrated, to realize that he could look so exuberantly relaxed. As he drank, he softened into sensual content. And I was more surprised to catch his eyes, just for a moment, in repose. His whole being that night exuded power, and happiness, and excitement at having someone with whom to match his wits. He smacked his lips after each tankard, and billowed with contented laughter. But there was one interval, perhaps only a minute long, when each of us was quiet. It was the only silent time between us, all that night. George had put his tankard down, and was staring past me, down the room and into vacant space. His eyes were large, blue, set in deep orbits; in excitement they flashed, but for that moment they were mournful and lost.

In the same way, I heard occasional tones in his speech that seemed to come from different levels from the rest. I listened with all my attention, as I was to go on listening for a good many years. He was more articulate than anyone I had heard, the words often a little stiff and formal, his turns of phrase rigid by contrast to the loud hearty voice with its undertone of a Suffolk accent. He described his career to me in that articulate fashion, each bit of explanation organized and clear. He was the son of a small town postmaster, had been articled to an Ipswich firm, had done well in his solicitors' examinations. George did not conceal his satisfaction; everything he said of his training was cheerful, abounding in force, rational, full of his own brimming optimism. Then he came to the end of his articles, and there was a change in tone that I was to hear so often. 'I hadn't any influence, of *course*,' said George Passant, his voice still firm, articulate, but sharp with shrinking diffidence. I recognized that trick in the first hour we talked, but there were others that puzzled me for years, to which I listened often enough but never found the key.

At Eden and Martineau's, George was called the assistant solicitor, but this meant no more than that he was qualified. He was in fact a qualified managing clerk on a regular salary. I could not be sure how much he earned, but I guessed about three hundred pounds a year. Yet he thought himself lucky to get the job. He still seemed a little incredulous that they should have appointed him, though it had happened nearly a year before. He told me how he had expected them to reject him after the interview. He believed robustly enough that he was a competent lawyer, but that was something apart. 'I couldn't expect to be much good at an interview, of course,' said George. He was naïf, strangely naïf, in speculating as to why they had chosen him. He fancied that Martineau, the junior partner, must have 'worked it'. George had complete faith and trust in Martineau.

'He's the one real spot of light', cried George, ramming down his tankard, 'among the Babbitts and bell-wethers in this wretched town!'

But we did not talk for long that night of our own stories. We wanted to argue. We had come together, struck fire, and there was no time to lose. We were at an age when ideas were precious, and we started with different casts of mind and different counters to throw into the pool. Such knowledge as I had picked up was human and literary; George's was legal and political. But it was not just knowledge with which he bore me down; his way of thinking might be abstract, but it was full of passion, and he made tremendous ardent plans for the betterment of man. 'I'm a socialist, of course,' he said vehemently. 'What else could I be?' I burst in that so was I. 'I assumed that,' said George, with finality. He added, still more loudly: 'I should like someone to suggest an alternative for a reasonable man today. I should welcome the opportunity of asking some of our confounded clients how I could reconcile it with my conscience if I wasn't a socialist. God love me, there are only two defensible positions for a reasonable man. One is to be a philosophical anarchist – and I'm not prepared to indulge in that kind of frivolity; the other', said George, with crushing and conclusive violence, 'is to be exactly what I am.'

As the evening passed he assaulted me with constitutional law, political history, how the common man had won his political freedom, how it was for us and our contemporaries to take the next step. He made my politics look childish. George had bills for nationalization ready in his head, clear, systematic, detailed, thought out with the concentration and mental horsepower that I had admired from a distance. 'The next few years', said George, having sandbagged all of my criticisms, 'are going to be a wonderful time to be alive. Eliot, my boy, have you ever thought how lucky you and I are – to be our age at this time of all conceivable times?'

Giddy with drink, with the argument and comradeship, I walked with him through the town. We had not finished talking for the night. We ate some sandwiches in a frowsty café by the station, and then strolled, still arguing, down the streets near our offices, deserted now until next morning, the streets that had once been the centre of the old market town – Horsefair Street, Millstone Lane, Pocklington's Walk. George's voice rang thunderously in the deserted streets, echoed between the offices and the dark warehouses. At the corner of Pocklington's Walk there shone the lighted windows of a club. We stood beneath them, on the dark and empty pavement. George's hat was tilted back, and I saw his face, which had been open and happy in the heat of argument all night long, turn rebellious, angry, and defiant. The curtains were not drawn, and we watched a few elderly men, prosperously dressed, sitting with glasses at their side in the comfortable room. It was a scene of somnolent and well-to-do repose.

'The sunkets!' cried George fiercely. 'The sunkets!' He added: 'What right do they think they've got to sit there as though they owned the world?'

In the next days I thought over that first meeting. From the beginning, I believed that I could enlist George's help. His fellow feeling was so strong, one could not doubt it, and he knew much more than I. Yet I found it painfully hard to explain my position outright and put the question in his hands. Not from scruple, but from pride. I was seeing George regularly now. He took me as an equal: I was more direct than he, I could meet him on something like equal terms; it was wounding to upset the companionship in its first days and confess that I was lost.

While George, for all his good will, made it more awkward because of his own heavy-footed delicacy. He was not the man to take a hint or breathe in a situation through his pores. He needed an explicit statement. But he was too deliberately delicate to ask. It was not for a fortnight that he discovered exactly what I did for a living. Even then, his approach was elaborate and oblique, and he seemed to disbelieve my answers.

It happened, George's first attempt to help me, on a Saturday afternoon, on our way to a league football match. George had a hearty taste for the mass pastimes, chiefly because he enjoyed them, and a little out of defiance. We were jostling among the crowd, the cloth-capped crowd that hustled down the back streets towards the ground; and George, looking straight in front of him, asked a labyrinthine question.

'I take it that when you've got to the top in the education office – which I assume will be in about ten years' time – you won't find it necessary to make the schools in this town change over to the more gentlemanly sport of rugger?'

I was already accustomed to George's outbursts of anti-snobbery, of social hatred. I grinned, and assured him that he could sleep easy; but I knew that I was evading the real question.

'By the way,' George persisted, 'I take it that my assumption is correct?'

'What assumption, George?'

'You will be properly recognized at the education office in ten years' time?'

I made myself speak plainly.

'In ten years' time,' I said, 'if I stay there – I might have gone up a step or two. As a clerk.'

'I'm not prepared to accept that,' said George. 'You're underestimating yourself.'

We came to the ground. As we passed through the turnstiles, I asked: 'Do you realize what my job is?'

'I've got a general impression,' said George uncomfortably, 'but I'm not entirely clear.'

We clambered up the terrace, and there I began to tell him. But George was not inclined to believe it. He proceeded to speak as though my job were considerably grander and had more future than I had ever, in all my wishes, dared to imagine.

'It may be difficult now,' said George, 'but it's obvious that you're marked down for promotion. It's perfectly clear that they must have some machinery for pulling people like you to the top. Otherwise, I don't see how local government is going to function.'

That was a typical piece of George's optimism. I was tempted to leave him with it. Like my mother, I had to struggle to admit the humble truth – even though I managed to keep a hold on it, sometimes a precarious one. It was bitter. Yet, again like my mother, I felt that I must swallow the bitterness in order not to miss a chance – to impress on George that I was nothing but a clerk.

'I'm a very junior clerk, George. I'm getting twenty-five shillings a week. I shall be ticking off names for the next five years. Just as I'm doing now.'

George was both angry and abashed. He swore, and the violence of his curse made some youths in white mufflers turn and gape at him. He hesitated to ask me more, and then did so. Awkwardly he tried to pretend that things were not as bad as I painted them. Then he swore again, and he was near one of his storms of rage.

He said brusquely: 'Something will have to be done about it.'

He was brusque with embarrassment. I too was speaking harshly.

'That's easy to say,' I replied.

'I shall have to take a hand myself,' said George, still in a rough and offhand tone.

Now I had only to ask for help. I wanted it acutely; I had been playing for it; now it was mine for the asking, I was too proud to move. I turned as awkward as George.

'I expect I shall be able to manage,' I said.

George was abashed again. He stared fixedly at the empty field, where the turf gleamed brilliantly under the sullen sky.

'It's time these teams came out,' he said.

13

The Hopes of Our Youth

GEORGE was embarrassed at having his interest repulsed. For days and weeks he made no reference to my career or even to my daily life. He did not see so much of me alone. Cross with myself, incensed at my own involuntary stiffness, I tried half-heartedly to open the conversation again. But George went by rule, not by shades of feeling. He had made a mistake which caused him to feel inept. More than most men, he was paralysed when he felt inept. So he studied his mistake, so as to teach himself not to repeat it.

Without any embarrassment at all, however, he plunged me into the centre of the 'group'. That was our name, then and always, for the young men and women who gathered round George and whose leader he became. Theirs was the laughter I had envied, walking on the other side of the road, before George took me up. In the future, although we had no foresight of it then, he was to devote to them a greater and a greater share of his vigour; until in the end he lived altogether in them and for them. Until in the end, through living in them and for them, he destroyed his own blazing promise – so that he, who had led us all, came to look down into the gulf of ruin.

But George's is a story by itself. When I first knew him, the crisis of his life was years ahead, and he was assembling the 'group' round him, heartening and melting everyone within it, so brimful of hope for each one of us that no one could stay cold. All the group were students at the School, and, though the number increased later, in my time it was never larger than ten. Most of them were girls – some from the prosperous middle class, who went to the School to pass their time before they found a husband, and saw in George an escape from the restrictions of their homes. Most of the group, however, were poor and aspiring – young women working in the town, secretaries and clerks or elementary schoolteachers like my friend Marion Gladwell. They went to the School to better themselves professionally, or because they were hungry for culture, or because they might there find a man. They were always the backbone of George's group, together with one or two eager and ambitious young men, such as I was then.

That was the material George had to work on. We sat hour after hour at night or on Sunday afternoons in dingy cafés up and down the town, the cafés of cinemas or, late at night, the lorry drivers' 'caff' beside the railway station. In those first years, George did not find it easy to collect the group together, but soon we developed the practice of all going to spend weekends in a farmhouse ten miles away, where we could cook our own food, pay a shilling a night for a bed, and talk until daybreak.

Under the pink-shaded lights at the picture-house café, round the oil lamp on the table at the farm, we sat while George made prophecies of our future, shouted us down for false arguments, set us on fire with hope. He gave us credit for having all his own qualities and more. I knew he was overestimating the others, and sometimes, even with the conceit of eighteen, I did not recognize myself in his descriptions, and wished uncomfortably that they were nearer to the truth. He endowed me with all varieties of courage, revolutionary and altruistic zeal, aggressive force, leadership, unbreakable resolution, and power of will. He used to regret, with his naïve and surprising modesty, that he was not blessed with the same equipment. I was inflated, and acted for a time as though George's picture of my character were accurate, but I had a suspicion lurking underneath – for I was already more suspicious of myself and other human beings than George would be at fifty – that I was quite unlike George's noble picture, and that so also were all living men.

Yet George gave us such glowing hope just because he was utterly unsuspicious of men's nature and the human condition. As a child I had been used to my mother's roseate hopes of a transformation in her life, but by those she meant nothing more nor less than a fulfilment for herself – sometimes that she might find love, always that she might live like a lady. George's hopes were as passionate as hers, and more violent, but they were different in kind. He believed, with absolute sincerity and with each beat of his heart, that men could become better; that the whole world could become better; that the restraints of the past, the shackles of guilt, could fall off and set us all free to live, happily in a free world; that we could create a society in which men could live in peace, in decent comfort, and cease to be power-craving, avaricious, censorious, and cruel. George believed, with absolute sincerity and with each beat of his heart, that all this would happen before we were old.

It was the first time, for Jack Cotery and me and the rest, that we had been near a cosmic faith. But these were the middle twenties, and the whole spirit of the time was behind George Passant. It was a time when political hope, international hope, was charging the air we breathed. Not only George Passant was full of faith as we cheered the Labour gains in the town hall square on the election nights in twenty-two and twenty-three. And it was a time of other modes of hope. Freud, D H Lawrence, Rutherford – messages were in the air, and in our society we did not listen to the warnings. It was a great climacteric of hope, and George embodied it in his flesh and bone.

At another period he would have thrown himself into a religion. As it was, he made a creed out of every free idea that spurted up in those last days of radical and rootless freedom. He believed that it was better to be alive in 1923 than at any other moment in the world's history. He believed – with great simplicity, despite his wild and complex nature – in the perfectibility of man.

That faith of his did not really fit me at all – though for a time it coloured many of my thoughts. In due course I parted from George on almost all of the profound human questions. For all his massive intelligence, his vision of life was so different from mine that we could not for long speak the same mental language. And yet, despite that foreignness, despite much that was to happen, I was grateful always that, for those years in my youth, I came under his influence. Our lives were to take us divergent ways. As I have said, we parted on all the profound human questions – except one. Though I could not for long think happily as he did of the human condition, I also could not forget the strength of his fellow feeling. I could not forget how robustly he stood by the side of his human brothers against the dark and cold. Human beings were brothers to him – not only brothers to love, but brothers to hate with violence. When he hated them, they were still men, men of flesh and bone – and he was one among them, in their sweat and bewilderment and folly. He hoped for so much from them – but if he had hoped for nothing, he would still have felt them as his brothers and struggled as robustly by their side. He took his place among them. By choice he would not move a step away from the odour of man.

There I never wanted to part from him. His fellow feeling had strengthened mine. There he was my master, and throughout my life I wished he would stay so until the end.

Quite soon after George took me into the group, our difference began to show. Yet I too was full of hope. I might attack George's Utopian visions, but then at times George provoked all my destructive edge. There were other times I remembered afterwards, in which I was as unshielded as my mother used to be, in which I had learned nothing of disappointment.

I remembered the first time that Marion Gladwell asked me to call on her at school. She had been promising to lend me a book, but whenever we met in the group she had forgotten it; I could have it, she said, if I went round to her school in the lunch hour.

The school was in Albion Street, near to the middle of the town, a diminutive red-brick barracks drawing in the children from the rows of red-brick houses in the mean streets near. Marion had only taught there a year, since she came out of her training college. She was twenty-one, and engrossed in her work. She often talked to us about the children, laughed at herself for being 'earnest', and then told us some more.

When I arrived in her classroom that afternoon she was just opening a window. The room was dark and small, and there was a faint, vestigial, milky smell of small children. Marion said, in her energetic, overemphatic, nervous fashion, that she must let some oxygen in before the next lesson. She moved rapidly to the next window, opened it, returned to the blackboard, shook the duster so that a cloud of chalk hung in the air.

'Sit down, Lewis,' she said. 'I want to talk to you.'

She stood by the blackboard, twisting the duster. At the group she was overemphatic, overdecisive, but no one minded it much from her, since she was so clearly nervous and anxious to be liked and praised. She was tallish and strong, very quick and active physically, but a little clumsy, and either her figure was shapeless or she dressed so sloppily that one could not see she had a waist. But she had an open, oval, comely face, and her eyes were striking. They were not large, but bright and continually interested. Despite her earnestness, they were humorous and gay.

That afternoon she wrung out the duster, unusually restless and nervous even for her.

'I'm worried about you,' she said.

'What's the matter?'

'You mustn't burn the candle at both ends.'

I asked what she meant, but I had a very good idea. Marion, like most of the girls in the group, came from a respectable lower-middle-class home, and their emancipation had still not gone far. So Marion and the others were shocked, some of them pleasantly shocked, at the gossip they heard of our drinking parties and visits to Nottingham. The gossip became far more lurid than the facts – Jack saw to that, who was himself a most temperate man – and George and the rest of us acquired an aura of sustained dissipation.

I was not displeased. It was flattering to hear oneself being snatched from the burning. I tried to pare off the more extravagant edges of the stories, but Marion wanted to believe them, and I should have had to be much more wholehearted to persuade her.

'You mustn't wear yourself out,' said Marion obstinately.

'I'm pretty good at looking after myself,' I said.

'I don't believe it,' said Marion. 'Anyway, you mustn't waste yourself. Think of all you've got to do.'

She was watching me with her clear, bright eyes. She must have seen a change in my expression. She knew that I was softened and receptive now. She gave up twisting the duster and put it in its box. In doing so she knocked down a piece of chalk, and cried, 'Oh, why do I always upset everything?' Her eyes were lit up with gaiety, and she leaned against the desk. Her voice was still decisive, but it was easy to confide.

'Tell me what you want to do. Tell me what you want.'

My first reply was:

'Of course, I want to see a better world.'

Marion nodded her head, as though she would have given the same answer. We were sufficiently under George Passant's influence to make such an answer quite unselfconsciously. We were children of our class and time, and took that hope as unchallengeable. That afternoon in Marion's schoolroom in 1923, both she and I expected it to be fulfilled.

'What do you want for yourself?' asked Marion.

'I want success.'

She seemed startled by the force with which I had spoken. She said:

'What do you call success?'

'I don't mean to spend my life unknown.'

'Do you want to make money, Lewis?'

'I want everything that people call success. Plus a few requirements of my own.'

'You mustn't expect too much,' said Marion.

'I expect everything there is,' I said. I went on: 'And if I fail, I shan't make any excuses. I shall say that it is my own fault.'

'Lewis!' she cried. There was a strange expression on her face. After a silence, she asked: 'Is there anything else you want?'

This time I hesitated. Then I said: 'I think I want love.'

Marion said, her voice emphatic and decisive, but her face still soft with pain:

'Oh, I haven't had time for that. There's too much else to do. I wonder if you'll have time.'

I was too rapt to attend to her. Just then, I was living in my imagination.

Marion contradicted herself; and said:

'Oh, I suppose you're right. I suppose we all want – love. But, Lewis, I wonder if we mean the same thing by love?'

I was living in my imagination, and I could not tell her the essence of my own hope, let alone come near perceiving hers. I had confessed myself to her with ardour. I began to inquire about what she would teach that afternoon.

14

An Act of Kindness

THAT winter I found the days in the office harder than ever to bear. At night I drank with George, stood at coffee stalls, sat in his room or my attic, tirelessly walked the streets until the small hours, while we stimulated each other's answers to the infinite questions of young men – man's destiny, the existence of God, the organization of the world, the nature of love. It was hard to wake up, with the echoes of the infinite questions still running through my head, to get to the office by nine and to stare with heavy eyes at the names of fee-paying children at one of the secondary schools.

Mr Vesey did not make it easier. He considered that I was living above my station, and he disapproved intensely. He had heard that I was seen in the London Road one night, excessively cheerful with drink. He had heard also of my political speeches. Mr Vesey was outraged that I should presume to do things he dared not do. He said ominously that the life of his clerks out of hours was part of his business, whatever we might think. He addressed the office in characteristically dark and cryptic hints: how some people deliberately drew attention to themselves, either by sucking up to authority or by painting the town red, with only one intention, which was to discredit their superior and obstruct his promotion.

He was watching for a chance to report me. But here his mania for promotion made him cautious. He knew that I was in favour higher up. He realized he must have a cast-iron case, unless he were to lose his reputation for 'knowing his men'. He would rather sacrifice his moral indignation, let me go unpunished for a time, than make a false move. 'One doesn't want to drop a brick,' said Mr Vesey cryptically to the office, 'just when *they* must be realizing that certain things are overdue.'

Of course, it made him dislike me more. The story of my relation with Mr Vesey became a good one with which to entertain the group but it was not so funny during the monotonous, drab, humiliating days. Dislike at close quarters can be very wearing, and it does not console one much if the dislike shows on a comic face. I used to look up from my desk and see the enormous spectacled eyes of Mr Vesey fixed upon me. I could not make myself impervious to the thought that I had become an obsession within him, part of his web of persecution. When I described him to George and the rest, he was a trim spectacled figure, crazed with promotion-fever, keeping in the public eye; but in the office, where I spent so many desert hours, he became a man, a feeling and breathing man, who loathed me, every action I performed and every word I spoke.

Sitting in the office on winter afternoons, looking out into the murk of Bowling Green Street, I was angry that I had delayed taking George's help, even by a week. I was paying for my pride. Very soon I was ready to humble myself, apologize, and ask his advice. It was early in twenty-four, not more than a couple of months after his first approach. But I was spared having to eat my words: George had been considering his 'mistake', and he was not prepared to let me waste more time. He got in first. Stiffly he said, one night, with the formality that came over him when he was feeling diffident about expressing concern or affection: 'I propose that we adjourn to my place. I want to make some points about your career. I don't feel justified in respecting your privacy any longer. I have certain suggestions to make.'

This time I fell over myself to accept.

It was not until we had reached his lodgings, and settled ourselves by the fire, that George began with his 'suggestions'. It surprised people that he, one of the most turbulent of men, should sometimes behave so punctiliously and formally, as though he were undertaking a piece of delicate official diplomacy. That night he propitiated his landlady into making us a pot of tea, propitiated her because she was truculent and did nothing for him. George lived among the furniture of an artisan's front room; all he contributed were pipes, a jar of tobacco, a few books, documents from the office, and sheaf upon sheaf of foolscap.

We drank our tea. At last George thought it was a fitting time to begin.

'Well,' he said, firmly and yet uncomfortably, 'I propose to start on the basis of your legacy. I assume that I should have been told if the position had altered to any material extent.'

Aunt Za's will had taken a long time to prove, and I had often thought how inevitably my mother would have seen the sinister hand of Uncle Will. But in fact I had actually received the three hundred pounds a few weeks before.

'Of course you would have been told,' I said. 'It's still there.'

'The sum is three hundred pounds?' asked George unnecessarily, for his memory was perfect.

'Less what I owe you,' I said.

'I don't intend to consider that,' said George, for the first time hearty and comfortable. With money, he was lavish, easy, warm-hearted, and prodigal. At the end of each month, when he received his pay, he had taken to asking if he could lend me a pound or two. 'I don't intend to consider that for a minute. Three hundred pounds is your basis. You've got to use it to establish yourself in a profession. That's the only serious question, and everything else is entirely irrelevant.'

'I'm not going to disagree.' I smiled. I was on tenterhooks, excited, vigilant.

'Excellent,' said George. 'Well, I expect other people have made suggestions, but unless you stop me I propose to present you with mine.'

'If other people had made suggestions,' I said, 'I should probably have got a move on by now. You don't realize how you've altered the look of things,' I went on, with spontaneous feeling – and with a hint of something he wanted to hear mixed in the feeling, for that too came just as naturally.

'I don't know about that,' said George, and hurried on with his speech. 'I can't see that there is any alternative to my case. (*a*) You've got to establish yourself in a profession. (*b*) You insist that you haven't any reasonable contacts anywhere, and (*c*) I haven't any influence, *of course*. With one exception that I regard as important, and that is obviously Martineau. Which brings up the possibility of my own profession and my own firm. (*d*) It goes without saying that you'd become an incomparably better solicitor than most of the bell-wethers and sunkets who disfigure what I still consider a decent profession for a reasonable man. I can tell you here and now, from what I've seen of your work, that you would pass the examinations on your head, if you only follow my old maxim and work when there is nothing else to do. If you manage three hours' work a night before you come out for a drink, there will be nothing to stop you. (*e*) Your basic sum of three hundred pounds is enough to pay the cost of your articles, even if Martineau can't manage to get you in free. I can't be expected to answer for other professions, but I haven't been able to think of another where you won't have financial difficulties. (*f*) Martineau can be persuaded to let you serve your articles in our firm, which would be very convenient for all concerned.' George leant back in his chair with an expression seraphic and complacent. 'I'm afraid I can't see any alternative,' he said contentedly. 'Everything points to your becoming articled to the old firm of Eden and Martineau. I propose you give the egregious Vesey a parting kick, and get your articles arranged in time for the spring. That's my case.' He stared challengingly at me. 'I should like to hear if you can find any objections.'

'How much would it need? What would it cost?'

George answered with mechanical accuracy. No one was ever more conversant with regulations.

'If there's any snag,' said George, 'I should expect you to look on me as your banker. I don't see how you can possibly need more than a hundred pounds on top of your basic sum. Somehow or other, that will have to be found. I insist that you don't let a trivial sum affect your decision.'

I tried to speak, but George stopped me with a crashing, final shout: 'I regard it as settled,' he cried.

But I did not. I was touched and affected and my heart was thumping, just as I was affected all my life by any kindness. For another to take a step on one's behalf – it was one of the most difficult things to become hardened to. And I was attracted by George's proposal. It was a way of escape, a goodish way compared with my meaningless and servile days in the education office. With George's praise to bolster me up, I did not doubt that I should make a competent solicitor. As my mother would have said, it would be 'better than nothing' – and, sitting in George's room, excited, touched by his comradeship, avid with the drawing near of my first leap, I thought for a moment how gratified my mother would have been, if she had seen me accept his suggestion, become a solicitor, set up in a country town, make some money and re-establish the glory of her Wigmore uncle when she was a girl.

I was softened and mellow with emotion. In the haze of George's tobacco my head was swimming. Through the haze, George's face, the mantelpiece, the framed diploma hanging over the whatnot, all shone out, ecstatically bright. For the first time, as though my sight had sharpened, I read some words in the diploma. Suddenly I was seized by laughter. George looked astonished, then followed my finger, started across the room at the diploma, and himself roared until the tears came. For it was a certificate, belonging presumably to his landlady's husband, which testified to a record of ten years' total abstinence – it was issued by one of Aunt Milly's organizations.

Yet, all the time, I was wondering. At bottom I was warier than George, shrewder, far more ambitious and more of a gambler. If I was going to take this jump, why not jump further? – that question was half-formed inside me. George was not a worldly man, I realized already. Outside the place where chance had brought him, he did not instinctively, know his way about. I never forgot the first night we talked, when George stood in the dark street and cursed up at the club windows; for him, it was always others who sat in the comfortable places, in the warm and lighted rooms.

With delight I accepted his invitation to take me to the next of Martineau's 'Friday nights' – 'To carry out our plan, which I regard as settled, in principle,' said George complacently. Yet there might be other ways for me. Even that evening, with the excitement still hot upon me, I found time to ask some questions about a barrister's career. Not that I was contemplating it for a moment myself, I said. Becoming a solicitor might be practicable: this was not. But, just as a matter of interest, how well should I cope with the Bar examinations? George thought the question trivial and irrelevant, but said again that, with three or four years' work, I should sail through them.

He might not be worldly, but he was a fine lawyer, whose own record in examinations was of the highest class. Decisions are taken before we realize them ourselves: above all, perhaps, with those that matter to us most. I did not know it, but my mind may have been made up from that moment.

15

An Intention and a Name

I SET out to win the support of Martineau and Eden. Whichever way I moved, I should need them. I could not afford to fail. When George took me, first to Martineau's house, then to Eden's office, I was nervous; but it was a pleasurable nervousness that sharpened my attention and my wits. Unlike George, who was embarrassed at any social occasion, I was enjoying myself.

I got airy encouragement from Martineau, but no more. Although none of us realized it then, he was losing all interest in his profession. He welcomed me to his 'Friday night' parties; it was the first salon I had ever attended, and knowing no others I did not realize how eccentric it was. I enjoyed being inside a comfortable middle-class house for the first time. I could not persuade him to attend to my career, though he made half-promises, chiefly I thought because he was so fond of George.

It was quite different with Eden. Before ever George introduced me, I knew that the meeting was critical, for Eden was the senior partner. I guessed that I had disadvantages to overcome. Before I had been in Eden's office three minutes, I felt with an extra tightening of the nerves that I had more than a disadvantage against me: I was struggling with Eden's unshakeable dislike of George.

The office was warm and comfortable, with a fire in an old-fashioned grate, leather-covered armchairs, sets of heavy volumes round the walls. Eden sat back in his chair, smoking a pipe, when

George awkwardly presented me; and then George stood for a time, not knowing whether to leave us or stay, with me still standing also. Eden was just going to speak, but George chose that moment to say that he did not agree with Eden's general line of instructions about a new case.

Eden was bald and frog-faced, substantial in body, comfortably and pleasantly ugly. His manner was amiable, but he ceased to be so bland when he replied to George. They had a short altercation, each of them trying hard to be courteous, Eden repressing his irritation, George insisting on his opinion and his rights. Soon Eden said:

'Well, well, Passant, this isn't the best time to discuss it. Perhaps you might leave me with this young man.'

'If you prefer it, Mr Eden,' said George, and backed away.

Eden might have been designed to extract the last ounce of misunderstanding out of George. He was a solid, indolent, equable, good-humoured man, modest about everything but his judgement. He was often pleased with his own tolerance and moderation. He respected George's intellect and professional competence — it was comfortable for him to respect the latter, for Eden was not overfond of work, and, having once assured himself of George's skill, was content to let that dynamo-like energy dispose of most of the firm's business. But everything else about George repelled him. George's 'wildness', formality, passion for argument, lack of ease — they infuriated Eden. In his private heart he could not abide George. Before he spoke to me, when George at last left us alone, I knew that I was under the same suspicion. Some of George's aura surrounded me also, in Eden's eyes. I had to please right in the teeth of a prejudice.

'Well, young man,' said Eden with a stiff, courteous but not over-amiable smile, 'what can I do for you?' I replied that above all things I needed the guidance of a man of judgement. And I continued in that vein.

My brashness and spasms of pride with George were not much like me, or at least not like the self that in years to come got on easily with various kinds of men and women. Even in the months between my meetings with George and Eden, I was learning. In casual human contacts, I was already more practised than George, who stayed all his life something like most of us at eighteen. I was much more confident than George that I should get along with Eden or with anyone that I met; and that confidence made me more ready to please, more unashamed about pleasing.

Eden became much less suspicious. He went out of his way to be affable. He did not make up his mind quickly about people, but he was very genial, pleased with himself for being so impartial, satisfied that one of Passant's friends could – unlike that man Passant – make so favourable an impression. Eden liked being fair. Passant made it so difficult to be fair – it was one of his major sins.

Eden did not promise anything on the spot, as Martineau had done. He told me indulgently enough that I should have to 'sober down', whatever career I took up. In a local paper he had noticed a few violent words from a speech of mine. The identical words would have damned George in Eden's mind, but did not damn me. At first sight he felt he could advise me, as he could never have advised George. 'Ah well! Young men can't help making nuisances of themselves,' he said amiably. 'As long as you know where to draw the line.'

It would have offended Eden's sense of decorum to form an impression in haste, or to make a promise without weighing it. He believed in taking his time, in gathering other people's opinions, in distrusting impulse and first impressions, and in ruminating over his own preliminary judgement. He spoke, so I heard, to Darby and the director. He had a word with my old headmaster. It was a fortnight or more before he sent across to the education office a note asking me if I would make it convenient to call on him.

When I did so, he still took his time. He sat solidly back in his chair. He was satisfied now that the investigation was complete and the ceremony of forming a judgement properly performed. He was satisfied to have me there, on tenterhooks, waiting on his words. 'I don't believe in jumping to conclusions, Eliot,' he said. 'I'm not clever enough to hurry. But I've thought round your position long enough now to feel at home.' Methodically he filled his pipe. At last he came to the point.

'Do you know, young man,' said Eden, 'I don't see why you shouldn't make a job of it.'

Unlike Martineau, he made a definite offer. If I wanted to serve my articles as a solicitor, he would accept me on the usual footing, I paying my fee of two hundred and fifty guineas. It was entirely fair: it was exactly as he had treated any other of the articled clerks who had gone through the firm. He explained that he was not making any concessions to partiality or to the fact that I was so poor. 'If we started that, young man, we should never know when to stop. Pay your way like everyone else, and we shall all be better friends,' said Eden, with the broad judgement-exuding smile that lapped up the corners of his mouth. But he knew that, when I had paid the fee, I should not have enough to live on. So he was prepared to allow me thirty shillings a week while I served my time. With his usual temperateness he warned me that, before I took articles in the firm, I ought to be reminded that there was not likely to be a future for me there 'when you become qualified, all being well'. For George Passant was not, so far as Eden knew, likely to move, and the firm did not need another qualified assistant.

I thanked him with triumph, with relief. I said that I ought to think it over, and Eden approved. He had no doubt that I was going to accept. I said that I might have other problems to raise, and Eden again approved. He still had no doubt that I was going to accept.

How much doubt had I myself, that day in Eden's room? Or back at my desk, under Mr Vesey's enormous and persecuted eyes, on those spring afternoons, waiting for the day's release at half past five? There is no doubt that, on the days after Eden's offer, I often steadied myself with the thought that I need not stand it. I had a safe escape now. I could end the servitude tomorrow. If I did not, it was of my own volition.

I assuaged each morning's heaviness with the prospect of that escape. Yet I had a subterranean knowledge that I should never take it. The nerves flutter and dither, and make us delay recognizing a choice to ourselves; we honour that process by the title of 'making up our minds'. But the will knows.

I had rejected George's proposition the minute it was uttered – and before I set out to work for Martineau's and for Eden's help. I wanted that help, but for another reason. I was going – there was at bottom no residue of doubt, however much I might waver on the surface – to choose the wilder gamble, and read for the Bar.

I had not yet admitted the intention to the naked light, even in secret; but it was forcing its way through, flooding me with a sense of champagne-like risk and power. It was hard to defend, which I knew better than all those I should have to argue with, for I felt the prickle of anxiety even before I admitted the intention to myself. If all went perfectly, I should have spent my 'basic sum' by the time I took Bar Finals. There was no living to look forward to immediately, nor probably for several years; it meant borrowing money or winning a studentship. It left no margin for any kind of illness or failure. I should have to spend two thirds of the three hundred pounds on becoming admitted to an Inn. If anything went wrong, I had lost that stake altogether, and so had no second chance.

I did not even escape the office. For I should leave myself so little money, after the fees were paid, that my office wages would be needed to pay for food and board. Instead of crossing Bowling Green Street and working alongside of George, I should have to discipline myself to endure the tedium, the hours without end of clerking, Mr Vesey. All my study for the Bar examinations I should have to do at night; and on those examinations my whole future rested.

In favour of the gamble, there was just one thing to say. If my luck held at every point and I came through, there were rewards, not only money, though I wanted that. It gave me a chance, so I thought then, of the paraphernalia of success, luxury and a name and, yes, the admiration of women.

There was nothing more lofty about my ambition at that time, nothing at all. It had none of the complexity or aspiration of a mature man's ambition – and also none of the moral vanity. Ten years later, and I could not have felt so simply. Yet I made my calculations, I reckoned the odds, I knew they were against me, almost as clear-sightedly as if I had been grown-up.

When I knew, with full lucidity, that the decision was irrevocably taken, I still cherished it to myself for days and weeks.

I was intensely happy, in that spring and summer of my nineteenth year. The days were wet; rain streamed down the office window; I was full of well-being, of a joyful expectancy, now that I knew what I had to do. I was anxious and had some of my first sleepless nights. But it was a happy sleeplessness, so that I looked with expectation on the first light of a summer dawn. Once I got up with the sun and walked the streets that were so familiar to George and me at the beginning of the night. Now in the dawn the road was pallid, the houses smaller, all blank and washed after the enchantment of the dark. I thought of what lay just ahead. There would be some trouble with Eden, which I must surmount, for it was imperative to keep his backing. Perhaps George might not be altogether pleased. I should have to persuade them. That would be the first step.

It was in those happy days that, attuned so that my imagination stirred to the sound of a girl's name, I first heard the name of Sheila Knight. I was attuned so that an unknown name invited me, as I had never been invited before, attuned because of my own gamble and the well-being which made the blood course through my veins, attuned too because of the amorous climate which lapped round our whole group on those summer evenings. For George's pleasures could not be long concealed from us at our age, thinking of love, talking of love, swept off our feet by imagined joys. In Jack's soft voice there came stories of delight, his conquests and adventures and the whispered words of girls. We were at an age when we were deafened by the pounding of our blood. We began to flirt, and that was the first fashion. Jack's voice murmured the names of girls, girls he had known or whom he was pursuing. I flirted a little with Marion, but it was the unknown that invited me. Sheila's name was not the first nor only one that plucked at my imagination. But each word about her gave her name a clearer note.

'She goes about by herself, looking exceedingly glum,' said Jack. 'She's rather beautiful, in a chiselled, soulful way,' said Jack. 'She'd be too much trouble for me. It isn't the pretty ones who are most fun,' said Jack. 'I advise you to keep off. She'll only make you miserable,' said Jack.

None of the group knew her, though Jack claimed to have spoken to her at the School. It was said that she lived in the country, and came to an art class one night a week.

One warm and cloudy midsummer evening, I had met Jack out of the newspaper office, and we were walking slowly up the London Road. A car drove by close to the pavement, and I had a moment's sight, blurred and confused, of a young woman's face, a smile, a wave. The car passed us, and I turned my head, but could see no more. Jack was smiling. He said: 'Sheila Knight.'

16

Denunciation

FOR weeks no one knew that, instead of taking articles, I was determined to try reading for the Bar. I delayed breaking the news longer than was decent, even to George, most of all to George. I was apprehensive of his criticisms; I did not want my resolution shaken too early. The facts were harsh: I could face them realistically in secret, but it was different to hear them from another. Also I was uneasy. Could I still keep Eden's goodwill? Could I secure my own way without loss? I screwed myself up to breaking the news one afternoon in September. I thought I would get it over quickly, tell them all within an hour.

I took the half-day off, incidentally raising Mr Vesey's suspicions to fever point. I went into the reference library, so as to pass the time before Eden returned from lunch. I meant to tell George first, but not to give myself long. The library was cool, aquarium-like after the bright day outside. Instead of bringing calm, the chill, the smell of books, the familiar smell of that room only made me more uneasy, and I wished more than ever that I had this afternoon behind me.

Just before my appointment with Eden I looked into George's office and told him what I was going to say. I saw his face become heavy. He said nothing. There was no time for either of us to argue, for we could hear Eden's deliberate footsteps outside the open door.

Eden settled himself in his armchair. Now that the hesitation was over, now that I was actually in the room to make the best of it, I plunged into placating him. I told him how his support had stimulated and encouraged me. If I was attempting too much, I said with the mixture of deference and cheek that I knew would please him, it was really his fault – for giving me too much support. I liked him more, because I was seeing him with all my nerves alive with excitement – with the excitement that, when plunged into it, I really loved. I saw him with great clarity, from the pleased, reluctant, admonishing smile to the peel of sunburn on the top of his bald head.

He was pleased. There was no doubt about that. But he was too solid a man to have his judgements shaken, to give way all at once, just because he was pleased. He was severe, reflective, minatory, shocked, and yet touched with a sneaking respect. 'These things will happen,' he said, putting his fingertips together. 'Young men will take the bit between their teeth. But I shouldn't be doing my duty, Eliot, if I didn't tell you that you were being extremely foolish. I thought you were a bit more level-headed. I'm afraid you've been listening to some of your rackety friends.'

I told him that it was my own free choice. He shook his head. He had obstinately decided that it must be Passant's fault, and the more I protested, the more obstinate he became.

'Remember that some of your friends have got through their own examinations,' he said. 'They may not be the best company for you, even if they seem about the same age. Still, you've got to make your own mistakes. I know how you feel about things, Eliot. We've all been young once, you know. I can remember when I wanted to throw my cap over the windmill. Nothing venture, nothing win, that's how you feel, isn't it? We've all felt it, Eliot, we've all felt it. But you've got to have a bit of sense.'

He was certain that I must have made up my mind in a hurry, and he asked me to promise that I would do nothing irrevocable without thinking it over for another fortnight. If I did not consent to that delay, he would not be prepared to introduce me to an acquaintance at the Bar, whose signature I needed to support me in some of the formalities of getting admitted to an Inn.

'I'm not sure, young man,' said Eden, 'that I oughtn't to refuse straight out – in your own best interests. In your own best interests, perhaps I should put a spoke in your wheel. But I expect you'll think better of it anyway, after you've cooled your heels for another fortnight.'

In one's 'own best interests' – this was the first time I heard that ominous phrase, which later I heard roll sonorously and self-righteously round college meetings, round committees in Whitehall, round the most eminent of boards, and which meant inevitably that some unfortunate person was to be dished. But Eden had not said it with full conviction. Underneath his admonishing tone, he was still pleased. He felt for me a warm and comfortable patronage, which was not going to be weakened. I left his room, gay, relieved, with my spirits at their highest.

Then, along the corridor, I saw George standing outside his own room, waiting for me.

'You'd better come out for a cup of tea,' he said in a tone full of rage and hurt.

The rage I could stand, and in the picture-house café I was denounced as a fool, an incompetent, a half-baked dilettante, an airy-fairy muddler who was too arrogant to keep his feet on the ground. But I was used to his temper, and could let it slide by. That afternoon I was prepared for some hot words, for I had behaved without manners and without consideration, in not disclosing my plans to him until so late.

I had imagined vividly enough for myself what he was shouting in the café, oblivious of the customers sitting by, shouting with the rage I had bargained on and a distress which I had not for a minute expected. The figures of 'this egregious nonsense' went exploding all over the café, as George became more outraged. He extracted them from me by angry questions and then crashed them out in his tremendous voice. Two hundred and eight pounds down! At the best, even if I stayed at that 'wretched boy's job' (cried George, rubbing it in brutally), which was ridiculous if I were to stand any chance in the whole insane venture – even if nothing unexpected happened and my luck was perfect, I should be left with eighty pounds. 'What about your fees as a pupil? In this blasted gentlemanly profession in which you're so anxious to be a hanger-on, isn't it obligatory to be rooked and go and sit in some nitwit's Chambers and pay some sunket a handsome packet for the privilege?' George, as usual, had his facts right. I wanted another hundred pounds for my pupil's fees, and support for whatever time it was, a time which would certainly be measured in years, before I began earning. Against that I had my contemptible eighty pounds, and any money I could win in studentships. 'Which you can't count on, if you retain any shred of sanity at all, which I'm beginning to doubt. What other possible source of money have you got in the whole wide world?'

'Only what I can borrow.'

'How in God's name do you expect anyone to lend you money? For a piece of sheer fantastic criminal lunacy – '

He and Aunt Milly were, in fact, the only living persons from whom I had any serious hope of borrowing money. When he was first persuading me to become articled as a solicitor, George had, of course, specifically offered to be my 'banker'. How he thought of managing it, I could not imagine; for his total income, as I now knew, was under three hundred pounds a year, he had no capital at all, and made an allowance to his parents. Yet he had promised to find a hundred pounds for me and, even that afternoon, he was conscience-stricken at having to take the offer back, As well as being a generous man, George had the strictest regard for his word. That afternoon he was abandoned to anger and distress. He washed his hands of my future, as though he were dismissing it once for all. But even then he felt obliged to say:

'I am sorry that any promise of mine may have helped to encourage you in this piece of lunacy. I took it for granted that you'd realize it was only intended for purposes within the confines of reason. I'm sorry.'

He went away from the café abruptly. I sat alone, troubled, guilty, anxious. I needed someone to confide in. There was a pall of trouble between me and the faces in the streets, as I walked up the London

Road, my steps leading me, almost like a sleepwalker, to Marion. I sometimes talked to her about my plans, and she scolded me for not telling her more. Now I found myself walking towards her lodgings. I was voraciously anxious for myself; and mixed with the anxiety (how could I set it right?) I felt sheer guilt – guilt at causing George a disappointment I could not comprehend. I had been to blame; I had been secretive, my secrecy seemed like a denial of friendship and affection. But secrecy could not have wounded George so bitterly.

His emotion had been far more violent than disappointment, it had been furious distress, coming from a depth that I found bafflingly hard to understand. Very few people, it did not need George's response to teach me, could give one absolutely selfless help. They were obliged to help on their own terms, and were pained when one struggled free. That was the pattern, the eternally unsatisfactory pattern, of help and gratitude. But George's distress was far more mysterious than that.

On the plane of reason, of course, every criticism he made was accurate. It was only years later, after the gamble was decided, that I admitted how reasonable his objections were. But no one, not even George, could become so beside himself because of a disagreement on the plane of reason. He had been affected almost as though I had performed an act of treachery. Perhaps that was it. In his heart, I think, I seemed like a deserter.

In his urge to befriend, George was stronger than any man. But he needed something back. On his side he would give money, time, thought, all the energy of his nature, all more than he could afford or anyone else could have imagined giving: in return he needed an ally. He needed an ally close beside him, in the familiar places. I should have been a good ally, working at his side in the office, continuing to be his right-hand man in the group, sharing his pleasures and enough of his utopian hopes. In fact, if I had accepted his plan, become articled to Eden and Martineau's, and stayed in the town, it might have made a difference to George's life. As it was, I went off on my own. And, from the beginning, from that violent altercation in the picture-house café, George felt in his heart that I had, without caring, left him isolated to carry on alone.

But that evening, as I told Marion, I could not see my way through. I could not understand George's violence; I was wrapped in my own anxiety. As soon as I went into her sitting-room, Marion had looked at me, first with a smile, then with eyes sharp in concern.

'What's the matter, Lewis?' she said abruptly.

'I've run into some trouble,' I said.

'Serious?'

'I expect I'll get out of it.'

'You're looking drawn,' said Marion. 'Sit down and I'll make you some tea.'

She lodged in the front room of a semi-detached house, in a neat privet-hedged street just at the beginning of the suburbs. The hedge was fresh clipped, the patch of grass carefully mown. She was only just returned from her holidays, and on her sofa there was a notebook open, in which she was preparing her lessons for the term. Outside in the sun, a butterfly was flitting over the privet hedge.

'Why haven't I seen you before?' said Marion, kneeling by the gas ring. 'Oh, never mind. I know you're worried. Tell me what the trouble is.'

I did not need to explain it all, for she had written to me during her holiday and I had replied. On paper she was less brisk and nervous, much softer and more articulate. She had asked when I was going to 'take the plunge', assuming like everyone else that I was following George's plan. In my reply I had told her, with jauntiness and confidence, that I had made up my mind to do something more difficult. She was the first person to whom I told as much. Even so, she complained in another letter about 'your cryptic hints', and as she gave me my cup of tea, and I was at last explicit about my intention, she complained again.

'Why do you keep things to yourself?' she cried. 'You might have known that you could trust me, mightn't you?'

'Of course I trust you.'

'I hope you do.' She was sitting on the sofa, with the light from the window falling on her face, so that her eyes shone excessively bright. Her hair had fallen untidily over her forehead; she pushed it back impatiently, and impatiently said: 'Never mind me. Is it a good idea?' (She meant my reading for the Bar.)

'Yes.'

'No one else thinks so – is that the trouble?' she said with startling speed.

'Not quite.' I would not admit my inner hesitations, the times that afternoon when my doubts were set vibrating by the others. Instead, I told her of the scene with George. I described it as objectively as I could, telling her of George's shouts which still rang word for word in my ears. I left out nothing of his fury and distress, speculated about it, asked Marion if she could understand it.

'That doesn't matter,' said Marion shortly. 'George will get over it. I want to know about you. How much does it mean to you?'

Though she was devoted to George, she would not let me talk about him. Single-mindedly, with an intense single-mindedness that invaded my thoughts, she demanded to know how much I was dependent on George's help. I answered that, without his coaching, I should find the work much more difficult, but not impossible; without a loan from him, I did not see how I could raise money even for my pupil's year.

Marion was frowning.

'I think you'll get his help,' she said.

She looked at me.

'And if you don't,' she said, 'shall you have to call it off?'

'I shan't do that.'

Still frowning, Marion inquired about George's objections. How much was there in them? A great deal, I told her. She insisted that I should explain them; she knew so little of a career at the Bar. I did so, dispassionately and sensibly enough. It was easy at times to face objection after objection, to lay them down in public view like so many playing cards upon the table. It was some kind of comfort to put them down and inspect them, as though they were not part of oneself.

Marion asked sharply how I expected to manage. I said that there were one or two studentships and prizes, though very few, if I came out high in the Bar Finals. 'Of course, you're clever,' said Marion dubiously. 'But there must be lots of competition. From men who've had every advantage that you haven't, Lewis.'

I said that I knew it. I mentioned Aunt Milly: with luck, I could conceivably borrow a hundred or two from her. That was all.

From across the little room, Marion was looking at me – not at my face, but looking me up and down, from head to foot.

'How strong are you, Lewis?' she said suddenly.

'I shall survive,' I said.

'I'm sure you're highly strung.'

'I'm tougher than you think.'

'You're packed full of vitality, I've told you that. But, unless you're careful, aren't you going to burn yourself out?'

She got up from the sofa and sat on a chair near mine.

'Listen to me,' she said urgently, gazing into my eyes. 'I wish you well. I wish you very well. Is it worth it? It's no use killing yourself. Why not swallow your pride and do what they want you to do? It's the sensible thing to do after all, And it isn't such a bad alternative, Lewis. It will give you a comfortable life – you might even make another start from there. It won't take anything like so much out of you. You'll have time for everything else you like.'

My hand was resting on the arm of my chair. She pressed hers upon it: her palm was very warm.

I met her gaze, and said: 'Do you think that I'm cut out to be a lawyer in a provincial town?'

She left her hand on mine, but her eyes shrank away.

'All I meant was – you mustn't damage yourself.'

Wretched after my day, I wanted to leave her. But before I went she made me promise that I would report what Eden said next, whether George came round. 'You must tell me,' said Marion. 'I want to know. You mustn't let me think I shouldn't have spoken. I couldn't help it – but I want everything you want, you know that, don't you?'

17

The Letter on the Chest of Drawers

IN fact, I soon had good news to tell Marion – and I did so at once, to make amends for having been angry with her. This time she did not stop me describing both George's words and Eden's.

George had spoken to me, only three or four days after our quarrel, stiffly, still half-furiously, in great embarrassment. He could not withdraw any single part of his criticisms. He regarded me as lost to reason; but, having once encouraged me to choose a career and offered his help, he felt obliged to honour his word. He would be behind me, so far as lay in his power. If I wanted money, he would do his best, though I must not count on much. He would, naturally, coach me in private for the Bar examinations. 'I refuse to listen to any suggestion that you won't find the blasted examinations child's play,' said George robustly. 'That's the one item in the whole insane project that I'm not worrying about. As for the rest, you've heard my opinions. I propose from now on to keep them to myself.'

He spoke with a curious mixture of stubborn irritation, diffidence, rancour, magnanimity, and warmth. I was disarmed and overjoyed.

As for Eden, when I told him that I had not changed my mind, he shook his head, and said: 'Well, I suppose young men must have their fling. If you are absolutely determined to run your head against a brick wall, I shan't be able to stop you.' That did not prevent him from giving me a series of leisurely sensible homilies; but he was willing to sign my certificates of character and to introduce me to a barrister. He wrote the letter of introduction on the spot (there were one or two technical difficulties about my getting admitted to an Inn). The name on the envelope was Herbert Getliffe.

All that was left, I said to Marion, was to pay my fee.

It was a few days later, in the October of 1924, on a beautiful day of Indian summer – I was just nineteen – that I announced that my admission was settled and the fee paid. Now it was irrevocable. I went to Aunt Milly's house on Friday evening, and proclaimed it first to Aunt Milly and my father. On recent visits there for tea, I had hinted that I might spend the legacy to train myself for a profession. Aunt Milly had vigorously remonstrated; but now I told them that I had paid two hundred pounds in order to start reading for the Bar, she showed, to my complete surprise, something that bore a faint resemblance to approval.

'Well, I declare,' said my father, equably, on hearing the news.

Aunt Milly rounded on him. 'Is that all you've got to say, Bertie?' she said. Having dismissed him, she turned to me with a glimmer of welcome. 'I shan't be surprised if it's just throwing good money after bad,' said Aunt Milly, automatically choosing to begin with her less encouraging reflections. 'It's your mother's fault that you want a job where you won't dirty your hands. Still, I'd rather you threw away your money failing in those examinations than see you putting it in the tills of the public houses.'

'I don't put it in the tills, Aunt Milly,' I said. 'Only the barman does that. I've never thought of being a barman, you know.'

Aunt Milly was not diverted.

'I'd rather you threw your money away failing in those examinations', she repeated, 'than see you do several things that I won't mention. I suppose I oughtn't to say so, but I always thought your mother might get above herself and put you in to be a parson.'

Aunt Milly seemed to be experiencing what for her was the unfamiliar emotion of relief.

I had arranged to meet George in the town that evening; he liked to have a snack before we made our usual Friday night call at Martineau's. 'Drop in for coffee – or *whatever's going*,' George remarked, chuckling, munching a sandwich. He was repeating

Martineau's phrase of invitation, which never varied. 'I'd been to half a dozen Friday nights before it dawned on me that coffee was always going – by itself.'

I broke in:

'This is a special occasion. The deed's done.'

'What deed?'

'I sent off the money this afternoon.'

'Did you, by God?' said George. He gazed at me with a heavy preoccupied stare, and then said:

'Good luck to you. You'll manage it, of course. I refuse to admit any other possibility.'

The street lamps shimmered through the blue autumnal haze. As we strolled up the New Walk George said, in a tone that was firm, resigned, and yet curiously sad:

'I accept the fact that you'll manage it. But don't expect me to forget that you've been as big a firebrand as I ever have. Some of the entries in my diary may embarrass you later – when you get out of my sight.'

Very rarely – but they stood out stark against his blazing hopes – George had moments of foresight, bleak and without comfort. In the midst of all his hope, he never pictured any concrete success for himself.

Then he went on heartily: 'It's essential to have a drink on it tonight. This calls for a celebration.'

We left Martineau's before the public houses closed. George, as always, was glad of the excuse to escape a 'social occasion': even in that familiar drawing-room, he felt that there were certain rules of behaviour which had paralysingly been withheld from him; even that night, when I was proclaiming my news to Martineau, I noticed George making a conscious decision before he felt able to sit down. But once outside the house, he drank to my action with everyone we met. There was nothing he liked more than a 'celebration', and he stood me a great and noisy one.

Arriving at my room after midnight, I saw something on the chest of drawers which I knew to be there, which I had remembered intermittently several times that evening, but which would have astonished all those who had greeted my 'drastic' step, George most of all. It was a letter addressed in my own handwriting. After midnight, I was still drunk enough from the celebration, despite our noisy procession through the streets, to find the envelope glaring under the light. I saw it with guilt. It was a letter addressed in my own handwriting to my prospective Inn. Inside was the money. It was the letter, which, for all my boasts, I had not yet screwed up my courage to send off. I had been lying. There was still time to back out.

They thought of me as confident. Perhaps they were right in a sense, and I had a confidence of the fibres. In the very long run, I did not doubt that I should struggle through. But they, who heard me boast, were taken in when they thought I took this risk as lightly as I pretended. They did not see the interminable waverings, the attacks of nerves, the withdrawals, the evenings staring out in nervous despondency over the roofs, the dread of tomorrow so strong that I wished time would stand still. They did not detect the lies which I told myself as well as them. They did not know that I changed my mind from mood to mood; I used an uprush of confidence to hearten myself on to impress Eden that I was absolutely firm. But a few hours later that mood had seeped away and I was left with another night of procrastination. That had gone on for weeks. My natural spirits were high, and my tongue very quick, or else the others would have known. But in fact I concealed from them the humiliating anxieties, the subterfuges, the desperate attempts to find an excuse, and then another, for not committing myself without any chance of return. They could not guess how many times I had shrunk back from paying the fee, so that I could still feel safe till another day. At last, that Friday, I had brought myself to sign the letter and the cheque; in ebullient spirits I had told them all, Aunt Milly, my father, George, Martineau, all the rest, that the plunge was taken, and that I was looking ahead without a qualm; but in the small hours of Saturday the letter was still glaring under the light, on the top of the chest of drawers.

It was Monday before I posted it.

Part Three

THE END OF INNOCENCE

18

Walking Alone

MY first meeting with Sheila became blotted from my memory. The first sight of her, as Jack and I walked up the London Road and she walked from her car, stayed clear always; so did the sound of her name, echoing in my mind before I had so much as seen her face. But there was a time when we first spoke, and that became buried or lost, irretrievably lost, so that I was never able to recapture it.

It must have been in the summer of 1925, when we were each nearly twenty. During the winter I had heard a rumour that she was abroad – being finished, said someone, for her health, said another. Her name dropped out of the gossip of the group; Jack forgot all about her and talked with his salesman's pleasure, persuading himself as well as his audience of the charms of other girls. It was the winter after I had taken the plunge, when I was trying to assuage my doubts by long nights of work: days at the office, evenings with George and the group, then nights in my cold room, working like a medieval student with blankets round my knees, in order to save shillings in the gas fire. There were times when, at two or three o'clock, I went for a walk to get my feet warm before I went to bed.

Sheila and I must have met a few months later, in the summer. I did not remember our first calling each other by name. But, with extreme distinctness, a few words came back whenever I tried to force my memory. They had been spoken not at our first meeting, but on an occasion soon after, probably the first or second time I took her out. They were entirely trivial, and concerned who should pay the bill.

We were sitting in a kind of cubicle in an old-fashioned café. From the next cubicle to ours sounded the slide and patter of draughts, for this was a room where boxes of chessmen and draughts stood on a table, and people came in for a late tea and stayed several hours.

Through the tobacco smoke, Sheila was staring at me. Her eyes were large and disconcertingly steady. At the corner of her mouth, there was a twitch that looked like a secret smile, that was in fact a nervous tic.

'I want to pay my share,' she said.

'No, you can't. I asked you to come out.'

'I can. I shall.'

I said no. I was insecure, not knowing how far to insist.

'Look. I've got some. You need it more than I do.'

We stared at each other across the table.

'You're here. In this town. I'm not far away.' Her voice was high, and sometimes had a brittle tone. 'We want to see each other, don't we?'

'Of course,' I said in sudden joy.

'I can't unless I pay for myself. I shouldn't mind you paying – but you can't afford it. Can you?'

'I can manage.'

'You can't. You know you can't. I've got some money.'

I was still insecure. Our wills had crossed. Already I was enraptured by her.

'Unless you let me pay for myself each time I shan't come again.' She added: 'I want to.'

If I had met her when I was older, and she had spoken so, I should have wondered how much it was an exercise of her will, how much due to her curious kindness. But that afternoon, after we had parted, I simply said to myself that I was in love. I had no room to think of anything but that.

I said to myself that I was in love. It was different from all I had imagined. I had read my Donne, I had listened to Jack Cotery, that cheerful amorist, and had agreed, out of the certainty of my inexperience, that the root of love was sensual desire, and that all that mattered was the bed. Yet it did not seem so, now that I was in love. Even though each moment had become enhanced, so that I saw faces in the evening light with a tenderness that I had never felt before. The faces of young men and women strolling in the late sunlight – I saw the bloom on the girls' cheeks, I saw them feature by feature, as though my eyesight had suddenly become ten times as acute, As I watched the steam rising from my teacup the next morning, I felt that I was seeing it for the first time, as though I had just been born with each sense fresh and preternaturally strong. Each moment was sensually enhanced because of the love inside me. Yet for her who inspired that love I had not in those first days a sensual thought.

I did not make dreams of her, as I had done of many other girls. That first state of love was delectable beyond my expectation; in its delight I did not stop to wonder that I had often imagined love, and imagined it quite wrong. I breathed in the delight with every breath, those first mornings. I did not stop to wonder why my thoughts of her were vague, why I was content to let her image – unlike those of everyone else I knew – lie vague within my heart.

It was the same when I pictured her face. I was used already to studying the bones and skin and flesh of those I met, and I could, as a matter of form and habit, have described Sheila much as I should have described Marion or even George or Jack. I could have specified the thin, fine nose; great eyes, which had not the lemur-like sadness of most large eyes, but were grey, steady, caught and held the light; front teeth which only the grace of God saved from protruding, and which sometimes rested on her lower lip. She was fair, and her skin was even, pale, and of the consistency that most easily takes lines – so that one could see, before she was twenty, some of the traces that would deepen in ten years. She was tallish for a woman, strong-boned and erect, with an arrogant toss to her head.

I should have described her in those terms, just as I might have described the others, but to myself I did not see her as I did them. For I thought of her as beautiful. It was an objective fact that others did so too. Few of my friends liked her for long, and almost none was easy with her; yet even George admitted that she was a handsome bitch, and the women in the group did not deny that she was good-looking. They criticized each feature, they were scornful of her figure, and it was all true; but they knew that she had the gift of beauty. At that time I believed it was a great gift – and so did she, proud in her looks and her youth. Neither of us could have credited that there would come a day when I was to see her curse her beauty and deliberately, madly, neglect it.

To me she was especially beautiful. And, in the first astonishment of love, I saw her, and thought of her, just like that. I did not see her, as I was to see her in the future, with the detailed fondness of an experienced love, in which I came to delight in her imperfections, the front teeth, the nervous, secret-smiling tic. No, I saw her as beautiful, and I was filled with love.

I did not mind, I noticed as it were without regarding, how in company she was apt to fall constrained and silent, pallid faced, the smile working her mouth as though she were inwardly amused. The first time Jack Cotery saw her and me together, we were alone, and she was laughing; afterwards, Jack proceeded to congratulate me. 'You're getting on,' he said good-naturedly. He was glad to witness me at last a captive. He was glad that I was sharing in his human frailty. He had always been half-envious that I was less distracted than he. And he was also glad that I was happy: like most carnal men, he was sorry if his friends were fools enough not to enjoy the fun. 'She's not my cup of tea.' He grinned. 'And I'm not hers. She'd just look through me with those searchlight eyes. But clearly she's the best-looking girl round here. And you seem to have made a hit. Just let yourself go, Lewis, just let yourself go.'

One day, however, she came with me to the group. She greeted them all high-spiritedly enough, and then, though they were talking of books which she and I had discussed together, she fell into an inhibited silence and scarcely spoke a word. Jack cross-questioned me about her. 'Is she often like that? Remember, they sometimes give themselves away, when they're not trying. It's easy to shine when someone's falling in love with you.' He shook his head. 'I hope she isn't going to be much of a handful. If she is, the best thing you can do is cut your losses and get out of it straight away.'

I smiled.

'It's all very well to smile. I know it would be a wrench. But it might be worse than a wrench if you get too much involved – and you can't trust the girl to behave.'

I paid no attention. Nor did I to the curious incidents which I noticed soon after we met, when, instead of seeing her silent and pallid in company, I found her sitting on the area-steps of my lodging house, chatting like a sister to the landlady. The landlady was a slattern, who came to life when she broke into ruminations about her late husband or the Royal Family. Sheila listened and answered, relaxed, utterly at ease. And she did the same with the little waitress in the café, who liked her and took her for granted as she did no other customer. Somehow Sheila could make friends, throw her self-consciousness away, if she was allowed to choose for herself and go where no one watched her.

But I did not try, or even want, to think what she was truly like. If Marion had performed those antics, I should have been asking myself, what kind of nature was this? In the first weeks of my love for Sheila, I was less curious about her than about any other person. It even took me some time to discover the simple facts, such as that she was my own age within a month, that she was an only child, the daughter of a clergyman, that her mother had money, that they lived in a village twelve miles outside the town.

Walking in the windy autumn nights, I thought of her with the self-absorption of young love. I chose to be alone on those nights, so that I could cherish my thoughts, with the lights twinkling and quivering in the wind.

I was self-absorbed, yet with the paradox of such a love I had not begun to ask, even in my thoughts, anything for myself. I had not kissed her. It was enough just then that she should exist. It was enough that she should exist, who had brought me to this bliss, who had transformed the streets I walked in so that, looking down the hill at the string of lights, I felt my throat catch with joy.

I thought of her as though she alone were living in the world. I had never seen her house, but I imagined her within it, in her own room, high and light. She sat with a reading lamp at her side, and for a time she was still. Then she crossed the room and knelt by the bookshelves: her hair was radiant in the shadow. She went back to her chair, and her fingers turned the page.

I saw her so, and that was all I asked, just then.

19

The Calm of a September Afternoon

I WAS diffident in making the first approach of love. It was not only that the magic was too delicate to touch. I was afraid that I had no charm for her. I had none of Jack's casual confidence that he could captivate nine women out of ten; and I had not that other confidence which underlay George's awkwardness and which was rooted in his own certainty of his great sensual power. At twenty I did not know whether any woman would love me with her whole heart. Most of all I doubted it with Sheila.

I tried to dazzle her, not with what I was, but with what I could do. I boasted of my plans. I told her that I should be a success. I held out the lure of the prizes I should win by my wits. She was quite unimpressed. She was clever enough to know that it was not just a young man's fantasy. She believed that I might do as I said. But she believed it half with amusement, half with envy.

'You ought to bring off something,' she teased me. 'With your automatic competence.'

It amused her that I could work in the office all day, talk to her at the café over pot after pot of tea until she caught her train, and then go off and apply my mind for hours to the law of torts. But it was an envious amusement. She had played with music and painting, but she had nothing to do. She felt that she too should have been driven to work.

'Of course you'll get somewhere,' she said. 'What happens when you've got there? You won't be content. What then?'

She would not show more than that faint interest in my workaday hopes. She had none of Marion's robust and comradely concern for each detail of what I had to achieve. Marion had learned the syllabuses, knew the dates of the examinations, had a shrewd idea of when I must begin to earn money unless I was to fail. Sheila had faith in my 'automatic competence', but her tone turned brittle as I tried to dazzle her, and it hurt me, in the uncertainty of love.

She was still amused, not much more than that, when I brought her a piece of good news. In September that year, just after I began to meet her regularly, I had a stroke of fortune, the kind of practical fortune that was a bonus I did not count on and had no right to expect. It happened through the juxtaposition, the juxtaposition which became a most peculiar alliance, of Aunt Milly and George Passant. The solicitor who dealt with Aunt Milly's 'bit of property' (as my mother used to describe it, in a humorous resentful fashion) had not long since died.

By various chances, Aunt Milly found her way to the firm of Eden and Martineau, and so into George's office; and there she kept on going.

Aunt Milly was aware that I knew him. It did not soften her judgement. As a matter of course, it was her custom to express disapproval after her first meeting with any new acquaintance. Since she knew George was my closest friend, she felt morally impelled to double the pungency of her expression.

'I suppose I oughtn't to tell you,' said Aunt Milly, 'but that young fellow Passant was smelling of beer. At half past two in the afternoon. It might be doing everyone a service if I told his employers what I thought of it.' She went on to give a brief sketch of George's character.

To my surprise, it did not take long before her indignation moderated. After a visit or two, she was saying darkly and grudgingly: 'Well, I can't say that he's as hopeless as that other jackass – which is a wonder, considering everything.'

Nevertheless, it came out of the blue when George told me, as though it were nothing particularly odd, that they had been discussing me and my future. 'I found her very reasonable,' said George. 'Very reasonable indeed.' And again it did not strike him as particularly odd, though he was looking discreet and what my mother would have called chuff, with the self-satisfaction of one holding a pleasant secret, when he summoned me to meet her one lunchtime.

'She's asked me to attend, as a matter of fact,' said George complacently, swinging his stick.

Our meeting place was the committee room of one of Aunt Milly's temperance organizations. It was in the middle of the town, on the third floor above a vegetarian café; Aunt Milly was not a vegetarian, but she did not notice what she ate, and when she was working in that room she always sent down for a meal. Our lunch that morning was nut cutlets, and Aunt Milly munched away impassively.

Eating that lunch, we sat, all three of us, at a long committee table at the end of the room, Aunt Milly in the chair, George at her right hand like a secretary, and me opposite to them. The room was dark and filled with small tables, each covered with brochures, pamphlets, charts, handbills, and maps. Near our end of the room was a special stand, on which were displayed medical exhibits. The one most visible, a yard or so from our lunch, was a cirrhosed liver. I caught sight of Aunt Milly's gaze fixed upon it, and then on George and me. She went on eating steadily.

On the walls were flaunted placards and posters; one of them proclaimed that temperance was winning. George noticed it, and asked Aunt Milly how many people had signed the pledge in 1924.

'Not enough,' said Aunt Milly. She added, surprisingly, in her loud voice: 'That poster's a lie. Don't you believe it. The movement is going through a bad time. We've gone downhill ever since the war, and we shan't do much better till those people stop running away from the facts.'

'You made the best of your position in the war,' said George, with an abstract pleasure in political chess. 'You couldn't possibly have hoped to keep your advantage.'

'That is as may be,' said Aunt Milly.

George argued with her. She was completely realistic and matter of fact about details. She did not shut her eyes to any setback, and yet maintained an absolute and unqualified faith that the cause would triumph in the end.

She broke off brusquely:

'This isn't what I wanted you for. I haven't got all the afternoon to waste. It's time we got down to brass tacks.'

Aunt Milly was offering to make me a loan. Presumably at George's instigation, certainly after consulting him about my chances in the Bar examinations, she had decided to help. George sat by her side, in solid if subdued triumph. I began to thank her, with real spontaneous delight, but she stopped me.

'You wait till I've finished,' she said. 'You may not like my conditions as much as all that. You can take it or leave it.'

The 'conditions' referred to the date of the loan. Aunt Milly would, if she got her own way, lend me two hundred pounds. When would it be most useful to me? She had her view, I had mine: they were, as usual, different. And they were the opposite of what one might have expected. Aunt Milly had got it into her head that I did not stand a dog's chance in Bar Finals unless I could give up the office and spend the next eighteen months reading law 'as though you were at college, like your mother wanted for you'. I could never understand how Aunt Milly became fixed in this opinion; her whole family had picked up their education at night classes, and she was the last woman to be moved by the claims of social pretension. Perhaps it was through some faint memory of my mother's longings, for Aunt Milly was capable of a certain buried sentiment. Perhaps it was that I was looking overtired: she was always affected by physical evidence, about which there was no doubt or nonsense, which she could see with her own eyes. Anyway, for whatever reason, she had got the idea into her head, and held it as obstinately as all her other ideas.

My view was the exact opposite. I could, I said, survive my present life until Bar Finals. I would take care, however much sleep I lost, that it would make no difference to the result. Whereas two hundred pounds, once I was in Chambers, would keep me going for two years and might turn the balance between failure and success.

George took up the argument with both of us. He was himself a very strong man physically, and he had no patience with the wear and tear that the effort might cost me. That was one against Aunt Milly. On the other hand, he told me flatly that I was underestimating the sheer time that I needed for work. If I did not leave the office now and have my days clear, I could not conceivably come out high in the list. That was a decisive one against me. On the other hand, he fired a broadside against Aunt Milly – it was ridiculous to insist that the whole loan should be used on getting me through the Bar Finals, when a little capital afterwards would be of incalculable value.

Aunt Milly liked to be argued with by George, powerfully, loudly, and not too politely. It was a contrast to the meek silences of her husband and her brother. Maybe, I thought, she would have been more placid married to such a man. Was that why, against all the rules, they got on so well?

But, despite her gratification at meeting her match, she remained immovably obstinate. Either I left the office within a month, or the loan was off. Aunt Milly had the power of the purse, and she made the most of it.

At last George hammered out a solution, although Aunt Milly emerged victoriously with her point. I was to leave the office at once: Aunt Milly nodded her head, her eyes protruding without expression, as though it were merely a recognition of her common sense. Aunt Milly would lend me a hundred pounds 'at three per cent, payments to begin in five years,' said Aunt Milly promptly.

'On any terms you like,' said George irascibly. The hundred pounds would just carry me through, doing nothing but study law, until Bar Finals. Then, if I secured a first in the examination, she would lend me the other hundred pounds to help towards my first year in Chambers.

George chuckled as we walked back to Bowling Green Street. 'I call that a good morning's work,' he said. 'She's a wonderful woman.'

He hinted that I need not worry about taking the money. Even if all went wrong, it would not cripple her. She and her husband were among those of the unpretentious lower middle-class who had their nest eggs tucked away. George would not tell me how much. He was always professionally discreet, in a fashion that surprised some who only knew him at night. But I gathered that they were worth two or three thousand. I also gathered that I was not to expect anything from her will. That did not depress me – two hundred pounds now was worth two thousand pounds in ten years' time. But I should have liked to know how she was leaving her money.

I wanted Sheila to rejoice with me when I told her the news. I did not write to her; I saved it up for our next meeting. She came into the town on a Saturday afternoon, a warm and beautiful afternoon in late September. We met outside the park, not far from Martineau's house, walked by the pavilion, and found a couple of chairs near the hard tennis courts. The park was full of people. All round the tennis courts there were children playing on the grass, women sitting on the seats with perambulators in front of them, men in their shirtsleeves. On the asphalt court there were two games of mixed doubles, youths in grey flannels, girls in cotton dresses.

Sheila sat back with the sunshine on her face, watching the play.

'I'm about as good as she is,' she said. 'I'm no good at tennis. But I can run quite fast.'

She spoke with a secret pleasure, far away, as though she were gazing at herself in a mirror, as though she were admiring her reflection in a pool. I looked at her – and, in the crowded park, for me we were alone, under the milk-blue sky.

Then I told her that I was leaving the office. She smiled at me, a friendly, sarcastic smile.

'Gentleman of leisure, are you?' she said.

'Not quite,' I said.

'What in the world will you do with yourself? Even you can't work all day.'

I could not leave it, I could not bear that she was not impressed. I told her, I exaggerated, the difference it ought to make to my chances.

'You'll do well anyway,' she said lightly.

'It's not quite as easy as all that.'

'It is for you.' She smiled again. 'But I still don't see what you're going to do with yourself all day. I'm sure you're not good at doing nothing. I'm much better at that than you are. I'm quite good at sitting in the sun.'

She shut her eyes. She looked so beautiful that my heart turned over.

Still I could not leave it. My tongue ran away, and I said that it was a transformation, it was a new beginning. She looked at me; her smile was still friendly, sarcastic, and cool.

'You're very excited about it, aren't you?'

'Yes, I am.'

'Then so am I,' she said.

But she responded in a different tone to another story that I told her, as we sat there in the sun. It concerned a piece of trouble of Jack's, which had sprung up almost overnight. It arose because Jack, not for the first time, had evoked an infatuation; but this time he was guiltless, and ironically this was the only time that might do him an injury. For the one who loved him was not a young woman, but a boy of fifteen. The boy's passion had sprung up that summer, it was glowing and innocent, but the more extravagant because it was so innocent. He had just given Jack an expensive present, a silver cigarette case; and by accident his family had intercepted a letter of devotion that was coming with it. There were all kinds of practical repercussions, which worried us and against which we were trying to act: Jack's future in his firm was threatened; there were other consequences for him, and, in the long run, most of all for George, who had thrown himself, with the whole strength of a man, into Jack's support.

Sheila listened with her eyes alight. She was not interested in the consequences, she brushed them impatiently aside. To her the core of the story, its entire significance, lay in the emotion of the boy himself.

'It must be wonderful to be swept away. He must have felt that he had no control over himself at all. I wonder what it was like,' she said. She was deeply moved, and our eyes met.

'He won't regret it.' She added, gently, 'I wish it had happened to me at his age.'

143

We fell into silence: a silence so charged that I could hear my heart beating. Between her fingers a cigarette was smouldering blue into the still air.

'Who is he, Lewis?' she said.

I hesitated for a fraction of a second. She was very quick. 'Tell me. If I know him, I might help. I shall go and say that I envy him.'

'He's a boy called Roy Calvert,' I said.

I had only met him for a few minutes in the middle of this crisis. What struck me most was that he seemed quite unembarrassed and direct. He was more natural and at ease than the rest of us, five years older and more, who questioned him.

Sheila shook her head, as though she were disappointed.

'He must be a cousin of your friend Olive, mustn't he?' (Olive was a member of the group.)

I told her yes, and that Olive was involved in the trouble.

'I can't get on with her,' said Sheila. 'She pretends not to think much of herself. It isn't true.'

Suddenly Sheila's mood had changed. Talking of Roy, she had been gentle, delicate, self-forgetful. Now, at the mention of Olive, whom she scarcely knew, but who mixed gaily and could forget herself in any company, Sheila turned angry and constrained.

'I once went to a dance at Olive's,' she said. 'We didn't stay long. We went by ourselves to the palais. That was a lot better.'

For the first time, I was learning the language of a beloved. I was learning the tension, the hyperaesthesia, with which one listens to the tone of every word, And I was learning too, in the calm of that September afternoon, the first stab of jealousy. That 'we', said so clearly, that reiterated 'we': was it deliberate, was her companion a casual acquaintance, was she threatening me with someone for whom she cared?

She looked at me. At the sight of my face, her tone changed again.

'I'm glad you told me about Roy,' she said.

'Why are you glad?'

'I don't know.'

'Sheila, why are you glad?'

'If I knew, I shouldn't tell you.' Her voice was high. Then she smiled, and said with all simplicity and purity: 'No, I should tell you. I should want to. It would mean I had found something important, wouldn't it?'

20

In the Rain

WHEN she was not there, I was happy in my thoughts. They were pierced, it is true, by the first thrusts of jealousy, the sound of that clear 'we' in the calm air, not so much a memory but as though the sound stayed in my ears. They were troubled by the diffidence of my love, so that I could not always think of her alone in her room, without needing some sign of love to calm me. But the rapture was so strong, it swept back after those intrusions; she existed, she walked the same earth, and I should see her in three days' time.

Once, meeting her after a week's absence, I felt incredulous, all the excitement deflated, all the enchantment dead. Her face seemed, at the first glance, not different in kind from other faces – pale, frigid, beaky, ill-tempered. Her voice was brittle, and grated on my nerves. Everything she thought was staccato. There was no flow or warmth about her, or about anything she said or did. I was, for a few minutes, nothing but bored. Nothing deeper than that, just bored. Then she gazed at me – not with a smile, but with her eyes steady and her face quite still; on the instant, the dead minutes were annihilated and I was once more possessed.

Later that day, I happened to tell her that the group were spending the following weekend out at the farm. She always took a curious, half-envious, half-mocking interest in the group's affairs. That afternoon she was speculating, like one left outside a party, about how we should pass the weekend. I knew her house was only two or three miles from the farm, and I begged her to drop in.

'I can't stand crowds,' she said. Then, as though covering herself, she retorted: 'Why shouldn't you come and see me? It's no further one way than the other.'

I was overjoyed.

She added: 'You'll have to meet my parents. You can study them, if you like.'

We arranged that I should walk over for tea on the Saturday afternoon. That Saturday, in the middle of October, was my last day in the office; and I was thinking of the afternoon as I said all my goodbyes. Mr Vesey reminded me that I was under his control until one o'clock; he told me three times not to be careless about leaving my papers in order, then he shook my hand, and said that he had not yet been provided with my successor, and that some people had never realized his difficulties. How could he be expected to run his section well if his one good clerk went and left him? Why did he never get a chance himself? 'Never mind, Eliot,' he said bravely, shaking my hand again. 'I don't expect to be in the limelight. I just carry on.'

I was thinking of the afternoon; but, stepping out of the office on to the wet pavement, leaving for the last time a place which for years had been a prison, I felt an ache of nostalgia, of loss, and of regret.

George and I went out by bus, through a steady drizzle, At half past three, when I started out from the farm, the rain was heavier; I was getting wet as I cut across the fields, down the country lanes, to Sheila's house. I was happy and apprehensive, happy because she had asked me, apprehensive because I was sensible enough to know that I could not possibly be welcome. She had asked me in innocence: that I took for granted. She would not care what her parents thought, if she wanted to see me. Through her actions there shone so often a wild and wilful innocence. And I, far more realistic than she in all other ways, had for her and with her the innocence of romantic love. So that, tramping through the mud that afternoon, I was happy whatever awaited me. I wanted nothing but the sight of her; I knew it, she knew it, and in that state of love there were no others.

But I assumed that her parents would see it differently. I might not have given a conscious thought to marrying her – and that, strange as it later seemed, was true, Her parents would never believe it. To them, I must appear as a suitor – possibly a suitor with an extremely dim outside chance, but nevertheless a suitor, and a most undesirable one. For they were rich, Sheila had both looks and brains; they were bound to expect her to make a brilliant marriage. They were not likely to encourage me. I had nothing whatever with which to mollify them. Some parents might have endured me because I was not a fool, but I guessed that even my wits were suspect. Sheila was capable of recounting my opinions, and then saying that she shared them. I did not know how I was going to carry it off. Yet I was joyful, walking those two miles through the rain.

The vicarage was a handsome Georgian house, lying back behind the trees at the end of the village. I was not far wrong about my welcome. But before Mrs Knight could start expressing herself there was a faintly farcical delay. For I arrived wet through. The maid who let me in did not know how to proceed; Sheila and her mother came out into the hall. Mrs Knight at once took charge. She was prepared to greet me coldly, but she became solicitous about my health. She was a heavily built woman, bigger than Sheila, but much more busy and fussy. She took me into the bathroom, sent the maid for some of the vicar's clothes, arranged to have mine dried. At last I entered the drawing-room dressed in a cricket shirt, grey flannels, pullover, dressing gown, and slippers, all belonging to Sheila's father, all the clothes much too wide for me and the slippers two sizes too big.

'I hope you won't take cold,' Mrs Knight rattled on busily. 'You ought to have had a good hot bath. I think you ought to have a nice stiff whisky. Yes, that ought to keep off the cold.'

She had none of her daughter's fine, chiselled features. She was broad-faced, pug-nosed, with a loud quacking voice; she was coarse-grained and greatly given to moral indignation; yet her eyes were wide open and childlike, and one felt, as with other coarse-grained women, that often she was lost and did not know her way about the world.

However, she was very far from lost when it came to details of practical administration. I was made to put down a couple of fingers of neat whisky. She decided that I was not wearing enough clothes, and Sheila was sent for one of the vicar's sports coats.

'He's upstairs in his study,' said Mrs Knight, talking of her husband with a rapt, childlike devotion, accentuating the 'he' in her worship. 'He's just polishing a sermon for tomorrow. He always likes to have them polished. He'll join us later for his tea, if he finishes in time. I should never think of disturbing him, of course.'

We sat down by the fire and began our tea, a very good one, for Mrs Knight liked her food. She expected everyone round her to eat as heartily as she did, and scolded Sheila for not getting on with the toast and honey. I watched Sheila, as her mother jockeyed her into eating. It was strangely comfortable to see her so, by the fireside. But she was silent in her mother's presence – as indeed it was hard not to be, since Mrs Knight talked without interruption and loud enough to fill any room. Yet Sheila's silence meant more than that; it was not the humorous silence of a looker-on.

The more I could keep Mrs Knight on the theme of physical comfort, the better, I thought to myself; and so I praised the house, the sight of it from the village, the drawing-room in which we sat. Mrs Knight forcefully agreed.

'It's perfect for our small family,' she said. 'As I was obliged to explain to my neighbour, Mrs Lacy, only yesterday. Do you know what she had been saying, Sheila? I shouldn't have believed my ears, if I hadn't heard Doris Lacy talk and talk and talk for the last twenty years. Of course, she's a great friend of mine and I'm devoted to her and I know she'd say the same of me' – Mrs Knight put in this explanation for my benefit – 'but the trouble is that she will talk without thinking. And she can't have been thinking at all – even she couldn't have said it if she'd thought for a single moment – she can't have been thinking at all when she talked about this house. She actually said' – Mrs Knight's voice was mounting louder as her indignation grew – 'that this house was *dark*. She said that this house was *dark*. She who doesn't get a ray of sun till half past three!'

She got fairly started on the misdeeds, the preposterous errors of judgement, the dubious gentility and mercenary marriage, of Mrs

Lacy. She kept asking Sheila for her support and then rushing off into another burst of indignation. It was some time before she turned on me. She collected herself, regarded me with open eyes, said how gallant it was for me to visit them on such an afternoon. Then, with elaborate diplomacy, she said:

'Of course, it doesn't feel like living in the country, now Sheila is growing up. She brings people to see us who are doing all kinds of interesting things. Why, it was only the other day we saw one of her friends who they say has a great future in his firm – '

The knife of jealousy twisted. Then I felt a flood of absolute relief, for Sheila said clearly: 'He's dense.'

'I don't think you can say that, Sheila.'

'I can.'

'You mustn't be too hard on your friends,' said Mrs Knight busily. 'You'll be telling me next that Tom Devitt isn't interesting. He's a specialist at the infirmary,' said Mrs Knight to me, and continued with enthusiasm, 'and they say he's the coming man. Sheila will be telling us that he's dense too. Or – '

The involuntary smile had come to Sheila's mouth, and on her forehead I could see the lines. The jealous spasm had returned, with Tom Devitt's name, with the others' (for Mrs Knight had by no means finished), but it merged, as I watched Sheila, into a storm of something that had no place in romantic love, something so unfamiliar in my feeling for her that I did not recognize it then. It only lasted for a moment, but it left me off my balance for Mrs Knight's next charge.

'I think I remember Sheila saying that you were kept very busy,' she remarked. 'Of course, I know we can't all choose exactly what we want, can we? Some of us have got to be content – '

'I've chosen what I want, Mrs Knight,' I said, a little too firmly.

'Have you?' She seemed puzzled.

'I'm a law student. That's what I've chosen to do.'

'In your spare time, I suppose?'

'No,' I said. 'I'm reading for the Bar. Full-time. I shan't do anything else until I'm called.' It was technically true. It had been true since one o'clock that day. 'I shan't earn a penny till I'm called.'

Mrs Knight was not specially quick in the uptake. She had to pause, so as to readjust her ideas.

'I do my reading in the town,' I said. 'Then I go up to my Inn once a term, and get through my dinners in a row. It saves money – and I shall need it until I get a practice going, you know.'

It was the kind of career talk she was used to hearing; but she was baffled at hearing it from me.

'All the barristers I've known', she said, 'have eaten their dinners while they were at college. I remember my cousin used to go up when he was at Trinity – '

'Did he ever get through an examination?' asked Sheila.

'Perhaps he wasn't clever at his books,' said Mrs Knight, becoming more cross, 'but he was a good man, and everyone respected him in the county.'

'My friends at the Inn', I put in, 'nearly all come from Cambridge.' Here I was stretching the truth. I had made one or two friendly acquaintances there, such as Charles March, who were undergraduates, but I often dined with excessively argumentative Indians.

Mrs Knight was very cross. She did not like being baffled and confused – yet somehow I had automatically to be promoted a step. She had to say, as though Sheila had met me at the house of one of their friends:

'I've always heard that a barrister has to wait years for his briefs. Of course, I suppose you don't mind waiting – '

I admitted that it would take time. Mrs Knight gave an appeased and comforted sigh, happy to be back on firm ground.

Soon after, there was a footfall outside the room, a slow footfall. Mrs Knight's eyes widened. 'He's coming!' she said. 'He must have finished!'

Mr Knight entered with an exaggeratedly drooping, an exaggeratedly languid step. He was tall, massive, with a bay window of a stomach that began as far up as his lower chest. He was wearing a lounge suit without a dog collar, and he carried a sheaf of manuscript in his hand. His voice was exaggeratedly faint. He was, at first glance, a good deal of an actor, and he was indicating that the virtue had gone out of him.

He said faintly to his wife: 'I'm sorry I had to be late, darling,' sat in the armchair which had been preserved for him, and half closed his eyes.

Mrs Knight asked with quacking concern whether he would like a cup of tea. It was plain that she adored him.

'Perhaps a cup,' he whispered. 'Perhaps just a cup.'

The toast had been kept warm on the hotplate, she said anxiously. Or she could have some fresh made in three minutes.

'I *can't* eat it, darling,' he said. 'I can't *eat* it, I can't eat *anything.*'

The faintness with which he spoke was bogus, Actually his voice was rich, and very flexible in its range of tone. He had a curious trick of repeating a phrase, and at the second turn completely altering the stress. Throughout his entry, which he enjoyed to the full, he had paid no attention to me, had not thrown me an open glance, but as he lay back with heavy lids drawn down he was observing me from the corner of an eye that was disturbingly sly and shrewd.

When at last he admitted to a partial recovery, Mrs Knight introduced me. She explained volubly the reason for my eccentric attire, taking credit for her speed of action. Then, since they seemed still to be worrying her, she repeated my statements about doing nothing but read for the Bar, as though trusting him to solve the problem.

Unlike his wife, Mr Knight was indirect. He gazed at Sheila, not at me.

'You never tell me anything, do you, my dear girl,' he said. 'You never tell me anything.'

Then slyly, still looking at her, he questioned me. His voice stayed carefully fatigued, he appeared to be taking a remote interest in these ephemeral things. In fact, he was astute. If he had been present, I should never have succeeded for a minute in putting up my bluff with Mrs Knight. Without asking me outright, he soon got near the truth. He took a malicious pleasure in talking round the point, letting me see that he had guessed, not giving me away to his wife.

'Isn't there a regulation', he inquired, his voice diminishing softly, 'by which you can't read for the Bar if you're following certain occupations? Does that mean one has to break away? I take it, you may have had to select your time to break away – from some other occupation?'

It was not the reason, but it was a very good shot. We talked for a few minutes about legal careers. He was proud of his ability to 'place' people and he was now observing me with attention. Sometimes he asked a question edged with malice. And I was learning something about him.

He and his wife were each snobbish, but in quite different fashions. Mrs Knight had been born into the comfortable moneyed middle class; she was a robust woman without much perception, and accepted those who seemed to arrive at the same level; just as uncritically, she patronized those who did not. Mr Knight's interest was far more subtle and pervading. To begin with, he was no more gently born than I was. I could hear the remains of a northern dialect in that faint and modulated voice. Mr Knight had met his wife, and captured her for good, when he was a young curate. She had brought him money, he had moved through the social scene, he had dined in the places he had longed for as a young man – in the heart of the county families and the dignitaries of the Church. The odd thing was, that having arrived there, he still retained his romantic regard for those very places. All his shrewdness and suspicion went to examine the channels by which others got there. On that subject he was accurate, penetrating, and merciless.

He was a most interesting man. The time was getting on; I was wondering whether I ought to leave, when I witnessed another scene which, though I did not know it, was a regular feature of the vicarage Saturday teas. Mrs Knight looked busily, lovingly, at her husband.

'Please, darling, would you mind giving us the sermon?' she said.

'I *can't* do it, darling. I can't *do* it. I'm too exhausted.'

'Please. Just give us the beginning. You know Sheila always likes to hear the sermon. I'm sure you'd like to hear the sermon.' Mrs Knight rallied me. 'It will give you something to think over on the way home. I'm sure you want to hear it.'

I said that I did.

'I believe he's a heathen,' said Mr Knight maliciously, but his fingers were playing with the manuscript.

'You heard what he said, darling,' urged Mrs Knight. 'He'll be disappointed if you don't give us a good long piece.'

'Oh well.' Mr Knight sighed. 'If you insist, If you insist.'

Mrs Knight began to alter the position of the reading lamp. She made her husband impatient. He was eager to get to it.

The faintness disappeared from his voice on the instant. It filled the room more effortlessly than Mrs Knight's. He read magnificently. I had never heard such command of tone, such control, such loving articulation. And I had never seen anyone enjoy more his own reading; occasionally he peered over the page to make sure that we were not neglecting to enjoy it too. I was so much impressed with the whole performance that I could not spare much notice for the argument.

He gave us a good long piece. In fact, he gave us the whole sermon, twenty-four minutes by the clock. At the end, he leaned back in the chair and closed his eyes. Mrs Knight broke into enthusiastic, worshipping praise. I added my bit.

'Water, please, darling,' said Mr Knight very faintly, without opening his eyes. 'I should like a glass of water. Just water.'

As I changed into my own clothes in the bathroom, I was wondering how I could say goodbye to Sheila alone. In the general haze of excitement, I was thinking also of her father. He was vain, preposterously and superlatively vain, and yet astute; at the same time theatrical and shrewd; malicious, hypochondriac, and subtle; easy to laugh at, and yet exuding, through it all, a formidable power. He was a man whom no one would feel negligible. I believed that it was not impossible I could get on with him. I should have to suffer his malice, he would be a more effective enemy than his wife. But I felt one thing for certain, while I hummed tunelessly in the bathroom: he was worried about Sheila, and not because she had brought me there that afternoon; he was worried about her, as she sat silently by the fire; and there had been a spark, not of liking, but of sympathy, between him and me.

On my way downstairs I heard Mrs Knight's voice raised in indignation.

'It's much too wet to think of such a thing,' came through the drawing-room door. When I opened it, Mrs Knight was continuing: 'It's just asking to get yourself laid up. I don't know when you'll begin to have a scrap of sense. And even if it were a nice night –'

'I'm walking back with you,' said Sheila to me.

'I want you to tell her that it's quite out of the question. It's utterly absurd,' said Mrs Knight.

'I don't know what it's like outside,' I said half-heartedly. 'It does sound rather wild.'

The wind had been howling round the house.

'If it doesn't hurt you, it won't hurt me,' said Sheila.

Mr Knight was still lying back with his eyes closed.

'She *oughtn't* to do it,' a whisper came across the room. 'She oughtn't to *do* it.'

'Are you ready?' said Sheila.

Her will was too strong for them. It suddenly flashed across my mind, as she put on a mackintosh in the hall, that I had no idea, no idea in the world, how she felt towards either of them.

The wind blew stormily in our faces; Sheila laughed aloud. It was not raining hard, for the gale was too strong, but one could taste the driven rain. Down the village street we were quiet; I felt rapturously at ease, she had never been so near. As we turned down a lane, our fingers laced, and hers were pressing mine.

We had not spoken since we left the house. Her first words were accusatory, but her tone was soft:

'Why did you play my mother's game?'

'What do you mean?'

'Pretending to be better off than you are.'

'All I said was true.'

'You gave her a wrong impression,' she said. 'You know you did.'

155

'I thought it was called for.' I was smiling.

'Stupid of you,' she said. 'I'd rather you said you were a clerk.'

'It would have shocked her.'

'It would have been good for her,' said Sheila.

The gale was howling, the trees dashed overhead, and we walked on in silence, in silence deep with joy.

'Lewis,' she said at last. 'I want to ask you something.'

'Darling?'

'Weren't you terribly embarrassed – ?'

'Whatever at?'

'At coming in wet. And meeting strangers for the first time in that fancy dress.'

She laughed.

'You did look a bit absurd,' she added.

'I didn't think about it,' I said.

'Didn't you really mind?'

'No.'

'I can't understand you,' she said. 'I should have curled up inside.' Then she said: 'You are rather wonderful.'

I laughed at her. I said that, if she were going to admire me for anything, she might choose something more sensible to admire. But she was utterly serious. To her self-conscious nerves, it was incredible that anyone should be able to master such a farce.

'I curled up a bit myself this afternoon,' she said, a little later.

'When?'

'When they were making fools of themselves in front of you.'

'Good God, girl,' I said roughly, lovingly, 'they're human.'

She tightened her grip on my hand.

At the end of a lane we came in sight of the farm. There was one more field to cross, and the lights blazed out in the windy darkness. I asked her to come in.

'I couldn't,' she said. I had an arm round her shoulders as we stood. Suddenly she hid her face against my coat. I asked her again.

'I must go,' she said. She looked up at me, and for the first time I kissed her, while the wind and my own blood sang and pounded in my ears. She drew away, then threw her arms round my neck, and I felt her mouth on mine.

'I must go,' she said. I touched her cheek, wet in the rain, and she pressed my hand. Then she walked down the lane, dark that night as a tunnel-mouth, her strong, erect stride soon losing her to sight against the black hedges. I waited there until I could hear nothing, no footsteps, nothing but the sound of the wind.

I returned to the group, who were revelling in a celebration. Jack was starting on his new business, and after supper George sat in our midst, predicting success for us all, for me most of all, complacent with hope about all our futures. It was not until the next, Sunday, night I spoke to George alone. The others had gone back by the last bus; I was staying till the morning, in order to have the first comfort of my emancipation. That night, when we were left alone, George confided more of his own strange, violent, inner life than he had ever done before. He gave me part of his diary, and there I sat, reading by the light of the oil lamp, while George smoked his pipe by my side.

When I had finished, George made an inquiry about my love affair. He had only two attitudes towards his friends' attachments. First, he responded with boisterous amusement. Then, when he decided that one was truly in love, he adopted an entirely different manner, circumlocutory, obscure, packed with innuendo, which he seemed to have decided was the height of consideration and tact. In the summer he had jovially referred to Sheila as that 'handsome bitch', but for some time past he had spoken of her, with infinite consideration, in his second manner. On that Sunday night his actual opening was:

'I hope you reached your destination safely yesterday afternoon?'

I said that I had.

'I hope that it all turned out to be' – George pulled down his waistcoat and cleared his throat – 'reasonably satisfactory?'

I said that it did.

'Perhaps I can assume', said George, 'that you're not completely dissatisfied with your progress?'

I could not keep back a smile – and it gave me right away.

21

Deceiving and Pleasing

EVEN after that visit to Sheila's house I still did not tell her simply how much I loved her. Her own style seemed to keep my tongue playful and sarcastic; I made jokes about joy and hope and anguish, as though it were all a game. I was not yet myself released.

Once or twice she kept me waiting at a meeting place. The minutes passed, the quarters; I performed all the tricks that a lover does to cheat time, to make it stand still, to pretend not to notice, so as suddenly to see her there. It was an anguish like jealousy, and, like jealousy, when at last she came, it was drowned in the flood of relief.

I complained. But still my words were light; I did not speak from the angry pain of five minutes before. I scolded her, I asked her not to expose me to looks of *schadenfreude* in the café – but I did it with the playful sarcasm that had become our favourite way of speaking to one another. Nevertheless, it was my first demand. She obeyed. At our next meeting, she was ten minutes early. She was trying to behave, and I was gay; but she was also strained and ill-tempered, as though it were an effort to subdue her pride even by an inch.

During my next visit to eat dinners at the Inn, I was waiting for a letter. It was the beginning of December, I was in London for my usual five nights, and I had made Sheila promise to write to me. Hopefully I looked for a letter on the hall table the morning after I arrived. I used to stay in a boarding house in Judd Street, rather as though, with a provincial's diffidence, I did not want to be separated too far from my railhead at St Pancras. The dining-room, the hall, the bedroom, all smelt heavily of beeswax and food; the dining-room was dark, and we used to sit down to breakfast at eight o'clock in the winter gloom; there were twelve or so round the table – maiden ladies living there on a pittance, clerks, transients like myself. Through having students pass through the house, the landlady had acquired the patter of examinations. With a booming heartless heartiness, she used to encourage them, and me in my turn, by giving them postcards on the day of their last paper. On the postcard she had already written 'I got through, Mrs Reed'; she exhorted one to post it to her as soon as the result was known.

After each breakfast on that stay, I went quickly to the hall table. There lay the letters, pale blue in the half-dark – not many in that house: none for me, on the first morning, the second, the third. It was the first time I had been menaced by the post.

Just as when I waited for her, I went through all the calculations of a lover. She could not have written before Monday night, it was more likely she would wait till Tuesday, there was no collection in the village after tea, it was impossible that I could get the letter by Wednesday morning. I was beginning to learn, in those few days, the arithmetic of anxiety and hope.

So, carrying with me that faint ache of worry, knowing that when I returned to the boarding house my eyes would fly to the hall table, I went out to eat my dinners at the Inn. On two of the nights I joined a party of my Cambridge acquaintances, Charles March among them; we went away from dinner to drink and talk, before they caught their train from Liverpool Street.

They were the kind of acquaintances on whom I should have sharpened my wits, if I had gone to a university. I had not yet spoken to Charles March alone, but him I felt kinship with, and wanted for a friend. The others I liked well enough, but no better than many of my friendly acquaintances in the town. I was soon easy among them, and we talked with undergraduate zest. When I was alone I compared their luck and mine. Some of them would be rivals. Now that I knew something of them, how did my prospect look?

I thought that, for intellectual machinery, between me and Charles March there was not much in it. I had no doubt that George Passant, both in mental equipment and in horsepower, was superior to both of us – but Charles March and I had a great deal more sense. Of those other Cambridge acquaintances, I did not believe that any of them, for force and precision combined, could compete with either Charles March or me, much less George Passant.

I was reassured to find it so. And I went on, once or twice, to envy them their luck. One of these young men was the son of an eminent KC, and another of a headmaster: Charles March's family I guessed to be very rich. With that start, what could I not have done? I should have given any of them a run for their money, I thought. By their standards, by the standards of the successful world from which they came, it would have been long odds on my being a success. Whereas now I had, in my young manhood, to take an effort and endure a strain that they did not even realize. I felt a certain rancour.

I was capable, however, of a more detached reflection. In one way I had a priceless advantage over these new acquaintances of mine. They had known, at first hand, successful men; and it often took away their confidence. They had lived in a critical climate. Their families had been bound to compare them, say, to an uncle who had 'come off'. There were times, even to a man as vigorous as Charles March, when all achievement seemed already over, all the great things done, all the books written. That was the penalty, and to many of them a crippling penalty, of being born into an old country and an established class. It was incomparably more easy for me to venture on my own. They were held back by the critical voices – or, if they moved at all, they tended to move, not freely, but as though they could only escape the critical voices by the deafening noise of their own rebellion.

I was far luckier. For I was, in that matter, free. From their tradition I could choose what I wanted. I needed neither to follow it completely, nor completely to rebel. I had never lived in a critical climate. There was nothing to hold me back. Far from it; I was pushed forward by the desires, longings, the inarticulate aspirations, of my mother and all her relatives, my grandfather and his companions arduously picking up their artisan culture, all my connexions who had stood so long outside the shop window staring at the glittering toys inside.

Later in my life I should not have wanted to alter any of that reflection. By twenty, in fact, I had a fair conception of most of my advantages and disadvantages, considered as a candidate in worldly affairs. I knew that I was quick-witted and adaptable – after meeting Charles March and the others, I was sure that I could hold my own intellectually. I could get on easily with a large number of human beings, and by nature I knew something of them. That seemed to me my stock-in-trade. But I left something out. Like most young men of twenty I found it impossible to credit that I had much will. George, for example, who had a will of Cromwellian strength, wrote of himself in his diary as being 'vacillating' and 'weak'. Often he thought, with genuine self-condemnation, that he was the most supine of men. It was much the same with me. I should have been surprised if I had been told that I had a tough, stubborn, deep-rooted will, and that it would probably be more use to me than my other qualities all added together.

A letter came. My heart leapt as I saw the envelope on the hall table. But it was the wrong letter. Marion wrote to say that she had a half holiday on the Thursday; she wanted to buy a hat, and she needed an impartial male opinion – she could trust me to be impartial, couldn't she? Could I spare her an hour that afternoon? And perhaps, if I were free, we might go to a play at eight. She would have to catch the last train home, so I should get her off my hands in good time.

I knew that she was fond of me, but there my imagination stopped. It was still so when I received this letter. I replied by return, saying that of course I should be glad to see her. That was true; but it was also true that I was full of chagrin at finding her letter instead of another, and that made me hasten to reply.

The other arrived, by a coincidence, on the day that Marion was due. It did not say much, it was like Sheila's speech, shut in, capricious, gnomic. But she referred, with a curious kind of intimacy, brittle and yet trusting, to one or two of our private jokes. That was enough to irradiate the dark hall. That was enough to make me happy all day, to keep the stylised phrases running through my mind, to give me delight abounding and overflowing, so that when Marion arrived I lavished some of it on her.

She told me how well and gay I looked. I smiled and said that I was both those things. She took it as a welcome. Her eyes were bright and I suddenly thought how pretty she could be.

She gave the impression, as usual, of being sloppily dressed. Quite why I could not decide, for she was now spending much attention on her appearance. That afternoon she was wearing the Russian boots fashionable that winter, and a long blue coat. She looked fresh, but nothing could stop her looking also eager and in a hurry. No one had less trace of the remote and arctic.

Practically, competently, she had discovered some hat shops in and near the Brompton Road – they were recommended as smart, she said, and not too dear.

Along we went. Neither she nor I knew much of London, and we traipsed up and down Kensington High Street before we found the first of her addresses. There was a slight fog, enough to aureole the lights and make the streets seem cosier; the shops were decked for Christmas, and inside them one felt nothing but the presence of furs, warm air, and women's scent. I was half irked, because I hated shopping, half glad to be among the lights and the crowds – cheerful because of the secret pleasure which she did not know, and also cheerful because of her enjoyment. I did not know it then, but I should have felt that second pleasure if I had been a more experienced man and deceiving her less innocently.

Marion tried on hat after hat, while I watched her.

'You must say what you think,' she said. 'My taste is very vulgar. I'm a bit of a slut, you know.'

There was one that I liked.

'I'm afraid it will show up my complexion,' she said. 'My skin isn't too good, is it?'

She was so straightforward. If Sheila had made that remark, I was thinking, I should have seen her skin as *strange*, transcendentally different from all others. While Marion's, when she drew my eyes to it, I saw just as skin, with a friendly familiar indifference, with the observant eye untouched by magic, just as I might have viewed my own.

I told her, as was true, that most women would envy her complexion. At last the hat was bought. It was expensive, and Marion grimaced. 'Still,' she said philosophically, 'a good hat ought to take a girl a bit farther. A bit farther than a deep interest in the arts. I always have had a deep interest in the arts, haven't I? and look what it's done for me.'

Over tea she tried to find out whether I had been seeing Sheila. But she soon stopped – for she had discovered that I became claustrophobic when she showed a possessive interest in my life. I shied from her just as – I did not realize it then – I shied from the possessive invasion of my mother. That afternoon, she was satisfied that I seemed untroubled and relaxed.

She did not ask a straight question or inquire too hard. We were still natural with each other. She told me stories of an inspector's visit to her school, and how he was terrified that she was chasing him. Marion had developed a self-depreciating mode of humour, and I found it very funny. The earnestness of manner was disappearing fast, now that she had discovered that she could amuse.

We laughed together, until it became time for me to go to my Inn. I had to score my dinner there, or otherwise I should need to stay an extra night; I left straight after and joined Marion at the theatre. She might be losing her earnestness, but she was still in the *avant garde* of the twenties and she had chosen to see a Pirandello. I bought the tickets. I was cross at her letting me do so; for she had a regular salary, and she knew that each shilling mattered to me. But when I saw her sitting by me, waiting for the curtain to go up, I could not grudge her the treat. She was as naïvely expectant, as blissful to be there, as a child at a pantomime. It was not that she was ungenerous with money, or unthoughtful, but that she consumedly loved being given a treat, being taken out. She was never disappointed. Every treat was always a success. She was disappointed if, immediately afterwards, one said it was a hopeless play. She did not like the gilt taken away at once, though a week later she would be as critical as any of us. That night, on our way to St Pancras by the tube, she was a little tender-minded because I made fun of Pirandello.

I desisted. I did not want to spoil her pleasure. And, on the foggy platform, I was warmed by affection for her – affection the more glowing (it did not seem shameful as I laughed at her) because of a letter in my pocket whose words I carried before my eyes. At St Pancras we coughed in the sulphurous fog.

'Fancy having to go back tonight,' said Marion. 'I shall be hours late. I pity the children tomorrow. I shall smack them and shout at them.'

'Poor dear, you'll be tired,' I said.

'I shan't get home till four,' she said. 'And I don't mind a bit. And that's as much in the way of thanks as is good for you.'

Instead of going straight from the station to Judd Street, I found a coffee stall along the Euston Road. The fog, thickening every minute, swirled in front of the lamp, and one inhaled it together with the naphtha fumes and the steam. As I drank a cup of tea, I felt the glow of affection with me still. Then I took out Sheila's letter and read it, though I knew it by heart and word for word, in the foggy lamplight. I felt giddy with miraculous content. The name stood out in the dim light, like no other name. I felt giddy, as though the perfection of the miracle would happen now, and I should have her by my side, and we should walk together through the swirling fog.

22

Christmas Eve

WHEN I next met Sheila she was strangely excited. I saw it before she spoke to me, saw it while she made her way through the café towards our table. She was electric with excitement; yet what she had to say, though it filled me with pleasure, did not explain why. Without any preliminary she broke out: 'You know the Edens, don't you?'

'I know him, of course. I've never been to the house.'

'We drink punch there every Christmas Eve,' she said, and added: 'I love punch,' with that narcissistic indrawn satisfaction which took her far away. Then, electric-bright again, she said: 'I can take anyone I like. 'Will you come with me?'

I was open in my pleasure.

'I want you to,' she said, and I still noticed the intensity of her excitement. 'Make a note of it. I shan't let you forget.'

I could not understand, in the days between, why she laid so much stress on it, but I looked forward happily to Christmas Eve. The more happily, perhaps, because it was like an anticipation in childhood; it was like waiting for a present that one knew all the time one was safely going to receive. I imagined beforehand the warmth of a party, Harry Eden's surprise, the flattery of being taken there by the most beautiful young woman in the room – but above all the warmth of a party and the certain joy of her presence by my side among the drinks and laughter.

On the day before Christmas Eve I was having a cup of tea alone in our habitual café. A waitress came up and asked if I was Mr Eliot: a lady wanted me on the telephone.

'Is that you?' It was Sheila's voice, though I had never heard it before at the other end of a wire. It sounded higher than in life, and remote, as though it came from the far side of a river.

'I didn't think they'd recognize you from my description. I didn't think I should find you.'

She sounded strung up but exhilarated, laughing to herself.

'It's me all right,' I said.

'Of course it's you.' She laughed. 'Who else could it be?' I grumbled that this was like a conversation in a fairy tale. 'Right. Business. About tomorrow night.' Her voice was sharp. My heart dropped.

'You're coming, darling?' I pleaded. I could not keep the longing back: she had to hear it. 'You must come. I've been counting on it – '

'I'll come.'

I exclaimed with relief and delight.

'I'll come. But I shall be late. Go to the party by yourself. I'll see you there.'

I was so much relieved that I would have made any concession. As a matter of form, I protested that it would have been nice to go together.

'I can't. I can't manage it. You can make yourself at home. You won't mind. You can make yourself at home anywhere.' She laughed again.

'But you will come?'

'I'll come.'

I was vaguely upset. Why was she keyed up to a pitch of excitement even higher than when she first invited me? I felt for a moment that she was a stranger. But she had never failed me. I knew that she would come. The promise of love, of romantic love, of love where one's imagination makes the beloved fit all one's hope, enveloped me again. Once more I longed for tomorrow night, the party, for her joining me as I sat among the rest.

The Edens lived outside the middle of the town, in the fashionable suburb. I strolled slowly across the park on Christmas Eve, up the

166

London Road; I heard a clock strike; the party began at nine o'clock, and I was deliberately a little late. A church stood open, light streaming through the doors. Cars rushed by, away from the town, but the pavement was almost empty, apart from an occasional couple standing beneath the trees in the mild night.

I came to where the comfortable middle-class houses stood back from the main road, with their hedges, their lawns, their gravel drives. Through the curtains of the drawing-rooms the lights glowed warm, and I felt curious; as I often did, walking any street at night, about what was going on behind the blinds. That Christmas Eve, the sight of those glowing rooms made me half-envious, even then, going to a rendezvous in my limitless expectancy; here seemed comfort, here seemed repose and a safe resting place; I envied all behind the blinds, even while, in the flush of youth and drunkenness of love, I despised them also, all those who stayed in the safe places and were not going out that night; I envied them behind the glowing curtains, and I despised them for not being on their way to a beloved.

The Edens' drawing-room was cheerful with noise when I entered. There was a great fire, and the party sitting round. On the hearth stood an enormous bowl, with bottles beside it, glinting in the firelight. All over the drawing-room there wafted a scent of rum, oranges, and lemons. Under the holly and mistletoe and tinsel drifted that rich odour.

Eden was sitting, with an air of extreme permanence, in an armchair by the fireplace. He greeted me warmly. 'I'm very glad to see you, Eliot. This is the young man I told you about – ' He introduced me to his wife. 'He's a friend of Sheila Knight's – but I've known him on my own account for, let me see, it must be well over a year. When you get to my age, Eliot, you'll find time goes uncomfortably fast.' He went on explaining me to his wife. 'Yes, I gave him some excellent advice which he was much too enterprising to take. Still, there's nothing like being a young man in a hurry.'

Mrs Eden was kneeling on the hearthrug, busy with hieratic earnestness at the mixing of the punch. The liquid itself was steaming in the hearth; she had come to the point of slicing oranges and throwing in the pieces. She was pale-faced, with an immensely energetic, jerky, and concentrated manner. She had bright, brown eyes, opaque as a bird's. She fixed them on me as she went on slicing.

'How long have you known Sheila, Mr Eliot?' she asked, as though the period were of the most critical importance.

I told her.

'She has such style,' said Mrs Eden with concentration.

Mrs Eden was enthusiastic about most things, but especially so about Sheila. She was quite unembarrassed by her admiration; it was easy to think of her as a girl, concentrated and intent, unrestrained in a *schwärmerei*, bringing some mistress flowers and gifts. At any rate, I wondered (I might be distorting her remarks through my own emotion) whether she too was not impatient for Sheila's arrival. With hieratic seriousness she went on cutting the oranges, dropping in the peel. It was luxuriously warm by the fire, the punch was smoking, Eden lay back with a sigh of reminiscent well-being, and began to talk to us – in those days,' he said, meaning the days of his youth, the turn of the century. I looked at the clock. It was nine-twenty. The others were listening to Eden, watching his wife prepare the punch. They were jolly and relaxed. I could scarcely wait for the minutes to pass and my heart was pounding.

To all of them except to Eden I was someone who Sheila Knight had picked up, how they did not know. They were a different circle from ours, more prosperous and more comfortably middle class. The Edens liked entertaining, and they had a weakness for youth, so nearly all the people round the fire were young, the sons and daughters of some of Eden's clients. The young men were beginning in their professions and in the local firms. Eden had once, with his fair-minded sense of etiquette, invited George to join one of the parties, but George, horrified at the prospect, had made a stiff excuse and kept away. So there were no links between us – they had never heard my name. Sheila, however, had visited the house quite often, possibly owing to the enthusiasm of Mrs Eden, and everyone there had either met her or knew her family – for Mrs Knight was prepared to include the prosperous town families in her ambit, as well as her county friends.

One or two of them inspected me inquisitively. I was quiet, apart from keeping Eden's reminiscences going. I was watching the clock. I did not take much part in the circle; the voices round were loud and careless, but as the minutes passed I was not listening to them, only for a ring at the bell outside.

'Punch is ready,' said Mrs Eden, suddenly and with energy.

'Ah well,' said Eden, 'I like the sound of that.'

'Shall we wait for Sheila?' Mrs Eden's eyes darted round the circle. Cheerily, the circle voted against.

'I really don't see why we should,' said Eden. 'Last come, last served. What do you think, Eliot? I fancy your friend Sheila won't mind if we proceed to the business of the meeting. You can explain to her afterwards that it's what happens to young women when they're late.'

The seconds were pounding on, but under Eden's affable badinage I felt proprietorial. I answered that I was sure she would not mind. The circle cheered. Mrs Eden dipped a ladle in the bowl and intently filled each glass but one.

The punch was hot, spiced, and strong. After the first round the circle became noisier, Eden's reminiscences had to give way, someone suggested a game. All the time I was listening. It was past ten o'clock. At last I heard, I heard unmistakably after the false hopes, the sound of a car in the drive. On the instant, I felt superlative content.

'Sheila,' said Mrs Eden with bright eyes.

For minutes I basked in well-being. I could sit back now she would soon be here, and not stare each moment at the door. I did not even need to listen too hard to the sounds outside.

The door opened. Sheila came in, radiant. Behind her followed a man.

Sheila came up to Mrs Eden, her voice sharp with excitement. 'I'm being extremely rude,' she said. 'Will you let me stay if I bring someone else? We've been having dinner, and I thought you wouldn't mind giving him some punch too. This is Doctor Devitt. He works at the infirmary.'

I heard Mrs Eden saying:

'We need another glass. That's all. Sit down, Dr Devitt. I'll get a glass for you.'

Her first response was always action. Perhaps she had not given a thought to what was happening. In any case, she could not resist Sheila, who only had to ask.

Through the haze I watched Eden smile politely, not his full, bland, melon-lipped smile, at Sheila and the other man. Eden looked at me. Was he puzzled? Did he understand? Was he looking at me with pity?

I had known, from the instant I saw her enter. It was not chance. It was deliberate. It was planned.

The room swam, faces came larger than life out of the mist, receded, voices were far away, then crashingly near. Somehow I managed to speak to Eden, to ask him some meaningless question.

The circle was being expanded, to bring in two more chairs. Sheila and Devitt sat down, Sheila between him and me. As Mrs Eden filled two glasses, Sheila said: 'Can Lewis have another one? Let me pass it.' She took my tumbler without a word between us. Intently, Mrs Eden filled it and gave it back to Sheila, who turned and put it into my hand.

'There,' she said.

Her face was smoother than I had ever seen it. It was open before me, and there seemed no trace or warning of her lines. Until her eyes swept up from the glass, which she watched into my fingers as though anxious not to spill a drop, until her eyes swept up and I could see nothing else, I watched (as if it had nothing to do with the mounting tides of pain, the sickness of misery, the rage of desire) her face – open, grave, pure and illuminated.

The circle went on with a game. It was a game in which one had to guess words. The minutes went by, they might have been hours, while I heard Sheila shouting her guesses from my side. Sometimes I shouted myself. And afterwards I remembered Eden, sitting quietly in his armchair, a little put out because the party chose to play this game instead of listening to him; Eden sitting quietly because he was not quick at guessing and so withdrew.

Midnight struck.

'Christmas Day,' said Mrs Eden; and, with her usual promptness, went on: 'Merry Christmas to you all.'

I heard Sheila, at my side, return the greeting.

Soon after, people began to stand up, for the party was ending. At once Sheila went to the other side of the hearth, and started to talk to Mrs Eden. Tom Devitt and I were standing close together – and, through the curious intimacy of rivals, we were drawn to speak.

He was much older than I was, and to me looked middle-aged. He was, I later found, in the middle thirties. His face was heavy, furrowed, kind, and intelligent. We were both tall, and our eyes met at the same level, but already he was getting fat, and his hair was going.

Awkwardly, with kindness, he asked about my studies. He said that Sheila had told him how I was working. He said, with professional concern, that I looked as though I might be overdoing it. Was I short of sleep? Had I anything to help me through a bad night?

I replied that it did not matter, and retaliated by telling him that there was a crack in one of his spectacles: oughtn't he to have it mended?

'It's too near the eye to affect vision,' said Tom Devitt. 'But I do need another pair.'

In the, clairvoyance of misery, I knew some vital things about him. I knew that he was in love with Sheila. I knew that he was triumphant to be taking her out that night. He was concerned for me because of his own triumph at being the preferred one. But I knew too that he was a kind, decent man, not at all unperceptive; he realized the purpose for which she had used him, and was angry; he had had no warning until he arrived in that room, and saw that I had already been invited as her partner.

We stood there, talking awkwardly – and we felt sorry for each other. We felt that, with different luck, we should have been friends.

Sheila beckoned to him. I followed them out of the room: at all costs I must speak to her. Any quarrel, any bitterness, was better than this silence.

But they were putting on their coats, and she stayed by Tom Devitt.

'I'm driving him to the infirmary,' she said to me, 'Can we give you a lift?'

I shook my head.

'Oh well.' She gazed at me. 'I'll see you soon.'

They went out of the door together. Just as they got to the car, I saw Devitt turn towards her, as though asking a question. His face was frowning, but at her reply it lightened with a smile.

The hum of the car died at last away. While I could hear it, she was not quite gone. Then I went home the way I had come, four hours before. I was blind with misery; yet as I crossed the park under the dark, low, starless sky, there were moments when I could not believe it, when absurdly I was invaded by the hope that had uplifted me on the outward journey. It was like those times in misery when one is cheated by a happy dream.

Blindly I came home to my room. Under the one bare light the chair and table and bed stood blank before my eyes. They were blank as the darkness into which I stared for hours, lying awake that night. I stared into the darkness while mood after mood took hold of me, as changeable as the fever and chill of an illness, as ravaging and as much beyond my control.

I could have cried, if only the tears would come. I twisted about in a paroxysm of longing. I was seized by a passion of temper, and I could have strangled her.

I had been humiliated once before – on that morning as a child, the memory of which possessed me for a moment in the night, when I offered my mother's ten-shilling note. As a rule, I did not look for or find humiliation. I was no George Passant, going through the world expecting affronts and feeling them to the marrow of his bones. For my age, I got off lightly, in being free from most of the minor shames. But when humiliation came, it seared me, so that all my hidden pride shrieked out, and in bitterness I vowed that this must be the end, that I would make sure that I never so much as saw her again, that I would act as though she had never been.

Yet, turning over on to the other side, praying for sleep, I hoped, hoped for a word that would put it right. It had been an accident, I thought; she was remote, she lived in a world of her own; she had just happened to see him that night. There must be a simple explanation. With the foolish detailed precision of love, I recalled each word between us since she invited me to go to the Edens'; and I proved to myself in that armistice of hope, that it was a series of coincidences, and none of it was meant. Tomorrow, no, the day after, I should receive a letter which would resolve it all. She might not know how I had been hurt. At the Edens' she had been light and friendly to me, as though we should meet soon after on our usual terms. Her manner had been the same to both of us. She had not looked at him lovingly.

Then I knew jealousy. Where had they gone after the car drove away? Had he kissed her? Had he slept with her? Were they, at this moment when I was lying sleepless, in each other's arms? For the first time in my thoughts of Sheila, my sensual imagination was active, merciless, gave me no rest.

The night ticked by, slower than my racing heart. Again I knew that it was all planned. Again, with detailed precision, but with another purpose, I went over each word that she had spoken since her invitation – her excitement when she first asked me to go, her tense exaltation, the tone in which she had telephoned at the cafe. It was the edge of cruelty. I had been hurt by motiveless cruelty on that morning of childish humiliation – but this was the first time I had felt cruelty in love. Did I know that night that it was the end of innocence? I felt much that I had imagined of love stripped from me by her outrage, and in the darkness, I saw in her and in myself a depth which was black with hate, and from which, even in misery, I shrank back appalled. I had always known it in myself, but kept my eyes away; now her outrage made me look.

In the creeping winter dawn, my thoughts had become just two. The first was, I must dismiss her from my mind, I must forget her name – and, as I got more tired, I kept holding to that resolve. The second was, how soon would she write to me, so that I could see her again?

23

The Lights of a House

THE days passed; and, working in my room, a veil kept coming between my eyes and the page. When the veil came, I would hear some phrase of Sheila's, and that set going my thoughts as through the sleepless night I sat there at my books, but I could not force my eyes to clear.

I heard nothing, I saw no one, I received no letter, for day after day. George and Jack and I had arranged to meet to see the new year in; but after one drink George went off to an 'important engagement', and Jack and I were left alone.

'He must have found somebody,' said Jack. 'Good luck to him.'

We argued about how we should spend the night. Jack's idea was that there could be no better way than of going to the local palais-de-danse and picking up two girls; but, at the mention of the word, I re-heard Sheila saying 'we went to the palais', and I could not face the faintest chance, the one chance in ten thousand, of seeing her there.

I wanted to stay in the public house, drinking. Jack was discontented, but, in his good-natured way, agreed. For him, it was a sacrifice. It was only to be convivial, and because he liked us, that he endured long drinking parties with George and me.

Amiably he sipped at his whisky, and made a slight face. He was so accommodating that I wanted to explain why I could not go to the palais; I was also longing to confide, and I knew that I should get sympathy and some kind of understanding; yet when I began, my pride clutched me, and the story came out, thin, half-humorous, so garbled that he could get no inkling either of my humiliation or my aching emptiness as each day passed. Even so, I got some relief, perhaps more than if I had exposed the truth.

'We all have lovers' quarrels,' said Jack.

'I suppose so,' I said.

'It's sweet when you make it up,' said Jack.

He smiled at me.

'You've got to be a bit firm,' he said. 'See that she apologizes. Box her ears and make her feel a little girl. Then be specially nice to her.' He went on: 'It's all right as long as you don't take it too tragically. You watch yourself, Lewis. Mind you don't get all the anguish and none of the fun. You'd better get her where you want her this time. I'll tell you how I managed it last week – '

Thus I spent the last hours of 1925 listening to Jack Cotery on the predicaments and tactics of a love affair; of how he had changed a reverse into a victory; of comic misfortune, of tears that were part of the game, of tears that turned into luxurious sighs. And, listening to his eloquence, I was solaced, I half believed that things would go that way for me.

The first days of January. Not a word. The voice of sense gave way, and I began to write a letter. Then my pride held me on the edge, and I tore it up. When I could not sleep, I dragged myself out of bed to work. I did not know how long such a state could last. I had nothing to compare it with. I went on – with 'automatic competence', a clear high voice taunted me, more piercing than any voice of those I met. I worked to tire myself, so that I should sleep late into the morning. I was living always for the next day.

Before Christmas the group had arranged to go out to the farm for the first weekend of the year. I had promised to join the party. But now I recoiled from company, I told George that I could not go. 'You're forgetting your responsibilities,' he said stiffly. There were other times when I craved for any kind of human touch. I went the round of pubs, talking to barmaids and prostitutes, anything for a smile. It was in one of those storms that I changed my mind again.

On the Friday night I sought George out, and told him that I should like to come after all. 'I'm glad to see you're back in your right mind,' said George. Then he asked formally: 'Nothing seriously wrong with your private affairs, I hope?'

For George, it was a great weekend. Everyone was there, and he could bask right in the heart of his 'little world', surrounded by people whom he loved and looked after, where all his diffidence, prickles, suspiciousness, and angry defiance were swept away, where he felt utterly serene. At the farm, surrounded by his group, one saw George at his best. He was a natural leader, though, because of the quirks of his nature, it had to be a leader in obscurity, a leader of a revolt that never came off. He was a strange character – many people thought him so bizarre as to be almost mad: yet no one ever met him, however much they suppressed their own respect, without thinking that he was built on the lines of a great man.

Seated at the supper table, outside the golden circle of the oil lamp, George was at his best. Each word he spoke was listened to, even in the gossip, chatter, and argument of the group. That night he talked to us of freedom – how, if we had the will (and that it would never have occurred to him to doubt), we could make our children's lives the best there had ever been in the world. Not only by making a better society, in which they would stand a fair chance, but also by bringing them up free and happy. 'The good in men is incomparably more important than the evil,' said George. 'Whatever happens, we've always got to remember that.'

The whole group was moved, for he had spoken from a great depth. That was his message, and it came from a man who struggled with himself. When Jack, the most impudent person there, twitted him and said the evil could be very delectable, George shouted: 'I don't call *that* evil. It's half the trouble that for hundreds of years all the priests and parents and pundits have tried to make us miserable by a load of guilt.'

I had not said much that supper time, for my mind was absent, thinking of a recent supper at that table, when I came in wet, alight with a secret happiness. For a moment I shook off my preoccupation, my own load, and looked at George. For I knew that he, more than most of us, was burdened by a sense of guilt – and so he demanded that we should all be free.

After supper, we broke into twos and threes, and Marion and I began to talk out in the window bay. She had just returned from her Christmas holidays, and it was three weeks since we had met.

'I need your help,' she said at once.

'What about?'

'I've got a problem for you.' Then she added: 'What were you thinking about just now?'

'What's your problem, Marion?' I said, wanting to evade the question.

'Never mind for a minute. What were you thinking about? I've never seen you look so far away.'

'I was thinking about George.'

'Were you?' she said doubtfully. 'When you're thinking of someone, you usually watch them – with those damned piercing eyes of yours, don't you? You weren't watching George. You weren't watching any of us.'

I had had time to collect myself, and I told her that I had been thinking of George's message of freedom compared with the doctrine of original sin. Often she would have been interested, for she tried to get me to talk about people; but just then she did not believe a word of it, she was angry at being put off. Impatiently, as though irrelevantly, she burst out:

'Why in heaven's name don't you learn to keep your tie straight? You're a disgrace.'

It was really a bitter cry, because I would not confide. I felt ashamed of myself because I was fond of her – but also I felt the more wretched, the more strained, because she was pressing me. It was by an effort that I kept back a cold answer. Instead, I said, as though we were both joking about our untidiness: 'I must say, that doesn't come too well from you.'

Jack was close by, talking to another girl, with an ear cocked in our direction. He moved away, as though he had not overhead anything of meaning in our words.

Again I asked about her problem.

'You won't be very interested,' said Marion.

'Of course I'm interested,' I said.

She hesitated about telling me; but she wanted to, she had it ready. She had been offered a job in her own town. It was a slightly better job, in a central school. If she were to make a career of teaching, it would be sensible to take it. She could live with her sister, and save a good deal of money.

She wanted me to say, without weighing any of her arguments, just: you're not to go. Increasingly I felt myself constrained, the offender (increasingly I longed for the lightness that came over me as I talked to Sheila), because I could not. I was tongue-tied, and all I had to say came heavily. My spontaneity had deserted me quite. Yet I should miss her, miss her with an ache of affection, if she went. I knew that somehow I relied on her, even as I tried to speak fairly and she watched me with mutinous eyes and gave me curt, rude answers. I tried to think only of what was best for her – and for that she could not listen to me or forgive me.

George called out heartily: 'Lewis, are you coming for a constitutional?'

This was a code invitation, devised to meet the need of his curious sense of etiquette in front of the young women: a 'constitutional' meant going down the road to the public house, sitting there for an hour or so, and then coming back, ready to talk until the next morning. That night I was glad to escape from the house; no one else stirred, and George and I went across the field together.

Suddenly, on an impulse that I could not drive down, I said: 'George, I'm going to leave you for an hour. I'm going for a walk.'

At first George was puzzled. Then, with extreme quickness, with massive tact, he said:

'I quite understand, old chap. I quite understand.' He gave a faint, sympathetic, contented chuckle. He proceeded to go through one of his elaborate wind-ups: 'I take it you might prefer me to practise a little judicious prevarication? If we walk back from the pub together, there's no compelling reason why our friends should realize that you've been engaged on – other activities.'

In fact, I had no thought of seeing Sheila. Alone in the dark, I made my way through the lanes, drawn as though by instinct towards her house. I could not have said why I was going except that each yard I covered gave me some surcease. I knew that I should not see her with the relic of reason and pride, I knew that it would have been disastrous to see her. Yet on the way, across the same fields that I had first seen in a downpour with so much joy, surrendered to the impulse that drew me across the fields, down the lanes, towards her house, I felt a peace, such as I had not known since Christmas Eve. It was a precarious peace, it might break at any moment; but I was closer to her, and my whole body melted into the mirage of well-being.

In the village, I drew up my coat collar. I could not bear the risk of being recognized, if one of the family happened to be out that night. I kept in the shadow, away from the lights of the cottage windows. From the bar parlour came loud and raucous singing. I went past the lych-gate: the spire was dark against the stars. I could see the serene lights of the vicarage. I stopped before the drive, huddled myself against a tree, hidden in case anyone should drive out: there I stood, without moving, without any thought or plan. The drawing room windows were lit up, and so was one on the next floor. I did not even know her room. Was that her room? – the real room, instead of that which, in the first rapture, I had pictured to myself. Was she there, away from anyone who pried, away from anyone who troubled her? Was she there at that moment, writing to me?

No shadow crossed the window. I did not feel the cold. I could not have said how many minutes passed, before I went back again, keeping to the dark side, down the village street.

24

The Key In the Lock

BACK in my room, I slept through broken nights and worked and gazed over the roofs, and all my longings had become one longing – just to be in touch again. The shock of Christmas Eve had been softened by now, and the pain dulled: pride alone was not much of a restraint to keep my hand from the pen, from the comfort of writing Dearest Sheila. Yet I did not write.

Monday went by, after the weekend when I stood outside her house. Tuesday. Wednesday. I longed that we could have some friend in common, so that I could hear of her and drop a remark, as though casually, that I was waiting. A friend could help us both, I thought, could put in a word for me. Apart from our meetings – I was glad to think so, for it shifted the blame outside ourselves, gave me something which could be altered and so a scrap of hope – we had none of the reminders of each other, the everyday gossip, of people who lived in the same circle. My friends inhabited a different world: so far as they knew her, they hated her; while hers I did not know at all.

I was impelled to discover what I could about Tom Devitt. I dug my nails into the flesh, and willed that I must put him out of my mind, together with the scene at the Edens' – together with Sheila and what I felt for her. On the Monday after I returned from the farm, however, I found myself making an excuse to go to the reference library. There was some point not covered by my textbook. In the library I looked it up, but I could safely have left it; it was of no significance at all, and for such a point I should never have troubled to come. I browsed aimlessly by the shelves which contained *Who's Who*, Whitaker, Crockford (where I had already long since looked up the Reverend Laurence Knight), and the rest. Almost without looking, I was puffing out the *Medical Directory*. *Devitt A T N*; the letters seemed embossed. It did not say when he was born, but he had been a medical student at Leeds and qualified in 1914 (when she and I were nine years old, I thought with envy). In the war, he had been in the RAMC, and had been given a Military Cross (again I was stabbed with envy). Then he had held various jobs in hospitals: in 1924 he had become registrar at the infirmary; I did not know then what the hospital jobs meant, nor the title registrar. I should have liked to know how good a career it had been, and what his future was.

The Thursday of that week was a bright cold sunny day of early January. In the afternoon I was working in my overcoat, with a blanket round my legs. When I looked up from my notebook I could see, for the table stood close to the window, the pale sunlight silvering the tiles.

Someone was climbing up the attic stairs. There was a sharp knock, and my door was thrown open. Sheila came into the room. With one hand she shut the door behind her, but she was looking at me with a gaze expressionless and fixed. She took two steps into the room, then stopped quite still. Her face was pale, hard, without a smile. Her arms were at her sides. I had jumped up, forgetting everything but that she was here, my arms open for her; but when she stayed still, so did I, frozen.

'I've come to see you,' she said.

'Yes,' I said.

'I haven't seen you since that night. You're thinking about that night.' Her voice was louder than usual.

'I'm bound to think of it.'

'Listen to this: I did it on purpose.'

'Why did you do it?'

'Because you made me angry.' Her eyes were steady, hypnotic in their glitter. 'I've not come to tell you that I'm sorry.'

'You ought to be,' I said.

'I'm not sorry.' Her voice had risen. 'I'm glad I did it.'

'What do you mean?' I said in anger.

'I tell you, I'm glad I did it.'

We were standing a yard apart. Her arms were still at her sides, and she had not moved. She said:

'You can hit me across the face.'

I looked at her, and her eyes flickered.

'You should,' she said.

As I looked at her, in the bright light from the window behind my back, I saw the whites of her eyes turn bloodshot. Then tears formed, and slowly trickled down her cheeks. She did not raise a hand to touch them. As she cried, dreadfully still, the hard fierce poise of her face was dissolved away, and her beauty, and everything I recognized.

I took her by the shoulders, and led her, very gently, to sit on the bed. She came without resistance, as though she were a robot. I kissed her on the lips, told her for the first time in words that I loved her, and wiped away the tears.

'I love you,' I said.

'I don't love you, but I trust you,' cried Sheila, in a tone that tore my heart open for myself and her. She kissed me with a sudden desperate energy, with her mouth forced on to mine; her arms were convulsively tight; then she let go, pressed her face into the counterpane, and began to cry again. But this time she cried with her shoulders heaving, with relief; I sat on the bed beside her, holding her hand, waiting till she was exhausted; and in those moments I was possessed by the certainty that no love of innocence, no love in which she had been only the idol of my imagination, could reach as deep as that which I now knew.

For now I had seen something frightening, and I loved her, seeing something of what she was. I felt for her a curious detached pity in the midst of the surge of love – and I realized that it was the first ignorant forerunner of pity that I had felt for her in her mother's drawing-room. I felt a sense of appalling danger for her, and, yes, for me: of a life so splintered and remote that I might never reach it; of cruelty and suffering that I could not soften. Yet I had never felt so transcendentally free. Holding her hand as she cried, I loved her, I believed that she in part loved me, and that we should be happy.

She raised her head, sniffed, blew her nose, and smiled. We kissed again. She said:

'Turn your head. I want to see you.'

She smiled, half-sarcastically, half-tearfully, as she inspected me. She said:

'You look rather sweet with lipstick on.'

I told her that her face, foreshortened as I saw it when I kissed her, was different from the face that others saw: its proportions quite changed, its classical lines destroyed, much more squashed, imperfect, and human.

I asked her again about Christmas Eve.

'Why did you do it?'

She said:

'I'm hateful. I thought you were too possessive.'

'Possessive?' I cried.

'You wanted me too much,' said Sheila.

I inquired about Tom. We were sitting side by side, with arms round each other. In the same heartbeat I was jealous and reassured.

'Do you love him?' I said.

'No,' said Sheila. She exclaimed in a high voice: 'I wish I did. He's a good man. He's too good for me He's a better man than you are.'

'He loves you,' I said.

'I think he wants to marry me,' she said. 'I can't. I don't love him.' Then she said: 'Sometimes I think I shall never love anyone.'

She pulled down my face and kissed me.

'I don't love you, but I trust you. Get me out of this. I trust you to get me out of this.'

I heard her say once more: 'I don't love you, but I trust you.'

I told her that I loved her, the words set free and pouring over: I was forced to speak, able to speak, deliriously happy to speak, as I had never yet spoken to a human being. 'Get me out of this' – that cry turned the key in the lock. I did not know what she meant, and yet it lured me on. I was utterly released, there was no pride, no reserve left, as there was when my mother, when Marion, invaded me with love. Seeing her at last as a person, not just an image in a dream, I threw aside my own burden of self. I told her, the words came bursting out, of every feeling that had possessed me since we first met. In this other nature, remote from anything I knew, I could abandon all, except my passion for her. In her arms, hearing that mysterious and remote cry, I lost myself.

Part Four

THE FIRST SURRENDER

25

A Piece of Advice

I HAD thought, when Marion took me shopping in London and talked of her complexion, of how the same words spoken by Sheila would have taken their special place, would have been touched by the enchantment of strangeness: so that I should remember them, as I remembered everything about her, as though they were illuminated. For everything she did, when I was first in love, was separated from all else that I heard or saw or touched; the magic was there, and the magic laid an aura round her; she might have been a creature from another species. For me, that was the overmastering transformation of romantic love. And in part it stayed so – until in middle age, a generation after I first met her, years after she was dead, there were still moments when she possessed my mind, different from all others.

It stayed so, after that January afternoon in my attic. There were nights when we had walked hand in hand through the bitter deserted streets, and I went back alone, rehearing the words spoken half an hour before, but hearing them as though they were magic words. The slightest touch – not a kiss, but the tap of her fingers on my pocket, asking for matches to light a cigarette – I could feel as though there had never been any other hands.

Yet that January afternoon had added much. That I knew even as she stood there, her face dissolved by tears. I could no longer shape her according to my own image of desire. I was forced to try to know her now. She was no longer just my beloved, she was a separate person

187

whose life had crashed head-on into mine. And I was forced to feel for her something quite separate from love, a strange pity, affection, compassion, inexplicable to me then as it was at the first intimation in her mother's drawing-room.

I began to learn the depth and acuteness of her self-consciousness. She could not believe that I was not tormented likewise. She wondered at it. Whereas she – she smiled sarcastically and harshly, and said: 'It would be hard to be more so. You can't deny it. You can't pretend I'm not.'

She was angry about it. She blamed her parents. Once she said, not angrily, but as a matter of fact: 'They've destroyed my self-confidence for ever.' She wanted ease at all costs, and used all her will to get it. If I could give her ease, she never thought twice about visiting me in my room. People might think she was my mistress; she knew now that I hungered for her; her parents would stop her if they could; she dismissed each of those thoughts with contempt, when the mood was on her and she felt that I alone could soothe her. Nothing else mattered, when her will was set.

I knew something else, something so difficult for a lover to accept that I could not face it steadily. Yet I knew that she was going round like a sleepwalker. She was looking for someone with whom to fall in love.

I knew that she was desperately anxious, so anxious that the lines deepened and the skin darkened beneath her eyes, that she would never manage it. She did not love me, but I gave her a kind of hope, an illusory warmth, as though through me she might break out into release – either with me or another, for as to that, in her ruthlessness, innocence, and cruelty, she would not give a second's thought.

Such was the little power I had over her.

She was afraid that she would never love a man as I loved her. It was from that root that came her acts of Christmas Eve, her deliberate cruelty.

For she was cruel, not only through indifference, but also as though in being cruel she could find release. In such a scene as that on

Christmas Eve, she could bring herself to the emotional temperature in which most of us naturally lived.

It was hard to take, at that age. The more so, as she played on a nerve of cruelty within myself — which I had long known, which except with her I could forget. Once or twice she provoked my temper, which nowadays I had as a rule under control. She made me quarrel: quarrels were an excitement to her, a time in which to immerse herself, to swear like a fishwife; to me, except in the height of rage, they were — because I had so little power over her — like death.

It was harder for me, because now I longed for her completely. The time was past when I could be satisfied, thinking of her alone in her room; each scrap of understanding, each wave either of compassion or anger, and the more I wanted her. On that January afternoon, when I had the first sight of her as a living creature, driven by her nature, I felt not only the birth of affection, as something distinct from love — but also I was trembling with desire. And that was the first of many occasions when she felt my hand shake, when she felt in me a passion which left her unmoved, which made her uneasy and cruel. For now I wanted her in the flesh. Although everything I knew made nonsense of the thought, I wanted her as my wife.

I had not enough confidence to tell her so. I had always been afraid that I had no charm for her. Sometimes, now that I wanted her so much, I hoped I had a little; sometimes, I thought, none at all. Occasionally she was warm and active and laughing in my arms; then, at our next meeting, irritated by my need for her, she would smoke cigarette after cigarette in an endless chain so as to give me no excuse to kiss her. I could not face the cold truth she might tell me if I took the cigarette away.

She caused me intense jealousy. Not only with Tom Devitt; in fact she quarrelled with him early in the year. I told her that I was suspicious of her quarrels. 'You needn't be this time,' she said. 'Poor Tom. It's a pity. He couldn't turn me into a doctor's wife.' She reflected, with a frown.

'The more helpless they are, the worse one treats them.' She looked at me. 'I know I'm unpleasant. You can tell me so if you like. But I'm telling the truth. It's also true of less unpleasant women. Isn't it so?'

'I expect it's true of us all,' I said.

'I've never found a man who made me helpless yet,' she said. 'I don't know what it would be like.'

'I've found you,' I said.

She shook her head.

'No,' she said. 'You're not so helpless. I shouldn't come to see you if you were.'

I ceased to be jealous of Tom Devitt, but there were others. They were nearly all misfits, waifs and strays, often – like Devitt – much older than she was. For the smart comely young businessmen who pursued her she had no use whatsoever. But she would find some teacher at the School timid with women or unhappily married, and I should hear a threatening, excited 'we' again. She had a very alert and hopeful eye for men whom she thought might fascinate her. In getting to know them, she rid herself of her self-consciousness; instead of shrinking into a corner, as she did in company, she was ready to take the initiative herself, exactly as though she were a middle-aged woman on the prowl for lovers. I could see nothing in common between those who pleased her. I knew that she herself imagined some implacably strong character, some Heathcliff of a lover who would break her will – but they were all weaker and gentler than she was.

Each of those sparks of interest guttered away, and she came back, sometimes pallid, ill-tempered, more divided than before, sometimes sarcastic and gay.

I was beyond minding in what state she came back. For each time I was bathed in the overwhelming reassurance of the jealous. After days spent in the degrading detective work of jealousy, I saw her in front of me, and the calculations were washed away. It was only the jealous, I thought later, who could be so ecstatically reassured. She had said that she went home by the eight-ten last night. Where had she been between teatime and the train, with whom had she been? Then she said that her mother had been shopping in the town, and they had gone to the pictures. Only the suspicious could be as simple and wholehearted in delight as I was then.

I did not spend much time with the group during those months. My first Bar examination happened in the summer, and whenever I could not see Sheila I was trying to concentrate upon my work. I went out at night with George and Jack, I still went to Martineau's on Fridays, but the long weekends at the farm I could no longer spare. There was, I knew, a good deal of gossip; by now it was common knowledge that I was head over heels in love with Sheila. Marion also began to keep away from the group, and we never met at all.

There was one pair of curious, observant eyes that did not let me keep my secrets unperceived. Jack Cotery was interested in me, and love was his special subject. He watched the vicissitudes in my spirits as day followed day. He went out of his way to meet Sheila once or twice. Then, in the summer, not long before I set off to London to take the examination, he exerted himself. He came up one night and said, in his soft voice:

'Lewis, I want to talk to you.'

I tried to put him off, but he shook his head.

'No. Clearly, it's time someone gave you a bit of advice.'

He was oddly obstinate. It was the only time I had known him make a determined stand about someone else's concerns. He insisted on taking me to the picture-house café. 'I'm more at home there.' He grinned. 'I'm tired of your wretched pubs.' There, under the pink-shaded lights, with girls at the tables close by, whispering, giggling, he was indeed at home. But that night he was keeping his eyes from girls. With his rolling muscular gait he led the way into the corner, where there was a table separate from the rest. The night was warm; we drank tea, and got warmer; Jack Cotery, in complete seriousness, began to talk to me.

Then I realized that this was an act of pure friendliness. It was the more pure, because I had recently been busy trying to stop one of his dubious projects. In the autumn he had borrowed money from George, in order to start a small wireless business. Since then he had launched out on a speculation that was, if one took the most charitable view, somewhere near the edge of the shady. He was pestering George for more money with which to extricate himself. I had used my influence with George to stop it. My motives were not all disinterested; I might still want to borrow from George myself, and so Jack and I were rivals there; but still, I had a keen nose for a rogue, I had no doubt that to Jack commercial honesty was without meaning, and thus early I smelt danger, most of all, of course, for George.

Jack was a good deal of a rogue, but he bore no grudges. No doubt he enjoyed advising me, showing off his expertness, parading himself where he was so much more knowledgeable, so much less vulnerable, than I. But he had a genuine wish, earthy and kind, to get me fitted up with a suitable bed-mate, to be sure that I was enjoying myself, with all this nonsensical anguish thrown away. He had taken much trouble to time his advice right. With consideration, with experienced eyes, he had been watching until I seemed temporarily light-hearted. It was then, when he felt sure that I was not worrying about Sheila, that he took me off to the picture-house café. He actually began, over the steaming tea:

'Lewis, things aren't so bad with your girl just now, are they?'

I said that they were not.

'That's the time to give her up,' said Jack, with emphasis and conviction. 'When you're not chasing her. It won't hurt your pride so much. You can get out of it of your own free will. It's better for you yourself to have made the break, Lewis, it will hurt you less.'

He spoke so warmly that I had to answer in kind.

'I can't give her up,' I said. 'I love her.'

'I've noticed that,' said Jack, smiling good-naturedly. 'Though why you didn't tell me earlier I just can't imagine. We might have dangled a few distractions before your eyes. Why in God's name should you fall for that – horror?'

'She's not a horror.'

'You know very well she is. In everything that matters. Lewis, you're healthy enough. Why in God's name should you choose someone who'll only bring you misery?'

I shrugged my shoulders.

'Once or twice', I said, 'I've been happier with her than I've ever imagined being.'

'Don't be silly,' said Jack. 'If you didn't get a spot of happiness when you're first in love, it'd be a damned poor lookout for all of us. Look here, I know more about women than you do. Or if I don't', he grinned, 'I must have been wasting my time. I tell you, she's a horror. Perhaps she's a bit crazy. Anyway, she'll only bring you misery. Now why did you choose her?'

'Has one any choice?' I said.

'With someone impossible,' said Jack, 'you ought to be able to escape.'

'I don't think I can,' I said.

'You've got to,' said Jack, with more vigorous purpose than I had ever heard from him. 'She'll do you harm. She'll make a mess of your life.' He added: 'I believe she's done you a lot of harm already.'

'Nonsense,' I said.

'I bet you don't know when to make love to her.'

The hit was so shrewd that I blushed.

'Damn the bitch,' said Jack. 'I'd like to have her in a bedroom with no questions asked. I'd teach her a thing or two.'

He looked at me.

'Lewis,' he said, 'it's the cold ones who can do you harm. I expect you wonder if any woman will ever want you.'

'Yes,' I said. 'Sometimes I do.'

'It's absurd,' said Jack, in his flattering, easy, soothing fashion. 'If you'd run across someone warm, you'd know how absurd it is. Why, with just a bit of difference, you'd have a better time than I do. You're sympathetic. You're very clever. You're going to be a success. And – you've got a gleam in your eye… It's like everything else,' he went on.

'You've got to believe in yourself. If she's ruined that for you, I shall never forgive her. I tell you, it's absurd for you to doubt yourself. There are hundreds of nicer girls than Miss Sheila who'd say yes before you'd had time to ask.'

When he cared, he was more skilful than anyone I knew at binding up the wounds.

Jack looked across the table. I was certain that he had something else to say, and was working his way towards it. He was using all his cunning, as well as his good nature.

'Now Marion', he said, as though casually, and I understood, 'would be a hundred times better – for any purpose that you can possibly imagine. I don't mind telling you, I've thought of her myself. I just can't understand why you've done nothing about it.'

'I've been pretty occupied,' I said. 'And I wasn't – '

'I should have thought', said Jack, 'that you might have found time to think of her. After all, she's been pining for you long enough.'

I was forced on to the defensive. I said, in confusion, that I knew she was rather fond of me, but he was exaggerating it beyond all reason.

'You bloody fool,' said Jack, 'she worships the ground you walk on.'

I still protested, Jack went on attacking me. If I did not realize it, he said roughly, it must be because I was blinded by Sheila. The sooner I got rid of her the better, if I could not notice what was going on round me. 'Remember too,' said Jack, 'if anyone falls in love with you, it is partly your own fault. It's not all innocence on your side. It never is. There's always a bit of encouragement. You've smiled at her, you've been sympathetic, and you've led her on.'

I felt guilty: that was another stab of truth. I argued, I protested again that he was exaggerating. I was confused: I half wanted to credit what he said, just for the sake of my own vanity; I half wanted to be guiltless.

'I don't care about the rights and wrongs,' said Jack. 'All I care about is that the young woman is aching for you. Just as much as you ache for your girl. And without any nonsense about it. She wants you, she knows she wants you. But remember she can't wait for ever. If I never advise you again, Lewis, I'm doing so now. Get free – not next week, tonight, go home and write the letter – and take Marion on. It will make all the difference to you... I'm not at all sure', he said surprisingly, 'that you wouldn't be wise to marry her.'

26

Meeting by Accident

THE examination did not trouble me overmuch. It was not a decisive one; my acquaintances who were taking law degrees, like Charles March, were exempt from it; unless I did disgracefully badly, nothing hung upon the result. Once I got started, I felt a cheerful, savage contempt for those who tried to keep me in my proper station. I had only taken one examination in my life, the Oxford, but I found again that, after the first half-hour, I enjoyed the game. In the first lunch interval, certain that I was not going to disgrace myself, I reflected realistically, as I had done before, that my performance this year would be a guide to my chances twelve months hence in the Bar Finals – on which, in my circumstances, all depended.

I stayed at Mrs Reed's, for no better reason than habit, but this time I did not have to look in entreaty at the hall table each time I entered the house. Sheila's letter arrived on my second morning, according to her promise. For I had seen her before I left town, not listening to Jack Cotery, despite the comfort he had given me. The letter was in her usual allusive style, but contained a passage which made me smile: 'My father has lost his voice, which is exceedingly just. He croaks pathetically. I have offered to nurse him – would you expect me to be good at the healing word?' And, a little farther on, she wrote: 'Curiously enough, he inquired about you the other day. He is probably thinking you might be useful some time for free legal consultations. My family are remarkably avaricious. I don't know whether I shall inherit it. Poor Tom used to have to prescribe for my father. But Tom was a moral coward. You are evasive and cagey, but you're not that.'

Evasive and cagey, I thought, in the luxury of considering a beloved's judgement, in the conceit of youth. Was it true? No one else had ever said so. So far as I knew, no one had thought so. She had seen me get on, in harmony, with all kinds of people – while she shrank into a corner. And she alone had seen me quite free.

She wrote in the same vein about her father, her mother, herself. She was unsparing; equally remote from moral vanity or visceral warmth; she saw no reason to give herself or anyone else the benefit of the doubt. Sometimes her judgements were lunatic, and sometimes they went painfully deep. Those judgements were her revenge. People got through life with their lies and pretences, with their spontaneity, with their gluey warmth denied to her. She was left out of the party. So she told them that the party was false and the good-fellowship just a sham, and in telling them so she was sometimes no truer than a hurt child; but sometimes she tore the façade off the human condition, and made us wince at the truth.

Her letter brought her near, and I went undisturbed through the rest of the papers. I saw Charles March at dinner, with his usual party of Cambridge friends. He undertook to find out my marks in detail; he had no idea why I was so curious, nor that next year's examination was a crisis in my career, but he was a sensitive, quick-witted man, pleased to be of help. I envied his assumption that it was easy to discover what was going on behind the scenes. Some day, I thought, I too must be as sure of myself, as much able to move by instinct among the sources of information and power. Twenty years ahead, and it was ironical to meet Charles March, and for us to be reminded that I had once resolved to emulate him.

I remained in London for an extra afternoon, in order to go to Lord's and watch some cricket. There, in the sunshine, I felt peace seep over me like a drug, steadying my heart, slowing my pulse. The examination was safe. Soon I should be seeing Sheila. There was not even the shadow of care, as there had been that day – it suddenly came back to memory and made me smile – when my father watched his first and only cricket match and I sat beside him, eight years old.

But that evening, as the train rushed through the midland fields and in half an hour I should be home, that mood of peace seemed separated from me by years or an ocean. I was fretted by anxiety, as though my mind were a vacuum, and immediately one ominous thought left it, another bored in. I had an irresistible sense that I was returning into trouble, every kind of trouble. I struggled with each item of anxiety, but the future was full of pain. I was angry with myself for being the prey of nerves. It was time to remember that I was strained by this kind of apprehension whenever I came home from a journey. I had just to accept it, like a minor disease. If I did not, I should become as superstitious as my mother. But as I stepped on to the station platform I was looking round in dread, expecting some news of Sheila that would break my heart. I bought an evening paper, dreading against all reason that she might have chosen this day to become engaged. I rang her up from the station; she sounded surprised, amused, and friendly, and had no news at all.

For a moment I was reassured, as though in a fit of jealousy. Then I felt anxious about George, and went to see him; in his case, there had been some faint cause for worry, though neither he nor I had taken it seriously; that night, it still seemed faint, though he did produce some mystifying information about Martineau.

My nerve-storm dropped away; and for weeks after my examination all was smooth. George had a piece of professional success, the alarm over Martineau began to seem unreal; Jack Cotery had begun, by luck or daring, to make some money. Sheila was uncapricious and gay, and had set herself the task of teaching me to take an interest in painting. My examination result appeared in *The Times*, and had gone according to plan. It reappeared in the local papers, having been sent there by Aunt Milly, who had now finally decided to admit that I was less foolish than most young men. Their curious alliance still operating, George impressed on her that I was fulfilling my share of the bargain. He went on 'to gain considerable satisfaction', as he said himself, by ramming the fact of my performance in front of anyone who had ever seemed to doubt me.

I received a few letters of congratulation, a bland one from Eden, an affectionate and generous one from Marion, a fantastically florid one from Mr Vesey – and a note from Tom Devitt. My father professed a comic gratification; and Sheila said: 'I didn't expect anything else. But if you make me celebrate, I shall quite like it.' It was my first taste of success, and it was sweet.

Nevertheless, I had returned into trouble. As the summer went on, some of the ominous thoughts of the journey came back; but this time they were not a trick of the nerves, they were real. The first trouble – the first sign that the luck had changed, I found myself thinking, in the superstitious way of which I was ashamed – was a mild one, but it harassed me. It followed close behind the congratulations, and was a disappointment about my examination. Charles March had kept his word. Somehow or other he had obtained the marks on my individual papers. They were not bad, but I was not high up the list of the first class. They were nothing like good enough if I were to make a hit next year.

There was no option. Next year I had to do spectacularly well. It was an unfair test, I thought, forgetting that I had once faced these brutal facts – when I first made my choice. But it was different facing facts from a long way off: and then meeting them in one's nerves and flesh. It was very hard to imagine a risk, until one had to live with it.

There was nothing for it. Next year I had to do better. I had to improve half a class.

I consulted George. At first, he was unwilling to accept that anything was wrong. I was exaggerating, as usual, said George stormily; I was losing my sense of proportion just because this man March, whom George had never heard of, reported that I had not done superlatively well in a couple of papers. No one was less ready than George to see the dangerous sign. He had to be persuaded against his will, in the teeth of his violent temper, that a disquieting fact could conceivably exist, particularly in a protégé's career. He denounced Charles March. 'I see no reason', shouted George, 'why I should be expected to kowtow to the opinions of your fashionable friends.' He denounced me for being an alarmist. I had to be rough and lose my own temper and tell him that, however much he deceived himself about others, he must not do it about me. These were the official marks, never mind how they were obtained. Brusquely I told him that it was just a problem of cramming; the facts were clear, and I was not going to argue about them: I wanted to know one thing – how could I pull up half a class?

Immediately, without the slightest rancour, George became calm and competent. He proceeded to analyse the marks with his customary pleasure in any kind of puzzle. Neither George nor I had been certain that I should need such a degree of detailed knowledge. 'Though', said George, 'I was under the impression that you had got hold of most of the classic cases. They didn't ask you much that was really out of the way. I imagined that you'd conquered most of this stuff months ago.'

It was too much of a temptation for George to resist saying tactfully: 'Of course, I realize there have been certain complications in your private life.'

'What's to be done?' I said.

'Your memory is first class,' said George. 'So you simply can't have read enough, that's all. We'd better invent a new reading programme for you. We'd better do it now.'

Without needing to look up a single authority, without asking me one question about the syllabus of the Bar examinations (which he had, of course, never taken himself) or what books I had already read, George drew up a working timetable for me for each week between that day and the date of the finals. 'Nine months to go,' said George with bellicose content, and wrote down the first week's schedule. He forgot nothing; the programme was well-ordered, feasible, allowed time for a fortnight's revision at the end, and then three days free from work. I preserved that sensible document, so neat and orderly, in George's tidy legal handwriting. It might have been the work of one of nature's burgesses.

But there were many days in the months ahead when George did not speak or act in the slightest respect like one of nature's burgesses; and that was the second trouble into which we were plunged. It seemed grave then. In retrospect it seemed more than grave, it seemed to mark the point where the curve of George's life began to dip. At this point, I need only say a few words about it. The upheaval in our circle began with Martineau. We had always known that he was restless and eccentric; but we expected him to continue his ordinary way of life, entertaining us on Friday nights, and safeguarding George's future in the firm. Suddenly he went through a kind of religious conversion. That autumn he relinquished his share in the practice. It was a few months later, early in 1927, that he completed his abnegation; then he sold all his remaining possessions, gave the money away, and at fifty-one began to wander round the country, begging his way, penniless and devout.

It was now left to Eden to decide whether George should ever become a partner. We all urged George at least to establish a *modus vivendi* with Eden. George, dogged by ill fortune and his own temperament, promptly performed a series of actions which made Eden, who already disliked him, rule him out of the running, not only then, but always. And so at twenty-seven George was condemned to be a managing clerk for the rest of his life. There were many consequences that none of us could have foreseen; a practical one was that George began to cooperate in Jack Cotery's business.

To me, that trouble was light, though, compared to a quarrel with Sheila – a quarrel which I said to myself must be the last. It came with blinding suddenness, after a summer in which most of our meetings had been happy, happier than any since the days of innocence a year before. We amused each other with the same kind of joke, youthful, reckless, and sarcastic. I had discovered that I could often coax and bully her out of her indrawn, icy temper. It was the serene hours that counted. I was not much worried when, in the early autumn, days followed each other when she sat abnormally still, her eyes fixed in a long-sighted stare, when if I took her hand it stayed immobile and I seemed to be kissing a dead cheek. I had been through it before, and that removed the warning. She would emerge. Meanwhile, she was not giving me any excuse for jealousy. For weeks she had not mentioned any other man. And, in those fits of painful stillness, she saw no one but me.

One day in September we had been walking in the country, and were resting on the grass beside the road. She had been quiet, wrapped deep in herself, all afternoon. Suddenly she announced:

'I'm going shooting.'

I laughed aloud, and asked her when and where. She said she was travelling to Scotland, the next week.

'I'm going shooting,' she repeated.

Again I laughed.

'What's funny about that?'

Her tone was sharp.

'It is funny,' I said.

'You'd better tell me why.'

Her tone was so sharp that I took her shoulders and began to shake her. But she broke loose and said:

'I suppose you mean that I only know these people because my father married for money. I suppose it is a wonderfully good joke that my mother was such a fool.'

With bewilderment I saw that she was crying. She was staring at me in enmity and hate. She turned aside, and dried the tears herself.

On the way back, I made one effort to tell her that nothing had been further from my mind. 'It doesn't matter,' she said, and we went along in silence. Intolerably slowly (and yet I could not bear to part), the miles went by. We came to the suburbs and walked in silence under the chestnut trees.

At the station entrance, she spoke.

'Don't see me off.' She added, as though she was forced to: 'I shall be away a month. I shan't write much. I'm too prickly. I'll tell you when I get back.'

In the days that followed, I was angry as well as wretched. It would be easy to cease to love her, I thought, making myself remember her cold inimical face. Then I cherished those unwilling words at the station. 'Prickly' – was she not trying to soften it for me, in the midst of her own bitterness? Why hadn't I made her speak? This was not a separation, I comforted myself, and wrote to her, as lightly as though that afternoon had not existed. As I wrote, I had the habitual glow, as if she must, through my scribble on the paper, be compelled at that moment to think of me. No answer came.

A fortnight after that walk in the country, I was strolling aimlessly through the market place. I was on edge, and sleeping badly; it was hard to steer myself through a day's work; I had come out that afternoon, hoping to freshen myself for another two hours later on. It was nearly teatime on a dark autumn day, with the clouds low, but bright and cosy in the streets, the shops already lighted. Smells poured out into the crowded streets, as the shop doors swung open – smells of bacon, ham, cheese, fruit – and, at the end of the market place, the aroma of roast coffee beans, which mastered them all, and for a moment dissolved all my anxiety and took me back to afternoons of childhood. In our less penurious days, before the bankruptcy, my mother used to take me shopping in the town, when I was a small child; and I smelt the coffee then, and watched the grinding machine in the window, and heard my mother assert that this was the only shop she could think of patronizing.

I watched the grinding machine again, sixteen years later (for I could not have been more than five when I accompanied my mother). I would have sworn that she had actually used the word 'patronizing'; and indeed it gave me a curious pleasure to think of her so – for few women could the word have been more apt, at that period, before she had been cast down.

At last I turned away. On the pavement, walking towards me, was Sheila. She was wearing a fur coat which made her look a matron, and her head was bent, staring at the ground, so that she had not seen me. At that instant it occurred to me we had never met by accident before.

I called her name, She looked up. Her face was cold and set.

'I didn't know you were back,' I said.

'I am,' said Sheila.

'You said you'd be away a month.'

'I changed my mind,' she said. She added fiercely: 'If you want to know, I hated it.'

'Why didn't you tell me?'

'I might have done in time.'

'I don't mean in time,' I said. 'You ought to have told me before today.'

'Try to remember this,' said Sheila. 'You don't own me. If I wanted you to own me, I should be glad to tell you everything. I don't want it.'

'You let me just run into you like this – ' I cried.

'I don't propose to send you word every time I come into the town,' she said. 'I'll let you know when I want to see you.'

'Will you have some tea?'

'No,' she said. 'I'm going home.'

We moved away from each other. I looked back, but not she.

That was all. That was the end, I thought.

I too was full of anger and hate, as I made my resolve that night. I could have stood jealousy, I could have stood her madnesses and cruelty, but this I could no longer stand. I had had too much. I strengthened myself by the pictures of her indrawn face, in which there was no regard for me. There were hours when I hoped that love itself had died.

I must cut her out of my heart, I thought. Jack was right; Jack had been right all along. I must cut her out of my heart; and I knew by instinct that, to do it, I must not see her again, speak to her, receive a word from her or write to her, even hear of her at second hand. That was my resolve; and this time, unlike Christmas Eve, I felt the wild satisfaction that I could carry it out.

I worked with a harsh gusto, staying in my attic when she might be in the town, going only to the reference library when there was no chance that we could meet. I took precautions to avoid her as elaborate as those I had once used to pin down each minute of her day. And then I wanted to distract myself. Jack was right. She had done me harm; she had left me lonely and unsure. I thought (as I had often done since that night in the café, as I had done after meetings where Sheila did not give an inch and I was humiliated) of the bait Jack had laid for me. I thought of Marion. Would she have me, if I went to her now?

I had wondered many times whether Jack was right about her too. Had she really been in love with me? I wanted it to be true. Just then, I was voracious for any kind of woman's love.

I believed that Marion had been fond of me. I believed that if I had wooed her, I could probably have persuaded her to love me. That was as far as I trusted Jack's propaganda. Yet now, unsure of myself, I wanted to meet Marion again. I had not seen her, except to wave to in the streets, for months. She was the most active of us, and it would have been right out of character for her to sit and mope. She had gone off and attached herself to the town's best amateur theatrical company. There she found a new circle: to my surprise, people spoke highly of her as a comic actress. I wished that we could be brought together again, without any contrivance of mine. I had, of course, a furtive, fugitive hope that Jack might not after all have been exaggerating, and that she would fall into my arms.

Strangely enough, it was through Martineau that I caught a glimpse of her at the theatre. It was a Friday night in November. Although we did not know it, Martineau was within a few days of renouncing his share in the firm, and we were to go to the house for only one more Friday night. Unconcerned, amiable, and light hearted, Martineau mentioned that *The Way of the World* was being acted the following week, and invited me to go with him to see it.

It was a singular choice of entertainment, I thought later, for a man who was on the point of trying to live like St Francis; but Martineau enjoyed every minute of it. He appeared in his wing collar, frock coat, and grey trousers, for, until he actually left the firm, he never relaxed in his dress. We sat near to the stage, and Martineau roared with laughter, more audibly than anyone in the house, at each bawdy joke. And he was particularly taken by Marion. She was playing Millamant, the biggest part she had had with this company, and she won the triumph of the evening. Her bright eyes flashed and cajoled and hinted; on the stage her clumsiness disappeared, she stood up straight, she had presence and a rakish air, and her voice lilted and allured. Despite her reputation, I had not expected anything like it. I felt very proud of her.

Martineau was captivated entirely.

'She's a stunner,' he said, using enthusiastically, as he often did, the slang of years ago. 'She's a perfect stunner.'

I told him that I knew her fairly well.

'Lucky old dog,' said Martineau. 'Lucky old dog, Lewis.' At the end of the play, Martineau was reluctant to leave the theatre. 'Lewis,' he said, 'what do you say to our paying respects to your young friend? Going round to the stage door, we used to call it.'

We had to wait, along with other friends of the cast, for the theatre was a makeshift one, and all the women dressed in one large room. At last we were allowed in. Marion was still shining in her greasepaint, surrounded by people praising her. She was lapping it up, from all quarters, both sexes, from anyone who had a word of praise, whatever its quality. She caught my eye, looked surprised, smiled, cried out 'Lewis, my dear', then turned to listen, her whole face open to receive applause, to a man who was telling her how wonderful she had been. The air was humming with endearments and congratulations. I took Martineau to Marion, and he added his share, and it was clear that she could not have enough of it.

A couple of young men were competing for her attention, but Martineau held her for a time. Apart from a smile of recognition, and a question upon how I liked the show, she had been too ecstatic in her triumph to come aside to me. She was glad I was there; but she was glad Martineau was there, she was glad everyone in the room was there; she was ready to embrace us all.

The company were holding a party, and we had to leave. Marion called goodbyes after Martineau, after me, after others who had been praising her.

Martineau and I went out into the cold night air.

'What a stunning girl,' said Martineau. 'I say, Lewis, your friend is something to write home about.'

I agreed. But I was lonely and dispirited. I wished I had not gone.

27

'I Believe In Joy'

ON winter afternoons, when I could not work any longer, I gazed from my attic window over the roofs. This time last year – the thoughts crept treacherously in – I might have been at tea with Sheila. Now the evening ahead was safe, quite safe. I was keeping my resolve. I had abstained from all the forbidden actions, in order to cut her out of my heart. Yet why – I could not help crying to myself – had she of all women the power to set me free?

I was not well that winter, and for days together slept badly and woke in a mysterious malaise. There was nothing I could be definite about, but I was worried, for the Bar Finals and the future, as I lay awake listening to the thudding of my heart. It was necessary, I knew, to take no notice. And I had to do my best to see that George was not too much damaged, now that Martineau had left the firm in November. Often, when I felt like lying in bed, I had to struggle through some work, and then drag myself off to an argument with George or Eden. There were other lives beside one's own; it was a discipline hard to learn, when one was young, ill, and empty with unrequited love.

Sometimes those discussions were a relief, simply because they took away from my loneliness. I had not the spirit to seek for Marion, away from her stage properties. That night at the theatre had been a misfire when I did not want another. It was out of loneliness that I returned to the group, for there I could find without effort the company of some young women. They welcomed me back. George began by saying: 'I take it that you're slightly reducing the extent of your other commitments.'

'It's over,' I said. I did not wish to speak of it.

'Thank God for that,' said George. 'I'm glad you've come to your senses.' And automatically, from that moment, George demoted Sheila in his speech. After being cloaked in euphemisms for a year, she was referred to once more as 'that damned countyfied bitch'.

Jack was listening, attentively and shrewdly. 'Good,' he said, but he looked troubled. I wondered if he noticed that, when I went out to the farm, I did not stir from the house for fear of the remote chance of meeting Sheila. I wondered too if he would pass any word to Marion.

With a considerateness that touched me, the Edens asked me to their Christmas Eve party, in my own right, asking me to bring a partner if I felt inclined. Eden went out of his way to drop the hint that they had 'rather lost touch with Sheila Knight'. I went alone. Just as last year, the drawing-room was redolent of rum and spice and orange; most of last year's party were there; all was safe, I listened to Eden, the fire blazed, Mrs Eden did not mention Sheila. In the early morning, when I left the house, it was colder than that last warm Christmas morning, and no car stood outside.

It was on a January morning, returning home from the reference library (I had changed my routine, so as never to be in the main shopping streets in the afternoon), that I found a telegram waiting at my lodgings. Before I opened it, I knew from whom it came. It read: YOU ONCE WANTED TO BORROW A BOOK FROM ME IT IS NOT A GOOD BOOK I SHALL BRING IT TO THE USUAL CAFÉ TOMORROW AT FOUR. It was signed SHEILA, and, luxuriating in the details, I noticed that it had been dispatched from her village that morning at nine-five. It gave me the pleasure of intimacy, silly and caressing, to think of her going to the post office straight after breakfast.

I made no struggle. I had two weapons to keep me out of danger – pain and pride. But I dismissed the pain, and thought only of my emptiness. As for pride, she had appeased that, for it was she who asked. I was infused by hope so sanguine that I felt the well-being pour through me to the fingertips. I watched motes dancing in the winter sunlight. Just as when I was first in love, it seemed that I had never seen things so fresh before.

The clock was striking four when I went through the café, past a pair of chess players already settled in for the evening, down to the last alcove. She was there, reading an evening paper, holding it as usual a long way from her eyes. She heard my footstep, and watched me as I sat down beside her.

She said: 'I've missed you.' She added: 'I've brought the book. You won't like it much.'

She set herself to talk as though there had been no interval. I was irritated, in one of those spells I had previously known. Was this she whose absence made each hour seem pointless? Yes, she was good-looking, but was that hard beauty really in my style? Yes, she was clever enough, but she had no stamina in anything she thought or did.

At the same instant I was chafing with impatience for reassurances and pledges. I did not want to listen to her, but to take her in my arms.

She saw that something was wrong. She frowned, and then tried to make me laugh. We exchanged jokes, and she worked at a curious awkward attempt to coax me. Once or twice the air was electric, but through my fault there were gaps of silence.

'When shall I see you again?' said Sheila, and we arranged a meeting.

I went away to drink with George, impatient with her, compelled by the habit of love to count the hours until I saw her next – but incredulous that I had not broken away. Perhaps it would have been like that, I thought, if our roles had been reversed and she had done the loving. There might have been many such teatimes. Perhaps it would have been better for us both. But when I drank with George there was no jubilation in my tone to betray that afternoon, even if he had been a more perceptive man.

By the first post of the day I was expecting her, I received a letter. My heart quickened, but as I read it I chuckled.

'I can't appear tomorrow afternoon', she wrote, 'because I have a shocking cold. I always get shocking colds. Come and see me, if you'd like to, and can face it. My mother will be out of the way, visiting the sick. If I were a parishioner, she would be visiting me, which would be the last straw.'

When I was shown into the drawing-room, I saw that Sheila was not exaggerating. She was sitting by the fire with her eyes moist, her lids swollen, her nostrils and upper lip all red; on the little table by her side were some books, an inhaler, and half a dozen handkerchiefs. She gave me a weak grin. 'I told you it was a shocking cold. Every cold I have is like this.' Her voice was unrecognisably low, as well as thick and muffled.

'You can laugh if you want to,' she said. 'I know it's comic.'

'I'm sorry, dear,' I said, 'but it is a bit comic.' I was feeling both affectionate and amused; she was so immaculate that this misadventure seemed like a practical joke.

'My father doesn't think so,' she said with another grin. 'He's terrified of catching anything. He refuses to see me. He stays in his study all day.'

We had tea, or rather I ate the food and Sheila thirstily drank several cups. She told the maid that she would not eat anything, and the maid reproached her: 'Feed a cold and starve a fever, Miss Sheila. You're hungrier than you think.'

'That's all you know,' Sheila retorted. In her mother's absence the maid and Sheila were on the most companionable terms.

While I was eating, Sheila watched me closely.

'You were cross with me the other day.'

'A little,' I said.

'Why?'

'It doesn't matter now.'

'I'm trying to behave,' she said. 'What have I done?'

'Nothing.' It was true. Not once had she been cruel, or indifferent, or dropped a hint to rouse my jealousy.

'Wasn't it a good idea to make it up?'

I smiled.

'Then what was the matter?'

I told her that I loved her totally, that no one could be more in love than I was, that no one could ever love her more. I had not seen her for three months and I had tried to forget her – three bitter months; then we met, and she expected me to talk amiably over the teacups as though nothing had happened.

Sheila blew her nose, wiped her eyes, and considered.

'If you want to kiss me now, you can,' she said. 'But I warn you, I don't really feel much like it.'

She pressed my hand. I laughed. Cold or no cold, her spirits were further from the earth than mine could ever be, and I could not resist her.

She was considering again.

'Come to a ball,' she said suddenly. She had been searching, I knew, for some way to make amends. With her odd streak of practicality, it had to be a tangible treat.

'I hate balls,' she said. 'But I'll go to this one if you'll take me.'

'This one' was a charity ball in the town; Mrs Knight was insisting that her husband and Sheila should go; it would annoy Mrs Knight considerably if I made up the party, Sheila said, getting a double-edged pleasure.

'My mother thinks you're a fortune hunter,' said Sheila with a smile. For a moment I was amused. But then I was seized by another thought, and felt ashamed and helpless.

'I can't come,' I said.

'Why can't you? You must come. I'm looking forward to it.'

I shook my head. 'I can't.'

'Why not?'

I was too much ashamed to prevaricate.

'Why not? It isn't because of Mother, is it? You never mind what people think.'

'No, it's not that,' I said.

'I believe my father doesn't dislike you. He dislikes nearly everyone.'

She unfolded a new handkerchief.

'I'm getting angry,' she said nasally, but she was still good-tempered. 'Why can't you come?'

'I haven't got the clothes,' I said.

Sheila sneezed several times and then gave a broad smile. 'Well!' she said. 'For you of all men to worry about that. I give up. I just don't understand it.'

Nor did I; it was years since I had been so preposterously ashamed.

'It has worried you, hasn't it?'

'I don't know why, but it has,' I confessed.

Sheila said, with acid gentleness:

'It's made me remember how young you are.'

Our eyes met. She was in some way moved. After a moment she said, in the same tone:

'Look. I want to go to this ball. They don't give me much money, but I can always get plenty. Let me give you a present. Let me buy you a suit.'

'I can't do that.'

'Are you too proud?'

'I suppose so,' I said.

She took my hand.

'If I'd made you happier', she said, 'and then asked if I could give you a present – would you still be too proud?'

'Perhaps not,' I said.

'Darling,' she said. It was rare for her to use the word. 'I can't be articulate like you when you let yourself go. But if I ask you to let me do it – because of what's happened between us?'

In a brand new dinner jacket, I arrived with the Knights at the charity ball. It was held in the large hall, close by the park, a few hundred yards away from where Martineau used to live. Perhaps that induced me at supper to tell the story of Martineau, so far as I then knew it; I had seen him leave the town on foot, with a knapsack on his back, only a few days before.

I told the story because someone had to talk. The supper tables were arranged in the corridors all round the main hall, and the meal was served before the dance began. As a party of four, we were not ideally chosen. Sheila was looking tired; she was boldly made up, much to her mother's indignation, but the powder did not hide the rings under her eyes, and the painted lips were held in her involuntary smile. She was strained in the presence of her parents, and some of her nervousness infected me, the more so as I was still not well. With her usual directness and simplicity, Mrs Knight resented my presence. She produced a list of young men who, in her view, would have been valuable additions – some of whom Sheila had been seeing in the last few months, though she had resisted the temptation to let fall their names. As for Mr Knight, he was miserable to be there at all, and he was not the man to conceal his misery.

He was miserable for several reasons. He refused to dance, and he hated others enjoying fun which he was not going to share. His wife and Sheila were active, strong women, who loved using their muscles (Sheila, once set on a dance floor, forgot she had not wanted to come, and danced for hours); Mr Knight was an excessively lazy man, who preferred sitting down. He also hated to be at any kind of disadvantage. In his own house, backed by everything Mrs Knight could buy for him, he was playing on his home ground. He did not like going out, where people might not recognize him or offer the flattery which sustained him.

I picked up an example right at the beginning of supper. Mrs Knight announced that the bishop had brought a party to the hall. Shouldn't they call on him during the evening? I could feel that she had not abandoned hope of getting her husband some preferment.

'Not unless he asks us, darling,' said Mr Knight faintly.

'You can't expect him to remember everyone,' said Mrs. Knight, with brisk common sense.

'He ought to have *remembered* me,' said Mr Knight. 'He *ought* to have.'

I guessed that conversation had been repeated often. She had always planned for him to go far in the Church; he was far more gifted than many who had climbed to the top. When she married him, she was prepared to find ways of getting all the bishops on the bench to meet him. But he would not do his share. As he grew older, he could not humble himself at all. He had too much arrogance, too much diffidence, to play the world's game. Later on, I ran across a good many men who had real gifts but who, in the worldly sense, were failures; and in most of them there was a trace of Mr Knight; like him, they were so arrogant and so diffident that they dared not try.

Mr Knight was miserable; Mrs Knight indignant; Sheila strained. We did not talk much for the first half of supper, and then, in desperation, I brought out the story of Martineau.

'He must be a crank,' said Mrs Knight as soon as I finished. 'Well, Mrs Knight,' I said, 'no one could call him an ordinary man.'

'Harry Eden', she decided, 'must be glad to see the back of him.'

'I don't think so,' I said. 'Mr Eden is devoted to him.'

'Harry Eden was always a loyal person,' said Mrs Knight.

Sheila broke in, clearly, as though she were thinking aloud: 'He'll enjoy himself!'

'Who will?' her mother asked obtusely.

'Your Martineau.' Sheila was looking at me. 'He'll enjoy every minute of it! It's not a sacrifice.'

'Of course', said Mr Knight, in his most beautifully modulated voice, 'many religions have sprung up from sources such as this. We must remember that there are hundreds of men like Martineau in every century, Those are the people who start false religions, but I admit that many of them have felt something true.' Mr Knight was theologically fair-minded; but his nose was out of joint. If anyone was to act as raconteur to that party, he should do so. He proceeded to tell a long story about the Oneida community. He told it with art, far better than I had told mine, and as we chuckled, he became less sulky. I thought (for I was irritated at not being allowed to shine in front of Sheila) that his story had every advantage, but that mine was at any rate first-hand.

After supper I danced with Sheila and Mrs Knight alternately. They had many acquaintances there, who kept coming up to claim Sheila. As I watched her round the hall, my jealous inquisitiveness flew back, like a detective summoned to an unpleasant duty: was this one with whom she had threatened me last year? But, when I danced with her, she did not mention any of her partners. Her father was behaving atrociously, she said with her usual ruthlessness. And she had to talk to all these other people; she wanted to be quiet with me. So, much of the night, we danced in a silence that to me was languorous.

It was far otherwise in my alternate dances. Mrs Knight disapproved of me, but she demanded her exercise, and dancing with her became vigorous and conversational. She took it heartily, for she had a real capacity for pleasure. I was an unsatisfactory young man, but I was better than no one to whirl her round. She got hot and merry, and as we passed her friends on the floor she greeted them in her loud horsy voice. And she surprised me by issuing instructions that I was to take care of myself.

'You're not looking so well as you did,' she said, in a brusque maternal stand-no-nonsense manner.

I explained that I had been working hard.

'You're not keeping fit. You're pale,' she said. 'How long is it to your exam?'

I knew that exactly. 'Ten weeks.'

'You mustn't crock up, you know.'

I knew that too. Yet, though I wished she was not Sheila's mother, I was coming to like her. And, dancing with her at that ball early in 1927, I had a curious thought. George and I and thoughtful persons round us used to predict that our lives were going to see violent changes in the world. At the ball, inside the Knights' house, those predictions seemed infinitely remote, a bubble no more real than others that George blew. Yet if they came true, if Mrs Knight lost all, lost servants and house and had to work with her hands and cook for her husband, I could imagine her doing it as heartily as she was dancing now. I should not like to be within the range of her indignation, but she would survive.

For one dance, both she and Sheila were taken off by others and I was left at our table with Mr Knight. Out of the corner of his eye, he must have noticed that my own glance was drawn time and again to follow Sheila. He was still bad-tempered at being ignored so much that night, and he did not intend to let me sit and dream. He required me as an audience and I had to listen to the main points of a letter that he thought of writing to *The Times*. Then, half-maliciously, he made me look at a dark-haired girl in a red dress, just dancing by our corner of the hall.

'I'm not certain of your standards, Eliot,' he said, 'but should you say that she was pretty?'

'Very,' I said.

'They live in my parish, but they don't attend. I'm afraid that she's broken a good many hearts.'

He was being deliberately oblique, I knew. He did not appear to be watching me, but he was making sure that I concentrated on the girl in the red dress.

'She ought to get married,' he said. 'She ought to get married. It's bad for anyone to break too many hearts. It shows there's something' – he paused – 'shall I say torn? inside their own.'

He was, of course, talking in code. That was the nearest he would come to mentioning Sheila. But he was so subtle and oblique that I could not be certain what he was telling me. Was he giving me a warning? Was he trying to share a worry, knowing that I loved her, feeling that I too was lost and concerned for what might happen to her? Was he, incredibly, encouraging me? Or was he just being malicious at my expense? I had no idea. In his serious moments, when he gave up acting, I never knew where I was with Mr Knight.

Soon after, Sheila said that she wanted some air. Instead of dancing, we walked outside the hall. There was nowhere to sit out, except in the colonnades which looked over the park. She took my arm, and we stood there. Couples were strolling behind us, though the March night was sharp. Right round the other side of the park, the tram-standards made a necklace of lights (we were looking in the direction that I walked, feet light with hope, the last Christmas Eve but one).

'Rather pretty,' said Sheila. Then she asked, unexpectedly: 'What does Martineau believe?'

I had to collect myself before I replied.

I said: 'I'm not sure that he knows himself. I think he'd say that the only way to live a Christian life was to live like Christ. But – '

'He's doing it because he wants to do it,' said Sheila. From the lights of the hall behind, I could see her face. She was lined, harassed, concentrated, and rapt. Her beauty was haggard; she was speaking with absolute certainty. 'All people are selfish, Though they make a better show of it than I do. He'll go about humbly helping his fellow men because it makes him feel good to do it.'

Looking into the dark stretches of the park, she said: 'What do you believe?'

I gripped her arm, but she said, in the same tone: 'I don't want to hear anything nice. What do you believe?'

I told her – and anything I said seemed flat after the rapt question – that I had no faith in any of the faiths. For me, there was something which took their place; I wanted to find some of the truths about human beings.

'Yes,' said Sheila. In a moment, she said: 'I believe in something.'

'What?'

She said: 'I believe in joy.'

We did not speak again before we returned to the Knights' table. The dance that we had left was not yet ended, and Mrs Knight looked gratified that we had come back so soon. Mr Knight reclined heavily in his chair, spreading himself in the company of his womenfolk. I had just heard an affirmation which sounded in my mind throughout Sheila's life and after, as clear, as thrilling, as vulnerable, and as full of hope, as when she stared over the park and spoke into the darkness. Yet that evening it vanished as quickly as a childhood dread. Just then it seemed only a remark, past and already half-forgotten, as, tired and subdued, she took her place by her father. Mr Knight's splendid voice rose, and we all listened to him.

28

Results of a Proposal

THERE were nights when it was a pleasure to lie awake. Outside, a train would rattle and roar over the bridge (I remembered, in the Zeppelin raids, my mother saying: 'The trains are our friends. When you can hear them, you feel that everything is going on all right.'). I had finished another textbook, and lay there, with a triumphant surge of mastery, because I knew it inside out; I would ask myself a question, answer it as though I were already in the examination hall, and then switch on the light to see if I had any detail wrong.

And, night after night, I did not want to sleep until I had re-cherished, like a collector going over his prints, each moment and each word of that absurd scene in the Knights' drawing-room, with Sheila snuffling her m's and n's, and saying 'I wadt you to cub to the ball.'

As I thought of her so, my prayers were cut in two, and my longings contradicted each other. On the one side, I begged: let me stay here, having known that comical delight, having known loving peace; let me stay cherishing it, for that afternoon was so delicate that it would perish at a touch. On the other, I wanted all, not just the tantalizing promise: I wanted to be sure of her, to fight my way Past the jealousies, to rely on such afternoons for the staple of my life, to risk any kind of pain until I had her for my own.

The first time we met after the ball, neither of us said a word that was not trivial. I was happy; it was an hour in a private world, in which

218

we lived inside a crystal shell, so fragile that either of us could speak and shatter it.

At our next meeting, she did speak. Although she was 'trying to behave', she had to let slip, for the first time since our reconciliation, that a new admirer was trying to rush her. After one dinner he was demanding some fixture for each day of the next week.

'Shall you go?'

'I shall go once,' Sheila said.

'Shall you go more than once?'

'It depends on how much I like him.' She was getting restive, and there was a harsh glint in her eyes.

There and then I knew I must settle it. I could not go on in this suspense. Even though, before we parted, Sheila said awkwardly: 'He's probably not a very useful young man.'

I must settle it, I thought. I decided how I must talk to her. We had arranged our next assignation in the usual place. I copied her action when she had her cold, and wrote to say that I was laid up. I could borrow some crockery from my landlady – would Sheila come and make some tea for me?

The March afternoon was cloudy; I turned the gas fire full on, and it snored away, brilliant in the dark room. I had tried to work, but gave it up, and was sitting on the bed, listening, for each footstep on the stairs.

At last I heard her. At last, but it was only a minute past the hour. The nerves at my elbows seemed stretched like piano strings. Sheila entered, statuesque in the light from the gas fire.

'You needn't have asked me to make tea,' she began without any preliminary. 'I should have done it without asking.'

We kissed. I hoped that she did not notice that my hands were shaking. She patted my shoulder.

'Well,' she said, 'what's the matter with you?'

'Nothing much,' I said. 'I'm a bit strung up, that's all.'

She switched on the light.

'I shall never have a bedside manner,' she said. 'Look, if you're worried, you ought to see poor Tom Devitt. He was a sensible doctor.'

I thought it was not meant to be cruel. In her innocence, that was over long ago.

'You rest,' she said. 'I'll make the tea. You needn't have asked me.'

She had brought some cakes, though she never ate them, some books, and, eccentrically, a tie. There was something random about her kindness: it was like a child trying to be kind. She was gay, putting the kettle on the gas ring, making tea, giving me my cup. She switched off the light again, and sat on the other side of the fire, upright on the hard chair. She talked on, light and friendly. The suspense was raging inside me. I answered absently, sometimes after a delay, sometimes not at all. She looked inquiringly:

'Are you all right?'

'Yes.'

I was quivering, so that I took hold of the bedrail.

She asked another question, about some book or person, which I did not hear. The blood was throbbing in my neck, and I could wait no longer.

'Sheila,' I said. 'Marry me.'

She gazed at me, and did not speak. The seconds spread themselves so that I could not tell how long a time had passed; I could hear the fire, whose noise was a roar in my ears, and my own heart.

'How ever would you manage', she asked, 'to keep us both?'

I had anticipated any response but that. I was so much astonished that I smiled. My hands were steadier, and for the first time that day I felt a respite.

'We might have to wait,' I said. 'Or I'd find a way.'

'I suppose you could. Yes, you've got plenty of resource.'

'But it's not important,' I cried. 'With you – '

'It might be important,' said Sheila. 'You never give me credit for any common sense.'

'It's not the point,' I said. 'And you know it's not.'

'Perhaps you're right,' she said, as though reluctantly.

'If you'll marry me,' I said, 'I'll find a way.'

'Do you mean it?'

'Do you think I'm playing?'

'No.' She was frowning. 'You know me better than anyone else does, don't you?'

'I hope so.'

'Yes, you do,' she said, 'That's why I came back. And you still want to marry me?'

'More than anything that I shall ever want.'

'Lewis, if I married you I should like to be a good wife. But I couldn't help it – I should injure you. I might injure you appallingly.'

'That is for me to face,' I said. 'I want you to marry me.'

'Oh,' she cried. She stood up, rested an elbow on the mantelpiece, arched her back, and warmed her calves in front of the fire. I watched the glow upon her stockings; she was silent, looking not at me but straight down the room. Then she spoke: 'If I marry, I shall hope to be in love.'

'Yes.'

'I'm not in love with you,' she said. 'You know that, and I've told you.' She was still not looking at me. 'I'm not in love with you,' she repeated. 'Sometimes I ask myself why I'm not. I ask myself what's the matter with me – or what's missing in me, if you like.'

A few times in my life, there came moments I could not escape. This was one. I could not escape the moment in which I heard her voice, high, violent, edged with regret and yet with no pity for herself or me.

In time, I asked: 'Must it always be so?'

'How do I know?' She shrugged her shoulders. 'You can answer that – maybe better than I can.'

'Tell me what you feel.'

'If you must hear,' she said, 'I think I shall never love you.' She added: 'You may as well hear the rest. I've been hoping I should love you – for a long time now. I'd rather love you than any of the others. I don't know why. You're not as nice as people think.'

At that, having heard the bitterest news of my young manhood, I burst out laughing, and pulled her down on to my knee to kiss her. That final piece of ruthless observation took away my recognition of what I had just heard; and suddenly she was glad to be caressed and to caress. For now she was radiant. Anyone watching us then, without having heard the conversation, would have guessed that she had just received a proposal she was avid to accept – or, more likely, that she was out to win someone of whom she was almost but not quite sure. She was attentive, sleek, and shining. She was anxious to stroke my face when I looked downcast. She wanted to rub away the lines until I appeared as radiant as she did. She was reproachful if, for a moment, I fell into silence. She made me lie on the bed, sat by me, and then went out to buy supper. About that we had what to all appearance was a mild, enjoyable lovers' quarrel. She proposed to fetch fish and chips: I told her that, despite her lack of snobbery, she was enough a child of the upper middle class to feel that the pastimes and diet of the poor were really glamorous. The romance of slumming, I said. You're all prostrating yourselves before the millions, I said. And I had a reasonable argument: I had to live in that room; her sense of smell was weak, but mine acute. She pouted, and I said that classical faces were not designed for pouting. We ended in an embrace, and I got my way.

She left late in the evening, so late that I wondered how she would get home. Wondering about her, suddenly I felt the lack of her physical presence in the room. Then – it came like a grip on the throat – I realized what had happened to me. The last few hours had been make-believe. She had spoken the truth. That was all.

It was no use going to bed. I sat unseeing, just where I sat while she answered my proposal. She had spoken with her own integrity. She was as much alone as I was – more, for she had none of the compensations that my surface nature gave me as I moved about the world. She had spoken out of loneliness, and out of her craving for joy. If my heart broke, it broke. If I could make her love me, well and good. It was *sauve qui peut*. In her ruthlessness, she had no space for the sentimentalities of compassion, or the comforting life. She could take the truth herself, and so must I.

Had I a chance? Would she ever love me? I heard her final voice – 'if you must hear' – and then I thought, why had she been so happy afterwards? Was it simply that she was triumphant at hearing a proposal? There was a trace of that. It brought back my mocking affection for her, which was strongest when I could see her as much chained to the earth as I was myself. She could behave, in fact, like an ordinary young woman of considerable attractions, and sit back to count her conquests. There was something predatory about her, and something vulgar. Yes, she had relished being proposed to. Yet, I believed, with a residue of hope, that did not explain the richness of her delight. She was happy because I had proposed to her. There was a bond between us, though on her side it was not the bond of love.

But that – I heard her final voice – was the only bond she craved.

I did not know how to endure it. Sitting on my bed, staring blindly at where she had stood, I thought what marriage with her would be like. It would only be liveable if she were subjugated by love. Otherwise she would tear my heart to pieces. Yet, my senses and my memories tore also at my heart, even my memories of that night, and I did not know how to endure losing her.

I did not know on what terms we could go on. I had played my last card, I had tried to cut my suspense, and I had only increased it. Would she sustain the loving make-believe of the last few hours? If she did not, I could not stand jealousy again. I was not strong enough to endure the same torments, with no light at the end. Now it rested in her hands.

I had not long to wait. The first time we met after my proposal, she was gay and airy, and I could not match her spirits. The second time, she told me, quite casually, that she had visited the town the day before.

'Why didn't you let me know?' The cry forced itself out.

She frowned, and said: 'I thought we'd cleared the air.'

'Not in that way.'

She said: 'I thought now we knew where we stood.'

I had no intention then. But, unknown to me, one was forming.

Three days later, we met again, in the usual alcove in the usual café. She had come from her hairdresser's, and looked immaculately beautiful. I thought, with resentment, with passion, that I had seen her dishevelled in my arms. Through tea we kept up a busy conversation. She made some sarcastic jokes, to which I replied in kind. She said that she was going to a dance. I did not say a word, but went back to the previous conversations. We were talking about books, as though we were high-spirited, literary-minded students, who had met by accident.

She went on trying to reach me – but she knew that I was not there. Her face had taken on an expression of puzzled, almost humorous distress. Her eyes were quizzically narrowed.

She asked the time, and I told her five o'clock.

'I've got lots of time. I needn't go home for hours,' she said.

I did not speak.

'What shall we do?' she persisted.

'Anything you like,' I said, indifferently.

'That's useless.' She looked angry now.

Automatically I said, as I used to: 'Come to my room.'

'Yes,' said Sheila, and began powdering her face.

Then my intention, which up to then I had not known, broke out.

'No,' I said. 'I can't bear it.'

'What?' She looked up from her mirror.

'Sheila,' I said, 'I am going to send you away.'

'Why?' she cried.

'You ought to know.'

She was gazing at me, steadily, frankly, unrelentingly. She said: 'If you send me away now, I shall go.'

'That's what I want.'

'Once I shouldn't have. I should have come back and apologized. I shan't do that now, if you get rid of me.'

'I don't expect you to,' I said.

'If I do go, I shall keep away. I shall take it that you don't want to see me. This time I shan't move a single step.'

'That's all I ask,' I replied.

'Are you sure? Are you sure?'

'Yes,' I said. 'I am sure.'

Without another word, Sheila pulled on her coat. We walked through the smoky café. I noticed our reflections in a steam-filmed mirror. We were both white.

At the door we said the bare word, goodbye. It was raining hard, and she ran for a taxi. I saw her go.

29

Second Meeting With a Doctor

ONE day, between my proposal to Sheila and our parting, I met Marion. I was refreshed to see her. I found time to speculate whether Jack had, in fact, slipped in a word. She was much more certain of herself than she used to be. Of us all, owing to her acting, she had become most of a figure in the town. She threw her head back and laughed, confidently and with a rich lilt. I had no doubt that she had found admirers, and perhaps a lover. Her old earnestness had vanished, though she would always stay the least cynical of women.

With me she was friendly, irritated, protective. Like many others at that time, like Mrs Knight at the ball, she noticed at once that I was looking physically strained. It was easy to perceive, for I had a face on which wear and tear painted itself. The lines, as with Sheila, were etching themselves while I was young.

Marion was perturbed and cross.

'We've got to deliver you in London on the –' It was like her to have remembered the exact date of Bar Finals. 'We don't want to send you there on a stretcher, Lewis.'

She scolded George.

'You mustn't let him drink,' she said. 'Really, you're like a lot of children. I think I'm the only grown-up person among the lot of you.'

Against my will, she made me promise that, if I did not feel better, I would go to a doctor.

I was afraid to go. Partly I had the apprehension of any young man who does not know much of his physical make-up. There might be something bad to learn, and I was frightened of it.

But also I had a short-term fear, a gambler's fear. Come what may, I could not stop working. It was imperative to drive myself on until the examination. Nothing should stop that; a doctor might try to. After the examination I could afford to drop, not now.

I parted from Sheila on a Friday afternoon. The next morning, as I got out of bed, I reeled with giddiness. The room turned and heaved; I shut my eyes and clutched the mantelpiece. The fit seemed to last, wheeling the room round outside my closed eyelids, for minutes. I sat back on the bed, frightened and shaken. What in God's name was this? Nevertheless, I got through my day's quota of reading. If I broke the programme now, I was defeated. I felt well enough to remember what I worked at. But the next morning I had another attack, and for two days afterwards, usually in the morning, once at night.

I was afraid: and above all I was savagely angry. It would be intolerable to be cheated at this stage. Despite Sheila, despite all that had happened to me, I had got myself well-prepared. That I knew. It was something I had to know; I should suffer too much if I deceived myself this time. George was speaking not with his cosmic optimism, but as a technical expert, when he encouraged me. Recently I had asked him the chances. George did not think naturally in terms of odds, but I pressed him. What was the betting on my coming out high in the first class? In the end, George had answered that he thought the chances were better than even.

It would be bitter beyond bearing to be cheated now. My mind was black with rage. But I was also ignorant and frightened. I had no idea what these fits meant. My fortitude had cracked. I had to turn to someone for help.

I thought of calling on old Dr Francis – but, almost involuntarily one evening, after struggling through another day's work, I began walking down the hill to the infirmary. I was going to ask for Tom Devitt. The infirmary was very near, I told myself, I should get it over quicker; Tom was a modern doctor, and the old man's knowledge must have become obsolete; but those were excuses. She had spoken of him the afternoon that I proposed, and I went to him because of that.

At the infirmary I explained to a nurse that I was an acquaintance of Devitt's, and would like to see him in private. She said, suspiciously, formidably, that the doctor was busy. At last I coerced her into telephoning him. She gave him my name. With a bad grace she told me that he was free at once.

I was taken to his private sitting-room. It overlooked the garden, from which, in the April sunshine, patients were being wheeled. Devitt looked at me with a sharp, open, apprehensive stare. He greeted me with a question in his voice. I was sure that he expected some dramatic news of Sheila.

'I'm here under false pretences,' I had to say. 'I'm presuming on your good nature – because we met once. I'm not well, and I wondered if you'd look me over.'

Devitt's expression showed disappointment, relief, a little anger.

'You ought to have arranged an appointment,' he said irritably. But he was a kind man, and he could no more forget my name than I could his.

'I'm supposed to be off duty,' he said. 'Oh well, You'd better sit down and tell me about yourself.'

We had met just the once. Now I saw him again, either my first impression had been gilded, or else he had aged and softened in between. He was very bald, his cheeks were flabby and his neck thickening. His eyes wore the kind of fixed, lost look that I had noticed in men who, designed for a happy, relaxed, comfortable life, had run into ill luck and given up the game. I should not have been surprised to hear that Devitt could not bear an hour alone, and went each night for comfort to his club.

There was also a certain grumbling quality which overlaid his kindness. He was much more a tired, querulous, professional man than I had imagined. But he was, I felt, genuinely kind. In addition, he was businesslike and competent, and, as I discovered when I finished telling him my medical history, had an edge to his tongue.

'Well,' said Tom Devitt, 'how many diseases do you think you've got?'

I smiled. I had not expected such a sharp question.

'I expect you must have diagnosed TB for yourself. It's a romantic disease of the young, isn't it – '

He sounded my lungs, said: 'Nothing there. They can X-ray you to make sure, but I should be surprised.' Then he set to work. He listened to my heart, took a sample of blood, went through a whole clinical routine. I was sent into the hospital to be photographed. When I came back to his room Devitt gave me a cigarette. He seemed to be choosing his words before he began to speak.

'Well, old chap,' he said, 'I don't think there's anything organically wrong with you. You've got a very slight mitral murmur – ' He explained what it was, said that he had one himself and that it meant he had to pay an extra percentage on his insurance premium. 'You needn't get alarmed about that. You've got a certain degree of anaemia. That's all I can find. I shall be very annoyed if the X-rays tell us anything more. So the general picture isn't too bad, you know.'

I felt great comfort.

'But still,' went on Tom Devitt, 'it doesn't seem to account for the fact that you're obviously pretty shaky. You are extremely run down, of course. I'm not sure that I oughtn't to tell you that you're dangerously run down.' He looked at me, simply and directly: 'I suppose you've been having a great deal of worry?'

'A great deal,' I said.

'You ought to get rid of it, you know. You need at least six months doing absolutely nothing, and feeding as well as you can – you're definitely undernourished – and without a worry in your head.'

'Instead of which,' I said, 'in a month's time I take the most important examination of my career.'

'I should advise you not to.'

At that point I had to take him into my confidence. I was not ready to discuss Sheila, even though he desired it and gave me an opening.

'Some men can have their health break down – through something like a broken engagement,' said Tom Devitt naïvely.

'I can believe that,' I said, and left it there. But I was quite open about my circumstances, how I was placed for money, what this examination meant. For every reason I had to take it this year. If my health let me down, I had lost.

'Yes,' said Devitt. 'Yes. I see.' He seemed taken aback, discomfited.

'Well,' he added, 'it's a pity, but I don't think there's a way out. I agree, you must try to keep going. Good luck to you, that's all I can say. Perhaps we can help you just a bit. I should think the most important thing is to see that you manage to sleep.'

I smiled to myself; on our only other meeting, he had been concerned whether I got enough sleep. He gave me a couple of prescriptions, and then, before I went, a lecture.

He told me, in an uncomfortable, grumbling fashion, that I was taking risks with my health; I was probably not unhealthy, but I was liable to over-respond; I was sympathetotonic; I might live to be eighty if I took care of myself. 'It's no use telling you to take care of yourself,' said Tom Devitt. 'I know that. You'll be lucky if you have a comfortable life physically, old chap.'

I thanked him. I was feeling both grateful and relieved, and I wanted him to have a drink with me. He hesitated. 'No. Not now,' he said. Then he clapped me on the shoulder. 'I'm very glad you came. I hope you pull it off. It would be nice to have been some good to you.'

I rejoiced that thought, and, though I had another bout of giddiness next day, I felt much better. Perhaps because of Devitt's reassurance, the bouts themselves seemed to become less frequent. I read and wrote with the most complete attention that I could screw out of myself. I was confident now that I should last the course.

On the Saturday I travelled out to the farm later than the rest, because I could not spare the afternoon. I had not said much to George about my health. To the little I told him, he was formally sympathetic; but in his heart he thought it all inexplicable and somewhat effeminate.

I was so much heartened that I needed to tell someone the truth, and as soon as I saw Marion among the group I took her aside and asked her to come for a walk. We struck across the fields – in defiance. I headed in the direction of the vicarage – and I remarked that I had kept my promise and gone to a doctor. Then I confessed about my symptoms, and what Devitt had said.

'I'm very much relieved, I really am,' cried Marion, 'Now you must show some sense.'

'I shall arrive at this examination,' I said. 'That's the main thing.'

'That's one thing. But you mustn't think you can get away with it for ever.' She nagged me as no one else would have done: I was too wilful, I tried to ride over my illnesses, I was incorrigibly careless of myself.

'Anyone else would have gone to a doctor months ago,' she said. 'That would have spared you a lot of worry – and some of your friends too, I may say. I'm very glad I made you go.'

I could hear those I's, a little stressed, assertive in the middle of her yearning to heal and soothe and cherish. In all tenderness such as hers, there was the grasp of an ego beneath the balm. I had never romanticised Marion. People said she was good, full of loving-kindness, so free from sentimentality in her unselfish actions that one took from her what one could not from another. Much of that was true. Some of us had generous impulses, but she carried hers out. She never paraded her virtues, nor sacrificed herself unduly. If she enjoyed acting, then she spent her time at it, took and revelled in the applause. She was no hypocrite, and of all of us she did most practical good. And so Jack Cotery and the rest admired her more than any of our friends.

I was very fond of her, and flattered because she was fond of me. Yet I knew that in a sense she was vainer than Sheila, more grasping than myself. I think I liked her more because she needed applause for her tender actions. In my eyes, she was warm, tenacious, tough in her appetite for life, and deep down surprisingly self-centred. It was her lively, self-centred strength that I drew most refreshment from; that and her feeling for me. There was no war inside her, her body and soul were fused and would in the end find fulfilment and happiness. As a result, her company often brought me peace.

She brought me peace that evening (in the lanes I had once walked wet through) in a cool twilight when, behind the lacework of the trees, the sky shone a translucent apple-green. There I confided to her, far more than I had to anyone, of what had happened between me and Sheila. I was too secretive to reveal the depth of my ecstasy, torments, and hope; some of it I wrapped up in mockery and sarcasm; but I gave her a history which, so far as it went, was true. She received it with an interest that was affectionate, greedy, and matter-of-fact. Perversely, so it seemed to me, she did not regard Sheila's behaviour as particularly out of the ordinary. She domesticated it with a curious, quasi-physical freemasonry, as though she or any other woman might have done the same. She did not consider Sheila either excessively beautiful or strange, just a young woman who was 'not quite certain what she wanted'. Marion's concern was directly for me, 'Yes, it was a pity you ran across her,' she said. 'Mind you, I expect you puzzled her as much as she did you – that is, if I know anything about you.'

I was wondering.

'Still, it's better for you that it's over. I'm glad.'

We had turned towards home. The green of the sky was darkening to purple.

'So you sent her away?' she said.

'Yes, I sent her away.'

'I don't expect she liked that. But I believe it was right for you.'

In the half-dark I put my arm round her waist. She leaned back, warm and solid, against me. Then, with a recoil of energy, she sprang away.

'No, my lad. Not yet. Not yet.' She was laughing.

I protested.

'Oh no,' said Marion. 'I've got something to say first. Are you free of Sheila?'

'Yes,' I said. 'I've told you. I've parted from her.'

'That's not the same,' said Marion. 'My dear, I'm serious. You ought to know I'm not a capricious girl. And', she said, firmly, confidently, reproachfully, 'you must think of me for once. I've given you no reason to treat me badly.'

'Less than anyone,' I said.

'So I want you to be honest. Answer my question again. Are you free of Sheila?'

The first stars were coming out. I saw Marion's eyes, bright, not sad but vigilant.

I wanted to know her love. But she forced me not to lie. I thought of how I had gone, as though hypnotized, to Tom Devitt, because his life was linked to Sheila's; I thought of my memories, and of waking at nights from dreams that taunted me. I said:

'Perhaps not quite. But I shall be soon.'

'That's honest, anyway,' Marion said, with anger in her voice. Then she laughed again. 'Don't be too long. Then take me out. I'm not risking you on the rebound.'

Decorously, she slipped an arm through mine.

'We're going to be late for supper, my lad. Let's move. We'll talk of something sensible – like your exam.'

In the late spring, in April and early May, even the harsh red brick of the town seemed softened, The chestnuts flowered along the road to Eden's house, the lilacs in the gardens outside Martineau's. I was near the end of my reading, George's calculations had not been fallible, and I had only two more authorities to master. In the mild spring days I used to take my books to the park, and work there.

But there were times when, sitting on a bench with my notebook, I was distracted. On the breeze, the odour of the blossoms reached me; I ached with longing; I was full of restlessness, of an unnamed hope. Those were the days when I went into the town in the afternoon; I looked into shop windows, stood in bookshops, went up and down the streets, searched among the faces in the crowd; I never visited our usual café, for she did not go there alone, but I had tea in turn in all those where I had known her meet her mother. I did not see her, neither there, nor at the station (I remembered her trains as I did my last page of notes). Was it just chance? Was she deliberately staying at home? Was she helping me to see her no more? I told myself that it was better. In the spring sunshine, I told myself that it was better.

On the day before I left for London and the examination, George, to whom formal occasions were sacred, had insisted that there must be a drinking party to wish me success. I had to go, it would have wounded George not to; but I, more superstitious and less formal, did not like celebrations before an event. So I was grateful when Marion gave me an excuse to cut the party short.

'I'll cook you a meal first,' she said. 'I'd like to be certain that you have one square meal before your first paper.'

I ate supper in her lodgings before I joined George at our public house. Marion was an excellent cook in the hearty English country style, the style of the small farmers and poor-to-middling yeomen stock from which she came. She gave me roast beef and Yorkshire pudding, an apple pie with cheese, a great Welsh rarebit. Eating as I did in snacks and pieces, being at my landlady's mercy for breakfast, and having to count the pennies even for my snacks, I had not tasted such a meal for long enough.

'Lewis,' said Marion, 'you're hungry.' She added: 'I'm glad I thought of it. Cooking's a bore, whatever anyone tells you, so I nearly didn't. Shall I tell you why I decided to feed you?'

Comfortably, I nodded my head.

'It's just laying a bait for large returns to come. When you're getting rich and successful, I shall come to London and expect the best dinners that money can buy.'

'You shall have them.' I was touched: this meal had been her method of encouraging me, practical, energetic, half-humorous.

'You see, Lewis, I think you're a pretty good bet.' Soon after, she said: 'You've not told me. Have you seen Sheila again?'

'No.'

'How much have you thought about her?'

I wished that she would not disturb the well-being in the room. Again I had to force myself to answer truly.

I said: 'Now and then – I see ghosts.'

She frowned and laughed.

234

'You are tiresome, aren't you? No, I mustn't be cross with you. I asked for it.' Her eyes were flashing. 'Go and polish off this exam. Then you must have a holiday. And then – ghosts don't live for ever.'

She smiled luxuriously, as though the smile spread over her whole skin.

'I'm afraid', she said, 'that I was meant to be moist and jealous and adoring.'

I smiled back. It was not an invitation at that moment. We sat and smoked in silence, in a thunderous comfort, until it was time for my parting drink with George.

30

The Examination

JUST as George, on the subject of how to prepare for an examination, advised me as though he were one of nature's burgesses, so I behaved like one. I went to London two days before the first paper; I obeyed the maxims that were impressed upon all students, and I slammed the last notebook shut with a night and a day to spare. Slammed it so that I could hear the noise in the poky, varnish-smelling bedroom at Mrs Reed's. Now I was ready. One way or the other, I thought, challenging the luck, I should not have to stay in that house again.

I spent a whole day at the Oval, with all my worries shut away but one. I did not think about the papers, but I was anxious lest, at the last moment, I might be knocked out by another turn of sickness. I had been feeling better in the past weeks, and I was well enough as I lolled on the benches for a day, and as I meandered back to Judd Street in the evening. I walked part of the way, over Vauxhall Bridge and along the river, slowly and with an illusion of calm. I stopped to gaze at a mirage-like sight of St Paul's and the city roofs mounted above the evening mist. Confidence seeped through me in the calm – except that, even now, I might be ill.

I slept that night, but I slept lightly. I had half woken many times, and it was early when I knew that it was impossible to sleep longer. I looked at the watch I had borrowed for the examination: it was not yet half past six. This was the day. I lay in bed, having wakened with the fear of the night before. Should I get up and test it? If I were going to be wrecked by giddiness that day, I might as well know now. Carefully I rose, trying not to move my head. I took three steps to the window, and threw up the blind, In streamed the morning sunlight. I was steady enough. Recklessly, I exclaimed aloud. I was steady enough.

I did not return to bed, but read until breakfast time, a novel I had borrowed from Marion; and at breakfast I was not put off either by Mrs Reed's abominable food or the threat of her abominable postcards. 'I've got one ready for you to take away,' she told me, with her ferocious *bonhomie*. 'I'll send you a bouquet,' I said jauntily, for the only way to cope with her was not to give an inch. I sometimes wondered if she had a nerve in her body; if she knew young men were nervous at examinations; if she had ever been nervous herself, and how she had borne it.

In good time, I caught a bus down to the Strand. Russell Square and Southampton Row and Kingsway shimmered in the clean morning light. My breath caught, in something between anticipation and fear, between pleasure and pain. Streams of people were crossing the streets towards their offices; the women were wearing summer dresses, for the sky was cloudless, there were all the signs of a lovely day.

The examination was to be held in the dining hall of an Inn. I was one of the first to arrive outside the doors, although there was already a small knot of candidates, mainly Indians. There I waited by myself, watching a gardener cut the lawn, smelling the new-mown grass. Now the nervousness was needle-sharp. I could not resist stealing glances at my watch, though it was only two minutes since I had last looked. A quarter of an hour to go. It was intolerably long, it was a no man's land of time, neither mine nor inimical fate's. Charles March came up with a couple of acquaintances, discussing, in his carrying voice, in his first-hand, candid, concentrated fashion, why he should be 'in a state' before an examination which mattered nothing and which even he, despite his idleness, presumably would manage to scrape through. I smiled. Later I explained to him why I smiled. As the doors creaked open, he wished me good luck.

I said: 'I shall need it.'

The odour of the hall struck me as I went quickly in. It made my heart jump in this intense expectancy, in this final moment. I found my place, at the end of a gangway. The question paper rested, white, shining, undisturbed, in the middle of the desk. I was reading it, tearing my way through it, before others had sat down.

At first I felt I had never seen these words before. It was like opening an innings, when one is conscious of the paint on the crease, of the bowler rubbing the ball, as though it were all unprecedented, happening for the first time. The rubrics to the questions themselves seemed sinister in their unfamiliarity: 'Give reasons why…', 'Justify the opinion that…' Although I had read such formulas in each examination paper for years past, the words stared out, dazzling, black on the white sheet, as if they were shapes unknown.

That horror, that blank in my faculties, lasted only a moment. I wiped the sweat from my temples; it seemed that a switch had been touched. The first question might have been designed for me, if George had been setting the paper. I read on. I had been lucky – astonishingly lucky I thought later, but in the hall I was simply filled by a throbbing, combative zest. There was no question I could not touch. It was a paper without options, and eight out of ten I had waiting in my head, ready to be set down. The other two I should have to dig back for and contrive.

I took off my wristwatch and put it at the top of the desk, within sight as I wrote. I had at my fingers' end the devices which made an answer easy to read. My memory was working with something like the precision of George's. I had a trick, when going so fast, of leaving out occasional words: I must leave five minutes, prosaically I reminded myself, to read over what I had written. Several times, as though I had a photograph in front of me, I remembered in visual detail, in the position they occupied in a textbook, some lines that I had studied. In they went to my answer, with a little lead-up and gloss. I was hot, I had scarcely lifted my eyes, obscurely I knew that Charles March was farther up the hall, on the other side of the gangway. This was the chance to try everything I possessed: and I gloried in it.

The luck remained with me throughout. Of all the past papers I had worked over, none had suited me as well as the set this year. Nearly all the specialized knowledge I had acquired from George came in useful (not the academic law he had taught me, but the actual cases that went through a provincial solicitor's hands). On the afternoon of the first day I was half-incredulous when I saw my opportunities. Then I forgot everything, fatigue, the beating of my heart, the sweat on my face, as for three hours I made the most of them.

I was jubilant that first night. Jubilant but still guarded and in training, telling myself that it was too early to shout. In the warm May evening, though, I walked at leisure down Park Lane and through the great squares. Some of the houses were brilliant with lights, and through the open doors I saw staircases curving down to the wide halls. Cars drove up, and women swept past me on the pavement into those halls, leaving their perfume on the hot still air. In my youth, in my covetousness and pride and excitement, I thought that my time would come and that I too should entertain in such a house.

The last afternoon arrived, and the last paper. The spell had not broken. It suited me as well as the first. Except that by now I was tired, I had spun out my energies so that I was near the end of my tether. I wrote on, noticing my tiredness not much more than the extreme heat. But my timing was less automatic; I had finished the paper, read it through, and still had five minutes to spare.

Ah well, I was thinking, it has been pretty good. Each paper up to the standard of the first, and one distinctly better. One better than I could have hoped. Then the room went round, sickeningly round, and I clutched the desk. It was not a long attack; when I opened my eyes, the hall stood hazily there. I smiled to myself, a little uneasily. That was too close a call to relish.

I was still sick and giddy as Charles March came down the aisle; but he joined me, we left the hall together, and after the civilities of inquiring about each other's performances we went to get some tea. I was glad of the chance. I had often wished to talk to him alone. We sat in a tea shop and did post mortems on the papers.

He was an active, rangily built young man with hair as fair as mine and excessively intelligent, inquiring eyes. At a glance, one could tell that he was a man of force and brains. He was also argumentative, which was in George's style rather than mine, and had a talent for telling one home truths with the greatest possible edge. But he was capable of a most concentrated sympathy. Somehow he had divined that this examination was of cardinal importance to me. That afternoon at tea, seeing me delighted with what I had done, yet still strained and limp, he asked me to tell him. Why did it matter seriously? I had obviously done far better than he had, or than any sane person would consider necessary. Why did it matter? Did I feel like telling him?

Yes, I felt like it. In the clammy tea shop, with the papers spread on the table, I explained my position, under Charles March's keen, hard, and appreciative eyes. It was out of my hands now, and I talked realistically and recklessly, frankly and with bravado. Until the result came out, I should have no idea what was to become of me.

'Yes,' said Charles March. 'It's too much to invest in one chance. Of course it is. You've done pretty well, of course.' He pointed to the papers. 'Whether you've done well enough – I don't see that anyone can say.'

He was understanding. He knew that I could not have stood extravagant rosy prophecies just then.

Charles had refrained from any kind of roseate encouragement; and he was right, for I could not have received it. Yet, in the theatre that night, listening to the orchestra, I was all of a sudden carried on a wave of joy, certain that all I wanted was not a phantom in the future but already in my hands. I was not musical, but in the melody I possessed all I craved for. A name was mine; I was transferred from an unknown, struggling, apprehensive young man; a name was mine. Riches were mine; all the jewels of the imagination glittered for me, the houses, the Mediterranean, Venice, all I had pictured in my attic, looking down to the red brick houses and the slate; I was one of the lords of this world.

Yes, and love was mine. In the music, I remembered the serene hours with Sheila, her beautiful face, her sarcastic humour, the times when her spirit made mine lighter than a mortal's, the circle of her arms round me and her skin close to.

I had not to struggle for her love. It was mine. I had the certainty of never-ending bliss. As I listened to the music, her love was mine.

31

Triumph and Surrender

WHEN I returned to the town I had four weeks to wait for the result. And I hid from everyone I knew. I paid my duty call on George, to show him the papers and be cross-questioned about my answers: he, less perceptive than Charles March, shouted in all his insatiable optimism that I must have done superbly well. Then I hid, to get out of sight, out of reach of any question.

I was half-tempted to visit Marion. But our understanding was clear – and also, and this kept me away for certain, I was not fit to be watched by affectionate, shrewd eyes. I did not want to be seen by anyone who knew me at all, much less one who, like my mother, would claim the right of affection to know me well. Just as I had never shared my troubles with my mother, so I could not share this suspense now.

Could I have shared it with Sheila, I thought once? I could have talked to her; yet such troubles were so foreign to her, so earth-bound beside her own, that she would not touch them.

Since the night at the theatre, she had been constantly present in my mind. Not in the forefront, not like the shadow of the result. I was not harassed about her. Even with my days quite empty, I never once walked the streets where I might meet her, and in my prowls at night I was not looking for her face. Underneath, maybe, I knew what was to come, what my next act must be.

Yet, one evening in June, my first thought was of her when my landlady bawled up the stairs that a telegram had arrived. I had only received one telegram in my life, and that from Sheila. The examination result, I assumed, would come by the morning post. I ran down, ripped the telegram open just inside the front door. It was not from Sheila, but the blood rushed to my face. I read: CONGRATULATIONS AND HOMAGE STUDENTSHIP PRIZE ACCORDING TO PLAN SEE YOU SOON MARCH.

I threw it in the air and hugged my landlady.

'Here it is,' I cried.

I only half realized that the waiting was over – just as I had only half realized it when my mother proclaimed the news of my first examination, that solitary piece of good news in her hopeful life. I was practising the gestures of triumph before I felt it. On my way to George's, telegram in hand, I was still stupefied. Not so George. 'Naturally,' he called out in a tremendous voice. 'Naturally you've defeated the sunkets. This calls for a celebration.'

It got it. George and I called on our friends and we packed into the lounge of the Victoria. George was soon fierce with drink. 'Drink up! Drink up!' he cried, like an angry lion, to astonished salesmen who were sitting quietly over their evening pint. 'Can you comprehend that this is the climacteric of our society?' That extraordinary phrase kept recurring through the mists of drink, the faces, the speeches and the songs. Drunkenly, happily, I impressed upon a commercial traveller and his woman friend how essential it was to do not only well, but competitively and superlatively well, in certain professional examinations. I had known, I said in an ominous tone, many good men ruined through the lack of this precaution. I was so grave that they listened to me, and the traveller added his contribution upon the general increase in educational standards.

'Toasts,' cried George, in furious cheerfulness, and at the end of each threw his glass into the fireplace. The barmaids clacked and threatened, but we had been customers for years, we were the youngest of their regulars, they had a soft spot for us, and finally

George, with formidable logic, demonstrated to them that this was, and nothing else could possibly be, the climacteric of our society.

It went on late. At midnight there was a crowd of us shouting in the empty streets. It was the last of my student nights in the town. George and I walked between the tramlines up to the park, with an occasional lorry hooting at us as it passed. There, in the middle of the road, I expressed my eternal debt to George. 'I take some credit,' said George magnificently. 'Yes, I take some credit.'

I watched him walk away between the tramlines, massive under the arc lights, setting down his feet heavily, carefully, and yet still with a precarious steadiness, whistling and swinging his stick.

All the congratulations poured in except the one I wanted. There was no letter from Sheila. Yet, though that made me sad, I knew with perfect certainty what I was going to do.

I went to London to arrange my new existence. I arranged my interview with Herbert Getliffe, whose Chambers I was entering, on Eden's advice; I found a couple of rooms in Conway Street, near the Tottenham Court Road. The rooms were only a little less bleak than my attic, for I was still cripplingly short of money, and might be so for years.

In something of the same spirit in which I had abandoned Aunt Milly's and spent money living on my own, I treated myself to a week in a South Kensington hotel. Then, since it was the long vacation, I should return to the attic for my last weeks in the town – and in October I was ready for another test of frugality in Conway Street. But in this visit, when I was arranging the new life, I deserted Mrs Reed's and indulged myself in comfort – just to prove that I was not frightened, that I was not always touching wood.

It was from that hotel that I wrote to Sheila, asking her to meet me.

I wrote to Sheila. Since the examination I had known that if she did not break the silence, I should. Despite the rebellion of my pride. Despite Jack Cotery's cautionary voice, saying: 'Why must you fall in love with someone who can only make you miserable? She'll do you harm. She can only do you harm.' Despite my sense of self-preservation. Despite any part of me that was sensible and controlled.

Prom within myself and without, I was told the consequences. Yet, as I took a sheet of the hotel notepaper and began to write, I felt as though I were coming home.

It was surrender to her, unconditional surrender. I had sent her away, and now I was crawling back. She would be certain in the future that I could not live without her. She would have nothing to restrain her. She would have me on her own terms. That I knew with absolute lucidity.

Was it also another surrender, a surrender within myself? I was writing that letter as a man in love. That was the imperative I should have found, however thoroughly I searched my heart. I should have declared myself ready to take the chances of unrequited love. And all that was passionately true. Yet was it a surrender within myself?

I did not hear that question. If I had heard it, writing to Sheila when I was not yet twenty-two, I should have laughed it away. I had tasted the promise of success. I was carving my destiny for myself. Compared with the ordinary run of men, I felt so free. I was ardent and sanguine and certain of happiness. It would have seemed incredible to hear that, in the deepest recess of my nature, I was my own prisoner.

I wrote the letter. I addressed it to the vicarage. There was a moment, looking down at it upon the writing table, when I revolted. I was on the point of tearing it up. Then I was swept on another surge, rushed outside the hotel, found a pillar box, heard the flop of the letter as it dropped.

I had written the first night of that week in London, asking Sheila to meet me in five days' time at Stewart's in Piccadilly. I was not anxious whether she would come. Of that, as though with a telepathic certainty, I had no doubt. I arrived at the café before four, and captured window seats which gave on to Piccadilly. I had scarcely looked out before I saw her striding with her poised, arrogant step, on the other side of the road. She too had time to spare; she glanced at the windows of Hatchard's before she crossed. Waiting for her, I was alight with hope.

Part Five

THE HARD WAY

32

Two Controllers

I WAS early for my first interview with Herbert Getliffe. It was raining, and so I could not spin out the minutes in the Temple gardens; I arrived at the foot of the staircase, and it was still too wet to stay there studying the names. Yet I gave them a glance.

LORD WATERFIELD

MR H GETLIFFE

MR W ALLEN

and then a column of names, meaningless to me, some faded, some with the paint shining and black. As I rushed into the shelter of the staircase, I wondered how they would find room for my name at the bottom, and whether Waterfield ever visited the Chambers, now that he had been in the cabinet for years.

The rain pelted down outside, and my feet clanged on the stone stairs. The set of Chambers was three flights up, there was no one on the staircase, the doors were shut, there was no noise except the sound of rain. On the third floor the door was open, a light shone in the little ball; even there, though, there was no one moving, I could hear no voices from the rooms around.

Then I did hear a voice, a voice outwardly deferential, firm, smooth, but neither gentle nor genteel.

'Can I help you, sir?'

I said that I had an appointment with Getliffe.

'I'm the clerk here. Percy Hall.' He was looking at me with an appraising eye, but in the dim hall, preoccupied with the meeting to come, I did not notice much about him.

'I suppose', he said, 'you wouldn't happen to be the young gentleman who wants to come here as a pupil, would you?'

I said that I was.

'I thought as much,' said Percy. He told me that Getliffe was expecting me, but was not yet back from lunch; meanwhile I had better wait in Getliffe's room. Percy led the way to the door at the end of the hall. As he left me, he said:

'When you've finished with Mr Getliffe, sir, I hope you'll call in for a word with me.'

It sounded like an order.

I looked round the room. It was high, with panelled walls, and it had, so Percy had told me, been Waterfield's. When Waterfield went into politics, so Percy again had told me, Getliffe had moved into the room with extreme alacrity. It smelt strongly that afternoon of a peculiar brand of tobacco. I was not specially nervous, but that smell made me more alert; this meeting mattered; I had to get on with Getliffe. I thought of the photograph that Eden had shown me, of himself and Getliffe, after a successful case. Getliffe had appeared large, impassive, and stern.

I was impatient now. It was a quarter of an hour past the time he had given me. I got up from the chair, looked at the briefs on the table and the picture over the fireplace, the books on the shelves. I stared out of the windows, high and wide and with their shutters folded back. Alert, I stared down at the gardens, empty in the dark, rainy, summer afternoon. And beyond was the river.

As I was standing by the window, there was a bustle outside the room, and Getliffe came in. My first sight of him was a surprise. In the photograph he had appeared large, impassive, and stern. In the flesh, as he came bustling in, late and flustered, he was only of middle height, and seemed scarcely that because of the way he dragged his feet. He had his underlip thrust out in an affable grin, so that there was something at the same time gay and shamefaced about his expression.

He suddenly confronted me with a fixed gaze from brown opaque and lively eyes.

'Don't tell me your name,' he began, in a slightly strident, breathless voice. 'You're Ellis – '

I corrected him.

With almost instantaneous quickness, he was saying: 'You're Eliot.' He repeated: 'You're Eliot,' with an intonation of reproof, as though the mistake had been my fault.

He sat down, lit his pipe, grinned, and puffed out smoke. He talked matily, perfunctorily, about Eden. Then he switched on his fixed gaze. His eyes confronted me. He said: 'So you want to come in here, do you?'

I said that I did.

'I needn't tell you, Eliot, that I have to refuse more pupils than I can take. It's one of the penalties of being on the way up. Not that one wants to boast. This isn't a very steady trade that you and I have chosen, Eliot. Sometimes I think we should have done better to go into the Civil Service and become deputy-under-principal secretaries and get two thousand pounds a year at fifty-five and our YMCA or XYZ some bright new year.'

At this time I was not familiar with Getliffe's allusive style, and I was slow to realize that he was referring to the orders of knighthood.

'Still one might be doing worse. And people seem to pass the word round that the briefs are coming in. I want to impress on you, Eliot, that I've turned down ten young men who wanted to be pupils – and that's only in the last year. It's not fair to take them unless one has the time to look after them and bring them up in the way they should go. I hope you'll always remember that.'

Getliffe was full of responsibility, statesmanship, and moral weight. His face was as stern as in the photograph. He was enjoying his own seriousness and uprightness, even though he had grossly exaggerated the number of pupils he refused. Then he said: 'Well, Eliot, I wanted you to understand that it's not easy for me to take you. But I shall. I make it a matter of principle to take people like you, who've started with nothing but their brains. I make it a matter of principle.'

Then he gave his shamefaced, affable chuckle. 'Also,' he said, 'it keeps the others up to it.' He grinned at me: his mood had changed, his face was transformed, he was guying all serious persons.

'So I shall take you,' said Getliffe, serious and responsible again, fixing me with his gaze. 'If our clerk can fit you in. I'm going to stretch a point and take you.'

'I'm very grateful,' I said. I knew that, as soon as the examination result was published, he had insisted to Eden that I was to be steered towards his Chambers.

'I'm very grateful,' I said, and he had the power of making me feel so.

'We've got a duty towards you,' said Getliffe, shaking me by the hand. 'One's got to look at it like that.' His eyes stared steadily into mine.

Just then there was a knock on the door, and Percy entered. He came across the room and laid papers in front of Getliffe.

'I shouldn't have interrupted you, sir,' said Percy. 'But I've promised to give an answer. Whether you'll take this. They're pressing me about it.'

Getliffe looked even more responsible and grave.

'Is one justified in accepting any more work?' he said. 'I'd like to see my wife and family one of these evenings. And some day I shall begin neglecting one of these jobs.' He tapped the brief with the bowl of his pipe and looked from Percy to me. 'If ever you think that is beginning to happen, I want you to tell me straight. I'm glad to think that I've never neglected one yet.' He gazed at me. 'I shouldn't be so happy if I didn't think so.

'Shall I do it?' Getliffe asked us loudly.

'It's heavily marked,' said Percy.

'What's money?' said Getliffe.

'They think you're the only man for it,' said Percy.

'That's more like talking,' said Getliffe. 'Perhaps it is one's duty. Perhaps I ought to do it. Perhaps you'd better tell them that I will do it – just as a matter of duty.'

When Percy had gone out, Getliffe regarded me.

'I'm not sorry you heard that,' he said. 'You can see why one has to turn away so many pupils? They follow the work, you know. It's no credit to me, of course, but you're lucky to come here, Eliot. I should like you to tell yourself that.'

What I should have liked to tell myself was whether or not that scene with Percy was rehearsed.

Then Getliffe began to exhort me: his voice became brisk and strident, he took the pipe out of his mouth and waved the stem at me.

'Well, Eliot,' he said. 'You've got a year here as a pupil. After that we can see whether you're ever going to earn your bread and butter. Not to speak of a little piece of cake. Mind you, we may have to tell you that it's not your vocation. One mustn't shirk one's responsibilities. Not even the painful ones. One may have to tell you to move a bit farther up the street.'

'Of course,' I said, in anger and pride.

'Still,' said Getliffe, 'you're not going to sink if you can help it. You needn't tell me that. You've got a year as a pupil. And a year's a long time. Your job is to be as useful as you can to both of us. Start whenever you like. The sooner the better. Start tomorrow.'

Breathlessly, with immense zest, Getliffe produced a list of cases and references, happy with all the paraphernalia of the law, reeling out the names of cases very quickly, waving his pipe as I copied them out.

'As for the root of all evil,' said Getliffe, 'I shall have to charge you the ordinary pupil's fees. You see, Eliot, one's obliged to think of the others. Hundred guineas for the year. October to October. If you start early, you don't have to pay extra,' said Getliffe with a chuckle. 'That's thrown in with the service. Like plain vans. A hundred guineas is your contribution to the collection plate. You can pay in quarters. The advantage of the instalment system', he added, 'is that we can reconsider the arrangement for the third and fourth quarters. You may have saved me a little bit of work before then. You may have earned a bit of bread and butter. The labourer is worthy of his hire.' He smiled, affably, brazenly, and said: 'Yes! The labourer is worthy of his hire.'

I think I had some idea, even then, of the part Herbert Getliffe was going to play in my career. He warmed me, as he did everyone else. He took me in often, as he did everyone else. He made me feel restrained, by the side of the extravagant and shameless way in which he exhibited his heart. On the way from his room to the clerk's, I was half aware that this was a tricky character to meet, when one was struggling for a living. I should not have been astonished to be told in advance the part he was going to play. But Percy Hall's I should not have guessed.

Percy's room was a box of an office, which had no space for any furniture but a table and a chair; Percy gave me the chair and braced his haunches against the edge of the table. He was, I noticed now, a squat powerful man, with the back of his head rising vertically from his stiff collar. No one ever bore a more incongruous Christian name; and it was perverse that he had a job where, according to custom, everyone called him by it.

'I want to explain one or two points to you, sir. If you enter these Chambers, there are things I can do for you. I could persuade someone to give you a case before you've been here very long. But' – Percy gave a friendly, brutal, good-natured smile – 'I'm not going to until I know what you're like. I've got a reputation to lose myself. The sooner we understand each other, the better.'

With a craftsman's satisfaction, Percy described how he kept the trust of the solicitors; how he never overpraised a young man, but how he reminded them of a minor success; how he watched over a man who looked like training into a winner, and how gradually he fed him with work; how it was no use being sentimental and finding cases for someone who was not fitted to survive.

Percy was able, I was thinking. He liked power and he liked his job – and he liked himself. It was a pleasure to him to be hard and shrewd, not to succumb to facile pity, to be esteemed as a clear-headed man. And he cherished a certain resentment at his luck. He had not had the chances of the men for whose work he foraged; yet he was certain that most of them were weaklings beside himself.

'I want to know what strings you can pull, sir,' said Percy. 'Some of our young gentlemen have uncles or connexions who are solicitors. It turns out very useful sometimes. It's wonderful how the jobs come in.'

'I can't pull any strings,' I said. He was not a man to fence with. He was rough under the smooth words, and it was wiser to be rough in return.

'That's a pity,' said Percy.

'I was born poor,' I said. 'I've got no useful friends. Apart from my studentship – you knew I'd got one?'

'I see Mr Getliffe's correspondence, sir,' said Percy complacently.

'Apart from that, I'm living on borrowed money. If I can't earn my keep within three years, I'm finished – so far as this game goes.'

'That's a pity,' said Percy. Our eyes met. His face was expressionless.

He said nothing for some moments. He seemed to be assessing the odds. He did not indulge in encouragement. He had, however, read Eden's letters and, with his usual competence, remembered them in detail. He reminded me that here was one solicitor with whom I had some credit. I said that Eden's was a conservative old firm in a provincial town.

'Never mind. They've paid Mr Getliffe some nice little fees.'

'Eden's got a very high opinion of him.'

'I suppose so, sir,' said Percy.

I was fishing for his own opinion, but did not get a flicker of response.

He had asked enough questions for that afternoon, and looked content. He banished my future from the conversation, and told me that he bred goldfish and won prizes for them. Then he decided to show me the place where I should sit for the next year. It was in a room close to Getliffe's, and the same size. There were already four people in it – Allen, a man well into middle age, who was writing at a roll-top desk, and two young men, one reading at a small table and two others playing chess. Percy introduced me, and I was offered a small table of my own, under one of the windows. The view was different from that in Getliffe's room: one looked across the gardens to another court, where an occasional light was shining, though it was teatime on a summer afternoon. The river was not visible from this window, but, as I turned away and talked to Allen and the others, I heard a boat hoot twice.

33

Manoeuvres

I CAME to know the view from that window in Chambers very well. I spent weeks in the long vacation there, though it was not realistic to do so. I learned little, and the others had gone away. Getliffe had asked me to produce some notes for him, but I could have taken my books anywhere. Yet I was restless, away from my place: it was as though I had to catch a train.

I was restless through that autumn and winter, through days when, with nothing to do, I gazed down over the gardens and watched the lights come on in the far court. There was nothing to do. Though Getliffe was good at filling in one's time, though I marked down every case in London that was not sheer routine, still there were days, stretches of days, when all I could do was read as though I were still a student and, instead of gazing from my garret over the roofs, look out instead over the Temple gardens. Some days, in that first year, when I was eating my heart out, that seemed the only change: I had substituted a different view, that was all.

I was too restless to enjoy knowing the others in Getliffe's chambers. At any other time I should have got more out of them. I struck up an acquaintance, it was true, with Salisbury, who worked in the other room; he had three years' start on me and was beginning to get a practice together. He boasted that he was earning seven hundred pounds a year, but I guessed that five hundred pounds was nearer the truth. Our acquaintance was a sparring and mistrustful one; he was a protégé of Getliffe's, which made me envy him, and in turn he saw me as a rival. I half knew that he was a kind, insecure, ambitious man who craved affection and did not expect to be liked; but I was distracted by the sight of his vulpine pitted face bent over his table, as I speculated how he described me to Getliffe behind my back.

Quite often we had a meal together, which was more than I ever did with any of the others. Of the three in my room, Allen was a precise spinster of a man, curiously happy, who said with simple detachment that he had none of the physical force and vitality of a successful barrister; he lived at his club, marked thousands of examination papers, edited volumes of trials, and for ten years past had averaged eight hundred or nine hundred pounds a year; he had a hope, at forty-five, of some modest permanent job, and made subfusc, malicious, aunt-like jokes at Getliffe's expense; they were cruel, happy jokes, all the happier because they got under Salisbury's skin. The other two were both pupils, only a term senior to me. One, Snedding, was hard-working and so dense that Percy erased him from serious consideration in his first month. The other, Paget, was a rich and well-connected young man who was spending a year or two at the Bar before managing the family estates. He was civil and deferential to us all in Chambers, and played an adequate game of chess; but outside he lived a smart social life, and politely evaded all invitations from professional acquaintances, much to the chagrin of Salisbury, who was a headmaster's son and longed for *chic*.

Paget was no fool, but he was not a menace. I was lucky, I told myself, that neither of those two was a competitor, for it meant that I might get more than my share of the minor pickings. I told myself that I was lucky. But all the luck was put off till tomorrow, and I fretted, lost to reason in my impatience, because tomorrow would not come.

No one was better than Getliffe at keeping his pupils occupied. So Salisbury said, who was fervently loyal to Getliffe and tried to counter all the gossip of the Inn dining table. There were plenty of times when I was too rancorous to hear a word in Getliffe's favour; yet in fact this one was true. From the day I entered the Chambers, he called me into his room each afternoon that he was not in court. 'How are tricks?'

he used to say; and, when I mentioned a case, he would expound on it with enthusiasm. It was an enthusiasm that he blew out like his tobacco smoke; it was vitalizing even when, expounding impromptu on any note I wrote for him, he performed his maddening trick of getting every second detail slightly wrong. Usually not wrong enough to matter, but just wrong enough to irritate. He had a memory like an untidy magpie; he knew a lot of law, but if he could remember a name slightly wrong he – almost as though on purpose – managed to. That first slip with my surname was just like him; and afterwards, particularly when he was annoyed, apprehensive, or guilty because of me, he frequently called me Ellis.

So, in the smell of Getliffe's tobacco, I listened to him as he produced case after case, sometimes incomprehensibly, because of his allusive slang, often inaccurately. He loved the law. He loved parading his knowledge and giving me 'a tip or two'. When I was too impatient to let a false date pass, he would look shamefaced, and then say: 'You're coming on! You're coming on!'

Then he got into the habit, at the end of such an afternoon, of asking me to 'try a draft' – 'Just write me a note to keep your hand in,' said Getliffe. 'Don't be afraid to spread yourself. You can manage three or four pages. Just to keep you from rusting.'

The first time it happened I read for several afternoons in the Inn library, wrote my 'opinion' with care, saw Getliffe flicker his eyes over it and say 'You're coming on!', and then heard nothing more about it. But the second time I did hear something more. Again I had presented the opinion as professionally as I could. Then one morning Getliffe, according to his custom, invited all three of us pupils to attend a conference. The solicitors and clients sat round his table; Getliffe, his pipe put away, serious and responsible, faced them. He began the conference with his usual zest. 'I hope you don't think that I'm a man to raise false hopes,' he said earnestly. 'One would rather shout the winners out at the back door. But frankly I've put in some time on this literature, and I'm ready to tell you that we should be just a little bit over cautious if we didn't go to court.' To my astonishment, he proceeded firmly to give the substance of my note. In most places he had not troubled to alter the words.

At the end of that conference, Getliffe gave me what my mother would have called an 'old-fashioned' look.

He repeated this manoeuvre two or three times, before, during one of our afternoon tête-à-têtes, he said:

'You're doing some nice odd jobs for me, aren't you?'

I was delighted. He was so fresh and open that one had to respond.

'I wanted to tell you that,' said Getliffe. 'I wanted to tell you something else,' he added with great seriousness. 'It's not fair that you shouldn't get any credit. One must tell people that you're doing some of the thinking. One's under an obligation to push your name before the public.'

I was more delighted still. I expected a handsome acknow-ledgement at the next conference.

I noticed that, just before the conference, Getliffe looked at the other pupils and not at me. But I still had high hopes. I still had them, while he recounted a long stretch from my latest piece of devilling. He had muddled some of it. I thought. Then he stared at the table, and said:

'Perhaps one ought to mention the help one sometimes gets from one's pupils. Of course one suggests a line of investigation, one reads their *billets-doux,* one advises them how to express themselves. But you know as well as I do, gentlemen, that sometimes these young men do some of the digging for us. Why, there's one minor line of argument in this opinion – it's going too far to say that I shouldn't have discovered it, in fact I had already got my observations in black and white, but I was very glad indeed, I don't mind telling you, when my Mr Ellis hit upon it for himself.'

Getliffe hurried on.

I was enraged. That night, with Charles March, I thrashed over Getliffe's character and my injuries. This was the first time he had taken me in completely. I was too much inflamed, too frightened of the future, to concede that Getliffe took himself in too. Actually, he was a man of generous impulses, and of devious, cunning, cautious afterthoughts. In practice, the afterthoughts usually won. I had not yet found a way to handle him. The weeks and months were running on. I did not know whether he would keep any of his promises, or how he could be forced.

He could not resist making promises – any more than he could resist sliding out of them. Charles March, who was a pupil in another set of Chambers, often went with me to hear him plead: one day, in King's Bench 4, it was all according to the usual pattern. Getliffe was only just in time. In he hurried, dragging his feet, slightly untidy and flurried – looking hunted as always, his wig not quite clean nor straight, carrying papers in his hand. As soon as he began to speak, he produced the impression of being both nervous and at ease. He was not a good speaker, nothing like so good as his opponent in this case; the strident note stayed in his voice, but it sounded thin even in that little court; yet he was capturing the sympathy of most people there.

At lunchtime, walking, in the gardens, Charles March and I were scornful of his incompetence, envious of his success, incredulously angry that he got away with it.

That night in his room I was able to congratulate him on winning the case. He looked at me with his most responsible air.

'One is glad to pull off something for the clients' sakes,' he said. 'It's the easiest fault to forget that they're the people most concerned. One has to be careful.'

'Still, it's very nice to win,' I said.

Getliffe's face broke into a grin.

'Of course it's nice,' he said. 'It gives me a bigger kick than anything in the world.'

'I expect I shall find it the same,' I said. 'If ever I manage it.'

Getliffe laughed merrily.

'You will, my boy, you will. You've got to remember that this ancient Inn wasn't born yesterday. It was born before HM Edward Three. No one's ever been in a hurry since. You've just got to kick your heels and look as though you like it. We've all been through it. It's good for us in the end. But I'll tell you this, Eliot' – he said confidentially – 'though I don't often tell it to people in your

261

position, that I don't see why next year you shouldn't be able to keep yourself in cigarettes. And even a very very occasional cigar.' He smiled happily at me. 'When all's said and done, it's a good life,' he said.

Years afterwards, I realized that, when I was his pupil, I crassly underestimated Getliffe as a lawyer. It was natural for me and Charles March to hold our indignation meetings in the Temple gardens; but, though it was hard for young men to accept, some of Getliffe's gifts were far more viable than ours. We overvalued power and clarity of mind, of which we both had a share, and we dismissed Getliffe because of his muddiness. We had not seen enough to know that, for most kinds of success, intelligence is a very minor gift. Getliffe's mind was muddy, but he was a more effective lawyer than men far cleverer, because he was tricky and resilient, because he was expansive with all men, because nothing restrained his emotions, and because he had a simple, humble, tenacious love for his job.

It was too difficult, however, for Charles March and me, in the intellectual arrogance of our youth, to see that truth, much less accept it. And I had a good deal to put up with. I had just discovered Getliffe's comic and pathological meanness with money. He had a physical aversion from signing a cheque or parting with a coin. In the evening, after a case, we occasionally went to the Feathers for a pint of beer. His income was at least four thousand a year, and mine two hundred, but somehow I always paid.

My pupil's year was a harassing one. I was restless. Often I was unhappy. Those nights with Charles March were my only respite from anxiety. They were also much more. Charles became one of the closest friends of my life, and he introduced me into a society opulent, settled, different from anything I had ever known. His story, like George Passant's, took such a hold on my imagination that I have chosen to tell it in full, separated from my own. All that I need say here is that, during my first year in London, I began to dine with Charles' family in Bryanston Square and his relatives in great houses near. It seemed my one piece of luck in all those months.

I had to return from those dinner parties to my bleak flat. Apart from the evenings with Charles, I had no comfort at all. On other nights I used to stay late in Chambers, and then walk up Kingsway and across Bloomsbury, round Bedford Square under the peeling plane trees, past the restaurants of Charlotte Street, up Conway Street to number thirty-seven, where there was a barber's shop on the ground floor and my flat on the third. Whenever I threw open the door, I looked at the table. The light from the landing fell across it, before I could reach the switch. There might be a letter or telegram from Sheila.

The sitting-room struck cold each night when I returned. I could not afford to have a fire all day, and my landlady, amiable but scatter-brained, could never remember which nights I was coming home. Most evenings the table was empty, there was no letter, my hopes dropped, and the room turned darker. I knelt on the hearth and lit a firelighter, before going out to make my supper off a sandwich at the nearest bar. Even when the fire had caught, it was a desolate room. There were two high-backed armchairs, covered with satin which was wearing through; an old hard sofa which stood just off the hearthrug and on which I kept papers and books; the table, with two chairs beside it; and an empty sideboard. My bedroom attained the same standard of discomfort, and to reach it I had to walk across the landing. The tenants of the fourth floor also walked across the same landing on their way upstairs.

I need not have lived so harshly. For an extra twenty pounds a year, I could have softened things for myself; and, by the scale of my debts, another twenty pounds paid out meant nothing at all, as I well knew. But, as though compelled by a profound instinct, I paid no attention to the voice of sense. Somehow I must live so as constantly to remind myself that I had nowhere near arrived. The more uncomfortable I was, the more will I could bend to my career. This was no resting place. When I had satisfied myself, it would be time to indulge.

I sat by the fire on winter nights, working on one of Getliffe's 'points', forcing back the daydreams, forcing back the anxious hope that tomorrow there would be a letter from Sheila. For I was waiting for letters more abjectly than for briefs. When I asked her to come back, I had surrendered. I had asked for her on her own terms, which were no terms at all. I had no power over her. I could only wait for what she did and gave.

It suited her. She came to see me quite often, at least once a month. With her nostalgia for the dingy, she used to take a room at a shabby Greek hotel a couple of streets away. And she came, out of her own caprices and because of her own needs. Her caprices had her usual acid tone, which I could not help but like. A telegram arrived: CANNOT BEAR MY FATHER'S VOICE PREFER YOURS FOR TWO DAYS SHALL APPEAR THIS EVENING. Once, without any warning, I found her sitting in my room when I got back late at night.

Occasionally we were happy, as though she were on the edge of falling in love with me. But she was flirting with man after man, lit up each time with the familiar hope that here at last was someone who could hypnotize her into complete love. I had to listen to that string of adventures, for she used her power over me to compel me into the role of confidant. She trusted me, she thought I understood her better than the others, she found me soothing. Sometimes I could smooth her forehead and lift the dread away. In part she relished playing on my jealousy, hearing me in torment as I questioned her, seeing me driven to another masochistic search.

One morning in February there was a postcard on my breakfast tray. At the sight of the handwriting my heart leaped. Then I read: 'I want you to dine with me at the Mars tomorrow (Tuesday). I may have a man with me I should like you to meet.'

I went as though I had no will.

The glass of the restaurant door was steamed over in the cold. Inside, I stared frenziedly round. She was sitting alone, her face pallid and scornful.

Still in my hat and coat, I went to her.

'Where is this man?' I said.

She said: 'He was useless.'

We talked little over the meal. But I could not rest without asking some questions. He was another of her lame dogs: she thought he was deep and mysterious, and then that he was empty. She was dejected. I tried to console her. I was stifling the rest, and fell silent.

Afterwards we walked into Soho Square, on the way home. Abruptly she said: 'Why don't you get rid of me?'

'It's too late.'

'You'd like to, wouldn't you?'

'Don't you think I should?' I said flatly, in utter tiredness. She pressed my fingers, and there was no more to say.

All through those months when I was struggling to get started, I could not talk to her about my worries. It was to Charles March that I had to trace and retrace the problems, boring to anyone else, acutely real to me. Was Percy giving me my share of the guinea and two-guinea briefs? Would Getliffe let me off the last instalments of my pupil's fees? Had I won any kind of backing yet? Would Getliffe give me a hand, if it cost him nothing, or would he stand in my way?

Sheila could not imagine that daily life of trivial manoeuvre, contrivance, petty gains and setbacks. She concerned herself about my need for money, and she bought presents which saved me dipping into my scholarship. In that way she was generous, for, since Mr Knight parted with money only a little more easily than Getliffe, she had to go without dresses, which she did not mind, and beg her father for an extra allowance, which she minded painfully. But the frets and intrigues – those she could not enter. Since we first met, she had taken it for granted that I should prevail. As for my struggles with Getliffe, they did not matter. She could not believe that I cared so much.

34

A Friend's Case

PERCY did me no favours in my first year. But he did me no disfavours either. He was neutral, as though I were still under supervision, might be worth backing or might have to be written off. I received my share of the 'running down' cases, the insignificant defences of motoring prosecutions, that came Percy's way. Percy also advised me how to pick up more at the police courts. I used to attend several, on the off chance of a guinea. Those courts were only a few miles apart, but in society the distance was vast – from the smart businessmen showing off their cars on the way home from the tennis court, to the baffled, stupid, foreign prostitutes, the ponces and bullies, the street bookmakers, the blowsy landladies of the Pimlico backstreets.

From that police-court work, in the year from October 1927 to July 1928, I earned just under twenty-five pounds. And that was my total professional income for the year. I mentioned the fact to Percy.

'Yes, sir,' he said impassively. 'It's just about what I should have expected.'

He took pleasure in being discreet. But he relented to the extent of telling me that many men, perhaps the majority of men, did worse. And he said, by way of aside, that I ought not to start lecturing or marking papers; I had plenty of energy, but I might need it all; this was a long-distance race, not a sprint, said Percy. It was then I realized that Percy was judiciously, cold-bloodedly, watching my health.

I intended to press Getliffe about my last instalment of fees. He had promised to remit it if I had earned my keep; I had done more than that, I had saved him weeks of work, and he must not be allowed to think that I was easy prey. I knew more of him now. The only way to make him honour a bargain, I thought, was to play on his general impulse and at the same moment to threaten: to meet expansiveness with expansiveness, to say that he was a fine fellow who could never break his word – but that he would be a low confidence trickster if he did.

The trouble was, as the time came near I found it impossible to get an undisturbed half an hour with him. He could smell danger from afar, or see it in one's walk. Somehow he became busier than ever. When, for want of any other opportunity, I caught him on the stairs, he said reprovingly and matily: 'Don't let's talk shop out of hours, Ellis. It can wait. Tomorrow is also a day.'

At the beginning of the long vacation he went abroad for a holiday; the first I knew of it was a genial wave from the door of our room and a breathless, strident shout: 'Taxi's waiting! Taxi's waiting!' He left with nothing settled, I still had not edged in a word. He also left me with a piece of work, arduous and complex, on a case down for October.

Two days after his return, at last I seized the chance to talk.

'I've not paid you my last quarter's fees,' I said. 'But – '

'All contributions thankfully received,' said Getliffe.

'I'd like to discuss my position,' I said. 'I've done some work for you, you know, and you said – '

Getliffe met my eyes with his straightforward gaze.

'I'm going to let you pay that quarter, Eliot,' he said. 'I know what you're going to say. I know you've done things for me, I know that better than you do. But I'm thinking of my future pupils, Eliot. I've tried to give you more experience than you'd have got in the Chambers of most of our learned friends. I make it a matter of principle to give my pupils experience, and I hope I always shall. But if I start letting them off their fees when they take advantage of their opportunities – well, I know myself too well, Eliot, I shall just stop putting things in their way. So I'm going to accept your cheque. Of course this next year we must have a business arrangement. This just wipes the slate clean.'

Before I could reply, he told me jollyingly that soon he would be inviting me to a party.

That party was dangled in front of me in many conversations afterwards. Now that my pupil's year was over, I was not called so often into Getliffe's room. For his minor devilling, he was using a new pupil called Parry. But for several cases he relied on me, for I was quick and had the knack of writing an opinion so that he could master its headings in the midst of his hurrying magpie-like raids among his papers. In return, I wanted to be paid – or better, recommended to a solicitor to take a brief for which Getliffe had no time. Some days promised one reward, some days another. When I was exigent, he said with his genial, humble smile that soon I should be receiving an invitation from his wife. 'We want you to come to our party' he said. 'We're both looking forward to it no end, L S' (He was the only person alive who called me by my initials.)

It was nearly Christmas before at last I was asked to their house in Holland Park. I found my way through the Bayswater streets, vexed and rebellious. I was being used, I was being cheated shamelessly – no, not shamelessly, I thought with a glimmer of amusement, for each of Getliffe's bits of sharp practice melted him into a blush of shame. But repentance never had the slightest effect on his actions. He grieved sincerely for what he had done, and then did it again. He was exploiting me, he was taking the maximum advantage of being my only conceivable patron. And now he fobbed me off with a treat like a schoolboy. Did he know the first thing about me? Was it all unconsidered, had he the faintest conception of the mood in which I was going to my treat?

Their drawing-room was large and bright and light. Getliffe himself looked out of place, dishevelled, boyishly noisy, his white tie not clean and a little bedraggled. He wife was elegantly dressed; she clung to my hand, fixed me with warm spaniel-like eyes, close to mine, and said: 'It is nice to see you. Herbert has said such a lot about you. He's always saying how much he wishes I had the chance of seeing you. I do wish I could see more of you all – '

Watching her later at the dinner table, I thought she was almost a lovely woman, if only she had another expression beside that of eager, cooing fidelity. She was quite young: Getliffe at that time was just over forty and she was a few years less. They were very happy. He had, as usual, done himself well. They talked enthusiastically about children's books, Getliffe protruding his underlip and comparing Kenneth Grahame and A A Milne, his wife regarding him with an eager loving stare, their warmth for each other fanned by the baby talk.

Once Mrs Getliffe prattled: 'Herbert always says you people do most of his work for him.' We laughed together.

They talked of pantomimes: they had two children, to what show should they be taken? Getliffe remarked innocently how, when he was an undergraduate, he had schemed to take his half-brother Francis to the pantomime – not for young Francis' enjoyment, but for his own.

That was the party. I said goodbye, in a long hand clasp with Mrs Getliffe. Getliffe took me into the hall. 'I hope you've enjoyed yourself, L S,' he said.

When I thanked him, he went on: 'We may not be the best Chambers in London – but we do have fun!'

His face was merry. On the way home, grinning at my own expense, I could not be certain whether his eyes were innocent, or wore their brazen, defiant stare.

In that bitterly cold winter of 1928-9 I reached a depth of discontent. I ached for this suspense to end. In my memory it remained one of the periods I would least have chosen to live through again. And yet there must have been good times. I was being entertained by the Marches, I was making friends in a new society. Long afterwards Charles March told me that I seemed brimming with interest, and even he had not perceived how hungry and despondent I became. That is how I remembered the time, without relief – I remembered myself dark with my love for Sheila, fretting for a sign of recognition in my job, poor, seeing no sign of a break. It was worse because Charles himself, in that December, was given his first important case. It was nothing wonderful – it was marked at twenty-five guineas – but it was a chance to shine, and for such a chance just then I would have begged or stolen.

Charles was working in the Chambers of a relation by marriage, and the case was arranged through other connections of his family. Nothing could be more natural as a start for a favourably born young man. As he told me, I was devoured by envy. Sheer rancorous envy, the envy of the poor for the rich, the unlucky for the lucky, the wallflower for the courted. I tried to rejoice in his luck, and I felt nothing but envy.

I hated feeling so. I had been jealous in love, but this envy was more degrading. In jealousy there was at least the demand for another's love, the sustenance of passion – while in such envy as I felt for Charles there was nothing but the sick mean stab. I hated that I should be so possessed. But I was hating the human condition. For as I saw more of men in society I thought in the jet-black moments that envy was the most powerful single force in human affairs – that, and the obstinate desire of the flesh to persist. Given just those two components to build with, one could construct too much of the human scene.

I tried to make conscious amends. I offered to help him on the brief; the case was a breach of contract, and I knew the subject well. Charles let me help, and I did a good share of the work. He was himself awkward and conscience-stricken. Once, as we were studying the case, he said:

'I'm just realizing how true it is – that it's not so easy to forgive someone, when you're taking a monstrously unfair advantage over him.'

The case was down to be heard in January. I sat by the side of Charles' father and did not miss a word. The judge had only recently gone to the bench, and was very alert and sharp-witted, sitting alone against the red upholstery of the Lord Chief Justice's court. Mr March and I placed ourselves for a day and a half near the door, so as not to catch Charles' eye. Charles' loud voice resounded in the narrow room;

his face looked thinner under his new, immaculate wig. The case was a hopeless one from the start. Yet I thought that he was doing well. He impressed all in court by his cross-examination of an expert witness. In the end he lost the case, but the judge went out of his way to pay a compliment: the losing side might, the judge hoped, take consolation from the fact that their case could not have been more lucidly presented.

It was a handsome compliment. It should have been mine, I felt again. Men stood around Charles, congratulating him, taking his luck for granted. I went to join them, to add my own congratulations. Partly I meant them, partly I was pleased – but I would not have dared to look deep into my heart.

I went back to Chambers and told Getliffe the result. It happened that his half-brother, Francis, had been a contemporary and friend of Charles' at Cambridge. Getliffe scarcely knew Charles, but he had a healthy respect for the powerful, and he assured me earnestly:

'Mark my words, Eliot, that young friend of ours will go a long way.'

'Of course he will.'

'Mind you,' said Getliffe, 'he's got some pull. He is old Philip March's nephew, isn't he? It helps in our game, Eliot, one can't pretend it doesn't help.'

Getliffe gazed at me, man to man.

'Don't you wish you were in that racket, Eliot?'

I explained, clearly and with some force, how the brief had arrived at Charles. As a pupil, he had not done much work for his master, Albert Hart, who stood to Charles as Getliffe did to me; but Hart had used much contrivance to divert this brief to Charles.

'I've been thinking', said Getliffe, his mood changing like lightning, 'that you ought to do some shooting yourself before very long. Would you like to, L S?'

'Wouldn't you in my place? Wouldn't you?'

'Well, one's roping in quite a bit of paper nowadays. I must look through them and see if there's one you could tackle. I should advise you not to start if you can help it with anything too ambitious. If you drop too big a brick, it means there's one firm of solicitors who won't leave their cards on you again.'

Then he looked at his most worried, and his voice took on a strident edge.

'I must see if I can find you a snippet for yourself one of these days. The trouble is, one owes a duty to one's clients. One can't forget that, much as one would like to.'

He pointed his pipe at me.

'You see my point, Eliot,' he said defiantly. 'One would like to distribute one's briefs to one's young friends. Why shouldn't one? What's the use of money if one never has time to enjoy it? I'd like to give you a share of my work tomorrow. But one can't help feeling a responsibility to one's clients. One can't help one's conscience.'

35

The Freezing Night

SOON after Charles' case, the temperature stayed below freezing point for days on end. For the first time since I went to London, I stayed away from Chambers. There was nothing to force me there. During two whole days I only went out into the iron frost for my evening meal, and came back to lie, as I had done all the afternoon, on my sofa in front of the fire.

The cold was at its most intense when Sheila visited me. It was nine o'clock on a bitter February night. She came and sat on the hearth rug, close to the fire; I lay still on the sofa.

We were quiet. For a moment there was noise, as she rattled the shovel in the coal scuttle. 'Don't get up. I'll do it,' she said, and knelt, shovelling the coals. Then she stared at the fire again, the darkened fire, cherry-red between the bars, with spurts of gas from the new coal.

We were quiet in the room, and outside the street was silent in the extreme cold.

I watched. She was kneeling, sitting back on her heels, her back straight; I could see her face in profile, softer than when she met me with her full gaze. The curve of her cheek was smooth and young, and a smile pulled on the edge of her mouth.

The fire was burning through, tinting her skin. She took the poker, stoked through the bars, then left it there. She studied the cave that formed as the poker began to glow.

'Queer,' she said.

The cave enlarged, radiant, like a landscape on the sun.

'Oh, handsome,' she said.

She was sitting upright. I saw the swell of her breast, I saw only that.

I gripped her by the shoulders and kissed her on the mouth. She kissed me back. For a moment we pressed together; then, as I became more violent, she struggled and shrank away.

In the firelight she stared up at me.

'Why are you looking at me like that?' she cried. 'No.'

I said: 'I want you.'

I seized her, forced her towards me, forced my lips upon her. She fought. She was strong, but I was possessed. 'I can't,' she cried. I tore her dress at the neck. 'I can't,' she cried, and burst into a scream of tears.

That sound reached me at last. Appalled, I let her go. She threw herself face downwards on the rug and sobbed and then became silent.

We were quiet in the room again. She sat up and looked at me. Her brow was lined. It was a long time before she spoke.

'Am I absolutely frigid?' she said.

I shook my head.

'Shall I always be?'

'I shouldn't think so. No.'

'I'm afraid of it. You know that.'

Then suddenly she rose to her feet.

'Take me for a walk,' she said. 'It will do me good.'

I said that it was intolerably cold. I did not want to walk: I had injured my heel that morning.

'Please take me,' she said. And then I could not refuse.

Before we went out she asked for a safety pin to hold her dress together. She smiled, quite placidly, as she asked, and as she inspected a bruise on her arm.

'You have strong hands,' she said.

Outside my room the cold made us catch our breath. On the stairs, where usually there wafted rich waves of perfume from the barber's shop, all scent seemed frozen out. In the streets the lights sparkled diamond-sharp.

We walked apart, down the back streets, along Tottenham Court Road. My heel was painful, and on that foot I only trod upon the sole. She was not looking at me, she was staring in front of her, but on the resonant pavement she heard me limping.

'I'm sorry,' she said, and took my arm.

In snatches she began to talk. She was a little released because I had tried to ravish her, She could not talk consecutively – so much of her life was locked within her; especially she could not bring out the secret dread and daydream in which she was obsessed by physical love. Yet, after her horror by the fireside, she was impelled to speak, flash out some fragment from her past, in the trust that I would understand. How she had, more ignorant than most girls, wondered about the act of love. How she dreaded it. There was nothing startling in what she said. But, for her, it was a secret she could only let out in a flash of words, then silence, then another flash. For what to another woman would have been matter-of-fact, for her was becoming an obsession, so that often, in her solitary thoughts, she believed that she was incapable of taking a man's love.

Trafalgar Square was almost empty to the bitter night, as she and I walked across arm in arm.

I did not know enough of the region where flesh and spirit touch. I did not know enough of the aberrations of the flesh, nor how, the more so because they are ridiculous except to the sufferer, they can corrode a life. If I had been older, I could perhaps have soothed her just a little. If I had been older and not loved her; for all my thoughts of love, all my sensual hopes and images of desire, belonged to her alone. My libido could find no other home; I had got myself seduced by a young married woman, but it had not deflected my imagination an inch from the girl walking at my side, had not diluted by a drop that total of desire, erotic and amorous, playful and passionate, which she alone invoked. Hers was the only body I wanted beside me at night. And so I was the wrong man to listen to her. If I had been twice my age, and not loved her, I could have told her of other lives like her own; I should have been both coarser and tenderer and I should have told her that, at worst, it is wonderful how people can come to terms and make friends of the flesh. But I was not yet twenty-three, I loved her to madness, I was defeated and hungry with longing.

So she walked, silent again, down Whitehall and I limped beside her. Yet it seemed that she was soothed. It was strange after that night, but she held my hand. Somehow we were together, and she did not want to part. We stood on Westminster Bridge, gazing at the black water; it was black and oily, except at the banks, where slivers of ice split and danced in the light.

'Too cold to jump,' she said. She was laughing. Big Ben struck twelve.

'How's the foot?' she said. 'Strong enough to walk home?'

I could scarcely put it to the ground, but I would have walked with her all night. She shook her head. 'No. I'm going to buy us a taxi.'

She came back to my room, where the fire was nearly out. She built it up again, and made tea. I lay on the sofa, and she sat on the hearthrug, just as we had done two hours before, and between us there was a kind of peace.

36

A Stroke of Luck

IN the early summer of 1929 I had my first great stroke of luck. Charles March intervened on my behalf. He was a proud man; for himself he could not have done what he did for me. No man was more sensitive to affronts, but for me he risked them. He was importunate with some of his connexions. I was invited to a garden party and scrutinized by men anxious to oblige Sir Philip March's nephew. I was asked to dinner, and met Henriques, one of the most prosperous of Jewish solicitors. Charles sat by as impresario, anxious to show me at my best. As it happened, I was less constrained than he. The Harts and Henriques were shrewd, guarded, professional men, but I was soon at my ease, as I had been with Eden. I had everything in my favour; they wished to please Charles, and I had only to pass muster.

In June the first case arrived. It lay on my table, in the shadow. Outside the window the gardens were brilliant in the sunlight, and a whirr came from a lawnmower cutting grass down below. I was so joyful that for a second I left the papers there, in the shadow. Then it all seemed a matter of everyday, something to act upon, no longer a novelty. The brief came from Henriques, bore the figures 20 + 1. The case was a libel action brought by a man called Chapman. It looked at a first reading straightforward and easy to win.

But there was little time to prepare. It was down for hearing in three days' time. Percy explained that the man to whom the case had first gone was taken suddenly ill; and Henriques had remembered me. It got him out of a difficulty, and did me a good turn, and after all I was certain to have three days completely free.

I was sent a few notes from the barrister who had thrown up the brief, and worked night and day. My four or five hours' sleep was broken, as I woke up with a question on my mind. I switched on the light, read through a page, made a jotting, just as I used to when preparing for an examination. I was strung-up, light-headed as well as lucid, and excessively cheerful.

Henriques behaved with a consideration that he did not parade, though it came from a middle-aged and extremely rich solicitor to a young and penniless member of the Bar. He called for a conference in person, instead of sending one of his staff; he acted as though this were a weighty brief being studied by the most eminent of silks. Getliffe was so much impressed by Henriques' attention that he found it necessary to take a hand himself, and with overflowing cordiality pressed me to use his room for the conference.

Henriques made it plain that we were expected to win. Unless I were hopelessly incompetent, I knew that we must. The knowledge made me more nervous: when I got on my feet in court, the judge's face was a blur, so were the jurors'; I was uncertain of my voice. But, as though a record was playing, my arguments came out. Soon the judge's face came clear through the haze, bland, cleft-chinned. I saw a juror, freckled, attentive, frowning. I made a faint joke. I was beginning to enjoy myself.

Our witnesses did all I wanted of them. I had one main fact to prove: that the defendant knew Chapman well, not merely as an acquaintance. As I finished with our last witness, I thought, though still anxious, still touching wood, that our central point was unshakable. The defence's only hope was to smear it over and suggest a coincidence. Actually my opponent tried that tack, but so tangled himself that he never made it clear. He seemed to have given up hope before the case began, and his speech was muddled and ill-arranged. He was a man of Allen's standing, with more force and a larger practice, but nothing like so clever. He only called three witnesses, and by the time two had been heard I was aglow. It was as good as over.

Their last witness came to the box. All I had to do was to make him admit that he and Chapman and the defendant had often met together. It was obviously so he could not deny it; it left our main point unassailable, and the case was clear. But I made a silly mistake. I could not let well alone; I thought the witness was malicious and had another interest in attacking Chapman. I began asking him about it. I was right in my human judgement, but it was bad tactics in law. First, it was an unnecessary complication: second, as the witness answered, his malice emerged – but so also did his view that Chapman was lying and I was sweating beneath my wig. I perceived what he was longing for the chance to say. I pulled up sharp. It was better to leave that line untidy, and bolt to the safe one; sweating, flustered, discomfited, I found my tongue was not forsaking me, was inventing a bridge that took me smoothly back. It happened slickly. I was cool enough to wonder how many people had noticed the break.

With the jury out, I sat back, uneasy. I went over the case: surely it stood, surely to anyone it must have appeared sound? Foolishly I had done it harm, but surely it had affected nothing?

The jury were very quick. Before I heard the verdict, I knew all was well. I did not want to shout aloud: I just wanted to sink down in relief.

'Very nice,' said Henriques, who had, with his usual courtesy, made another personal appearance. 'My best thanks. If I may say so, you had it in hand all the way. I apologize again for giving you such short notice. Next time we shan't hurry you so much.'

Charles took my hand, and, as Henriques left, began to speak.

'I'm glad,' he said. 'But whatever possessed you to draw that absurd red herring?'

Just then, I should have liked to be spared Charles' tongue. No one expressed the unflattering truth more pointedly. I thought that I had recovered well, I should have liked some praise.

'I'm very glad,' said Charles. 'But you realize that it might have been a serious mistake? You missed the point completely, don't you agree?'

On the other hand, Getliffe assumed responsibility for my success. He came into my room in Chambers (I still had my table in Allen's room) and spoke at large as though he had done it himself. He decided to organize a celebration. While I was writing to Sheila, Getliffe booked a table at the Savoy for dinner and telephoned round to make the party. They were gathered in Getliffe's haphazard manner – some were friends of mine, some I scarcely knew, some, like Salisbury, were acquaintances none too well pleased that at last I should begin to compete. That did not worry Getliffe. Incidentally, though the members of the party were invited haphazard, there was nothing haphazard about the arrangements for payment: Getliffe made sure that each of the guests came ready to pay for himself.

Charles did not come. He was already booked for a dinner party, but Getliffe expressed strong disapproval. 'He ought to have put anything else off on a night like this! Still,' said Getliffe, 'it's his loss, not ours. We're going to have a good time!' Then Getliffe added, in his most heartfelt tone: 'And while we're talking, L S, I've always thought young March might have done a bit more for you. He might have pulled a rope or two to get you started. Instead of leaving everything to your own devices – plus, of course, the bits and pieces I've been able to do for you myself.'

I wondered if I had heard aright. It was colossal, Yet, as he spoke, Getliffe was believing every word. That was one of his gifts.

At the party I was seated next to a good-looking girl. Tired, attracted to her, half-drunk, triumphant, I spread myself in boasting, as I had not boasted since my teens.

'I feel extremely jubilant,' I said.

'You look it,' she replied.

'I've often wished that I'd chosen a different line,' I went on. 'I mean, something where one got started quicker. But this is going to be worth waiting for when it comes.'

Provocatively she talked about friends at the Bar.

'I could have done other things,' I went on bragging. 'I'd have backed myself to come off in several different jobs!'

The irony of the party made me laugh aloud. My first victory – and here I was being drunk to by Getliffe, his smile merry, wily, and open. My first victory – not an intimate friend there, but a good many rivals instead. My first victory – instead of having Sheila in my arms, I was boasting wildly to this cool and pretty girl. Yet I had won, and I laughed aloud.

Within three days I received something more than congratulations. Percy spoke to me one morning in the hall, in his usual manner, authoritative under the servility:

'I should like a word with you, Mr Eliot.'

I went into his cubby hole.

'I've got something for you,' he said.

As I thanked him, Percy's smile was firm but gratified, the smile of power, the smile of a conferrer of benefits.

'Well, sir,' said Percy, 'you've given me a bit to go on now. I can tell them that you won the Chapman case for Henriques. It's not much, but it's better than nothing!'

In fact, Percy had decided that it was safe to give me a minor recommendation. He had been watching me for two years, with interest, never letting his sympathy – though whether he had sympathy I was not sure – interfere with his judgement. He had eked out the driblets, the guineas and the two guineas, to keep me from despair, but he would go no further. Now someone else had taken the risk, Percy was ready to speak in my favour just as much as the facts justified.

This case came from solicitors who had no contact at all with my Jewish friends. It was a case which happened to be rather like Charles' first. It would bring me thirty guineas.

Between July 1928 and July 1929, I had earned eighty-eight pounds. But of this sum, fifty-two pounds ten had arrived since June, on my first two cases. It was more promising than it looked. I dared not tell myself so, but the hope was there. I hoped I was coming through.

37

Value In Others' Eyes

I BEGAN to see how luck attracts luck. Before the long vacation, I received my biggest case so far, from one of Charles March's connexions, and, at the same time heard that another was coming from Henriques. In high spirits, I felt the trend ought to be encouraged, and so I set to work playing on Getliffe's better nature. I was determined not to let him wriggle out of every promise; now the stream was running with me, I intended to make Getliffe help. We had several most moving and heartfelt conversations. I told him that I could not afford a holiday, unless I was certain of earning three hundred pounds next year.

Getliffe said: 'You know, L S, it's an uncertain life for all of us. How much do you think I'm certain of myself? Only a few hundred. That's the meal ticket, you understand. I manage to rake in a bit more by way of extras. But as a steady income I can't count on as much as the gentleman who reads my income tax return.' He was grave with emotion at this thought. 'Then I think of taking silk!' he said. 'It'd be just throwing the steady bread and butter out of the window. I expect I shall some day. One never counts one's blessings. And I can tell you this,' he added, 'if and when I do take silk, there'll be plenty of confetti coming into the Chambers for chaps like you.'

'I'd like a bit more now,' I said.

'So should we all, L S,' said Getliffe reprovingly.

But I was becoming more practised with him.

'Look,' I said. 'I'm getting a few briefs now. Charles March has done more than his share. So has Henriques. I think you should do yours now. You've promised to find me some work. I think this would be a good time.'

Getliffe looked at me with a sudden, earnest smile.

'I'm very glad you've spoken like that, L S. I believe you've spoken like a friend. People sometimes tell me I'm selfish. I get worried. You see, I'm not conscious of it. I should hate to think of myself like that. I want my friends to pull me up if ever they think I'm doing wrong.'

Next day, though, he might think better of it. There was a very strong rumour – I never knew whether it was true – that whenever he took a holiday he tried to divert any cases which might be on the way. He did not divert them to bright young men, but to a middle-aged and indifferently competent figure who came so seldom into Chambers that I scarcely knew him. That rumour might be true, I thought: Getliffe did not welcome the sound of youth knocking at the door. Still, I should make him keep his promise.

As I told Getliffe, I could not afford a holiday, but I spent a week that summer with my old friends in the town. I had been in close touch with them since I came to London, George Passant visited me regularly once a quarter, but I had only returned myself for odd days, when Eden sent me a two-guinea brief on the Midland Circuit. To many people it seemed strange, and they thought me heartless.

That was not accurate. I was an odd fish, but my affections were strong; my friendship with George, like all my others, would only end with death. When I stayed in London and avoided the town, it was for a complex of reasons – partly I had to think of the railway fare, partly I was shy of dogging Sheila's tracks, partly I had an instinct to hide until I could come back successful. But the strongest reason was also the simplest: George and the group did not particularly want me. They loved me, they were proud of me, they rejoiced in any victory I won – but I had gone from their intense intimate life, I was no longer in the secrets of the circle, and it was an embarrassment, almost an intrusion, when I returned. So, as the train drew into the station on an August evening, I was unreasonably depressed. From the carriage window I had seen the houses gleam under the clear night sky; the sulphurous smell of the station, confined within the red brick walls, was as it used to be, when I returned home from dining at the Inn; my heart sank. George greeted me like a conquering hero, and so did the group. In my mood that night, it made me worse to have others overconfident about my future. I explained sharply that I had made an exceptional start for an unknown young man, but that was all. I had been lucky in my friends, I had the advantage in solicitors' eyes of looking older than I was – but the testing time was the next two years. It was too early to cheer. George would not listen to my disclaimers. Robustly, obtusely, he shouted them away. He was not going to be deprived of his drinking party. They all drank cheerfully; they were drinking harder than ever, now that they were a little less impoverished; they would rather have been at the farm, without a revenant from earlier days, but nevertheless they were happy to get drunk. But it was sadly that I got drunk that night.

Afterwards, George and I walked by ourselves to his lodgings. I asked about some of our old companions: then I felt the barrier come between us. George was content and comfortable in my presence so long as I left the group alone. I asked about Jack, who had not met me that evening.

'Doing splendidly, of course,' said George, and hurried to another subject.

But it was George who volunteered information on one old friend. Marion was engaged to be married. George did not know the man, or the story, and had scarcely seen her, but he had heard that she was overwhelmingly happy.

I should have wished to be happy for her. But I was not. In the pang with which I heard the news, I learned how infinitely voracious one is. Any love that comes one's way – it is bitter to let go. I had not seen Marion for eighteen months, all my love was given to another. Yet it was painful to lose her. It was the final weight on that sad homecoming.

But I was soon cheered up by a ridiculous lunch at the Knights'. Sheila and I had gone through no storms that summer; she had been remotely affectionate, and she had not threatened me with the name of any other man. And she was pleased at my success. In front of her parents she teased me about the income I should soon be earning, about the money and honours on which I had my eye. It seemed to her extremely funny.

It did not seem, however, in the least funny to her father and mother. It seemed to them a very serious subject. And at that lunch I found myself being regarded as a distinctly more estimable character.

They were beginning to be worried about Sheila. Mrs Knight was a woman devoid of intuition, and she could not begin to guess what was wrong. All Mrs Knight observed were the rough-and-ready facts of the marriage market. Sheila was already twenty-four and, like me, often passed for thirty. For all her flirtations, she had given no sign of getting married. Lately she had brought no one home, except me for this lunch. To Mrs Knight, those were ominous facts. Whereas her husband had been uneasy about Sheila's happiness since her adolescence, and had suppressed his uneasiness simply because in his selfish and self-indulgent fashion he did not choose to be disturbed.

Thus they were each prepared, if not to welcome me, at least to modify their discouragement. Mr Knight went further. He took me into the rose garden, lit a cigar, and, as we both sat in deckchairs, talked about the careers of famous counsel. It was all done at two removes from me, with Mr Knight occasionally giving me a sideways glance from under his eyelids. He showed remarkable knowledge, and an almost Getliffian enthusiasm, about the pricing of briefs. I had never met a man with more grasp of the financial details of another profession. Without ever asking a straightforward question he was guessing the probable curve of my own income. He was interested in its distribution – what proportion would one earn in High Court work, in London outside the High Court, on the Midland Circuit? Mr Knight was moving surreptitiously to his point.

'I suppose you will be appearing now and then on circuit?'

'If I get some work.'

'Ah. It will *come*. It *will* come. I take it', said Mr Knight, looking in the opposite direction and thoughtfully studying a rose, 'that you might conceivably appear some time at the local assizes?'

I agreed that it was possible.

'If that should happen,' said Mr Knight casually, 'and if ever you want a quiet place to run over your documents, it would give no trouble to slip you into this house.'

I supposed that was his point. I hoped it was. But I was left half-mystified, for Mr Knight glanced at me under his eyelids, and went on: 'You won't be disturbed. You won't be. My wife and daughter might be staying with their relations. I shan't disturb you. I'm always tired. I sleep night and day.'

Whatever did he mean by Sheila and her mother staying with relations, I thought, as we joined them. Was he just taking away with one hand what he gave with the other? Or was there any meaning at all?

I was very happy. Sheila was both lively and docile, and walked along the lanes with me before I left. It was my only taste of respectable courtship.

The Michaelmas Term of 1929 was even more prosperous than I hoped. I lost the case Percy had brought me, but I made them struggle for the verdict, and the damages were low. Percy went so far as to admit that the damages were lower than he expected, and that we could not have done much better in this kind of breach of contract. Henriques' second case was, like the first, straightforward, and I won it. I earned most money, however, from the case in which I did nothing but paperwork: this was the case which had come from connexions of Charles March just before the vacation. It took some time to settle, and in the end we brought in a KC as a threat. The engineering firm of Howard and Hazlehurst were being sued by one of their agents for commission to which he might be entitled in law though not in common sense. The case never reached the courts, for we made a compromise: the KC's brief was marked at one hundred and fifty guineas, and according to custom I was paid two-thirds that fee.

After those events, and before the end of term, at last I scored a point in my long struggle of attrition with Getliffe. I kept reminding him of his promise to unload some of his briefs; I kept telling him, firmly, affectionately, reproachfully, in all the tones I could command, that I still had not made a pound through his help. As a rule, I disliked being pertinacious, but with Getliffe it was fun. The struggle swayed to and fro. He promised again; then he was too busy to consider any of his briefs; then he thought, almost tearfully, of his clients; then he offered to pay me a very small fee to devil a very large case. At last, on a December afternoon, his face suddenly became beatific. 'Old H-J (a solicitor named Hutton-Jones) is coming in soon! That means work for Herbert. Well, L S, I'm going to do something for you. I'm going to say to H-J that there's a man in these Chambers who'll do that job as well as I should. L S, I can't tell you how glad I am to do something for you. You deserve it, L S, you deserve it.'

He looked me firmly in the eyes and warmly clasped my hand.

It happened. A ten-guinea brief in the West London County Court came to me from Hurton-Jones: and it had, unquestionably, been offered to Getliffe. Later on, I became friendly with Hutton-Jones, and his recollection was that the conversation with Getliffe went something like this: 'H-J, do you really want me to do this? Don't get me wrong. Don't think I'm too high-hat to take the county court stuff. It's all grist that comes to the mill, and you know as well as I do, H-J, that I'm a poor man. But I have got a young chap here – well, I don't say he could do this job, but he might scrape through. Mind you, I like Eliot. Of course, he hasn't proved himself. I don't say that he's ripe for this job – '

Hutton-Jones knew something of Getliffe, and diverted the brief to me. I argued for a day in court, and then we reached a settlement. I had saved our clients a fair sum of money. Getliffe congratulated me, as man to man.

It was a long time before another of his cases found its way to me, but now, by the spring of 1930, I was well under way. Percy judged that he could back me a little farther; Henriques and the Harts were speaking approvingly of me in March circles; Hurton-Jones was trying me on some criminal work, legally dull but shot through with human interest. I was becoming busy. I even knew what it was, as summer approached, to have to refuse invitations to dinner because I was occupied with my briefs.

Just about that time a letter came from Marion, out of the blue. I had written to congratulate her on her engagement, and I had heard that she was married. Now she said that she would much like to visit me. I had a fleeting notion, flattering to my vanity, that she might be in distress and had turned to me for help. But the first sight of her, as she entered my sitting-room, was enough to sweep that daydream right away. She looked sleek, her eyes were shining, she had become much prettier, and she was expensively dressed: though, just as I remembered, she had managed to leave a patch of white powder or scurf on the shoulder of her jacket.

'Not that you can talk,' she grumbled, as I dusted it off.

'I needn't ask whether you're happy,' I said.

'I don't think you really need,' she said.

She was all set to tell me her story. Before we went out to dinner she had to describe exactly how it all happened. She had met Eric at a drama festival and had fallen romantically in love with him, body and soul, she said. And he with her. They fell passionately in love, and decided to get married. According to her account, he was modest, shy, very active physically. It was only after they were engaged that she discovered that he was also extremely rich.

'That's the best example of feminine realism I've ever heard,' I said.

Marion threw a book at me.

They were living in a country house in Suffolk. It was all perfect, she said. She was already with child.

'What's the use of waiting?' said Marion briskly.

'I must say, I envy you.'

She smiled. 'You ought to get married yourself, my boy.'

'Perhaps,' I said.

She asked suddenly: 'Are you going to marry that woman?'

I was slow to answer. At last I said:

'I hope so.'

Marion sighed.

'It will be a tragedy,' she said. 'You must realize that. You're much too sensible not to see what it would be like. She'll ruin you. Believe me; Lewis, this isn't sour grapes now.'

I shook my head.

'I hate her,' Marion burst out. 'If I could poison her and get away with it, I'd do it like a shot.'

'You don't know all of her,' I said.

'I know the effect she's had on you. No, I don't want you for myself, my dear. I shall love Eric for ever. But there's a corner in my heart for you.' She looked at me, half-maternally. 'Eric's a much better husband than you'd ever have been,' she said. 'Still, I suppose I shan't meet another man like you.'

As we parted she gave me an affectionate kiss.

She had come to show off her happiness, I thought. It was no more than her right. I did not begrudge it. I felt somewhat desolate. It made me think of my own marriage.

For, as I told Marion, I had never stopped hoping to marry Sheila. Since my first proposal I had not asked her again. But she knew, of course, that, whether I was too proud to pester her or not, she had only to show the slightest wish. In fact, we had lately played sometimes with the future. For months past she had seemed to think more of me; her letters were sometimes intimate and content. She had told me, in one of the phrases that broke out from her locked heart: 'With you I don't find joy. But you give me so much hope that I don't want to go away.'

That exalted me more than the most explicit word of love from another woman. I hoped, I believed as well as hoped, that the bond between us was too strong for her to escape, and that she would marry me.

And marriage was at last a practical possibility. I did my usual accounting at the beginning of July 1930. In the last year I had made nearly four hundred and fifty pounds. The briefs were coming in. Without touching wood, I reckoned that a comfortable income was secure. More likely than not, I should earn a large one.

Just a week after I went through my accounts I woke in the morning with an attack of giddiness. It was like those I used to have, at the time of the Bar Finals. I was a little worried, but did not think much of it. It took me a day or two to accept the fact that I was unwell. I was forced to remember that I had often felt exhausted in the last months. I had gone home from court, stretched myself on the sofa, been too worn out to do anything but watch the window darken. I tried to pretend it was nothing but fatigue. But the morning giddiness lasted, my limbs were heavy; as I walked, the pavement seemed to sink.

By instinct, I concealed my state from everyone round me. I asked Charles March if he could recommend a doctor; I explained that I had not needed one since I came to London, but that now I had a trivial skin complaint.

I went to Charles' doctor, half anxious, half expecting to be reassured as Tom Devitt had reassured me. I got no decision on the first visit. The doctor was waiting for a blood count. Then the result came; it was not clear-cut. I explained to the doctor, whose name was Morris, that I had just established my practice, and could not leave it. I explained that I was hoping to get married. He was kindly and worried. He tried to steady me, 'It's shocking bad luck,' he said. 'But I've got to tell you. You may be rather ill.'

38

Some Kinds of Suffering

IN the surgery, my first concern was to put on a stoical front. Alone in my room, I stared out at the summer sky. The doctor had been vague, he was sending me to a specialist. How serious was it? I was enraged that no one should know, that the disaster should be so nebulous, that instead of having mastered the future I could no longer think a month ahead. Sometimes, for moments together, I could not believe it – just as, after Sheila's first cruel act, I walked across the park and could not credit that it had happened. Then I was chilled with dread. How gravely was I ill? I was afraid to die.

Already that afternoon, however, and all the time I was visiting the specialist, there was one direction in which my judgement was clear. No one must know. It would destroy my practice if the truth were known. No one would persevere with a sick young man. That might not matter, I thought grimly. But it was necessary to act as though I should recover. So no one must know, not even my intimates.

I kept that resolve throughout the doctors' tests, Fortunately, it was the Long Vacation, and Getliffe was away; his inquisitive eyes might have noticed too much. Fortunately also, although I was very pale, I did not look particularly ill; in fact, having had more money and so eating better, I had put on some weight in the past year. I forced myself to crawl tiredly to Chambers, sit there for some hours, make an effort to work upon a brief. I thought that Percy had his suspicions, and I tried to deceive him about my spirits and my energy.

I mentioned casually that I felt jaded after a hard year and that I might go away for a holiday and miss the first few days of next term.

'Don't be away too long, sir,' said Percy impassively. 'It's easy to get yourself forgotten. It's easy to do that.'

From the beginning the doctors guessed that I had pernicious anaemia. They stuck to the diagnosis even when as I afterwards realised – they should have been more sceptical. There was some evidence for it. There was no doubt about the anaemia; my blood counts were low and getting lower; but that could have happened (as Tom Devitt had said years ago) through strain and conflict. But also some of the red cells were pear-shaped instead of round, and some otherwise misshapen; and since the doctors were ready to believe in a pernicious anaemia, that convinced them.

But the reason why they originally guessed so puzzled me for a long time. For they were sound, cautious doctors of good reputation. It was much later that Charles March, after he had changed his profession and taken to medicine, told me that my physical type was common among pernicious anaemia cases – grey or blue eyes set wide apart, smooth tough skin, thick chest, and ectomorphic limbs. Then at last their diagnosis became easy to understand.

They were soon certain of it, assured me that it ought to be controllable, and fed me on hog's stomach. But my blood did not respond: the count went down; and then they did not know what to do. All they could suggest was that I should go abroad and rest, and continue, for want of any other treatment, to eat another protein extract.

This was at the beginning of August. I could leave, as though it were an ordinary holiday. I still kept my secret, although there were times when my nerve nearly broke, or when I was beyond caring. For my resistance was weakening now. Charles March, who knew that I was ill, but not what the doctor had told me, bought my tickets, and booked me a room at Mentone: I was tired out, and glad to go.

I had not seen Sheila since I went to be examined. Now I wrote to her. I was not well, I said, and was being sent abroad for a rest. I was travelling the day after she would receive this letter. I was anxious to see her before I left.

It was my last afternoon in England, and I waited in my room. I knew her trains by heart, That afternoon I did not have long to wait. Within ten minutes of the time that she could theoretically arrive, I heard her step on the stairs.

She came and kissed me. Then she stood back and studied my face.

'You don't look so bad,' she said.

'That's just as well,' I said.

'Why is it?'

I told her it was necessary to go on being hearty in Chambers. It was the kind of sarcastic joke that she usually enjoyed, but now her eyes were strained.

'It's not funny,' she said harshly.

She was restless. Her movements were stiff and awkward. She sat down, pulled out a cigarette, then put it back in her case. Timidly she laid a hand on mine.

'I'd no idea there was anything wrong,' she said.

I looked at her.

'It must have been going on for some time,' she said.

'I think it has.'

'I'm usually fairly perceptive,' she said in a tone aggrieved, conceited, and remorseful. 'But I didn't notice a thing.'

'I expect you were busy,' I said.

She lost her temper. 'That's the most unpleasant thing you've ever told me.'

She was white with anger, right at the flashpoint of one of her outbursts of acid rage. Then, with an effort, she calmed herself.

'I'm sorry,' she cried. 'I don't know – '

In the lull we talked for a few minutes, neutrally, of where we should dine that night.

Sheila broke away from the conversation, and asked: 'Are you ill?'

I did not reply.

'You must be, or you wouldn't let them send you away. That's true, isn't it?'

'I suppose it is,' I said.

'How badly are you ill?' she asked.

'I don't know. The doctors don't know either.'

'It may be serious?'

'Yes, it may be.'

She was staring full at me.

'I don't think you'll die in obscurity,' she said in a high, level voice, with a curious prophetic certainty. She went on: 'You wouldn't like that, would you?'

'No,' I said.

Somehow, in her bleak insistence, she made it easier for me. Her eyes were really like searchlights, I thought, picking out things that no one else saw, then swinging past and leaving a gulf of darkness.

She tried to talk of the future. She broke away again: 'You're frightened, aren't you?'

'Yes.'

'I think you're more frightened than I should be.' She considered. 'Yet you can put on a show to fool your lawyer friends. There are times when you make me feel a child.'

The day went on. Once she said, without any preliminary: 'Darling, I wish I were a different woman.'

She knew that I was begging her for comfort.

'Why didn't you love someone else? No decent woman could let you go like this.'

I had said not a word, I had not embraced her that day. She knew that I was begging for the only comfort strong enough to drive out fear. She knew that I craved for the solace of the flesh. She had to let me go without.

At Mentone I sat on the terrace by the sea, happy in the first few days as though I were well again, as though I were sure of Sheila. I had never been abroad before, and I was exhilarated by the sight of the warm sea, the quickening of all the senses which I felt by that shore. Some of my symptoms dropped away overnight, as I basked in the sun. The sea was so calm that it lost its colour. Instead it stretched like a mirror with a soft and luminous sheen to the edge of the horizon, where it darkened to a stratum of grey silk. It stretched like a mirror without colour, except where, in the wake of each boat that was painted on the surface, there was pencilled, heightening the calm, a dark unbroken line.

And when the Mediterranean summer broke into storms, I still had a pleasure, a reassurance of physical well-being, as I stood by the bedroom window at night and, through the rain and wind, smelt the bougainvillea and the arbutus. Turning back to see my bed in the light of the reading lamp, I was ready to forget my fears and sleep.

An old Austrian lady was living in the hotel. Because of her lungs she had spent the last ten years by the Mediterranean; she had a viperine tongue and a sweet smile, and I enjoyed listening to her talk of Viennese society in the days of the Hapsburgs. Inside a fortnight we became friends. I used to take her for gentle walks through the gardens, and I confided in her. I told her as much about my career as I had told Charles March; and I told her more of my love for Sheila and my illness than I had told anyone alive.

Slowly that respite ended. Slowly the illness returned, at first by stealth, so that I did not know whether a symptom was a physical fact or just an alarm of the nerves; one day I would be abnormally fatigued, and then, waking refreshed next morning, I could disbelieve it. Gradually but certainly, after the first mirage-like week, the weakness crept back, the giddiness, the sinking of the ground underfoot. I had provided myself with an apparatus so that I could make a rough measure of my blood count. While I felt better, I left it in my trunk. Later, as I became suspicious of my state, I tried to keep away from it. Once I had used the apparatus, quite unrealistically I began going through the process each day, as though in hope or dread I expected a miracle. It was difficult to be accurate with the little pipette, I had not done many scientific experiments, I longed to cheat in my own favour, and then overcompensated in the other direction. By the third week in August I knew that the count was lower than in July. It seemed more likely than not that it was still going down.

I used to wake hour by hour throughout the night. Down below was the sound of the sea, which in my first days had given me such content. I was damp with sweat. I thought of all I had promised to do – instead, I saw nothing but the empty dark. In my schooldays I had seen a master in the last stage of pernicious anaemia – yellow-skinned, exhausted, in despair. I had not heard of the disease then. Now I knew what his history must have been, step by step. I had read about the intermissions which now, reconstructing what I remembered, I realised must have visited him. For six months or a year he had come back to teach, and seemed recovered. If one were lucky – I thought how brilliant my luck had been, how, despite all my impatience and complaints, no one of my provenance had made a more fortunate start at the Bar – one might have such intermissions for periods of years. Lying awake to the sound of the sea, I felt surges of the fierce hope that used to possess my mother and which was as natural to me. Even if I had this disease, then still I might make time to do something.

Sometimes, in those nights, I was inexplicably calmed. I woke up incredulous that this could be my fate. The doctors were wrong. I was frightened, but still lucid, and they were confused. Apart from the misshapen cells, I had none of the true signs of the disease. There were no sores on my tongue. Each time I woke, I tested my tongue against my teeth. It became a tic, which sometimes, when I felt a pain, made me imagine the worst, which sometimes gave me the illusion of safety.

In those hot summer nights, with the sea slithering and slapping below, I thought of death. With animal fear, once or twice with detachment. I should die hard, I knew. If the time was soon to come, or whenever it came, I was not the kind to slip easily from life. Like my mother, I might manage to put a face on it, while others were watching: but in loneliness, in the extreme loneliness before death, I should, again like her, be cowardly and struggling, begging on my knees for every minute I could wrench out of the final annihilation. At twenty-five, when this blow struck me, I begged more ravenously. It would be bitterly hard to die without knowing, what I had longed for with all the intensity of which I was capable, any kind of achievement or love fulfilled. But once or twice, I thought, with a curious detachment, that I should have held on as fearfully and tenaciously if it came twenty or forty years later. When I had to face the infinite emptiness, I should never be reconciled, and should cry out in my heart 'Why must this happen to *me*?'

After such a night, I would get up tired, prick my finger, extract a drop of blood and go through my meaningless test, then I had breakfast on the terrace, looking out at the shining sea. My Austrian friend would come slowly along, resting a hand on the parapet. She used to look at me and ask: 'How is it this morning, my dear friend?'

I said often:

'A little better than yesterday, I think. Not perfect –' For it was difficult to disappoint her. A bright concern came to her eyes, intensely alive in the old face.

'Ah,' she said, 'when autumn is here, perhaps we shall both be better.'

Then each day I had to wait for the post from England. It arrived just before teatime; and as soon as it arrived I was waiting for the next day. I had written to Sheila on my first morning there, a long, loving, hopeful letter; the days passed, the days became weeks, August was turning into September, and I had heard nothing. For a time it did not worry me. But suddenly, one afternoon, as I waited while the porter ran through the bundle, it seemed that all depended on the next day – and so through afternoons of waiting, of watching the postman bicycle along the road, of the delay while they were sorted. At last, each afternoon, the sad and violent anger when there was nothing from her.

In cold blood, knowing her, I could not understand it. Was she ill herself? She could have told me. Had she found another man? In all her caprices she had never neglected a kind of formal etiquette towards me. Was it an act of cruelty? Had I thrown myself too abjectly on her mercy, that last day? It seemed incredible, even for her, I thought, with my temper smouldering, on those evenings as the lights came out along the shore. I had loved her for five years. I would not have treated the most casual acquaintance so, let alone one in my state.

Whatever she was feeling, she knew my state. I could not forgive her. I wanted her to suffer as I did.

I wrote again, and then again.

There were other letters from England, some disquieting rumours about George's indiscretions in the town; the news of the birth of Marion's child, a girl; a story of Charles March's father; and, surprisingly, a letter from Salisbury, saying that he had thought I was not so tireless as usual last term and that – if this was not just his imagination – I might like to know that he himself had a minor collapse just after he began to make a living at the Bar. Was he probing, I thought? Or was it a generous impulse? Perhaps both.

From all that news I got no more than a few minutes' distraction. I was more self-centred than ever in my life. I had no room for anything but my two concerns – my illness, and my obsession with Sheila. All else was trivial; I was utterly uninterested in the passing scene and, for once, in other human beings. I knew that my two miseries played on each other. I had the sense, which all human beings dread, which I was to see dominate another's existence, of my life being outside my will. However much we may say and know that we are governed by forces outside our control, and that the semblance of volition is only an illusion to us all, yet that illusion, when it is challenged, is one of the things we fight for most bitterly. If it is threatened, we feel a horror unlike anything else in life.

In its extreme form, this horror is the horror of madness, and most of us know its shadow, for moments anyway, when we are in the grip of an overmastering emotion. The emotion may give us pleasure or not, for most of its duration we can feel ourselves in full control; but there are moments, particularly in love, particularly in such a love as mine for Sheila, when the illusion is shattered and we see ourselves in the hands of ineluctable fate, our voices, our protests, our reasons as irrelevant to what we do as the sea sounding in the night was to my wretchedness, while I lay awake.

It was in such moments that I faced the idea of suicide. Not altogether in despair – but with the glint of a last triumph. And I believed the idea had come in that identical fashion to other men like me, and for the same reason. Not only as a relief from unhappiness, but also a sign, the only one possible, that the horror is not there, and that one's life is, in the last resort, answerable to will. At any rate, it was so with me.

In much the same spirit as I entertained the idea of suicide, I made plans for the future that ignored both physical health and Sheila. I've been unhappy for long enough, I thought. I'm going to forget her and get better. I must settle what steps to take. Framing plans that assumed that the passion was over, that I could make myself well by a resolution, plans of all the things I should never be able to do.

Beyond the horror of having lost my will, there was another, a simpler companion of those days. That was suffering. Suffering unqualified and absolute, so that at times the anger fled, the complaints and assertions became squallings of my own conceit, and there was nothing left but unhappiness. It was a suffering simple, uneventful, and complete. It lay upon me as weakness lay on my body. I thought I could never be as unhappy again.

It was the middle of September. I had known this suffering for some weeks, during which it was more constantly with me than any emotion I had known. I was sitting by the rocks, looking over to the mountains, arid in brown and purple, overhung by rotund masses of cloud. The water was as calm as in my first days there, and the clouds threw long reflections towards me – thin strips of white across the burnished sea. Mechanically I puzzled why these lattice-like separate strips should be reflected from clouds which, seen from where I sat, were flocculent masses above the hills.

It was as tranquil a sight as I had seen.

Then, for a moment, I knew that I was crying out against my fate no more. I knew that I was angry with Sheila no more (I was thinking of her protectively, reflecting that she must be restless and distressed); that all my protests and plans and attempts to revive my will were as feeble as a child's crying to drown the storm; that my arrogance and spirit had left me, that I could no longer keep to myself the pretence of self-respect. I knew that I had been broken by unhappiness. In that clear moment – whatever I protested to myself next day – I knew that

I had to accept my helplessness, that I had been broken and could do nothing more.

October came. Term would begin in a few days. I had to make a practical decision, Should I return?

In the past weeks letters had arrived from Sheila, one every other day, remotely apologetic, without any reason for her silence, yet intimate with a phrase or two that seemed to ask my help. I tried to dismiss those letters as I made my decision. I had to dismiss all I had felt by that shore or seen within myself.

My physical condition was no better, but not much worse. Or rather my blood count was descending, though the rate of descent seemed to have slowed. In other respects I was probably better. I was deeply sunburned, which caused me to look healthy except to a clinical eye. That would be an advantage, I thought, if I tried to brazen it out.

If I were not going to get better, it did not matter what I did.

For any practical choice, I had to assume that I should get better.

That assumed, was it wiser to return to Chambers, persist in concealing that I was ill, and try to carry it off? Or to stay away until I had recovered?

There was no doubt of the answer. If, at my stage, I stayed away long, I should never get back. One term's absence would do me great harm, and two would finish me. I might scrape a living or acquire a minor legal job, but I should have been a failure.

No, I must return. Now, before the beginning of term, as though nothing had happened.

There were grave risks. I was very weak. I might, with discipline and good management, struggle through the paper work adequately; but I was in no physical state to fight any case but the most placid. I might disgrace myself. Instead of losing my practice by absence, I might do so by presence.

That was a risk I must take. I might contrive to save myself exhaustion. To some extent, I could pick and choose my cases; I could eliminate the police courts straight away. I should have to alter the régime of my days, and use my energies for nothing but the cardinal hours in court.

Whatever came of it, I must return.

On my last evening the sun was falling across the terrace, shining in the pools left by the day's rain. The arbutus smelt heavily as my friend and I came to the end of our last walk. 'We shall meet again,' she said. 'If not next year, then some other time.' Neither of us believed it.

When the car drove through the gates, and I looked back at the sea, I felt the same distress that, years before, overcame me when I left the office for the last time. But on that shore I had been more unhappy than ever in my youth, and so was bound more tightly. More than ever in my youth, I did not know what awaited me at the end of my journey. So, looking back at the sea, I felt a stab of painful yearning, as though all I wanted in the world was to stay there and never be torn away.

39

Sheila's Room

MY luck in practical affairs was remarkable. Looking back from middle-age, I saw how many chances had gone in my favour; and I felt a kind of vertigo, as though I had climbed along a cliff, and was studying the angle from a safe place. How well should I face it, if required to do the same again?

My luck held that autumn, as, dragging my limbs, I made my way each morning across the Temple gardens. Mist lay on the river, the grass sparkled with dew in the October sunshine. They were mornings that made me catch my breath in exhilaration. I was physically wretched, I was training myself to disguise my weakness, but the sun shone through the fresh mist and I caught my breath. And I got through the days, the weeks, the term, without losing too much credit. I managed to carry off what I had planned by the sea at Mentone; I took defeats, strain, anxiety, and foreboding, but, with extraordinary luck, I managed to carry off enough to save my practice.

I met some discouragement. Each time I saw him, Getliffe made a point of asking with frowning man-to-man concern about my health. 'I'm very strong, L S,' he told me, as though it were a consolation. 'I've always been very strong.'

What was more disturbing, I had to persuade Percy that it was sensible to cut myself off from the county court work. It was not sensible, of course. My income was not large enough to bring any such step within the confines of sense. My only chance was to persuade Percy that I was arrogantly sure of success, so sure that I proposed to act as though I were already established, It was bad enough to have to convince him that I had not lost my head; it was worse, because I believed that he suspected the true reason. If so, I knew that I could expect no charity. Percy's judgement of my future had been − I had long since guessed − professional ability above average, influence nil, health doubtful; as a general prospect, needs watching for years. He would be gratified to have predicted my bodily collapse. It was more important to be right than to be compassionate.

'If you don't want them, Mr Eliot,' said Percy, 'there are plenty who do. In my opinion, it's a mistake. That is, if you're going on at the Bar.'

'In five years,' I said, 'you'll be able to live on my briefs.'

'I hope so, sir,' said Percy.

Going away that afternoon, so tired that I took a taxi home, I knew that I had handled him badly. All through that Michaelmas Term, although briefs came to me from solicitors whose cases I had previously fought, there was not a single one which Percy had foraged for. He had written me off.

Fortunately, there were a number of solicitors who now sent work to me. I received several briefs, and there was only one case that autumn where my physical state humiliated me. That was a disgrace. My stamina failed me on the first morning, I could not concentrate, my memory let me down, I was giddy on my feet; I lost a case that any competent junior should have won. Some days afterwards, a busybody of an acquaintance told me there was a whisper circulating that Eliot was ill and finished. In my vanity I preferred them to say that than take that performance as my usual form,

But, as I have said, by good luck I wiped out most of that disaster. The whispers became quieter. First I nursed myself through a case of Henriques', where, though I lost again, I knew I did pretty well. Charles March said it was my best case yet, and Henriques was discreetly satisfied. And then I had two magnificent strokes of fortune. In the same week I received two cases of a similar nature; in each the arguments were intricate and needed much research, and the cases were unlikely to come to court. Nothing could have been better designed for my condition. There was every chance to cover my deficiency. In actual fact, I made some backers through one of those cases; the other was uneventful; each was settled out of court, and I earned nearly two hundred and fifty pounds for the two together. They made the autumn prosperous. They hid my illness, or at least they prevented it becoming public. I thought I had lost little ground so far. It was luck unparalleled.

In November, without giving me any warning, Sheila came to live in London. She had compelled her father, so she wrote, to guarantee her three hundred pounds a year. An aunt had just died and left her some money in trust, and so she was at last independent. She had taken a bed-sitting-room in Worcester Street, off Lupus Street, where I could visit her. It was unexpected and jagged, like so many of her actions – like our last meeting, at Victoria Station on my return from France. The train was hours late; she had sent no word; but there she was, standing patiently outside the barrier.

Fog was whirling round the street lamps on the afternoon that I first went to Worcester Street. The trees of St George's Square loomed out of the white as the bus passed by. From the pavement, it was hard to make out the number of Sheila's house. She was living on the first floor: there was a little cardboard slip against her bell – MISS KNIGHT – for all the world like some of my former clients, prostitutes down on their luck, whom for curiosity's sake I had visited in those decaying streets.

Her room struck warm. It was large, with a substantial mantelpiece and obsolete bell pushers by the side. In the days of the house's prosperity, this must have been a drawing-room. Now the gas fire burned under the mantelpiece, and, near the opposite wall, an oil stove was chugging away and throwing a lighted pattern on the ceiling.

'How are you?' said Sheila. 'You're not better yet.'

I had come straight from the courts, and I was exhausted. She put me in a chair with an awkward, comradely kindness, and then opened a cupboard to give me a drink. I had never been in a room of hers before; and I saw that the glasses in the cupboard, the crockery and bottles, were marshalled with geometrical precision, in neat lines and squares. That was true of every piece of furniture; she had only been there three days, but all was tidy, was more than tidy, was so ordered that she became worried if a lamp or book was out of its proper line.

I chaffed her: how had she stood my disarray?

'That's you,' she said. 'We're different.' She seemed content, secretively triumphant, to be looking after me in a room of her own. As she knelt by the glasses and poured the whisky, her movements had lost their stylised grace. She looked more fluent, comfortable, matter-of-fact, and warm. Perhaps I was seeing what I wanted to see. I was too tired to care, too happy to be sitting there, with her waiting upon me.

'It's time you got better,' said Sheila, as I was drinking. 'I'm waiting for you to get better.'

I took her hand. She held mine, but her eyes were clouded.

'Never mind,' I said.

'I must mind,' she said sharply.

'I may be cheating myself,' I said, 'but some days I feel stronger.'

'Tell me when you're sure.' There was an impatient tone in her voice, but I was soothed and heartened, and promised her, and, so as not to spoil the peace of the moment, changed the subject.

I reminded her how often she had talked of breaking away from home and 'doing something'; the times that we had ploughed over it; how I had teased her about the sick conscience of the rich, and how bitterly she had retorted. Like her father, I wanted to keep her as a toy. My attitude to her was Islamic, I had no patience with half her life. Now here she was, broken away from home certainly, but not noticeably listening to her sick conscience. Instead, she was living like a tart in Pimlico.

Sheila grinned. It was rarely that she resented my tongue. She answered good-humouredly: 'I wish I'd been thrown out at sixteen, though. And had to earn a living. It would have been good for me.'

I told her, as I had often done before, that the concept of life as a moral gymnasium could be overdone.

'It would have been good for me,' said Sheila obstinately. 'And I should have been quite efficient. I mightn't have had time – ' She broke off. That afternoon, as I lay tired out in my chair (too tired to think of making love – she knew that; did it set her free?), she did not mind so much being absurd, She even showed me her collection of coins. I had heard of it before, but she had shied off when I pressed her. Now she produced it, blushing but at ease. It stood under a large glass case by the window: the coins were beautifully mounted, documented, and indexed; she showed me her scales, callipers, microscope, and weights. The collection was restricted to Venetian gold and silver from the fifteenth century to the Napoleonic occupation. Mr Knight, who begrudged her money for most purposes, had been incongruously generous over this one, and she had been able to buy any coin that came into the market. The collection was, she said, getting on towards complete.

When she had mentioned her coins previously, I had found it sinister – to imagine her plunged into such a refuge. But as I studied her catalogue, in the writing that I had so often searched for a word of love, and listened to her explanations, it seemed quite natural. She was so knowledgeable, competent, and curiously professional. She liked teaching me. She was becoming gayer and more intimate. If only her records had arrived, she would have begun educating me in music, as she had long wanted to do. She insisted that she must do it soon. As it was, she said she had better instruct me in the science of numismatics. She drew the curtains and shut out the foggy afternoon. She stood above me, looking into my eyes with a steady gaze, affectionate and troubled; then she said: 'Now I'll show you how to measure a coin.'

After that afternoon, I imagined the time when I could tell her that I was well. Would it come? As soon as I came back to London, my doctors had examined me again. They had shaken their heads, The blood count was perceptibly worse than when I went to France. The treatment had not worked, and, apart from advising me to rest, they were at a loss. In the weeks that followed I lost all sense of judgement about my physical state. Sometimes I thought the disease was gaining. There were mornings, as I told Sheila, when I woke and stretched myself and dared to hope. I had given up taking any blood counts on my own. It was best to train myself to wait. With Sheila, with my career, I thought, I had had some practice in waiting. In time I was bound to know whether I should recover. It would take time to see the answer, yes or no.

But others were not so willing to watch me being stoical. I had let the truth slip out, bit by bit, to Charles March as well as to Sheila. Charles was a man whose response to misery or danger or anxiety was very active. He could not tolerate my settling down to endure – before he had dragged me in front of any doctor in London who might be useful. I told him it would waste time and money. Either this was a psychosomatic condition, I said, which no doctor could reach and where my insight was probably better than theirs. If that was the explanation, I should recover. If not, and it was some rare form of pernicious anaemia untouched by the ordinary treatments, I should in due course die. Either way, we should know soon enough. It would only be an irritation and distress to have more doctors handling me and trying to make up their minds.

Charles would not agree. His will was strong, and mine was weakened, after that November afternoon, by Sheila's words. And also there were times just then when I wanted someone to lean on. So I gave way. Until the end of term I should keep up my bluff; but I was ready to be examined by any of his doctors during the Christmas vacation.

Charles organized it thoroughly. At the time, December 1930, he was, by a slight irony, a very junior medical student, for he had recently renounced the Bar and started what was to be his real career. He had not yet taken his first MB – but his father and uncle were governors of hospitals. It did not take long to present me to a chief physician. I was installed in a ward before Christmas. The hospital had orders to make a job of it: I became acquainted with a whole battery of clinical tests, not only those, such as barium meals, which might be relevant to my disease.

I loathed it all. It was hard to take one's fate, with someone forcing a test-meal plunger down one's throat. I could not sleep with others round me. I had lost my resignation. I spent the nights dreading the result.

On the first day of the new year, the chief physician talked to me.

'You ought to be all right,' he said. 'It's much more likely than not.' He dropped his eyelids.

'You'd better try to forget the last few months. Forget about this disease. I'm confident you've not got it. Forget what you were told,' he said. 'It must have been a shock. It wasn't a good experience for you.'

'I shall get over it,' I said, in tumultuous relief.

'I've known these things leave their mark.'

Having set me at rest, he went over the evidence. Whatever the past, there were now no signs of pernicious anaemia; no achlorhydria; nothing to support the diagnosis. I had had a moderately severe secondary anaemia, which should improve. That was the optimistic view. No one could be certain, but he would lay money on it. He talked to me much as Tom Devitt had once done – with more knowledge and authority but less percipience. Much of the history of my disease was mysterious, he said. I had to learn to look after myself. Eat more. Keep off spirits. Find yourself a good wife.

After I had thanked him, I said: 'Can I get up and go?'

'You'll be weak.'

'Not too weak to get out,' I said; and, in fact, so strong was the suggestion of health, that as I walked out of the hospital, the pavement was firm beneath my feet, for the first time in six months.

The morning air was raw. In the city, people passed anonymously in the mist. I watched a bank messenger cross the road in his top hat and carrying a ledger. I was so light-hearted that I wanted to stop a stranger and tell him my escape. I was light-hearted, not only with relief but with a surge of recklessness. Miseries had passed; so would those to come. Somehow I survived. Sheila, my practice, the next years, danced through my thoughts. It was a time to act. She was at home for Christmas – but there was another thing to do. In that mood, reckless, calculating, and confident, I went to find Percy in order to have it out.

There was no one else in Chambers, but he was sitting in his little room, reading a sporting paper. He said 'Good morning, Mr Eliot,' without curiosity, though he must have been surprised to see me. I asked him to come out for a drink. He was not over-willing, but he had nothing to do. 'In any case,' I said, 'I must talk to you, Percy. You may as well have a drink while you listen.'

We walked up to the Devereux, and there in the bar-room Percy and I sat by the window. The room was smoky and noisy, full of people shouting new-year greetings. Percy drank from his tankard, and impassively watched them.

I began curtly: 'I've been lying to you.'

Instead of watching the crowd, he watched me, with no change of expression.

'I've been seriously ill. Or at least they thought I was.'

'I saw you weren't up to the mark, Mr Eliot,' he said.

'Listen,' I said. 'I want us to understand each other. They thought that I might have a fatal disease. It was a mistake. I'm perfectly well. If you need any confirmation,' I smiled at him, 'I can produce evidence. From Sir—' And I said that I had that morning come from the hospital, I told him the story without any palaver.

He asked: 'Why didn't you let any of us know?'

'That's a bloody silly question,' I said, 'How much change should I have got – if everyone heard I was a bad life?'

For once, his eyes flickered.

'How much work would you have brought me?' I asked.

He did not answer.

'Come to that – how much work did you bring me last term?'

He did not prevaricate. He could have counted briefs which passed through his hands but which he had done nothing to gain. But he said, as brutally as I had spoken:

'Not a guinea's worth. I thought you were fading out.'

'I don't grumble,' I said. 'It's all in the game. I don't want charity. I don't need it now. But you ought to be careful not to make a fool of yourself.'

I went on. I was well now, I should be strong by the summer, the doctors had no doubt that I should stand the racket of the Bar. I had come through without my practice suffering much. I had my connexions, Henriques and the rest. It would be easy for me to move to other Chambers. A change from Getliffe, a change from Percy to a clerk who believed in me – I should double my income in a year.

Even at the time, I doubted whether that threat much affected him. But I had already achieved my end. He was a cross-grained man. He despised those who dripped sympathy and who expected a flow of similar honey in return. His native language, though he got no chance to use it, was one of force and violence and temper, and he thought better of me for speaking that morning in the language that he understood. He had never done so before, but he invited me to drink another pint of beer.

'You needn't worry, Mr Eliot,' he said. 'I don't make promises, but I believe you'll be all right.'

He stared at me, and took a long gulp.

'I should like to wish you', he said, 'a happy and prosperous new year.'

40

Listening to Music

IT was still the first week in January, and I was walking along Worcester Street on my way to Sheila's. She had returned the day before, and I was saving up for the luxury of telling her my news. I could have written, but I had saved it up for the glow of that afternoon. I was still light-hearted, light-hearted and lazy with relief. The road glistened in the drizzle, the basement lights were gleaming, here and there along the street one could gaze into lighted rooms – books, a table, a lamp-shade, a piano, a curtained bed. Why did those sights move one so, was it the hint of unknown lives? It was luxurious to see the lighted rooms, walking down the wet street on the way to Sheila.

I had no plan ready-made for that afternoon. I did not intend to propose immediately, now all was well. There was time enough now. Before the month was over I should speak, but it was luxurious to be lazy that day, and my thoughts flowed round her as they had flowed when I first fell in love. It was strange that she should be lodging in this street. She had always felt a nostalgia for the scruffy; perhaps she had liked me more, when we first met, because I was a shabby young man living in a garret.

I thought of other friends, like her comfortably off, who could not accept their lives. The social climate was overawing them. They could not take their good luck in their stride. If one had a talent for non-acceptance, it was a bad generation into which to be born rich. The callous did not mind, nor did the empty, nor did those who were able not to take life too hard; but among my contemporaries I could count half a dozen who were afflicted by the sick conscience of the rich.

Sheila was not made for harmony, but perhaps her mother's money impeded her search for it. If she had been a man, she might, like Charles March, have insisted on finding a job in which she could feel useful; one of Charles' reasons for becoming a doctor was to throw away the burden of guilt; she was as proud and active as he, and if she had been a man she too might have found a way to live. If she had been a man, I thought idly and lovingly as I came outside her house, she would have been happier. I looked up at her window. The light shone rosy through the curtains. She was there, alone in her room, and in the swell of love my heart sank and rose.

I ran upstairs, threw my arm round her waist, said that it had been a false alarm and that I should soon be quite recovered. 'It makes me feel drunk,' I said, and pressed her to me.

'You're certain of it?' she said, leaning back in the crook of my elbow.

I told her that I was certain.

'You're going to become tough again? You'll be able to go on?'

'Yes, I shall go on,'

'I'm glad, my dear. I'm glad for your sake.' She had slipped from my arms, and was watching me with a strange smile. She added: 'And for mine too,'

I exclaimed. I was already chilled.

She said: 'Now I can ask your advice.'

'What do you mean?'

'I'm in love. Quite honestly. It's very surprising. I want you to tell me what to do.'

She had often tortured me with the names of other men. There had been times when her eye was caught, or when she was making the most of a new hope. But she had never spoken with this authority. On the instant, I believed her. I gasped, as though my lungs were tight. I turned away. The reading lamp seemed dim, so dim that the current might be failing. I was suddenly drugged by an overwhelming fatigue; I wanted to go to sleep.

'I had to tell you,' she was saying.

'Why didn't you tell me before?'

'You weren't fit to take it,' she said.

'This must be the only time on record', I said, 'when you've considered me.'

'I may have deserved that,' she replied. She added: 'Believe me. I'm hateful. But this time I tried to think of you. You were going through enough. I couldn't tell you that I was happy.'

'When did it happen?'

'Just after you went to France,'

I was stupefied that I had not guessed.

'You didn't write to me for weeks,' I said.

'That was why. I hoped you'd get well quickly.' She shrugged her shoulders. 'I'm no good at deceit.'

I sat down. For a period that may have been minutes – I had lost all sense of time – I stared into the room. I half knew that she had brought up a chair close to mine. At last I said:

'What do you want me to do?'

Her reply was instantaneous:

'See that I don't lose him.'

'I can't do that,' I said roughly.

'I want you to,' she said. 'You're wiser than I am. You can tell me how not to frighten him away.' She added: 'He's pretty helpless. I've never liked a man who wasn't. Except you. He can't cope very well. He's rather like me. We've got a lot in common.'

I had heard other 'we's' from her, taunting my jealousy, but not in such a tone as this. She dwelt on it with a soft and girlish pleasure. I was chained there. I fell again into silence. Then I asked peremptorily who he was.

She was eager to tell me. She spoke of him as Hugh. It was only some days later, when I decided to meet him, that I learned his surname. He was a year or two older than Sheila and me, and so was at that time about twenty-seven. He had no money, she said, though

313

his origins were genteel. Some of his uncles were well off, and he was a clerk at a stockbroker's, being trained to go into the firm. 'He hates it,' she said. 'He'll never be any good at it. It's ridiculous.' He had no direction or purpose; he did not even know whether he wanted to get married.

'Why is he the answer?' I could not keep the question back.

She answered: 'It's like finding part of myself.'

She was rapt, she wanted me to rejoice with her. 'I must show you his photograph,' she said. 'I've hidden it when you came. Usually it stands – ' She pointed to a shelf at the head of the divan on which she slept. 'I like to wake up and see it in the morning.'

She was more girlish, more delighted to be girlish, than a softer woman might have been. She went to a cupboard, bent over, and stayed for a second looking at the photograph before she brought it out. Each action and posture was, as I had observed the first time I visited that room, more flowing and relaxed than a year ago. When I first observed that change, I did not guess that she was in love. Her profile was hard and clear, as she bent over the photograph; her lips were parted, as though she wanted to gush without constraint. 'It's rather a nice face,' she said, handing me the picture. It was a weak, and sensitive face. The eyes were large, bewildered, and idealistic. I gave it back without a word. 'You can see', she said, 'that he's not much good at looking after himself. Much less me. I know it's asking something, but I want you to help. I've never listened to anyone else, but I listen to you. And so will he.'

She tried to make me promise to meet him. I was so much beside myself that I gave an answer and contradicted myself and did not know what I intended. It was so natural to look after her; to shield this vulnerable happiness, to preserve her from danger. At the same time, all my angry heartbreak was pent up. I had not uttered a cry of that destructive rage.

She was satisfied. She felt assured that I should do as she asked. 'Now what shall I do for you?' she cried in her rapture. 'I know,' she said, with a smile half-sarcastic, half-innocent as she brought out her anticlimax. 'I shall continue your musical education.' Since my first visit to Worcester Street, she had played records each time I went – to disguise her love. Yet it had been a pleasure to her. She knew I was unmusical, often she had complained that it was a barrier between us, and she liked to see me listening. She could not believe that the sound meant nothing. She had only to explain, and my deafness would fall away.

That afternoon, after her cry 'What shall I do for you?', she laid out the records of Beethoven's Ninth Symphony. Side by side, we sat and listened. Sheila listened, her eyes luminous, transfigured by her happiness. She listened and was in love.

The noise pounded round me. I too was in love.

The choral movement opened. As each theme came again, Sheila whispered to make me recognize it. 'Dismisses it,' she said, sweeping her hand down, as the first went out. 'Dismisses it,' she said twice more. But at the first sound of the human voice, she sat so still that she might have gone into a trance.

She was in love, and rapt. I sat beside her, possessed by my years of passion and devotion, consumed by tenderness, by desire, and by the mania of revenge, possessed by the years whose torments had retraced themselves to breaking point as she stood that night, oblivious to all but her own joy. She was carried away, into the secret contemplation of her love. I sat beside her, stricken and maddened by mine.

Part Six

A SINGLE ACT

41

The Sense of Power

THAT night, after Sheila told me she was in love, I stayed in the street, my eyes not daring to leave her lighted window. The music had played round me; I had said goodbye; but when I came out into the cold night, I could not go home. Each past storm of jealousy or desire was calm compared to this. The evening when I slipped away from George and stood outside the vicarage, just watching without purpose – that was nothing but a youth's lament. Now I was driven.

I could find no rest until I saw with my own eyes whether or not another man would call on her that night. No rest from the calculations of jealousy: 'I shall want some tea,' she had said, and that light phrase set all my mind to work, as though a great piece of clockwork had been wound up by a turn of the key. When would she make him tea? That night? Next day? No test from the torments, the insane reminders, of each moment when her body had allured me; so that standing in the street, looking at her window, I was maddened by sensual reveries.

It was late. A drizzle was falling, silver and sleety as it passed the street lamps. Time upon time I walked as far up the street as I could go, and still see the window. Through the curtains her light shone – orange among the yellow squares of other windows, the softest, the most luxurious, of all the lights in view. Twice a man came down the pavement, and as he approached her house my heart stopped. He passed by. A desolate prostitute, huddled against the raw night, accosted me. Some of the lights went out, but hers still shone.

The street was deserted, At last – in an instant when I turned my eyes away – her window had clicked into darkness. Relief poured through me, inordinate, inexpressible relief. I turned away; and I was drowsing in the taxi before I got home.

For days in Chambers I was driven, as violently as I had been that night. Writing an opinion, I could not keep my thoughts still. At a conference, I heard my leader talk, I heard the clients inquiring – between them and me were images of Sheila, images of the flesh, the images that tormented my senses and turned jealousy into a drill within the brain. And in the January nights I was driven to walk the length of Worcester Street, back and forth, hypnotized by the lighted window; it was an obsession, it was a mania, but I could not keep myself away.

One night, in the tube station at Hyde Park Corner, I imagined that I saw her in the crowd. There was a thin young man, of whom I only saw the back, and a woman beside him. She was singing to herself. Was it she? They mounted a train in the rush, I could not see, the doors slid to.

Soon afterwards – it was inside a week since she broke her news – the telephone rang at my lodgings. The landlady shouted my name, and I went downstairs. The telephone stood out in the open, on a table in the hall. I heard Sheila's voice: 'How are you?'

I muttered.

'I want to know: how are you, physically?'

I had scarcely thought of my health. I had been acting as though I were tireless. I said that I was all right, and asked after her.

'I'm *very* well.' Her voice was unusually full. There was a silence, then she asked: 'When am I going to see you?'

'When you like.'

'Come here tonight. You can take me out if you like.'

Once more an answer broke out.

'Shall you be alone?' I said.

'Yes.' In the telephone the word was clear; I could hear neither gloating nor compassion.

When I entered her room that evening she was dressed to dine out, in a red evening frock. Since I had begun to earn money, we had taken to an occasional treat. It was the chief difference in my way of life, for I had not changed my flat, and still lived as though in transit. She let me do it; she knew that I had my streak of childish ostentation, and that it flattered me to entertain her as the Marches might have done. For herself, she would have preferred our old places in Soho and round Charlotte Street; but, to indulge me, she would dress up and go to fashionable restaurants, as she had herself proposed that night.

She was bright-eyed and smiling. Before we went out, however, she said in a quiet voice: 'Why did you ask whether I should be alone?'

'You know.'

'You're thinking', she said, her eyes fixed on me, 'of what I did to you once? At the Edens' that night – with poor Tom Devitt?'

I did not reply.

'I shan't do that again,' she said. She added: 'I've treated you badly. I don't need telling it.'

She walked into the restaurant at the Berkeley with me behind her. Just then, at twenty-five, she was at the peak of her beauty. For a young girl, her face had been too hard, lined, and over-vivid. And I often thought, trying to see the future, that long before she was middle-aged her looks would be ravaged. But now she was at the age which chimed with her style. That night, as she walked across the restaurant, all eyes followed her, and a hush fell. She made the conversation. Each word she said was light with her happiness, more than ever capricious and sarcastic. Sometimes she drew a smile, despite myself. Then, in the middle of the meal, she leaned across the table, her eyes full on me, and said, quietly and simply: 'You can do something for me.'

'What?'

'Will you?' she begged.

321

I stared at her.

'You can be some good to me,' she said.

'What do you want?'

She said: 'I want you to see Hugh.'

'I can't do it,' I burst out.

'It might help me,' she said.

My eyes could not leave hers.

'You're more realistic than I am,' she said. 'I want you to tell me what he feels about me. I don't know whether he loves me.'

'What do you think I am?' I cried, and violent words were quivering behind my lips.

'I trust you,' she said. 'You're the only human being I've ever trusted.'

There was silence. She said:

'There is no one else to ask. No one else would be worth asking.'

In exhaustion, I replied at last: 'All right. I'll see him.'

She was docile with delight. When could I manage it? She would arrange any time I liked. 'I'm very dutiful to Hugh,' she said, 'but I shall make him come – whenever you can manage it.' What about that very night? She could telephone him, and bring him to her room. Would I mind, that night?

'It's as good as any other,' I said.

She rang up. We drove back to Worcester Street. In the taxi I said little, and I was as sombre while we sat in her room and waited.

'He's highly strung,' she said. 'He may be nervous of you.'

A car passed along the street, coming nearer, and I listened. Sheila shook her head.

'No,' she said. 'He'll come by bus.' She asked: 'Shall I play a record?'

'If you like.'

She grimaced, and began to search in her shelf. As she did so, there pattered a light step down below. 'Here he is,' she said.

He came in with a smile, quick and apologetic. Sheila and I were each standing, and for a second he threw an arm round her waist. Then he faced me, as she introduced us.

'Lewis, this is Hugh Smith.'

He was as tall as me, but much slighter. His neck was thin and his chest sunken. He was very fair. His upper lip was petulant and vain, but when he smiled his whole face was merry, boyish, and sweet. He looked much younger than his years, much younger than either Sheila or me.

He was taken up with Sheila's dress.

'I've not seen you in that before, have I?' he said. 'Yes, it's very very nice. Let me see. Is it quite right at the back –?' he went on with couturier's prattle.

Sheila laughed at him.

'You're much more interested than my dressmaker,' she said.

Hugh appealed to me: 'Aren't you interested in clothes?'

His manner was so open that I was disarmed.

He went on talking about clothes, and music, and the plays we had seen. Nothing could have been lighter-hearted, more suited to a polite party. She made fun of him, more gentle fun than I was used to. I asked a question about his job, and he took at once to the defensive; I gave it up, and he got back to concerts again. Nothing could have been more civilized.

I was watching them together. I was watching them with a desperate attention, more concentrated than I had ever summoned and held in all my life before. Around them there was no breath of the heaviness and violence of a passion. It was too friendly, too airy, too kind, for that. Towards him she showed a playful ease which warmed her voice and set her free. When she turned to him, even the line of her profile seemed less sharp. It was an ease that did not carry the deep repose of violent love; it was an ease that was full of teasing, half-kittenish and half-maternal. I had never seen her so for longer than a flash.

I could not be sure of what he felt for her. He was fond of her, was captivated by her charm, admired her beauty, liked her high spirits – that all meant little. I thought that he was flattered by her love. He was conceited as well as vain. He lapped up all the tributes of love. He was selfish; very amiable; easily frightened, easily overweighted, easily overborne.

Sheila announced that she was going to bed. She wanted Hugh and me, I knew, to leave together, so that I could talk to him. It was past midnight; the last buses had gone; he and I started to walk towards Victoria. It was a crisp frosty night, the black sky glittering with stars.

On the pavement in Lupus Street, he spoke, as though for safety, of the places we lived in and how much we paid for our flats. He was apprehensive of the enmity not yet brought into the open that night. He was searching for casual words that would hurry the minutes along. I would have welcomed it so. But I was too far gone. I interrupted:

'How long have you known her?'

'Six months.'

'I've known her six years.'

'That's a long time,' said Hugh, and once more tried to break on to safe ground. We had turned into Belgrave Road.

I did not answer his question, but asked: 'Do you understand her?'

His eyes flickered at me, and then away.

'Oh, I don't know about that.'

'Do you understand her?'

'She's intelligent, isn't she? Don't you think she is?' He seemed to be probing round for answers that would please me.

'Yes,' I said.

'I think she's very sweet. She is sweet in her way, isn't she?'

Our steps rang in the empty frost-bound street.

'She's not much like the other girls I've known!' he ventured. He added with his merry childlike smile: 'But I expect she wants the same things in the end. They all do, don't they?'

'I expect so.'

'They want you to persuade them into bed. Then they want you to marry them.'

I said: 'Do you want to marry her?'

'I think I'd like to settle down, wouldn't you?' he said. 'And she can be very sweet, can't she?' He added: 'I've always got out of it before. I suppose she's a bit of a proposition. Somehow I think it might be a good idea.'

The lights of the empty road stretched ahead, the lights under the black sky.

'By the way,' he said, 'I'm frightfully sorry if I've been poaching. I am sorry if I've got in your way. These things can't be helped, though, can they?'

For minutes the lights, the sky, had seemed shatteringly bright, reelingly dark, as though I were dead drunk.

Suddenly my mind leapt clear.

'I should like to talk about that,' I said. 'Not tonight. Tomorrow or the next day.'

'There isn't much to talk about, is there?' he said, again on the defensive.

'I want to say some things to you.'

'I don't see that it'll do much good, you know,' he replied.

'It's got to be done,' I said.

'I'm rather full up this week – '

'It can't be left,' I said.

'Oh, if you want,' he gave way, with a trace of petulance. Before we parted, we arranged to meet. He was shy of the place and time, but I made him promise – my flat, not tomorrow but the evening after.

The fire was out when I returned to my room. I did not think of sleep, and I did not notice the cold. Still in my overcoat, I sat on the head of the sofa, smoking.

I stayed without moving for many minutes. My thoughts were clear. They had never seemed so clear. I believed that this man was right for her. Or at least with him she might get an unexacting happiness. Knowing her with the insight of passionate love, I believed that I saw the truth. He was lightweight, but somehow his presence made her innocent and free. Her best chance was to marry him.

Would he marry her? He was wavering. He could be forced either way. He was selfish, but this time he did not know exactly what he wanted for himself. He had made love to her, but was not physically bound. She had little hold on him; yet he was thinking of her as his wife. He was irresolute. He was waiting to be told what to do.

Thinking back on that night, as I did so often afterwards, I had to remember one thing. It was easy to forget, but in fact many of my thoughts were still protective. Her best chance was to marry him. I thought of how I could persuade him, the arguments to use, the feelings to play on. Did he know that she would one day be rich? Would he not be flattered by my desire to have her at any price, would not my competition raise her value? I imagined her married to him, light and playful as she had been that night. It was a sacrificial, tender thought.

If I played it right, my passion to marry her would spur him on.

Yes. Her best chance was to marry him. I believed that I could decide it. I could bring it off – or destroy it.

With the cruellest sense of power I had ever known, I thought that I could destroy it.

42

Steaming Clothes Before the Fire

I HAD two days to wait. Throughout that time, wherever I was, to whomever I was speaking, I had my mind fixed, my whole spirit and body, bone and flesh and brain, on the hour to come. The sense of power ran through my bloodstream. As I prepared for the scene, my thoughts stayed clear. Underneath the thoughts, I was exultant. Each memory of the past, each hope and resolve remaining – they were at one. All that I was, fused into the cruel exultation.

I went into Chambers each of those mornings, but only for an hour. I conferred with Percy. On Thursday we were to hear judgement in an adjourned case: that would be the morning after Hugh's visit, I thought, as Percy and I methodically arranged my timetable. February would be a busy month.

'They're coming in nicely,' said Percy.

Those two days were cold and wet, but I did not stay long in Chambers or in my room. I was not impatient, but I was active. It was a pleasure to jostle in the crowds. My mind was planning, and at the same time I breathed in the wet reek of Covent Garden, the whispers of a couple behind me at the cinema, the grotesque play of an enraged and pompous woman's face.

I did not hurry over my tea on the second day. He was due at half past six; I had to buy a bottle of whisky on the way home, but there was time enough. I had been sitting about in cafés most of that afternoon, drinking tea and reading the evening papers. Before I set off for home, I bought the latest edition and read it through. As people came into the café their coats were heavy with the rain, and at the door men poured trickles of water from their hat-brims.

When I reached my door the rain had slackened, but I was very wet. I had to change; and as I did so I thought with sarcastic tenderness of the first occasion that I arrived at Sheila's house. In the mirror I saw myself smiling. Then I got ready for Hugh's visit. I made up the fire. I had not yet drawn the blinds, and the reflections of the flames began to dance behind the window panes. I put the bottle of whisky and a jug of water and glasses on the table, and opened a box of cigarettes. Then at last I pulled down the blinds and shut the room in.

He should be here in ten minutes. I was feeling exalted, braced, active with physical well-being; there was a tremor in my hands.

Hugh was a quarter of an hour late. I was standing up as he came in. He gave his bright, flickering smile. I said that it was a nasty night, and asked if he were soaked. He replied that he had found a taxi, but that his trousers were damp below the knees. Could he dry them by the fire? He sat in a chair with his feet in the fireplace. He remarked, sulkily, that he had to take care of his chest.

I invited him to have a drink. First he said no, then he changed his mind, then he stopped me and asked for a very small one. He sat there with glass in hand while I stood on the other side of the hearth. Steam was rising from his trousers, and he pushed his feet nearer to the grate.

'I'm sorry to have brought you out on a night like this,' I said.

'Oh well, I'm here.' His manner, when he was not defending himself, was easy and gentle.

'If you had to turn out tonight,' I said, 'it's a pity that I've got to tell you unpleasant things.'

He was looking at me, alert for the next words. His face was open.

I said casually: 'I wonder if you'd rather we went out and ate first. If so, I won't begin talking seriously until we come back. I must have you alone for what I've got to say. I don't know what the weather's like now.'

I left the fireplace, went to the window, and lifted the bottom of the blind. The rain was tapping steadily. Now that our eyes were not meeting, he raised his voice sharply:

'It can't possibly take long, can it? I haven't the faintest idea what it's all about – '

I turned back.

'You'd rather I spoke now?' I said,

'I suppose so.'

I sat down opposite to him. The steam was still wafted by the draught, and there was a smell of moist clothes. His eyes flickered away, and then were drawn back. He did not know what to expect.

'Sheila wants to marry you,' I said. 'She wants to marry you more than you want to marry her.'

His eyelids blinked. He looked half-surprised that I should begin so.

'Perhaps that's true,' he said.

'You're quite undecided,' I said.

'Oh, I don't know about that.'

'You're absolutely undecided,' I said. 'You can't make up your mind. It's very natural that you shouldn't be able to.'

'I shall make it up.'

'You're not happy about it. You've got a feeling that there's something wrong. That's why you're so undecided.'

'How do you know that I feel there's something wrong?'

'By the same instinct that is warning you,' I said. 'You feel that there are reasons why you shouldn't marry her. You can't place them, but you feel that they exist.'

'Well?'

'If you knew her better', I said, 'you would know what those reasons are.'

He was leaning back in the chair with his shoulders huddled.

'Of course, you're not unprejudiced,' he said.

'I'm not unprejudiced,' I said. 'But I'm speaking the truth, and you believe that I'm speaking the truth.'

'I'm very fond of her,' he said. 'I don't care what you tell me. I shall make up my mind for myself.'

I waited, I let his eyes dart towards me, before I spoke again.

'Have you any idea', I said, 'what marriage with her would mean?'

'Of course I've an idea.'

'Let me tell you. She has little physical love for you – or any man.'

'More for me than for anyone.' He had a moment of certainty.

I said: 'You've made love to other women. What do you think of her?'

He did not reply. I repeated the question. He was more obstinate than I had counted on – but I was full of the joy of power, of revenge, of the joy that mine was the cruel will. Power over him, that was nothing, except to get my way. He was an instrument, and nothing else. In those words I took revenge for the humiliation of years, for the love of which I had been deprived. It was she to whom I spoke.

I said: 'She has no other love to give.'

'If I feel like marrying her,' he said, 'I shall.'

'In that case,' I said, and now I knew the extreme of effort, the extreme of release, 'you'll be marrying an abnormal woman.'

He misunderstood me.

'No,' I said. 'I don't mean that. I mean that she is hopelessly unstable. And she'll never be anything else.'

I could feel his hate. He hated me, he hated the force and violence in my voice. He longed to escape, and yet he was fascinated.

'But you'd take her on,' he said. 'If only she'd have you. You can't deny it, can you?'

'It is true,' I said. 'But I love her, which is the bitterest fate in my life. You don't love her, and you know it. I couldn't help myself, and you can. And if I married her, I should do it with my eyes open. I should marry her, but I should know that she was a pathological case.'

He avoided my gaze.

'You've got to know that too,' I said.

'Are you saying that she will go mad?'

'Do you know', I said, 'when madness begins or ends?' I went on: 'If you ask me whether she'll finish in an asylum, I should say no. But if you ask me what it would be like to go home to her after you were married, I tell you this: you would never know what you would find.'

I asked him if he had ever heard the word schizoid. I asked if he had noticed anything unusual about her actions. I told him stories of her. All the time my exultation was mounting higher still; from his whole bearing, I was certain that I had not misjudged him. He would never marry her, He wanted to escape, as soon as he decently could, from a storm of alien violence. He was out of his depth with both her and me. His feeling for her had always been mild; his desire to marry her not much more than a fancy; now I had destroyed it. He hated me, but I had destroyed it.

I despised him, in the midst of passionate triumph, in the midst of my mastery over her, for not loving her more. At that moment I felt nothing but contempt for him. I was on her side as I watched him begin to extricate himself.

'I shall have to think it over,' he said. 'I suppose that it's time I made up my mind.'

He knew that his decision was already taken. He knew that it was surrender. He knew that he would slip from her, and that I was certain of it.

I demanded that, as soon as he told her, he should tell me too.

'It's only between her and me,' he said with an effort of defiance.

'I must know.'

He hated me, but for the last time he gave way.

Right at the end, he asserted himself. He would not come with me to dinner, but went off on his own.

43

Mr Knight Tries to be Direct

THE next morning I went into court to hear a judgement. It was in one of the London police courts; the case was a prosecution for assault which I had won the week before; the defendant had been remanded for a medical report. He had been pronounced sane, and now the stipendiary sentenced him. There was a shadow of blackmail in the case, and the magistrate was stern. 'It passes my comprehension how anyone can sink to such behaviour. No words are too strong to express the detestation which we all feel for such men as you – '

It had often seemed to me strange that men should be so brazen with their moral indignation. Were they so utterly cut off from their own experience that they could utter these loud, resounding, moral brays and not be forced to look within? What were their own lives like, that they could denounce so enthusiastically? If baboons learned to talk, the first words they spoke would be stiff with moral indignation. I thought it again, without remorse, as I sat in court that Thursday morning.

Without either remorse or regret, though fourteen hours had passed. I was still borne up by my excitement, I was waiting to hear from Hugh, but I had no doubt of the answer. Just then, I had one anxiety about my action, and only one: would Sheila learn of it? If so, should I have lost her for good? How could I get her back?

Hugh called on me early the following Sunday, while I was at my breakfast.

'I said that I'd tell you, didn't I?' he said, in a tone weary and unforgiving. He would not sit down. 'Well,' he went on, 'I've written to tell her that I'm walking out.'

'What have you said?'

'Oh, the usual things. We shouldn't get on for long, and it would be mostly my fault. What else could I say?'

'Have you seen her', I asked, 'since we talked?'

'Yes.'

'Did she guess what was coming?'

'I didn't tell her.' Then he said, with a flash of shrewdness: 'You needn't worry. I haven't mentioned you. But you've given me some advice, and I'm going to do the same to you. You'd better leave her alone for a few months. If you don't, you're asking for trouble.'

Within two days, I was telephoning her. At first, when I got no answer but the ringing tone, I thought nothing of it. She must be out for the evening. But when I had put through call after call, late into the night, I became alarmed. I had to imagine the bell ringing on and on in her empty room. I tried again the next morning as soon as I woke, and went straight round to Worcester Street. Sheila's landlady opened the door to me in the misty morning twilight. Miss Knight had gone away the day before. She hadn't said where she was going, or left an address. She might come back or she might not, but she had paid three months' rent in advance (my heart leapt and steadied with relief).

I asked if I might glance at Sheila's room. There was a book I had lent her, I went on persuading. The landlady knew me, and had a soft spot for Sheila, like everyone who waited on her; so I was allowed to walk round the room, while the landlady stood at the door, and the smell of frying bacon came blowing up the stairs. The room looked high in the cold light. The coins had gone, the records, her favourite books.

I wrote to her, and sent the letter to the vicarage address. I heard nothing, and within a week wrote again. Then I made inquiries through friends in the town – not George Passant and the group, but others who might have contact with the Knights. Soon one of them, a girl called Rosalind, sent me some news. Sheila was actually living at home. She was never seen outside the house. No one had spoken to her. She would not answer the telephone. No one knew how she was.

I could see no way to reach her. That weighed upon me, it was to that thought that I woke in the night, not to the reproach that this had happened through my action.

Yet I sometimes faced what I had done. Perhaps sometimes I exaggerated it. Many years later I could at last ask fairly: would he really have transformed her life? How much difference had my action made? Perhaps I wanted to believe that I had done the maximum of harm. It took away some of the reproach of staying supine for so long.

Often I remembered that evening with remorse. Perhaps, as I say, I cherished it. But at other times I remembered it with an utterly different, and very curious, feeling. With a feeling of innocence, puzzled and incredulous.

I had noticed this in others who performed an action which brought evil consequences on others and themselves. But I had to undergo it myself before I understood. The memory came back with the innocence of fact…an act of the flesh, bare limbs on a bed…a few words on a sheet of paper…was it possible that such things could shake a life? So it was with me. Sometimes I remembered that evening, not with remorse, but just as words across the fireplace, steam rising from the other man's trousers, some words spoken as I might have spoken them on any evening. All past and gone. How could such facts hag-ride me now, or hold out threats for the years to come?

The summer began, and quite irrelevantly, I had another stroke of practical luck. Getliffe at last took silk. Inevitably, much of his practice must come to me.

For years he had bombarded us with the arguments for and against. He had threatened us with his own uncertainties; he had taken advice from his most junior pupil as well as his eminent friends at the Bar. He had delayed, raised false hopes, changed his mind, retracted. I had come to think that he would never do it – certainly not that summer,

1931, with a financial crisis upon us and the wise men prophesying that legal work would shrink by half.

He told me on an evening in June. I was alone in Chambers, working late; he had spent all the day since lunchtime going from one acquaintance to another. He called me into his room.

It was a thundery overcast evening, the sky black beyond the river, with one long swathe of orange where the clouds had parted. Getliffe sat magisterially at his desk. In the dark room his papers shone white under the lamp. He was wearing a raincoat, the collar half-turned up. His face was serious and also a little rebellious.

'Well,' he said, 'I've torn it now. I'm taking the plunge. If — is going to be one of His Majesty's counsel, I might as well follow suit. One has to think of one's duty.'

'Is it definite?' I said.

'I never bore my friends with my intentions', Getliffe reproved me, 'until they're cut and dried.'

Getliffe gave me his fixed man-to-man stare.

'Well, there's the end of a promising junior,' he said. 'Now I start again. It will ruin me, of course. I hope you'll remember that I expect to be ruined.'

'In three years', I said, 'you'll be making twice what you do now.'

He smiled.

'You know, L S, you're rather a good sort.' Then his tone grew threatening again. 'It's a big risk I'm taking. It's the biggest risk I've ever had to take.'

He enjoyed his ominous air; he indulged himself in his pictures of sacrifice and his probable disaster. Yet he was not much exaggerating the risk. At that moment, it was a brave step. I was astonished that he should do it. I admired him, half-annoyed with myself for feeling so. In that last year as a junior his income was not less than five thousand pounds. Even if the times were prosperous, his first years as a silk were bound to mean a drop. In 1931, with the depression spreading, he would be fortunate if he made two thousand pounds: he might not climb to his old level for years, perhaps not ever.

It could have deterred many men not overfond of money. Whereas Getliffe was so mean that, having screwed himself to the point of taking one to lunch, he would arrive late so that he need not buy a drink beforehand. It must have been an agony for him to face the loss. He can only have endured it because of a force that I was loath to give him credit for – his delight in his profession, his love of the legal honours not only for their cash value but for themselves. If ever the chance came, I ought to have realized, he would renounce the most lucrative of practices in order to become Getliffe J, to revel in the glory of being a judge.

Whatever the results for Getliffe, his move was certain to do me good, now and henceforward. His work still flowed into our Chambers: much of it, as a silk, he could not touch. His habits were too strong to break; he was no more reconciled to youth knocking at the door, and he did his best, in his furtive ingenious fashion, to direct the briefs to those too dim to be rivals. But he could not do much obstruction, and Percy took care of me. In the year 1930–1, despite my illness, I had earned seven hundred and fifty pounds. The moment Getliffe took silk I could reckon on at least a thousand pounds for each year thereafter. It was a comfort, for these last months I had half felt some results of illness and my private grief. I had not thrown myself into my cases with the old absorption. I did not see it clearly then, but I was not improving on my splendid start. I should still have backed my chances for great success, but a shrewd observer would have doubted them. Still, I had gone some distance. I was now certain of a decent income. For the first time since I was a child, I was sure of my livelihood.

Once I imagined that I should be overjoyed, when that rasp of worry was conquered. I had looked forward to the day, ever since I began to struggle. It should have marked an epoch. Now it had come, and it was empty. She was not there. All that I had of her came in the thoughts of sleepless nights. On the white midsummer nights, those thoughts gave me no rest. The days were empty. My bit of success was the emptiest of all. Right to the last I had hoped that when it came she would be with me. This would have been the time for marriage.

In fact, I had not the slightest word from her. I tried to accept that I might never see her again.

I went out, on the excuse of any invitation. Through the Marches and acquaintances at the Bar, my name was just finding a place on some hostesses' lists. I was a young man from nowhere, but I was presumably unattached and well thought of at my job. I went to dances and parties, and sometimes a girl there seemed real and my love a nightmare from which I had woken. I liked being liked; I lapped up women's flattery; often I half-resolved to find myself a wife. But I was not a man who could marry without the magic being there. Leaving someone who should have contented me, I was leaden with the memory of magic. With Sheila, I should have remembered each word and touch, whereas this – this was already gone.

One morning in September, soon after I had returned from a holiday, a letter stared from my breakfast tray. My heart pounded as I saw the postmark of her village; but the letter had been redirected from my Inn, and the handwriting was a man's. It came from Mr Knight, and read:

> My dear Eliot, Even one who hides himself in the seclusion of a remote life and simple duties cannot always avoid certain financial consultations. Much as I dislike coming to London I shall therefore be obliged to stay at the club for the nights of Monday and Tuesday next week. Owing to increasing age and disinclination, I know few people outside my immediate circle, and shall be free from all engagements during this enforced visit. It is, of course, too much to hope that you can disentangle yourself from your professional connexions, but if you should remember me and be available, I should be glad to give you the poor hospitality the club can offer at luncheon on either of those days.
>
> Very truly yours.

The letter was signed with a flamboyant 'Lawrence Knight'.

The 'club' was the Athenaeum. I knew that from private jokes with Sheila. He had devoted intense pertinacity to get himself elected, and

337

then never visited it. It was like him to pick up the jargon, particularly the arrogant private-world jargon, of any institution, and become a trifle too slick with it.

He must want to talk of Sheila. He must be deeply troubled to get in touch with me – and he had done it without her knowledge, for she would have told him my address. Reading his elaborate approach again, I guessed that he was making a special journey. He was so proud and vain that only a desperate trouble would make him humble himself so. Was she ill? But if so, surely even he, for all his camouflage, would have told me.

In some ways I was as secretive as Mr Knight, but my instinct in the face of danger was not to lose a second in knowing the worst. When I entered the Athenaeum, I was on tenterhooks to have all my anxieties settled. How was she? What was the matter? Had she spoken of me? But Mr Knight was too adroit for me. I was shown into the smoking-room and he began at once:

'My dear fellow, before we do anything else, I insist on your drinking a glass of this very indifferent sherry. I *cannot* recommend it. I cannot *recommend* it. I expect you to resolve my ignorance upon the position of our poor old pound – '

He did not speak hurriedly, but he gave me no chance to break in. He appeared intent on not getting to the point. I listened with gnawing impatience. Of all the interviews at which I had been kept waiting for news, this was the most baffling. Mr Knight was not at home in the Athenaeum, and it was essential for him to prove that no one could be more so. He called waiters by their names, had our table changed, wondered why he kept up his subscription, described a long talk that morning with the secretary. He proceeded over lunch to speculate intricately about the gold standard. On which – though no talk had ever seemed so meaningless – he was far more detached than most of my acquaintances. 'Of course we shall go off it,' said Mr Knight, with surprising decision and energy. 'They're talking complete nonsense about staying on it. It's an economic impossibility. At least I should have thought so, but I never think about these things. I gave up thinking long ago, Eliot. I'm just a poor simple country parson. No doubt this nonsense about the gold standard was convenient for removing our late lamented government, that is, if one had no high opinion of their merits.'

Mr Knight went on, with one of his sly darts, to wonder how warmly I regarded them. It was remarkable, in his view, how increased prosperity insensibly produced its own little effect, its own almost imperceptible effect, on one's political attitude…'But it's not for me to attribute causes,' said Mr Knight.

No talk had ever seemed so far away, as though I were going deaf. At last he took me upstairs for coffee, and we sat outside on one of the small balconies, looking over the corner of Waterloo Place and Pall Mall. The sunshine was hot. Buses gleamed in the afternoon light. The streets smelt of petrol and dust.

Suddenly Mr Knight remarked in an aside: 'I suppose you haven't had any experience of psychiatrists, professional or otherwise? They can't have come your way?'

'No, but…'

'I was only asking because my daughter – you remember that she brought you to my house once or twice, perhaps? – my daughter happened to be treated by one recently.'

I was riven by fear, guilt, sheer animal concern.

'Is she better?' I cried out of it all.

'She wouldn't persevere,' said Mr Knight. 'She said that he was stupider than she was. I am inclined to think that these claims to heal the soul…' He was taking refuge in a disquisition on psychology and medicine, but I had no politeness left.

'How is she?' I said roughly. 'Tell me anything. How is she?'

Mr Knight had been surveying the street. For a moment he looked me in the face. His eyes were self-indulgent but sad.

'I wish I knew,' he said.

'What can I do for her?'

'Tell me,' he said, 'how well do you know my daughter?'

'I have loved her ever since I met her. That is seven years ago. I have loved her without return.'

'I am sorry for you,' he said.

339

For the first time I had heard him speak without cover.

In an instant he was weaving his circumlocutions, glancing at me only from the corner of his eye.

'I am an elderly man,' he remarked, 'and it is difficult to shoulder responsibility as one did once. There are times when one envies men like you, Eliot, in the prime of your youth. Even though one may seem favoured not to be bearing the heat and burden of the day. If my daughter should happen to live temporarily in London, which I believe she intends to, it would ease my mind that you should be in touch with her. I have heard her speak of you with respect, which is singular for my daughter. If she has no reliable friends here, I should find my responsibility too much of a burden.'

Mr Knight looked down his nose, and very intently, at the passers-by across the place.

'It is just possible', he said, in an offhand whisper, 'that my daughter may arrive in London this week. She is apt to carry out her intentions rather quickly. She speaks of returning to a house which she has actually lived in before. Yes, she has lived in London for a few months. I think I should like to give you the address, then perhaps if you ever find yourself near – The address is 68 Worcester Street SW1.'

He wrote it on a piece of club paper which he pulled from his pocket. He wrote it very legibly, realizing all the time that I knew that address as well as my own.

44

Beside the Water

I RANG the familiar number on the day that Mr Knight hinted that it was 'just possible' she might return. She answered. Her voice was friendly. 'Come round,' she said, as she might have done at any previous time. 'How did you guess? I don't believe it was clairvoyance.' But she did not press me when we met. She took it for granted that I should be there, and seemed herself unchanged. She made no reference to Hugh, nor to her visit to the psychiatrist.

We sauntered hand in hand that night. For me, there was no future. This precarious innocent happiness had flickered over us inexplicably for a few days, perhaps adding up to a week in all, in our years together. Now it had chosen to visit us again.

She was sometimes airy, sometimes remote, but that had always been so. I did not want to break the charm.

For several days it seemed like first love. I said no word of her plans or mine. If this were an illusion, then let it shine a little longer. People called me clear-sighted, but if this were an illusion I did not want to see the truth.

On a warm September night we dawdled round St James's Park, and sat by the water at the palace end. It was the calmest and most golden of nights. The lamps threw bars of gold towards us, and other beams swept and passed from cars driving along the Mall. On the quiet water, ducks moved across the golden bars and left a glittering shimmer in their wake.

'Pretty,' she said.

The sky was lit up over the Strand. From the barracks the Irish bagpipers began to play in the distance, marched round until the music was loud, and receded again.

We were each silent, while the band made several circuits. She was thinking. I was enchanted by the night.

She said: 'Was it you who sent him away?'

I answered: 'It was.'

The skirling came near, died away, came near again. Our silence went on. Her fingers had been laced in mine, and there stayed. Neither of us moved. We had not looked at each other, but were still gazing over the water. A bird alighted close in front of us, and then another.

She said: 'It makes it easier.'

I asked: 'What does it make easier?'

She said: 'I'm no good now. I never shall be. I've played my last cards. You can have me. You can marry me if you like.'

Her tone was not contemptuous, not cruel, not bitter. It was resigned. Hearing her offer in that tone. I was nevertheless as joyful as though, when I first proposed to her in my student's attic, she had said yes. I was as joyful as though we had suffered nothing – like any young man in the park that halcyon night, asking his girl to marry him and hearing her accept. At the same time, I was melted with concern.

'I want you,' I said. 'More than I've ever done. But you mustn't come to me if you could be happier any other way.'

'I've done you great harm,' she said. 'Now you've done the same to me. Perhaps we deserve each other.'

'That is not all of us,' I said. 'I have loved you. You have immeasurably enriched my life.'

'You have done me great harm,' she said, relentlessly, without any malice, speaking from deep inside. 'I might have been happy with him. I shall always think it.'

I cried: 'Let me get him back for you. I'll bring him back myself. If you want him, you must have him.'

'I forbid you,' she said, with all her will.

'If you want him –'

'I might find out that it was not true. That would be worse.'

I exclaimed in miserable pity, and put my arm round her. She leant her head on my shoulder; the band approached; a long ripple ran across the pond, and the reflections quivered. I thought she was crying. Soon, however, she looked at me with dry eyes. She even had the trace of a sarcastic smile.

'No,' she said. 'We can't escape each other. I suppose it's just.'

She stared at me.

'I know it's useless,' she said. 'But I want to tell you this. You need a wife who will love you. And look after you. And be an ally in your career. I can do none of those things.'

'I know.'

'I'll try to be loyal,' she went on. 'That's all I can promise. I shan't be much good at it.'

A couple, arms round each other's waists, passed very slowly in front of us. When they had gone by, I looked once more at the lights upon the water, and then into her eyes.

'I know all this,' I said. 'I am marrying you because I can do nothing else.'

'Yes.'

'Why are you marrying me?'

I expected a terrible answer – such as that we had damaged each other beyond repair, that, by turning love into a mutual torment, we were unfit for any but ourselves. In fact, she said: 'It's simple. I'm not strong enough to go on alone.'

Part Seven

THE DECISION

45

An Autumn Dawn

LYING awake in the early morning, I listened to Sheila breathing as she slept. It was a relief that she had gone to sleep at last. There had been many nights since our marriage when I had lain awake, restless because I knew that in the other bed she too was staring into the darkness. It had been so a few hours before, worse because at the end of our party with the Getliffes she had broken down.

The chink in the curtain was growing pale in the first light of day. I could just make out the shape of the room. It was nearly a year since we first slept there, when, after our marriage, we moved into this flat in Mecklenburgh Square. I could make out the shape of the room, and of her bed, and of her body beneath the clothes. I felt for her with tenderness, with familiar tenderness, with pity, and, yes, with irritation, irritation that I was forced to think only of her, that looking after her took each scrap of my attention, that in a few hours I should go to the courts tired out after a night of trying to soothe her.

I had thought that I could imagine what it would be like. One can never imagine the facts as one actually lives them, the moment-by-moment facts of every day. I had known that she dreaded company, and I was ready to give up all but a minimum. It seemed an easy sacrifice. After our marriage, I found it a constant drain upon my tenderness. Each sign of her pain made me less prepared to coax her into another party. She was cutting me off from a world of which I was fond — that did not matter much. She kept me away from the 'useful' dinner tables, and professionally I should suffer for it. I saw another thing. She was not getting more confident, but less. More completely since our marriage, she believed that she could not cope.

Often I wondered whether she would have been healed if she had known physical love. Mine she could tolerate at times: she had no joy herself, though there were occasions, so odd is the flesh, when she showed a playful pleasure, which drew us closer than we had ever been. I tried to shake off the failure and remorse, and tell myself that the pundits are not so wise as they pretend. In sexual life there is an infinite variety; and many pairs know the magic of the flesh in ways which to others would be just a mockery. In cold blood, I thought that those who write on these topics must have seen very little of life. But that reflection did not comfort me, when she was too strained for me to touch her.

I hoped for a child, with the unrealistic hope that it might settle all: but of that there was no sign.

She wanted to meet no one – except those she discovered for herself. She had only visited her parents once since we married: that was at Christmas, as she kept some of her sense of formal duty. I myself had seen much more of Mr Knight, for we had struck up a bizarre companionship. Sheila let me go to the vicarage alone, while she hid herself in the flat or else went out in search of some of her nondescript cronies. They were an odd bunch. As in her girlhood, she was more relaxed with the unavailing, the down-and-out, even the pretentious, so long as they were getting nowhere. She would sit for hours in a little café talking to the waiter; she became the confidante of typists from decayed upper-class families who were looking for a man to keep them; she went and listened to writers who somehow did not publish, to writers who did not even write.

Some of my friends thought that, among that army of the derelict, she took lovers. I did not believe it. I did not ask; I did not spy any longer; I should have known. I did not doubt that she was faithful to me. No, from them she gained the pleasure of bringing solace. She had her own curious acid sympathy with the lost. She was touched by those, young and old, whose inner lives like her own were comfortless. It was in part that feeling which drew her to my attic in my student days.

I did not spy on her any longer. My obsessive jealousy had died soon after I possessed her. When she told me, as she still did, of some man who had taken her fancy, I could sympathize now, and stroke her hair, and laugh. I was capable of listening without the knife twisting within. I thought I should be capable, if ever I discovered a man who could give her joy, of bringing him to her arms. I thought I could do that; I who had, less than two years before, watched her window for hours in the bitter night – I who had deliberately set out to break her chance of joy.

Since then I had made love to her. Since then I had lain beside her in such dawns as this. Hugh was gone now, married, dismissed further into the past in her mind than in mine (I was still jealous of him, when all other jealousy was washed away). If ever she felt with another that promise of joy, I believed that I would scheme for her and watch over her till she was happy.

I did not think it was likely to happen. Her fund of interest seemed to have run low. She had gone farther along life's road than I had, though we were the same age and though my years had been more packed than hers. It was to me she turned, hoping for a new idea to occupy her. At times she turned to me as though to keep her going, as though I had to live for two. It was that condition of blankness and anxiety that I feared most in her, and which most wore me down. Even in perfect love it would be hard to live for another. In this love it was a tax beyond my strength.

She looked after the flat with the same competence that she spent on her coins. She was abler than I had thought, and picked up any technique very quickly. She did more of the housework than she need have done, for we could have afforded another servant; perhaps as an expiation, perhaps to console me, Mr Knight had surprised us with a lavish marriage settlement, and between us our income was about two thousand pounds a year. She spent little of it on herself. Sometimes she helped out her cronies, or bought records or books. That was almost all. I should have welcomed any extravagance. I should have welcomed anything into which she could pour out her heart.

I had threatened Hugh that if he married her he would never know what to expect when he arrived home. No cruel prophecy had ever recoiled more cruelly. After a year of marriage, I used to stay in Chambers of an evening with one care after another piling upon me. My career. I was slipping: if I were to achieve half my ambition, this was the time when I ought to take another jump forward. It was not happening. My practice was growing very slightly, but no more. I could guess too clearly that I was no longer talked about as a coming man.

There was another care which had become darker since the summer. Hints kept reaching me of a scandal breaking round George Passant and the group. I had made inquiries, and they did not reassure me. George would not confide, but I felt there was danger creeping up. Oblivious and obstinate, George shut me out. I was terrified of what might happen to him.

With those cares upon me, I would leave Chambers at last, and set out home. I wanted someone to talk to, with the comfort of letting the despondency overflow. 'My girl,' I wanted to say, 'things are going badly. My bit of success may have been a flash in the pan. And there's worse news still.' I wanted someone to talk to, and, in fact, when I got home, I might find a stranger. A stranger to whom I was bound, and with whom I could not rest until I had coaxed her to find a little peace. She might, at the worst, be absolutely still, neither reading nor smoking, just gazing into the room. She might have gone out to one of her down-at-heel friends. I could never sleep until she returned, although she tiptoed into the spare room, there to spend the night on the divan. Once or twice I had found her there in the middle of the night, smoking a chain of cigarettes, playing her records still fully dressed.

There was not one night that autumn of 1932, when I could reckon on going back to content.

My unperceptive friends saw me married to a beautiful and accomplished woman, and envied me. My wiser friends were full of resentment. One or two, guessing rightly that I was less a prisoner than before my marriage, dangled other women in front of me. They thought that I was being damaged beyond repair. Not even Charles March, whose temperament was closest to my own, had much good to say of her. No one was wise enough to realize that there was one sure way to please me and to win my unbreakable gratitude: that was to say not that they loved her – she received enough of that – but simply that they liked her. I wanted to hear someone say that she was sweet, and tried to be kind, and that she was harming only herself. I wanted them to be sorry for her, not for me.

Yet, lying beside her, I did not know how long I could stand it.

I was facing the corrosion of my future.

What idea had she of my other life? It seemed to her empty, and my craving for success vulgar. She did not invade me, she did not possess me, she did not wish to push me on. She knew me as a beseeching lover: she turned to me because I knew her and was not put off. For the rest, she left me inviolate and with my secrets. There was none of the give and take of equal hearts.

Lying beside her in the silver light of the October dawn, I did not know how long I could stand it.

She bore the same sense of formal duty to me as to her parents. Just as she visited them for Christmas, so she offered, once or twice, to entertain some legal acquaintances. 'You want me to. I shall do it,' she said. I did want it, but I knew before her first dinner party that nothing would be more of an ordeal. It was only recently that I had let her try again: and the result had been our dinner of the previous night.

I had mentioned that it was months since Henriques sent me a brief. She made some indifferent response; and then, some days later, she asked if she should invite the Henriques to the flat. I was so touched by the sign of consideration that I said yes with gusto, and told her (for the sake of some minor plan) to ask the Getliffes as well. For forty-eight hours before the dinner, she was wretched with apprehension. It tore open her diffidence, it exposed her as crippled and inept.

351

Before they arrived, Sheila stood by the mantelpiece; I put an arm round her, tried to tease her into resting, but she was rigid. She drank four or five glasses of sherry standing there. It was rare for her to drink at all. But for a time the party went well. Mrs Getliffe greeted us with long, enthusiastic stares from her doglike brown eyes, and cooed about the beauties and wonders of the flat. Her husband was the most valuable of guests; he was always ready to please, and he conceived it his job to make the party go. Incidentally, he provided me with a certain amusement, for I had often heard him profess a cheerful anti-Semitism. In the presence of one of the most influential of Jewish solicitors, I was happy to see that his anti-Semitism was substantially modified.

We gave them a good meal. With her usual technical competence, Sheila was a capable cook, and though I knew little of wine I had learned where to take advice. At any party, Getliffe became half-drunk with his first glass, and stayed in that expansive state however much he drank. He sat by Sheila's side; he had a furtive eye for an attractive woman, and a kindly one for a self-conscious hostess who needed a bit of help. He chatted to her, he drew the table into their talk. He was not the kind of man she liked, but he set her laughing. I had never felt so warm to him.

Henriques was his subdued, courteous, and observant self. I hoped that he was approving. With his wife, I exchanged gossip about the March family. I smiled down the table at Sheila, to signal that she was doing admirably, and she returned the smile.

It was Getliffe, in the excess of his bonhomie, who brought about the change. We had just finished the sweet, and he looked round the table with his eyes shining and his face open.

'My friends,' he said, 'I'm going to call you my friends at this time of night' – he gazed at Henriques with his frank man-to-man regard. 'I've just had a thought. When I wake up in the night, I sometimes wonder what I should do if I could have my time over again. I expect we all do, don't we?'

Someone said yes, of course we did.

'Well then,' said Getliffe triumphantly, 'I'm going to ask you all what you'd really choose – if God gave you the chance on a plate. If He came to you in the middle of the night and said "Look here, Herbert Getliffe, you've seen round some of this business of life by now. You've done a lot of silly little things. Now you can have your time over again. It's up to you. You choose." '

Getliffe gave a laugh, fresh, happy, and innocent.

'I'll set the ball rolling,' he said. 'I should make a clean sweep. I shouldn't want to struggle for the prizes another time. Believe me, I should just want to do a bit of good. I should like to be a country parson – like your father' – he beamed at Sheila: she was still –'ready to stay there all my life and giving a spot of comfort to a few hundred souls. That's what I should choose. And I bet I should be a happier man.'

He turned to Mrs Henriques, who said firmly that she would devote herself to her co-religionists, instead of trying to forget that she was born a Jewess. I came next, and said that I would chance my luck as a creative writer, in the hope of leaving some sort of memorial behind me.

On my left, Mrs Getliffe gazed adoringly at her husband. 'No, I shouldn't change at all. I should ask for the same again, please. I couldn't ask anything better than to be Herbert's wife.'

Surprisingly, Henriques said that he would elect to stay at Oxford as a don.

We were all easy and practised talkers, and the replies had gone clockwise round at a great pace. Now it was Sheila's turn. There was a pause. Her head was sunk on to her chest. She had a wineglass between her fingers; she was not spinning it, but tipping it to and fro. As she did so, drops of wine fell on the table. She did not notice. She went on tipping her glass, and the wine fell.

The pause lasted. The strain was so acute that they turned their eyes from her.

At last: 'I pass.' The words were barely distinguishable, in that strangulated tone.

Quick to cover it up, Getliffe said: 'I expect you're so busy taking care of old L S – you can't imagine anything else, either better or worse, can you! For better, for worse,' he said, cheerfully allusive. 'Why, I remember when L S first pottered into my Chambers – '

The evening was broken. She scarcely spoke again until they said goodbye. Getliffe did his best, the Henriques kept up a steady considerate flow of talk, but they were all conscious of her. I talked back, anything to keep the room from silence; I even told anecdotes; I mentioned with a desperate casualness places and plays to which Sheila and I had been and how we had argued or agreed.

They all went as early as they decently could. As soon as the front door closed, Sheila went straight into the spare room, without a word.

I waited a few minutes, and then followed her in. She was not crying: she was tense, still, staring-eyed, lying on the divan by her gramophone. She was just replacing a record. I stood beside her. When she was so tense, it did harm to touch her.

'It doesn't matter,' I said.

'Speak for yourself.'

'I tell you, it doesn't matter.'

'I'm no good to you. I'm no good to myself. I never shall be.' She added, ferociously: 'Why did you bring me into it?'

I began to speak, but she interrupted me: 'You should have left me alone. It's all I'm fit for.'

As I had so often done, I set myself to ease her. I had to tell her once again that she was not so strange. It was all that she wanted to hear. At last I persuaded her to go to bed. Then I listened, until she was breathing in her sleep.

She slept better than I did. I dozed off, and woke again, and watched the room lighten as the morning light crept in. Pity, tenderness, morbid annoyance crowded within me, took advantage of my tiredness, as I lay and saw her body under the clothes. The evening would do me harm, and she had not a single thought for that. She turned in her sleep, and my heart stirred.

It was full dawn. By ten o'clock I had to be in court.

46

The New House

ONE night that autumn I arrived home jaded and beset. I had been thinking all day of the rumours about George Passant. One explanation kept obtruding itself that: George had shared with Jack Cotery in a stupid, dangerous fraud. George – in money dealings the most upright of men. Often it seemed like a bad dream. That night I could not laugh it away.

Sheila brought me a drink. It was not one of her light-hearted days, but I had to talk to her.

'I'm really anxious,' I said.

'What have I done?'

'Nothing special.' I could still smile at her. 'I'm seriously anxious about old George.'

She looked at me, as though her thoughts were remote. I had to go on.

'I can hardly believe it,' I said, 'but he and some of the others do seem to have got themselves into a financial mess. I hope to God it's not actionable. There are rumours that they've gone pretty near the edge.'

'Silly of them,' she said.

I was angry with her. My own concerns, the lag in my career, the dwindling of my prospects, those she could be indifferent to, and I was still bound to cherish her. But now at this excuse my temper flared, for the first time except in play since we were married. I cried:

'Will you never have a spark of ordinary feelings? Can't you forget yourself for a single instant? You are the most self-centred woman that I have ever met.'

She stared at me.

'You knew that when you married me.'

'I knew it. And I've been reminded of it every day since.'

'It's your own fault,' she said. 'You shouldn't have married someone who didn't pretend to love you.'

'Anyone who married you', I said, 'would have found the same. Even if you fancied you loved him. You're so self-centred that you'd be a drag on any man alive.'

She said in a clear, steady voice: 'I suppose you're right.'

For several days she was friendly and subdued. She asked me about one of my cases. Then, after sitting silent through a breakfast time, she said, just as I was leaving for Chambers:

'I'm going away. I might come back. I don't know what I shall do.'

I said little in reply, except that I should always be there. My first emotion was of measureless relief. Walking away from Mecklenburgh Square, I felt free, light-footed, a little sad, above all exhilarated that my energies were my own again.

My sense of relief endured. I wrote an opinion that day with a total concentration such as I had not been capable of for months. I felt a spasm of irritation at the thought of explaining to the maid that Sheila was taking a holiday: I was too busy for that kind of diplomacy. But I was free. I had a long leisurely dinner with a friend that night, and returned late to Mecklenburgh Square. The windows of the flat were dark. I went into each room, and they were empty. I made myself some tea, relaxed and blessed because I need not care.

I did a couple of hours' good work before I went to bed. It was lonely to see her empty bed, lonely but a relief.

So I went on for several days. I missed her, but I should have said, if Charles March had examined me, that I missed her as I missed the seashore of my illness, with the nostalgia of the prison. I should have said that I was better off without her. But habits are more obstinate than freedoms: the habits of patience, stamina, desire, protective love.

I told myself that my cruel words had driven her away. I could not trust my temper even now. I had made the accusations which would hurt her most; they were true, but I had done her enough harm before. I did not like the thought of her wandering alone.

In much that I thought, I was deceiving myself. She was still dear to me, selfishly dear, and that was truer than tenderness or remorse. Yet even so my relief was so strong that I did not act as I should have done only a few months earlier. I worked steadily in Chambers and in the flat at night. I wrote for news of George. I did not walk among the crowds in the imbecile hope of seeing her face. All I did was telephone her father: they had had no word. Mr Knight's sonorous voice came down the wire, self-pitying and massively peevish, reproaching me and fate that his declining years and delicate health should be threatened by such a daughter. Then I inquired of some of her acquaintants, and called at the cafés where she liked to hide. No one had seen her.

I began to be frightened about her. Through my criminal cases I had some contact with the police, and I confided in an inspector at the Yard whom I knew to be sensible. They had no information. I could only go home and wait.

I became angry with her. It was her final outrage not to let me know. I was frightened. She was not fit to be alone. I sat in the flat at night, pretending to work, but once more, and for a different reason, her shadow came between me and the page.

Six days after she left, I was sitting alone. The front door clicked, and I heard a key in the lock. She walked into the room, her face grey and strained, her dress bedraggled. Curiously, my first emotion was again of relief, of tried but comforting relief.

'I've come back,' she said.

She came towards me with a parcel in her hands.

'Look, I've brought something for you,' she said.

Under her eyes, I unwrapped the paper. She had kept a childlike habit of bringing me presents at random. This was a polished, shining, rosewood box: I threw open the lid, and saw a curious array of apparatus. There were two fountain pens lying in their slots, bottles of different coloured inks, writing pads, a circular thermometer, a paper-weight in the shape of a miniature silver-plated yacht. It was the least austere and the most useless of collections, quite unlike her style.

'Extremely nice,' I said, and drew her on to my knees.

'Moderately nice,' she corrected me, and buried her head in my shoulder.

I never knew exactly where she had spent those days. She had certainly slept two or three nights in a low lodging house near Paddington Station. It was possible that she tried to find a job. She was not in a state to be questioned. She was miserable and defeated. Once more I had to find something to which she could look forward. Make her look forward – that was all I could do for her. Should we go abroad at Christmas? Should we leave this flat, where, I said, bad luck had dogged us, and start again in a new house?

It astonished me, but that night she caught almost hysterically at the idea. She searched through the newspapers, and would have liked me to telephone one agent without waiting till the morning. Midnight had gone, but she was full of plans. To buy a house – it seemed to her like a solution. She felt the pathetic hope that sets the heartbroken off to travel.

So, on the next few afternoons, I had to get away early from Chambers in order to inspect houses along the Chelsea reach. The wind was gusty, and the autumn leaves were being whirled towards the bright cloud-swept sky. I begrudged the time. Once again, it meant a brief prepared ten per cent less completely than if I were settled. Yet it was a joy, in those windy evenings, to see her safe. She had decided on Chelsea; she had decided that we must have a view of the river; and we looked at houses all along the embankment from Antrobus Street to Battersea Bridge. In a few days she discovered what she wanted, at the east end of Cheyne Walk, It was a good-looking early-Victorian house with a balcony and a strip of garden, thirty yards by ten, running down to the pavement. I had to pay for a fifteen-year lease. I borrowed the money from Mr Knight. He agreed with me that, if this house might make her tranquil, she must have it.

Avaricious as he was, he would have lent more than that so as not to have her on his conscience.

As I signed the lease, I wondered where she and I would be living in fifteen years.

We moved in by the middle of November. On our first evening the fog rolled up from the river, so thick that, walking together up and down the garden, we could not make out people passing by outside. We heard voices, very clear, from a long way down the embankment. Now and then the fog was gilded as a car groped past. We were hidden together as we walked in the garden; we might have been utterly alone; and there, in the cold evening, in the dark night, I embraced her.

When we went in to dinner, we left the curtains undrawn, so that the fire shone on the writhing fog behind the panes. On the river a boat's horn gave a long stertorous wail. We were at peace.

That visitation of happiness remained for a few days. Then all became as it had been in the flat. Once more I dreaded to go home, for fear of what awaited me. The familiar routine took charge. Once more the night was not over until I knew she was asleep. In the new house, she sat alone beside her gramophone in a high bright room.

One December evening, I was reading, trying to pluck up the fortitude to go into that room and calm her, when the telephone rang. It was to tell me that the police had begun their inquiries into George Passant's affairs, that I was needed that night and must catch the next train.

47

Another Night In Eden's Drawing-Room

GEORGE'S friends had sent for me because I was a lawyer. Before I had talked to him for half an hour that night, I thought it more likely than not that he would be prosecuted. I was relieved that I had something to do, that I was forced to think of professional action. It would have been harder just to listen helplessly to his distress.

He was both massive and persecuted. He was guarding his group: sometimes he showed his old unrealistic optimism, and believed that this 'outrage' would blow over. I could not be certain how much he was concealing from me, though he was pathetically grateful for my affection. Even in the fear of disgrace, his mind was as powerful and precise as ever. It was astonishing to listen to a man so hunted, and hear a table of events, perfectly clear and well ordered, in which he and Jack Cotery had taken part for four years past.

I did not understand it all until near the end of the trial; but from George's account, in that first hour, I could put together most of the case that might be brought against them.

George and Jack had been engaged in two different schemes for making money; and the danger was a charge of obtaining this money by false pretences, and (for technical reasons) of conspiracy to defraud.

The schemes were dissimilar, though they had used the same financial technique. After giving up his partnership with Eden, Martineau had played with some curious irrelevant ventures before he finally made his plunge and renounced the world; one of those was a

360

little advertising agency, which had attached to it the kind of small advertising paper common in provincial towns.

Jack Cotery had persuaded George that, if they could raise the money and buy out Martineau's partner, the agency was a good speculation. In fact, it had turned out to be so. They had met their obligations and made a small, steady profit. It looked like a completely honest business, apart from a misleading figure in the statement on which they had raised money. No sensible prosecution, I thought both then and later, would bring a charge against them on that count – if there existed one single clinching fact over the other business.

They had gone on from their first success to a project bigger altogether; they had decided to buy the farm and some other similar places and run them as a chain of youth hostels. In George's mind it was clear that one main purpose had been to possess the farm in private, so as to entertain the group. Jack had ranged about among their acquaintances, given all kinds of stories of attendances and profits, and on the strength of them borrowed considerable sums of money. I could imagine him doing it; I had little doubt that, whatever George knew of those stories, Jack Cotery had not kept within the limits of honesty, though he might have been clever enough to have covered his tracks. From the direction of the first inquiries, there seemed a hope that nothing explicitly damning had come to light. Looking at the two businesses together, however, I was afraid that the prosecution would have enough to go on. I went from George to Eden's house, where I was staying the night; and there, by the fireside in the drawing-room, where I had once waited with joy for Sheila, I told Eden the story to date, and what I feared.

'These things will happen,' said Eden, with his usual impenetrable calm. 'Ah well! These things will happen.'

'What do you think?'

'You're right, of course, we've got to be prepared.'

His only sign of emotion was a slight irritability; I was surprised that he was not more upset about the credit of his firm. 'I must say they've been very foolish. They've been foolish whatever they've been doing. They oughtn't to try these things without experience. It's the sort of foolishness that Passant would go in for. I've told you that before – '

'He's one of the biggest men I've met. That still holds after meeting a few more,' I said, more harshly than I had ever spoken to Eden. For a moment, his composure was broken.

'We won't argue about that. It isn't the time to argue now. I must consider what ought to be done,' he said; his tone, instead of being half-friendly, half-paternal, as I was used to, had become the practised cordial one of his profession. He did not like his judgement questioned, especially about George. 'I can't instruct you myself. My firm can't take any responsible part. But I can arrange with someone else to act for Passant. And I shall give instructions that you're to be used from the beginning. That is, if this business develops as we all hope it won't...'

I wanted to take the case. For, above all, I knew what to conceal.

I knew that the case might turn ugly. George was frightened of his legal danger: he was a robust man, and it was the simple danger of prison that frightened him most; but there was another of which he was both terrified and ashamed. The use of the farm; the morals and 'free life' of the group; they might all be dragged through the court. It would not be pretty, for the high thinking and plain living of my time had changed by now. The flirtations which had been the fashion in the idealistic days had not satisfied the group for long. Jack's influence had step by step played on George's passionate nature. Jack had never believed in George's ideals for an instant; and in that relation there could only be one winner. George had his great gift for moral leadership, but he was weak, a human brother, a human hypocrite, uncertain of the intention of his own desires. With someone like Jack who had no doubt of his desires or George's or any man's, George was in the long run powerless. And so it happened that he, who was born to be a leader, was in peril of being exposed to ridicule and worse than ridicule as the cheapest kind of provincial Don Juan.

I tried to think of any tactic that would save him. Back in London I sat over the papers night after night. Sheila was in her worst mood, but I could do little for her, and made nothing of an attempt. I could not drag myself to her room, if it only meant the usual routine. For once I prayed for someone who would give me strength, instead of bleeding away such as I had.

For some days Hotchkinson, the solicitor to whom Eden had deputed the case, sent me no news. I had a fugitive hope that the police had found the case too thin. Then a telegram arrived in Chambers to say 'clients arrested applying for bail'. It was the middle of December, and term would soon be over. After that morning, the next hearing in the magistrates' court was fixed for 29 December. I had no case in London till January; I thought I could be more use if I lived in the town for the next fortnight.

I went home to Chelsea to tell Sheila so. I wondered if she would perceive the true reason – that only away from her could I be free enough to work for them all out. I could suffer no distraction now.

She was quiet and sensible that morning, when I told her of the arrests.

'I'm sorry,' she said. 'I suppose it's been worrying you.'

I smiled a little.

'I did my best to warn you,' I said.

'I've been a bit – caged in.' It was the word she often used; she was ruthless in talking of herself, but sometimes she wanted to domesticate her own behaviour.

I said that I ought to stay at Eden's until the New Year.

'Why?'

'I must win this case.'

'Will it help you? Going away like that?' She was staring at me.

'It's rather a tangled case. Remember, they'll tell me everything they can – '

'Is it more tangled than all the others? You've never been away before.'

She said nothing more, except that she would go to her parents for Christmas Day. 'If you think that my father won't find out that you're staying at Eden's,' she said with her old sarcastic grin, 'you're very much mistaken. I'm not going to make your excuses for you. You'd better come over at Christmas and have a shot yourself.'

In the next fortnight I spent much of my time with George, and I saw Jack whenever he wanted me. Step by step they came to feel secure, as though I were still among them. George learned to believe that I had not altered, and both then and always was on his side. So far as I had altered, in fact, it was in a direction that brought me nearer to him in his trouble. When I was younger and he had known me best, I was struggling, but failure was an experience that I neither knew nor admitted as possible for myself. I believed with a hard, whole, confident heart that success was to be my fortune. I had the opaqueness of the successful, and the impatience of the successful with those so feeble and divided that they fell away. Since then, in my weeks of illness, I had acknowledged absolute surrender – and that I could not forget. I had known the depth of failure, and from that time I was bound to anyone who started with gifts and hope, and then felt his nature break him; I was bound not by compassion or detached sympathy, but because I could have been his like, and might still be. So, in those threatening days, I came near to George.

And yet, as I walked from Eden's to George's through the harsh familiar streets, I was often hurt by the changes in his life – not the fraud, but the transformation of his ideal society into a Venusberg. I wished that it had not happened. I was hurt out of proportion, considering the world in which I lived. Did I, who thought I could take the truth about any human being, wish to shut my eyes to half of George? Or was I trying to preserve the days of my young manhood, when George was spinning his innocent, altruistic, Utopian plans, and I was happy and expectant because of the delights to come?

It was that pain, added to George's, which led me into an error in legal tactics. I knew quite well that the prosecution's case was likely to be so strong that we had no chance of getting it dismissed in the police court on the 29th. The only sane course was to hold our defence and let it go to the assizes; on the other hand, if the lucky chance came off, and we defended and won in the police court, we might keep most of the scandal hidden. It was a false hope, and I was wrong to have permitted it. But George's violence and suffering over-persuaded me: if the prosecution in the police court was weaker than we feared, I might risk going for an acquittal there.

It did no positive harm to hold out such a hope. But I had to explain it to Eden and Hotchkinson. They were cool-headed men, and they strongly disagreed. It was much wiser, they said, to make up our minds at once. The case was bound to go to the assizes. Surely I must see that? Eden was troubled. I was young, but I had a reputation for good legal judgement. Both he and Hotchkinson thought I had been a more brilliant success at the Bar than was the fact. They treated me with an uneasy respect. Nevertheless, they were sound, sensible solicitors. They believed that I was wrong in considering such tactics for a moment; they believed that I was wrong, said so with weight, and firmly advised me against it.

That discussion took place on Christmas Eve. During my stay so far, I had not felt like visiting my relations and acquaintances in the town, and after the disagreement I felt less so than ever. But I wanted to avoid attending Eden's party, and so I went off to call on Aunt Milly and my father. I had to tell them about the case, which had already been mentioned in the local papers. Aunt Milly, very loyal when once she had given her approval, was indignant about George. She was sure that he was innocent, and could only have been involved through unscrupulous persons who had presumed on his good nature and what she called his 'softness'. Aunt Milly was now in the sixties, but still capable of vigorous and noisy indignation. 'My word!' said my father, full of simple wonder that I should be appearing in public in the town. 'Well, I'll be blowed!' He was just about to slink out of Aunt Milly's house for a jocular Christmas Eve going round singing with the waits. Getting me alone for two minutes, he at once asked me to join the party. 'Some of these houses do you proud,' said my father, with an extremely knowing look. 'I know where there's a bottle or two in the kitchen – '

I spent next day at the Knights'. It was the most silent time I had known inside that house. The four of us were alone. I was hag-ridden by the case.

When I looked at Sheila, I saw only an inward gaze. She had not made a single inquiry throughout the day. We walked for a few minutes in the rose garden. She said that she would have liked to talk to me. Not one word about the case. I was angry with her, angry and tired. I could not rouse myself to say that soon I should have time, soon I should be home refreshed and ready to console her.

All that day I wanted to get her out of my sight.

Mrs Knight was unusually quiet. She knew that something was wrong with our marriage, and, though she blamed me, it was out of her depth. As for Mr Knight, he would scarcely speak to me. Not because his daughter was miserable. Not because I was so beset that my voice was dead. No, Mr Knight would not speak to me for the simple reason that he was huffed. And he was huffed because I had chosen to live in Eden's house and not in his.

No explanation was any good – that I must see George and the others night and day, that I could not drive in and out from the country, that, whatever happened, even if we got them off, Eden was George's employer and it was imperative for me to keep his good will. No explanation appeased Mr Knight. And, to tell the truth, I was too far gone to make many.

'No one bothers to see me,' he said. 'No one bothers to see me. I'm not worth the trouble. I'm not worth the trouble.'

He only broke his dignified silence because his inquisitiveness became too strong. No one loved a scandal, or had a shrewder eye for one, than Mr Knight. Despite being affronted, he could not rest when he had the chief source of secret information at his dinner table.

I drank a good deal that night, enough to put me to sleep as soon as we went to bed. When I woke, Sheila was regarding me with a quizzical smile.

'The light's rather strong isn't it?' she said.

She made me a cup of tea. There were occasions when she enjoyed nursing me. She said:

'You got drunk. You got drunk on purpose.' She stared at me, and said: 'You'll get over it.'

As I kissed her goodbye, I reminded her that the case came up on the 29th. In a tone flatter and more expressionless than she had used that morning, she wished me luck.

In the police court, I had not listened to the prosecutor's speech for half an hour before I knew that Eden and Hotchkinson had been right. There was no chance of an acquittal that day. There never had been a chance. I should have to reserve our defence until the assizes. At the lunch break I said so, curtly because it was bitter to wound him more, to George.

When I told Eden, he remarked: 'I always thought you'd take the sensible view before it was too late.'

The next night Eden and I had dinner together in his house. He was at his most considerate. He said that I had been 'rushing about' too much; it was true that I was worn by some harrowing scenes in the last twenty-four hours. He took me into the drawing-room, and stoked the fire high in the grate. He gave me a substantial glass of brandy. He warmed his own in his hands, swirled the brandy round, smelt and tasted, with a comfortable, unhurried content. Just as unhurriedly, he said:

'How do you feel about yesterday?'

'It looks none too good.'

'I completely agree. As a matter of fact,' he said thoughtfully, 'I've been talking to Hotchkinson about it during the afternoon. We both consider that we shall be lucky if we can save those young nuisances from what, between ourselves, I'm beginning to think they deserve. But I don't like to think of their getting it through the lack of any possible effort on our part. Don't you agree?'

I knew what was coming.

Eden's voice was grave and cordial. He did not like distressing me, and yet he was enjoying the exercise of his responsibility.

'Well then, that's what Hotchkinson and I have been considering. And we wondered whether you ought to have a little help. You're not to misunderstand us, young man. I'd as soon trust a case to you as anyone of your age, and Hotchkinson believes in you as well. Of course, you were a trifle over-optimistic imagining you might get a dismissal in the police court, but we all make our mistakes, you know. This is going to be a very tricky case, though. It's not going to be just working out the legal defence. If it was only doing that in front of a judge, I'd take the responsibility of leaving you by yourself – '

Eden entered on a disquisition about the unpredictable behaviour of juries, their quirks and obstinacies and prejudices. I wanted to be spared that, in my impatience, in my wounded vanity. Soon I broke in:

'What do you suggest?'

'I want you to stay in the case. You know it better than anyone already, and we can't do without you. But I believe, taking everything into consideration, you ought to have someone to lead you.'

'Who?'

'I was thinking of your old chief – Getliffe.'

Now I was savage.

'It's sensible to get someone,' I said with violence, 'but Getliffe – seriously, he's a bad lawyer.'

'No one's a hero to his pupils, you know,' said Eden. He pointed out, as was true, that Getliffe was already successful as a silk.

'I dare say I'm unfair. But this is important. There are others who'd do it admirably.' I rapped out several names.

'They're clever fellows.' Eden gave a smile, obstinate, displeased, unconvinced. 'But I don't see any reason to go beyond Getliffe. He's always done well with my briefs.'

I was ashamed that the disappointment swamped me. I had believed that I was entirely immersed in the danger to my friends. I had lain awake at night, thinking of George's suffering, of how he could be rescued, of plans for his life afterwards. I believed that those cares had driven all others from my mind. And in fact they were not false.

Yet, when I heard Eden's decision, I could think of nothing but the setback to myself. It was no use pretending. No one can hide from himself which wound makes him flinch more. This petty setback overwhelmed their disaster. It was a wound in my vanity, it was a wound in my ambition. By its side, my concern for George had been only the vague shadow of an ache.

It lay bare the nerve both of my vanity and of my ambition. Much had happened to me since first in this town they had begun to drive me on; sometimes I had forgotten them; now they were quiveringly alive. They were, of course, inseparable; while one burned, so must the other. In all ambitions, even those much loftier than mine, there lives the nerve of vanity. That I should be thought not fit to handle a second-rate case! That I should be relegated in favour of a man whom I despised! I stood by the fire in Eden's drawing-room after he had gone to bed. If I had gone further, I thought, they would not have considered giving me a leader. I knew, better than anyone, that I had stood still this last year, and longer than that. They had not realized it, they could not have heard the whiffs of depreciation that were beginning to go round. But if I had indisputably arrived, they would not have passed me over.

There was one reason, and one reason only, I told myself that night, why I had not indisputably arrived. It was she. The best of my life I had poured out upon her. I had lived for two. I had not been left enough power to throw into my ambition. She not only did not help; she was the greatest weight I carried. She alone could have kept me back. 'Without her, I should have been invulnerable now. It was she who was to blame.

48

Two Men Rebuild Their Hopes

IN the assize court, Getliffe began badly. He took nearly all the examinations himself, he did not allow me much part. Once, when he was leading me, he had said with childlike earnestness: 'It's one of my principles, L S – if one wants anything done well, one must do it oneself.' The case went dead against us. Getliffe became careless, and in his usual fashion got a name or figure wrong. It did us harm. At those moments – though once in court I was passing him a junior's correcting notes, I was carried along by my anxiety about George's fate – I felt a dart of degrading satisfaction. They might think twice before they passed me over for an inferior again.

But then Getliffe stumbled on to a piece of luck. Martineau was still wandering on his religious tramps, but he had been tracked down, and he attended to give evidence about the advertising agency. In the box he allowed Getliffe to draw from him an explanation of the most damning fact against George – for Martineau took the fault upon himself. It was he who had misled George.

From that point, Getliffe believed that he could win the case. Despite the farm evidence which he could not shift; in fact, he worried less about that evidence than about the revelations of the group's secret lives. The scandals came out, and George's cross-examination was a bitter hour. They had raised much prejudice, as Getliffe said. Nevertheless, he thought he could 'pull something out of the bag' in his final speech. If he could smooth the prejudice down,

Martineau's appearance ought to have settled it. It was the one thing the jury were bound to remember, said Getliffe with an impish grin.

It had actually made an impression on Getliffe himself. Like many others, he could not decide whether Martineau had committed perjury in order to save George.

Before the end of the trial, I was able to settle that doubt. I listened to a confession, not from George or Jack but from their chief associate.

George had started the agency venture in complete innocence; but he realized the truth before they had raised the whole sum. He realized that the statement he had quoted, on Martineau's authority, was false. He tried to stop the business then, but Jack's influence was too strong. From that time forward, Jack was George's master. He was the dominant figure in the farm transactions – Jack's stories, on which they borrowed the money, were conscious lies, and George knew of them.

In his final speech, Getliffe kept his promise and 'pulled something out of the bag'. Yet he believed what he said; in his facile emotional fashion, he had been moved by the stories both of Martineau and of George, and he just spoke as he felt. It was his gift, naïve, subtle, and instinctive, that what he felt happened to be convenient for the case. He let himself go; and as I listened, I felt a kind of envious gratitude. As the verdict came near, I was thankful that he was defending them. He had done far better than I should ever have done.

He dismissed the charge over the agency, and the one over the farm, already vague and complicated enough, he made to sound unutterably mysterious. Then we expected him to sit down; but instead he set out to fight the prejudice that George's life had roused. He did so by admitting the prejudice himself. 'I want to say something about Mr Passant, because I think we all realize he has been the leader. He is the one who set off with this idea of freedom. It's his influence that I'm going to try to explain. You've all seen him… He could have done work for the good of the country and his generation – no one has kept him from it but himself. No one but himself and the ideas he has persuaded himself to believe in: because I'm going a

371

bit further. It may surprise you to hear that I do genuinely credit him with setting out to create a better world.

'I don't pretend he has, mind you. You're entitled to think of him as a man who has wasted every gift he possesses. I'm with you.' Getliffe went on to throw the blame on to George's time. As he said it, he believed it, just as he believed in anything he said. He was so sincere that he affected others. It was one of the most surprising and spontaneous of all his speeches.

The jury were out two hours. Some of the time, Getliffe and I walked about together. He was nervous but confident. At last we were called into court.

The door clicked open, the feet of the jury clattered and drummed across the floor. Nearly all of them looked into the dock.

The clerk read the first charge, conspiracy over the agency. The foreman said, very hurriedly: 'Not guilty.'

After the second charge (there were nine items in the indictment), the 'Not guilty' kept tapping out, mechanically and without any pause.

It was not long before George and I got out of the congratulating crowd, and walked together towards the middle of the town. The sky was low and yellowish-dark. Lights gleamed into the sombre evening. We passed near enough to see the window of the office where I had worked. For a long time we walked in silence.

Then George said, defiantly, that he must go on. 'I've not lost everything,' he said. 'Whatever they did, I couldn't have lost everything.'

Then I heard him rebuild his hopes. He could not forget the scandal; curiously, it was Getliffe's speech, that perhaps saved him from prison, which brought him the deepest rancour and the deepest shame. From now on, he would often have to struggle to see himself unchanged. Yet he was cheerful, brimming with ideas and modest plans, as first of all he thought of how he would earn a living. He wanted to leave the town, find a firm similar to Eden's, and then work his way through to a partnership.

He developed his plans with zest. I was half-saddened, half-exalted, as I listened. It brought back the nights when he and I had first walked in those streets. Just as he used to be, he was eager for the future, and yet not anxious. He was asking only a minor reward for himself. That had always been so; I remembered evenings similar to this, with the shop windows blazing and the sky hanging low, when George was brimful of grandiose schemes for the group, of grandiose designs for my future. For himself, he had never asked more than the most improbable of minor rewards, a partnership with Eden. I remembered nights so late that all the windows were dark; there were no lights except on the tram standards; we had walked together, George's great voice rang out in that modest expectation – and the dark streets were lit with my own ravenous hopes.

Walking by his side that evening, I felt the past strengthen me now. Just as I used to be, I was touched and impatient at his diffidence, heartened by his appetite for all that might come. Yet, even for him, it would be arduous beyond any imagining to rebuild a life. With the strength and hope he had given me as a young man and which, even in his downfall, he gave me still, I thought of his future – and of mine.

We went into a café, sat by an upstairs window, and looked over the roofs out to the wintry evening sky. George was facing what it would cost to rebuild his life. As he came to think of his private world, the group that had started as Utopia and ended in scandal, his face was less defiant and sanguine than his words. He could not blind himself to what he must go through, and yet he said: 'I'm going to work for the things I believe in. I still believe that most people are good, if they're given the chance. No one can stop me helping them, if I think another scheme out carefully and then put my energies into it again. I haven't finished. You've got to remember I'm not middle-aged yet. I believe in goodness. I believe in my own intelligence and will. You don't mean to tell me that I'm bound to acquiesce in crippling myself?'

He was so much braver than I was. He was facing self-distrust, which as a young man he had scarcely known at all. He realized that there were to be moments when he would ask what was to become of him. Yet he would cling to some irreducible fragment of his hope. It was born with him, and would die only when he died. And it strengthened me, sitting by him in the café that evening, as I heard it struggle through, as I heard that defiant voice coming out of his scandal, downfall, and escape.

It strengthened me in my different fashion. I should never be so brave, nor have so many private refuges. My life up to now had been more direct than his. I had to come to terms with a simpler conflict. Listening to George that evening, I was able to think of my ambition and my marriage more steadily than I had ever done.

My ambition was as imperative now as in the days when George first helped me. I did not need proof of that – but if I had, Eden's decision would have made it clear. It was not going to dwindle. If I died with it unfulfilled, I should die unreconciled: I should feel that I had wasted my time. I should never be able to comfort myself that I had grown up, that I had gone beyond the vulgarities of success. No, my ambition was part of my flesh and bone. In ten years, the only difference was that now I could judge what my limits were. I could not drive beyond them. They seemed to be laid down in black and white, that evening after George's trial.

Much of what I had once imagined for myself was make-believe. I never should be, and never could have been, a spectacular success at the Bar. That I had to accept. At the very best, I could aim at going about as far as Getliffe. It was an irony, but such was my limit. With good luck I might achieve much the same status – a large junior practice, silk round forty, possibly a judgeship at the end.

That was the maximum I could expect. It would need luck, It would mean that my whole life should change before too late. As it was now, with Sheila unhinging me, I should not come anywhere near. As it was now – steadily I envisaged how I should manage. One could make it too catastrophic, I knew. I should not lose much of my present practice. I might even, as my friends became more influential, increase it here and there. Perhaps, as the years went on, I should harden myself and be able to work at night without caring how she was. At the worst, even if she affected me as in the last months, I could probably earn between one thousand pounds and two thousand pounds a year, and do it for the rest of my life. I should become known as a slightly seedy, mediocre barrister – with the particular seediness of one who has a brilliant future behind him.

Could I leave her? I thought of her more lovingly now than in my anger after Eden's decision. I remembered how she had charmed me. But the violence of my passion had burned out. Yes, I could leave her – with sorrow and with relief. At the thought, I felt the same emancipation as when, that morning at breakfast, she announced that she might not return. I should be free of the moment-by-moment extortion. I could begin, without George's bravery but with my own brand of determination, to rebuild my hopes – not the ardent hopes of years before, nothing more than those I could retain, now I had come to terms. They were enough for me, once I was free.

There was nothing against it, I thought. She was doing me harm. I had tried to look after her, and had failed. She would be as well off without me. As for the difference to me – it would seem like being made new.

George and I were still sitting by the café window. Outside, the sky had grown quite dark over the town. More and more as I grew older, I had come to hide my deepest resolves. George was always the most diffident of men at receiving a confidence – and that day of all days, he had enough to occupy him.

Yet suddenly I told him that my only course was to separate from Sheila, and that I should do so soon.

49

Parting

I WAITED. I told myself that I wished to make the break seem unforced: I was waiting for an occasion when, for her as well as me, it would be natural to part. Perhaps I hoped that she would go off again herself. Nothing was much changed. Week after week I went to Chambers tired and came home heavy-hearted. All the old habits returned, the exhausted pity, the tenderness that was on the fringe of temper, the reminder of passionate and unrequited love. It was a habit also to let it drift. For my own sake, I thought, I had to fix a date.

In the end, it was the early summer before I acted, and the occasion was much slighter than others I had passed by. I had given up any attempt to entertain at our house, or to accept invitations which meant taking her into society. More and more we had come to live in seclusion, as our friends learned to leave us alone. But I had a few acquaintances from my early days in London, who had been kind to me then. Some of them had little money, and had seen me apparently on the way to success, and would be hurt if I seemed to escape them. Theirs were the invitations I had never yet refused, and since our marriage Sheila had made the effort to go with me. Indeed, of all my various friends, these had been the ones with whom she was least ill at ease.

At the beginning of June we were asked to such a party. It meant travelling out to Muswell Hill, just as I used to when I was penniless and glad of a hearty meal in this same house. I mentioned it to Sheila, and as usual we said yes. The day came round; I arrived home in the evening, an hour before we were due to set out. She was sitting in the drawing-room, thrown against the side of an armchair, one hand dangling down. It was a windy evening, the sky dark over the river, so that I did not see her clearly until I went close to. Of late she had been neglecting her looks. That evening her hair was not combed, she was wearing no make-up; on the hand dangling beside her chair, the nails were dirty. Once she had been proud of her beauty. Once she had been the most fastidious of girls.

I knew what I should hear.

'It's no use,' she said. 'I can't go tonight. You'd better cry off.'

I had long since ceased to persuade and force her. I said nothing, but went at once to the telephone. I was practised in excuses: how many lies had I told, to save her face and mine? This one, though, was not believed. I could hear the disappointment at the other end. It was an affront. We had outgrown them. They did not believe my story that she was ill. They were no more use or interest to us, and without manners we cancelled a date.

I went back to her. I looked out of the window, over the embankment. It was a grey, warm, summer evening, and the trees were swaying wavelike in the wind.

This was the time.

I drew up a chair beside her.

'Sheila,' I said, 'this is becoming difficult for me.'

'I know.'

There was a pause. The wind rustled.

I said slowly: 'I think that we must part.'

She stared at me with her great eyes. Her arm was still hanging down, but inch by inch her fingers clenched.

She replied: 'If you say so.'

I looked at her. A cherishing word broke out of me, and then I said: 'We must.'

'I thought you mightn't stand it.' Her voice was high, steady, uninflected. 'I suppose you're right.'

'If I were making you happy, I could stand it,' I said. 'But – I'm not. And it's ruining me. I can't even work – '

'I warned you what it would be like,' she said, implacably and harshly.

'That is not the same as living it.' I was harsh in return, for the first time that night.

She said: 'When do you want me to go?'

No, I said, she should stay in the house and I would find somewhere to live.

'You're turning me out,' she replied. 'It's for me to leave.' Then she asked: 'Where shall I go?'

Then I knew for certain that she was utterly lost. She had taken it without a blench. She had made none of the appeals that even she, for all her pride, could make in lesser scenes. She had not so much as touched my hand. Her courage was cruel, but she was lost.

I said that she might visit her parents.

'Do you think I could?' she flared out with hate. 'Do you think I could listen to them?' She said: 'No, I might as well travel.' She made strange fantasies of places she would like to see. 'I might go to Sardinia. I might go to Mentone. You went there when you were ill, didn't you?' she asked, as though it were infinitely remote. 'I made you unhappy there.' All of a sudden, she said clearly: 'Is this your revenge?'

I was quiet while the seconds passed. I replied: 'I think I took my revenge earlier, as you know.' Curiously, she smiled.

'You've worried about that, haven't you?'

'Yes, at times.'

'You needn't.'

She looked at me fixedly, with something like pity.

'I've wondered whether that was why you've stood me for so long,' she said. 'If you hadn't done that, you might have thrown me out long ago.'

Again I hesitated, and then tried to tell the truth.

'I don't think so,' I said.

Then she said: 'I shall go tonight.'

I said that it was ridiculous.

She repeated: 'I shall go tonight.'

I said: 'I shan't permit it.'

She said: 'Now it is not for you to permit.'

I was angry, just as I always had been when she was self-willed to her own hurt. I said that she could not leave the house with nowhere to go. She must stay until I had planned her movements. She said the one word, no. My temper was rising, and I went to take hold of her. She did not flinch away, but said: 'You cannot do that, now.'

My hands dropped. It was the last stronghold of her will.

Without speaking, we looked at each other.

She got up from her chair.

'Well, it's over,' she remarked. 'You'd better help me pack.'

Her attention was caught by the wind, as mine had been, and she glanced out of the window. The trees swayed to and fro under the grey sky. They were in full June leaf, and the green was brilliant in the diffuse light. Through the window blew the scent of lime.

'I liked this house,' she said, and with her strong fingers stroked the window sill.

We went into her sitting-room. It was more dishevelled than I had noticed it; until that evening, I had not fully realized how her finicky tidiness had broken down; just as a husband might not observe her looks deteriorate, when it would leap to the eye of one who had not seen her for a year.

She walked round the room. Though her dress was uncared for, her step was still active, poised, and strong. She asked me to guard her coins. They were too heavy, and too precious, to take with her if she was moving from hotel to hotel. The first thing she packed was her gramophone.

'I shall want that,' she said. Into the trunk she began to pack her library of records. As I handed some to her, she gave a friendly smile, regretful but quite without rancour. 'It's a pity you weren't musical,' she said.

I wanted her to think of clothes.

'I suppose I shall need some,' she said indifferently. 'Fetch me anything you like.'

379

I put a hand on her shoulder.

'You must take care of yourself.' Despite the parting, I was scolding her as in our occasional light-hearted days.

'Why should I?'

'You're not even troubling about your face.'

'I'm tired of it,' she cried.

'For all you can do, it is still beautiful.' It was true. Her face was haggard, without powder, not washed since that morning or longer, but the structure of the bones showed through; there were dark stains, permanent now, under her eyes, but the eyes themselves were luminous.

'I'm tired of it,' she said again.

'Men will love you more than ever,' I said, 'but you mustn't put them off too much.'

'I don't want it.'

'You know that you've always attracted men – '

'I know. If I had attracted them less, it might have been better for me. And for you as well.'

She went on stacking books in the trunk, but I stopped her.

'Listen to me once more. I hope you will find a man who will make you happy. It is possible, I tell you.'

She looked at me, her face still except for the faint grimace of a smile.

'You must believe that,' I said urgently. 'We've failed. But this isn't the end.'

She said: 'I shan't try again.'

She sat down and began, with the competence that had once surprised me, to discuss the matter-of-fact arrangements. She would finish packing within an hour, and would spend that night at an hotel. I did not argue any more. Her passport was in order, and she could travel tomorrow. I would transfer money to her in Paris. It was summer, too hot for her to go south immediately. I thought it strange that, even now, she should be governed by her dislike of the heat. She would probably spend the summer in Brittany, and wait till October before she made her way to Italy. After that, she had no plans. She assumed that sooner or later I should want to marry again. If so, I could divorce her whenever I wished.

'If you are in trouble,' I said, 'you must send for me.'

She shook her head.

'I shan't do that.'

'I should want you to.'

'No,' she said. 'I might want to, but I shan't. I've done you enough harm.'

She rose and turned her face from me, looking out of the window, away from the room. Her shoulders were rigid, and her back erect.

'You may need –'

'It doesn't matter what I need.'

'Don't say that,'

Quite slowly she turned again to face me.

'It doesn't matter.' She spoke with absolute control. Her head was high. 'For a good reason. You said that this wasn't the end for me, didn't you?'

'Yes.'

'You were wrong.'

She was seeing her future; she was asking for nothing. She did not move an inch towards me. She stood quite straight, with her arms by her sides.

'Leave me alone,' she said in a clear voice. 'I'll call you when I go.'

50

Walk In the Garden

I WALKED in the garden. As I turned at the bottom, by the street gate, I saw that Sheila had switched on a light, so that her window shone into the premature dusk. Out of doors, in the moist air, the scent of lime was overpoweringly sweet. Sometimes the warm wind carried also a whiff of the river smell; but over all that night hung the sweet and heavy scent, the scent of a London June.

I could not send her away. I could not manage it. I knew with complete lucidity what it meant. If I were ever to part from her, this was the time. I should not be able to change my mind again. This had been my chance: I could not take it. I was going to call her back, and fall into the old habit. I was about to sentence myself for life.

Yet there was no conflict within me. I was not making a decision. Like all the other decisions of my life, this had been taken before I admitted it – perhaps when I knew that she was lost, certainly when I saw her, upright in her pride, asserting that there was nothing for her. She faced it without pretence. I had never known her pretend. And she would set her will to live accordingly. She would move from hotel to hotel, lonely, more eccentric as each year passed.

I could not bear to let her. There was no more to it than that. Whatever our life was like, it was endurable by the side of what she faced. I must stay by her. I could do no other. I accepted it, as the warm wind blew in my face and I smelt the lime. There was no getting out of it now. Somehow I should have to secure some rest for myself: now it was for life, I must find some way of easing it. In my practical and contriving fashion, I was already casting round – I could bear it better if she did not imprison me quite. But that would be only a relief. It was for life, and I must be there when she wanted me.

I sneezed. Some pollen had touched my nostrils. Perhaps it brought back the sensation of the chalky air in Marion's classroom, ten years before. Anyway, for a second, I remembered how I had challenged the future then. I had longed for a better world, for fame, for love. I had longed for a better world; and this was the summer of 1933. I had longed for fame: and I was a second-rate lawyer. I had longed for love: and I was bound for life to a woman who never had love for me and who had exhausted mine.

As I remembered, I was curiously at one with myself. I smiled. No one could call it a good record. The world's misfortunes, of course, had nothing to do with me – but my own, yes, they were my fault. Another man in my place would not have chosen them. I had not seen enough of my life yet to perceive the full truth of what my nature needed. I could not distinguish the chance from the inevitable. But I already knew that my bondage to Sheila was no chance. Somehow I was so made that I had to reject my mother's love and all its successors. Some secret caution born of a kind of vanity made me bar my heart to any who forced their way within. I could only lose caution and vanity, bar and heart, the whole of everything I was, in the torment of loving someone like Sheila, who invaded me not at all and made me crave for a spark of feeling, who was so wrapped in herself that only the violence and suffering of such a love as mine brought the slightest glow.

My suffering over Sheila was the release of my vanity. At twenty-eight, walking in the garden on that night after I had tried to escape, they were the deepest parts of myself that I had so far seen. It was not the picture that others saw, for I passed as a man of warm affections, capable of sympathy and self-effacingness. That was not altogether false – one cannot act a part for years; but I knew what lay in reserve. It was not tenderness that was to stop me sending Sheila away, at this time when I knew the cost of keeping her and when my passion was spent. It was simply that she touched the depth of my vanity and suffering, and that this was my kind of love. Yet, like George after his trial, I was still borne up by hope. More realistic than he was, I had seen something of myself, and something of my fate. In detail, I did not burke the certain truths. I should never be able to shelve my responsibility for her. That was permanent – but did I think that one day I should find true love in another? I should now never make a success at the Bar – did I think one day I might get a new start?

I was twenty-eight, and I could still hope. Those random encouragements were blowing in the warm wind, and I felt, as well as the strength of acceptance, a hope of the fibres, a hope of young manhood. That night, I had come to terms with what I must do. But I breathed the scent of the limes, and the half-thought visited me: 'She said that she had come to the end. As for me, I am nowhere near the end.'

I looked up at her window. I had delayed going in to her, but I could delay no longer. The house was quiet. I opened the door of her room. She was standing, so still that she might have been frozen, by the trunk.

She said: 'I told you to leave me alone.'

I said: 'I can't let you go.'

For a second her face was smooth as though with shock. Then it hardened again.

'I've told you, I shall go tonight.'

I said: 'I can't let you go at all.'

She asked: 'Do you know what you're saying?'

I said: 'I know very well.' I added: 'I'm saying that I shall never speak to you as I did tonight. Not as long as we live.'

'You know what you'll lose?'

I repeated: 'I know very well.'

'I trust you,' she cried. 'I trust you.' Her control was near to snapping, but suddenly she braced herself again and said harshly: 'It won't be any different. I can't make it any easier for you.'

I nodded my head, and then smiled at her.

In the same harsh tone, she said: 'You're all I've got.' Her face was working. She said again: 'You're all I've got.'

She crumpled up, almost as if she were fainting. I sat on the sofa, and she sank her head into my lap, without another word or sound. Time and time again I stroked her hair. Outside the window, the tops of the trees were swaying in the wind.

C P Snow

A Coat of Varnish

Humphrey Leigh, retired resident of Belgravia, pays a social visit to an old friend, Lady Ashbrook. She is waiting for her test results, fearing cancer. When Lady Ashbrook gets the all clear she has ten days to enjoy her new lease of life. And then she is found murdered.

'An impressive novel, as elegant and capacious as the Belgravia houses in which it is set' – *New Statesman*

The Conscience of the Rich

Seventh in the *Strangers and Brothers* series, this is a novel of conflict exploring the world of the great Anglo-Jewish banking families between the two World Wars. Charles March is heir to one of these families and is beginning to make a name for himself at the Bar. When he wishes to change his way of life and do something useful he is forced into a quarrel with his father, his family and his religion.

C P Snow

Homecomings

Homecomings is the sixth in the *Strangers and Brothers* series and sequel to *Time of Hope*. This complete story in its own right follows Lewis Eliot's life through World War II. After his first wife's death his work at the Ministry assumes a larger role. It is not until his second marriage that Eliot is able to commit himself emotionally.

In Their Wisdom

Economic storm clouds gather as bad political weather is forecast for the nation. Three elderly peers look on from the sidelines of the House of Lords and wonder if it will mean the end of a certain way of life. Against this background is set a court struggle over a disputed will that escalates into an almighty battle.

C P Snow

The Light and the Dark

The Light and the Dark is the second in the *Strangers and Brothers* series. The story is set in Cambridge, but the plot also moves to Monte Carlo, Berlin and Switzerland. Lewis Eliot narrates the career of a childhood friend. Roy Calvert is a brilliant but controversial linguist who is about to be elected to a fellowship.

'A novel written with the intuition of a woman and the grasp of broad essentials generally reserved for men... As full of life as life itself' – *John Betjeman*

The Search

This story, told in the first person, starts with a child's interest in the night sky. A telescope begins a lifetime's interest in science. The narrator goes up to King's College, London, to study. As a fellow at Cambridge he embarks on love affairs and searches for love at the same time as career success. Finally, contentment in love exhausts his passion for research.

OTHER TITLES BY C P SNOW AVAILABLE DIRECT
FROM HOUSE OF STRATUS

Quantity		£	$(US)	$(CAN)	€
	THE AFFAIR	8.99	14.99	19.49	15.00
	A COAT OF VARNISH	8.99	14.99	19.49	15.00
	THE CONSCIENCE OF THE RICH	8.99	14.99	19.49	15.00
	CORRIDORS OF POWER	8.99	14.99	19.49	15.00
	DEATH UNDER SAIL	8.99	14.99	19.49	15.00
	GEORGE PASSANT	8.99	14.99	19.49	15.00
	HOMECOMINGS	8.99	14.99	19.49	15.00
	IN THEIR WISDOM	8.99	14.99	19.49	15.00
	LAST THINGS	8.99	14.99	19.49	15.00
	THE LIGHT AND THE DARK	8.99	14.99	19.49	15.00
	THE MALCONTENTS	8.99	14.99	19.49	15.00
	THE MASTERS	8.99	14.99	19.49	15.00
	THE NEW MEN	8.99	14.99	19.49	15.00
	THE SEARCH	8.99	14.99	19.49	15.00
	THE SLEEP OF REASON	8.99	14.99	19.49	15.00
NON-FICTION					
	THE PHYSICISTS	12.99	20.99	28.49	21.00
	TROLLOPE	12.99	20.99	28.49	21.00

ALL HOUSE OF STRATUS BOOKS ARE AVAILABLE FROM GOOD BOOKSHOPS
OR DIRECT FROM THE PUBLISHER:

Internet: www.houseofstratus.com including author interviews, reviews, features.

Email: sales@houseofstratus.com please quote author, title and credit card details.

Hotline: UK ONLY: 0800 169 1780, please quote author, title and credit card details.
INTERNATIONAL: +44 (0) 20 7494 6400, please quote author, title and credit card details.

Send to: House of Stratus Sales Department
24c Old Burlington Street
London
W1X 1RL
UK

Please allow for postage costs charged per order plus an amount per book as set out in the tables below:

	£(Sterling)	$(US)	$(CAN)	€(Euros)
Cost per order				
UK	2.00	3.00	4.50	3.30
Europe	3.00	4.50	6.75	5.00
North America	3.00	4.50	6.75	5.00
Rest of World	3.00	4.50	6.75	5.00
Additional cost per book				
UK	0.50	0.75	1.15	0.85
Europe	1.00	1.50	2.30	1.70
North America	2.00	3.00	4.60	3.40
Rest of World	2.50	3.75	5.75	4.25

PLEASE SEND CHEQUE, POSTAL ORDER (STERLING ONLY), EUROCHEQUE, OR INTERNATIONAL MONEY ORDER (PLEASE CIRCLE METHOD OF PAYMENT YOU WISH TO USE)
MAKE PAYABLE TO: STRATUS HOLDINGS plc

Cost of book(s): _____ Example: 3 x books at £6.99 each: £20.97

Cost of order: _____ Example: £2.00 (Delivery to UK address)

Additional cost per book: _____ Example: 3 x £0.50: £1.50

Order total including postage: _____ Example: £24.47

Please tick currency you wish to use and add total amount of order:

☐ £ (Sterling)   ☐ $ (US)   ☐ $ (CAN)   ☐ € (EUROS)

VISA, MASTERCARD, SWITCH, AMEX, SOLO, JCB:

☐☐☐☐☐☐☐☐☐☐☐☐☐☐☐☐☐☐☐☐

Issue number (Switch only):

☐☐☐

Start Date: Expiry Date:

☐☐/☐☐   ☐☐/☐☐

Signature: _____

NAME: _____

ADDRESS: _____

_____

POSTCODE: _____

Please allow 28 days for delivery.

Prices subject to change without notice.
Please tick box if you do not wish to receive any additional information. ☐

House of Stratus publishes many other titles in this genre; please check our website (**www.houseofstratus.com**) for more details.